THE MASK OF COMMAND

IAN ROSS has been researching and
writing about the later Roman world
and its army for over a decade. He
lives in Bath. Visit his website:
www.ianjamesross.com,
or find him on Twitter:
@IanRossAuthor.

TWILIGHT OF EMPIRE

War at the Edge of the World
Swords Around the Throne
Battle for Rome

WOL

County Council

Libraries, books and more.........

RECEIVED

1 0 JAN 2017

W/TON LIBRARY

- 3 FEB 2017

- 9 MAR 2017

Bollongate Book Drop

KESWICK

WITHDRAWN FROM STOCK

Please return/renew this item by the last date due.
Library items may also be renewed by phone on
030 33 33 1234 (24 hours) or via our website

www.cumbria.gov.uk/libraries

Cumbria Libraries

Interactive Catalogue

Ask for a CLIC password

IAN ROSS

TWILIGHT OF EMPIRE IV

THE MASK OF COMMAND

HEAD of ZEUS

First published in the UK in 2017 by Head of Zeus Ltd.

9 7 5 3 1 2 4 6 8

A CIP catalogue record for this book is available
from the British Library.

ISBN (HB) 9781784975258
ISBN (XTPB) 9781784975265
ISBN (E) 9781784975241

Typeset by Ben Cracknell Studios
Printed and bound by CPI Group (UK) Ltd, Croydon, CR0 4YY

Head of Zeus Ltd
Clerkenwell House
45–47 Clerkenwell Green
London EC1R 0HT

www.headofzeus.com

Galea diademate, sceptris pila mutentur: auri praemium ferri labore meruisti.

Let helmet be exchanged for diadem, spear for sceptre: you earned the reward of gold with the work of iron.

Symmachus

In tranquillo esse quisque gubernator potest.

In a calm sea, anyone can hold the helm.

Publilius Syrus

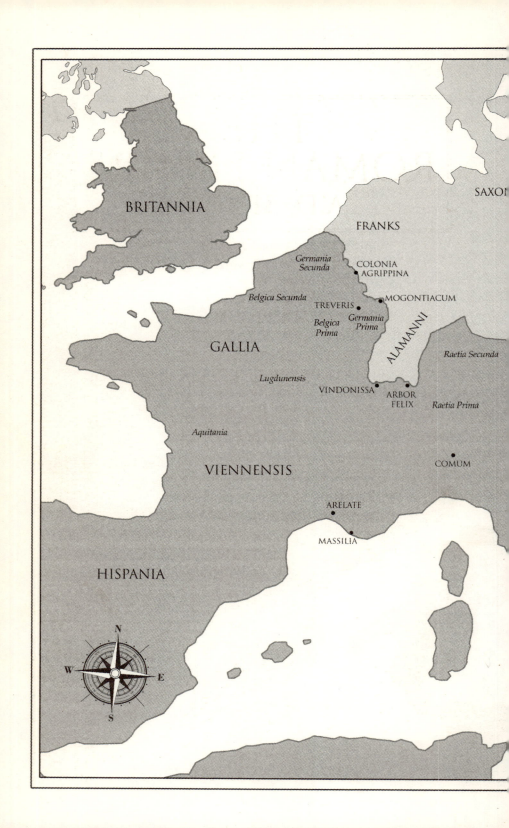

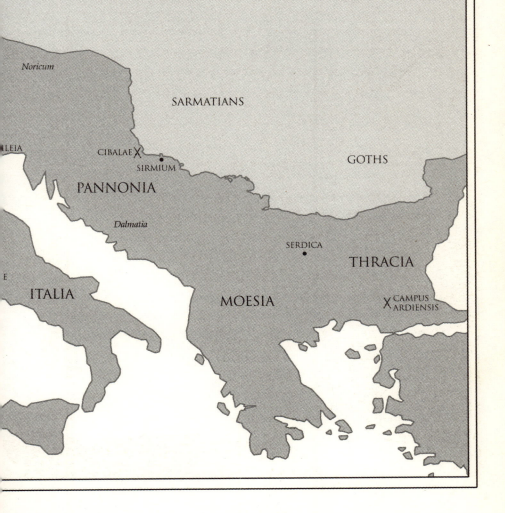

THE
ROMAN EMPIRE
A.D. 317–318

Noricum

SARMATIANS

LEIA

CIBALAE X

SIRMIUM

GOTHS

PANNONIA

Dalmatia

SERDICA

THRACIA

E

ITALIA

MOESIA

X CAMPUS ARDIENSIS

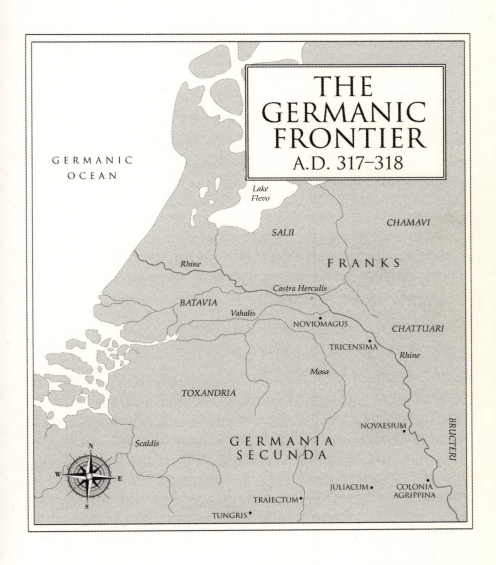

THE GERMANIC FRONTIER
A.D. 317–318

GERMANIC
OCEAN

Lake
Flevo

CHAMAVI

SALII

Rhine

F R A N K S

Castra Herculis

BATAVIA

Vahalis

NOVIOMAGUS

CHATTUARI

TRICENSIMA

Rhine

Mosa

TOXANDRIA

NOVAESIUM

BRUCTERI

Scaldis

G E R M A N I A
S E C U N D A

JULIACUM

COLONIA
AGRIPPINA

TRAIECTUM

TUNGRIS

N
W E
S

HISTORICAL NOTE

Over four years have passed since Emperor Constantine seized Rome and gained supremacy in the west. His ally Licinius, having destroyed their mutual rival Maximinus Daza, has claimed the eastern territories. United by treaty, the two men have agreed to rule the empire between them.

But already this delicate alliance is collapsing into war. Once again, Roman marches against Roman as Licinius and Constantine vie for sole power, with the disputed territories of the Danube provinces as their battleground.

Constantine's favoured religion, Christianity, continues to gain influence and attract followers. Meanwhile, on the frontiers of the empire, new enemies grow in strength and wait for the moment when Rome's weakness will allow them to strike.

PROLOGUE

Campus Ardiensis, Thracia, January AD *317*

The plain was covered with the wrack of war.

Many times the opposing armies had clashed, drawn back, and then clashed again, arrows and javelins flickering beneath winter clouds that boiled like dark smoke. Now the coarse and frost-stiffened grass and the ice-rimed pools bristled with spent missiles and shattered shields. The bodies of men and horses clogged the bloodied turf. Iron gleamed dull in the fading light, and the wind made the battle cries and the trumpet calls indistinguishable from the wails of the dying.

On a low ridge to the north of the plain, a group of men crouched below a stand of twisted black hawthorns, gazing out over the battlefield. The banners and shield blazons were lost in the gathering murk, and for a few long moments it was impossible for the observers to say which army fought for Constantine and which for Licinius. Impossible to say who was winning, and what had been lost. But already the first snow was whirling in from the south, and the men on the ridge knew that few of the wounded left between the battle lines would survive the night.

The youngest of the group, a supernumerary centurion with a wind-reddened face, threw out an arm suddenly and pointed. 'I see it!' he cried. 'Just to the right of the centre – the imperial standard! Constantine must be there...' He turned to the big man beside him, who knelt, impassive, wrapped in his cloak. 'Dominus,' the centurion said. 'Should we give the order to advance? The track will take us straight down onto the plain – we can reinforce the battle line at the centre...'

The senior officer unlaced his gilded helmet and lifted it from his head. He squinted, and his coarse heavy features bunched as he seemed to sniff the breeze.

'No,' he said. The word steamed in the frigid air.

'But, dominus... why delay any longer? Surely the emperor needs us...?' The centurion was young, untested in war and eager to prove himself. Behind them, on the track, five thousand soldiers waited in column with their baggage and equipment. Two days' forced march had brought them here – surely now they could turn the tide of the battle?

'I said *no*.'

The big man rubbed a palm along his jaw, through the rasp of stubble and the ugly scar that knotted his cheek. He studied the battlefield before him, and the young centurion saw the calculation in his eyes. He put his helmet back on.

'The army's strong enough at the centre,' he said. 'There's another track to our left, running along the rear of this ridge. It should take us down onto the plain to the east. We swing around that way and we can hit the enemy on their flank.'

The centurion blinked, and then stared at the land ahead of him. Snowflakes whirled in the wind, almost hypnotic.

'Well, what are you waiting for?' the commander said curtly. 'Get down there, find the emperor and report our position! Tell him that I intend to outflank the enemy lines on the left. Go!'

'Dominus!' the centurion said, saluting as he leaped to his feet. He turned and ran down the slope to where the horses were tethered. The commander watched the young man vault into the saddle, then spur his horse into a gallop down the trail towards the distant standards at the centre of the battle line. He exhaled, breathing a curse as he recalled the old adage. *War is sweet to the untried. An experienced man fears it with all his heart.*

Aurelius Castus, Tribune and Protector of the Sacred Retinue, *praepositus legionum* and commander of the detached column, was forty years old and had spent over half his life in the armies of Rome. He knew war intimately, as he knew fear. But he also knew that the centurion was right; there was no time for delay now. For over a month he had been leading his column through the barren hills of central Thracia, trying to intercept Licinius before he could link up with his reinforcements from Byzantium. Two days before, scouts had brought word that the enemy had evaded him; Licinius had already gathered an army at Adrianople, and Constantine himself was advancing to confront him. The last two days' rapid march had been shadowed by the threat of disgrace, of failure. Now, Castus and his men had a chance to redeem themselves. But there was so little time, and any mistake could bring disaster.

Striding back down from the ridge, he could see the men of his column waiting on the track to the north. He knew that all of them were weary, hungry and cold after marching sixty miles on muddy hill tracks in freezing rain, with no hot food and little sleep, their baggage carts and oxen abandoned far behind them. Castus had ordered a rest while he went forward to reconnoitre, a brief pause for the men to eat and drink from their canteens. But already many of them were back on their feet and forming up in line of march, grim-faced as they huddled in their cloaks, gripping their shields and weapons with numbed hands. In the fading light Castus saw their faces, pinched and grey; he saw the exhaustion in their eyes. He felt it too, but he carried the burden of command.

At the core of the column were a thousand men of Castus's own legion, II Britannica, veterans who had fought for Constantine for nearly a decade on the Rhine and in Italy. Them he could trust. His only cavalry were the mounted scouts and a few hundred troopers of the Equites Mauri. But the rest of his command was made up of half-trained recruits, barbarian *auxilia* and men conscripted from among the prisoners of war. Would they manage a difficult flanking march in gathering darkness, and then a charge into the heart of the battlefield?

'Pass the word down the line,' Castus ordered his deputy as he returned to the horses. 'No signals, no trumpets – keep silent. Every man to dump kit and cloak and prepare for battle. Mules and slaves to the rear – the Raetovarii to remain here as baggage guards, the rest to advance on my command.' He called to the leader of his mounted scouts: 'Decurion, have your men spread out along the north side of the ridge. Check the track's clear, and flush out any scouts or enemy skirmishers you find.'

The decurion saluted, then wheeled his horse. From the far side of the ridge came the distant cries of trumpets, the roar of combat. The fighting was intensifying once more. All along the column men stiffened, raising their heads, as if they might hear the screams of death carried on the air. A ripple passed through them: fear mixed with resolve.

Castus swung himself up onto his horse. His heart was beating heavily, and he tried to slow his breathing. He needed to appear perfectly calm and fearless now, perfectly in control of the situation. So much depended on his judgement, and his officers needed to see him and be reassured by him. The wind shoved at the plume of black feathers on his helmet. Reaching up, Castus fumbled at the heavy gold brooch that secured his cloak. It was inscribed with Constantine's name; the emperor himself had presented it to him, two years before in Rome, on the tenth anniversary of his rule. Remembering that day brought other thoughts: his wife Sabina had been with him then, and she was in Rome now. His wife, and their young son with her. When would he see them again?

Castus swore under his breath. His cold-clumsy fingers could barely flex the brooch pin from its socket. It came free, and he tried to hide the tremors in his hands as he let the cloak drop.

Behind him the troops were forming up, the centurions' voices carrying as hushed snarls. Castus urged his horse forward as his orderly took his cloak and his mounted bodyguard assembled. A quick glance back: the troops were ready, the confused mill of figures on the track forming into a single tight column behind their standards. Castus raised his hand, then let it drop, and with a low rumble of thudding boots and clinking metal, muffled curses and hissed orders, the column lurched into motion.

Thorn bushes lined the track below the ridge, and the soldiers moved rapidly and in silence. The wind boomed and whined above them, and the snow was beginning to settle in sheltered places among the thorns and on the higher slopes to either side. As he rode, Castus remembered the night march that the Caesar Galerius had made many years before, when he outflanked the Persian king's army. Castus himself had been a legionary then, in the ranks, but he remembered the uncanny fear of it, the sure sense that they would be discovered at any moment, that the darkness was filled with watching enemies. He knew that many of the men behind him now would be feeling the same way, those whose minds were not too deadened by exhaustion. If he closed his eyes he could sense the land around him, the proximity of the battlefield, the angle of their march. He prayed silently that his gamble would pay off, that he was not leading thousands of men to their deaths for nothing. But even as he prayed, he knew that the gods were seldom just.

This, after all, was a battle that should not have happened.

Nobody seemed sure any more what had caused the rupture between Constantine and Licinius. Some dispute, some accusation. The soldiers did not care; to them it was obvious that two men could not share the empire between them. Back in early October they had fought Licinius, on the plain outside the town of Cibalae, and defeated him. But, with his army destroyed, Licinius had managed to escape the field with his mounted bodyguard and flee. Now Constantine had to face him again, and his new army gathered from the eastern provinces. This time, Castus thought, there must surely be a conclusive victory. But in the gathering darkness and the falling temperature, the threatening snow, the chances of that were fading fast.

Ahead the track narrowed, the thorn trees closing in on either side. Castus's breath caught in his chest: what if this was a dead end, with no exit onto the plain to the south? His stomach churned, acid heat rising to the back of his throat. But then he saw the scouts ahead of him. He kicked his horse into a canter and joined them.

'Dominus,' the decurion said, saluting. The man had snow in his beard, and his breath sent up a plume of steam. 'The track drops into a defile just ahead, curving to the right. It's narrow, but it opens after about a hundred paces onto the plain. We've checked all along the ridge, and the enemy haven't sighted us yet.' He was grinning as he spoke, and Castus grinned too. The gods had been generous so far at least.

Turning in the saddle, Castus waved to the junior tribune heading the column that snaked back up the track. A moment later he saw the standards dip and swing, and the line of marching men doubled their pace. He was grateful for the wind now; the noise of the advance seemed very loud here, but nobody down on the plain would hear it.

Drawing aside, he sat on his horse with his bodyguards and staff officers around him, watching the column as it marched down towards the defile. The light troops and half the cavalry had passed him already; now the men of II Britannica were filing along the track. He had commanded this legion for years, and among them he saw many faces he recognised. Some of them called out to him, greeting him by name; others just raised their hands in salute.

For a moment more Castus paused, giving orders to the tribunes. He heard the snap in his voice, the note of anger that covered his nerves. Messengers were galloping back along the column, carrying his orders to the unit leaders. So much hung on his words now. As soon as his column cleared the defile they would be visible to the enemy.

Around the bend in the track, Castus entered the narrows. The wind caught him, driving snow into his eyes. He blinked, wiped his face, and then the open plain was before him. He felt his breathing slow, his chest contracting inside his burnished cuirass.

From his vantage point on the ridge the battle had seemed clear enough, the lines and dispositions easy to read. But from down here it was formless, a chaos of milling figures in the murk. Castus could not even tell whether his advance had brought him out facing the enemy flank, or that of Constantine's army. Panic quickened his blood, and he fought it down. There was no time left for consideration, no time for further plans. Everything was about speed now, about aggression.

Already the light troops had cleared the defile and were fanning out across the sloping ground that dropped to the plain. Behind them the advance units of II Britannica were pressing forward, massing into attack formation. As Castus watched them he felt a surge of pride rising through him. His mounted bodyguard were gathered close around him now, and his personal standard-bearer carrying the long blood-red draco banner hissing and snapping in the wind. Castus loosened the sword in his scabbard, took a long breath, and then slid down from the saddle, throwing the reins to his orderly. As he marched towards the head of the formation a voice cried after him, one of the staff tribunes.

'Dominus! You should remain here – your place is with us!'

Castus shook his head. This would be an infantry fight, and he wanted to be where he was needed.

'Would you have me send another man to do what I will not?' he called back in a voice that all the front-rank troops could hear. He drew his sword, and the cheers strengthened him.

Now he could see the enemy lines far away across the plain beginning to re-form, the cries of the officers reaching him on the wind as they tried to wheel the men of their reserves into a line to oppose this new threat on their flank. Their accents were unfamiliar, and Castus did not recognise the blazons on their white shields. He gave a low grunt of relief; surely these were Licinius's troops. There were trumpet calls from away to his right, sounds of fighting, but in the flurrying snow and the gathering dusk he could not make out what was happening there. It did not matter; his only task now was to smash at the enemy flank with all the force he could bring to bear.

Still he waited. He wanted only to give the signal to attack, but the longer he could delay the more of his men would be able to clear the defile and assemble in attack formation. *O greatest gods: Sol Invictus, Mars and Jupiter... do not let me fail now...*

Tension rippled through his body. He felt it from the men behind him as well, the ranks bunching forward, every soldier taut with the anticipation of battle. Another few heartbeats: then he had waited long enough.

'Constantine!' he yelled, raising his sword. A rush of breath, and the cry was echoed back in a massed shout. Then a din of spears clashed against shield rims, of screamed curses and shouts of defiance, cut through with trumpet blasts. Nothing would hold his men back now. Castus swung his sword down, took a step forward, and heard the command to advance bellowed all along the front ranks.

Three hundred paces to the enemy formation. The wind was roaring all around him, barbed with ice, and the whirling snow confused his vision.

Battle cries from the enemy lines, carrying through the murk: '*LICINIUS! APOLLINARIS!*' Castus squinted into the snow. He recognised the accents now. Legion XV Apollinaris was based in Cappadocia, hundreds of miles to the east on the Armenian frontier. Had Licinius really drawn troops from so far away? He remembered the jokes about the soldiers of Asia and Syria: soft and debauched, made effete by luxury. Castus had seen the eastern troops himself during the Persian war, and they had seemed tough enough. But the men before him now had been fighting all day, only now to face a fresh assault; even in the gathering gloom he could see that their ranks were in disarray.

Already the advance had closed more than half the distance to the enemy line. Castus glanced back over his shoulder, then called to the hornblower to sound the charge. Before the brassy notes had faded, he was running.

Shields on both sides, massed spears raised to strike; in the next rank men had javelins and darts ready to hurl. The Second

Britannica were famed for this: the blunt-headed charging wedge the soldiers called the *boar's head*. One thousand men bellowing as they ran, and Castus was yelling with them, his wind-numbed face stretched in fury. They powered forward into the funnel of the wind, like swimmers breasting a racing tide.

Castus barely noticed as the easterners broke. He saw a white shield go down, then he slammed another aside and he was in among them, striking at the fugitives as their formation collapsed into panic. His column scarcely missed a step as they drove into the enemy, blasting aside the frayed cordon and pushing onwards, deep into the exposed side of Licinius's right phalanx. Castus was still yelling, punching out with his shield boss and cutting down anyone who appeared before him.

Hands seized him, dragging him back. A centurion grinning at him, shouting through the noise. 'Got to re-form, dominus! Cavalry on our left!'

Castus could only nod, staggering as he tried to stand. The beating of his own blood seemed to be echoing inside his helmet and he could not speak. He heard the high scream of trumpets, the wail of horns and the cries of the centurions. '*Prepare to repel cavalry!*' He saw the shields of his own troops battering together into a solid wall, spears and javelins levelled. Voices in Latin, in Greek, in what sounded like Syriac. '*CONSTANTINE…! LICINIUS! LICINIUS!*'

The ground was covered with the bodies of the slain and dying. A hand grasped at his ankle, bloodied fingers sliding on his bronze greave, and Castus kicked it away. When he looked out between the shields he saw that the light had completely gone; the battlefield was eclipsed by darkness. Snowflakes whirled white against the black land and the black sky, and everywhere figures stumbled in confusion, moving like men lost in fog or overwhelmed by smoke.

A flurry of arrows struck somewhere to his left. A javelin with a bent shank arced out of the darkness and clattered off his shield. Castus felt his strength ebbing fast, the breath heaving in his chest as the last reserves of stamina burned through his limbs. Age was counting against him; he was no longer a young man. Then a moment later the darkness thickened into a line of advancing infantry, and all his thoughts were lost in the fury of combat.

It may have lasted only moments, or hours. Castus could no longer determine time. He was still on his feet, calling out for reports, and his orderly was at his side forcing him to drink from a canteen. From somewhere to his right he could hear the din of battle, and he knew that the emperor had thrown his full strength against the centre of the enemy line. Had they broken through? Was the battle won? He sucked down vinegar wine, choked and gasped, then drank again. It tasted like honey.

A figure was striding towards him out of the murky darkness, perhaps a dismounted cavalry officer, with a sword in his hand and other men advancing behind him. Castus stiffened, readying his shield, sensing the troops to either side of him doing the same. He lifted his sword, the reddened blade ready to strike.

But the figure kept coming, raising an open hand now, and Castus heard him calling his name. With only three paces between them, he recognised the man. Tribune Vitalis, serving with Constantine's main division.

'Aurelius Castus!' Vitalis said again. 'You took your time getting here, brother! But when you did, it was worth it!' He grabbed Castus by the shoulder, pulling him close and slamming his chest in a fierce embrace.

'Have they broken?' Castus managed to say, pulling himself back. Vitalis was grinning, his teeth gleaming in the dark.

'Broken and fled the field, brother. And if the gods are smiling, this is victory!'

Castus tipped back his head and sucked in air, feeling the cold freckling of snow on his tongue. All around him men were raising shields and spears, their hoarse voices crying out into the freezing night. '*VICTORY! VICTORY!*'

But the gods were not smiling.

Four days later, on a snow-covered plain ten miles south-east of the town of Adrianople, Constantine and Licinius met to declare a truce. The two emperors rode out from the ranks of their assembled armies, Constantine on a black horse that snorted and stamped, Licinius on a placid grey. Behind them, each had their mounted standard-bearer and a pair of Protectores. They approached slowly, with due dignity, crossing the unmarked snow until they reined in their horses side by side. Then both men leaned from the saddle and they embraced, kissing each other in a bond of brotherhood.

From his position with the other senior officers in the front rank of Constantine's army, Castus watched the two emperors on the open white field. He kept his face impassive. There was no shame in this, he told himself. No capitulation. In the confused closing hours of the battle at Campus Ardiensis, Licinius had managed to withdraw most of his left wing and his cavalry intact from the field. Under cover of darkness he had marched them north-east into the hills, and when morning came Constantine had led his troops south-east, following a decoy force on the road towards Byzantium. By the time the ruse was discovered, Licinius had manoeuvred to block Constantine's supply route, seize his baggage train and close his line of retreat. Both armies were exhausted, hungry and worn down by months of marching and fighting. All knew that the war was at an end, for now.

Castus remembered the day in Mediolanum, nearly four years before, when Constantine and Licinius had first met in solemn brotherhood. Maxentius was defeated, and Licinius was wedded to Constantine's half-sister to seal the pact between the new masters of the world. A glorious occasion, or so it had seemed at the time. Castus was there, of course, standing in the ranks of Constantine's officers, his white cloak and tunic stiff with gold and silver embroidery. He had helped secure the alliance himself, long before, by carrying a message to Licinius through barbarian country. That desperate journey had been in winter, too, in cold almost as harsh as this. How simple everything had seemed back then.

'When we fight them again,' Vitalis said quietly, standing at Castus's shoulder, 'let's hope it's summer, and our bellies are full!'

But as the trumpets sounded the imperial salute, Castus could think only of the field on the morning after the battle, the frozen corpses thinly blanketed by snow. Nearly all of them were Roman soldiers, and thousands like them had died in these three months of war. They had given their lives for a quarrel between two men, a quarrel that was now officially suspended. Constantine had won himself another five hundred miles of territory: all of Pannonia and most of Moesia. But whatever grand and empty words the two emperors were exchanging out there on the field between their armies, many more would die for them in years to come.

Back in the great camp of Constantine's army, Castus paced along the muddy avenue between the tent lines. Woodsmoke curled in the air, and he heard laughter, women's voices. At least now that the campaign was suspended the troops could return to more comfortable quarters. The thought gladdened him. He too had something to look forward to: in the spring, he would be back at Sirmium and his wife and child would be joining him there. He had not seen Sabina, or his son, for nearly a year; his wife loved Rome, and disliked travelling, but she had promised to make the journey into the cold and inhospitable north to stay with him again, for a few months at least. Besides, Sirmium was one of the great cities of the empire. It was not Rome, but neither was it short of luxuries.

He reached the enclosure of his command tent, returned the salute of the sentries, then paused to stamp the worst of the mud from his boots before going inside. Brazier-warmth met him, and the familiar smell of damp leather. His orderly brought a folding stool for Castus to sit on, and a cup of spiced and heated wine.

Castus drank, and felt the wine lifting his spirits further. Soon he would be with his family again. His son would be six years old this coming summer; Castus had seen so little of the boy that every time they met he had to re-establish a bond between them. Every time it was harder. This time, he told himself, he would make sure to spend much longer with Sabinus. None could fault him for that.

The thought of seeing his wife again brought conflicting feelings. Their marriage had not been easy; her betrayal of him five years before was forgiven now, but neither of them could forget it. It was almost as if, Castus thought, she was unable to forgive herself, or did not want to. As if she wanted that twisting guilt always to be between them. What did she fear would happen if she allowed it to fade? Sabina had always been a mystery to him. Maddening, too, but he loved her even so. He had long ago ceased to wonder whether she loved him in return. The passion that they shared during their few and scattered meetings seemed sincere, but Castus knew that it was laced with remorse. He shook his head, drank more, and felt the heat of the wine warming his chest. In the spring he would see her again, and somehow he knew that things would be better between them then.

'Dominus,' his secretary Diogenes said, 'there are some documents here that require your attention, I'm afraid to say.' He raised an eyebrow, rueful. He was sitting at a trestle table to one side of the tent, a mass of tablets and scrolls heaped before him. War, and the winter season, had held up the despatches and now a mass of correspondence had arrived at once, much of it months late.

'Put aside the ones I need to look at, and deal with as many of the rest as you can,' Castus told him. Diogenes had already performed great labours with the mass of documents, it appeared. Castus watched the man as he worked. He had known Musius Diogenes for well over a decade, ever since the ex-schoolteacher had been conscripted into the old Legion VI Victrix back in northern Britain. He had come to appreciate the man's odd wit, even his frequently bizarre notions. But as he looked at him now, Castus saw only the signs of age upon his face. Diogenes was barely older than him, but his scalp was balding and what hair he retained was mostly grey. Then again, Castus thought, while he himself had been destined for the military life – his father had been an army veteran and it was in his blood – Diogenes had forced himself into the mould of a soldier, and the effort had aged him. But one day, Castus knew, the years would take their toll on him as well. He had not forgotten his fatigue on the battlefield, his body's near-surrender.

'There's something else here,' Diogenes said, looking up. 'A letter for you. Personal correspondence.'

'Who from?'

Diogenes lifted the tablet, turning the face to the light and then the rear.

'Your wife's cousin, it seems,' he said, with a quizzical frown. 'The clarissimus Domitius Latronianus, in Rome. Or, at least, that appears to be his seal...'

Castus grimaced sourly. He had cared little for Latronianus. The man was a senator, an aristocrat, recently governor of Sicily; he had never hidden his disgust that his well-bred cousin had married a common soldier, a blacksmith's son from some Danubian backwater, no matter how exalted the rank he now held. Then again, Castus thought, he had once threatened to choke Latronianus with a lavatory sponge, and somehow the two of them had never quite managed to laugh the incident off...

'Open it and read it to me,' he said. 'Let's see what he wants.'

Sabina, he thought. Surely it was about his wife. What other reason would the senator have for writing to him directly? He felt a quick pinch of anxiety: the news would not be good. Latronianus, he felt sure, would not hesitate to inform him of some affair, some new adultery, if he thought the knowledge of it would wound Castus and drive him from Sabina. Castus had worried about that himself, of course, over all these long months of separation. His wife had never demonstrated a great regard for fidelity.

'Well?' he said. Diogenes had opened the tablet and run his eyes over the words, but was still staring down at it. 'What does it say?'

'Dominus, I...' Diogenes began, but then his voice failed. With a shock Castus noticed that the secretary's jaw was trembling, his face was pale, and there were tears in his eyes. He stood up quickly, the stool clattering behind him. Annoyance shifted at once to panicked dread, to swift anger.

'Speak!' he demanded, his fists clenching at his sides. 'Speak, curse you! What does it say?'

'Dominus, I'm sorry.' Diogenes cleared his throat, then recited in a hollow monotone. 'The clarissimus reports that your wife, the domina Valeria Domitia Sabina, was taken ill with a sudden fever last November...' He paused again, blinking, and then raised his eyes.

'Brother,' he said. 'Your wife is dead.'

Castus felt the breath punch against the back of his throat. For a few heartbeats his mind was blank, uncomprehending. He stood swaying, speechless. There was a strange ringing in his ears, and through it he heard Diogenes' voice, still in that dead flat tone. '... assures you that the family attended to the funeral with all due solemnity, and requests that you come to Rome at your earliest convenience to discuss matters relating to your late wife's property, and to the future of your son...'

A sudden lurching step, and Castus was flinging the tent flap aside. Whiteness glared in his eyes; it was snowing again, thick white flakes drifting slowly in the still air. He took another step, then another. The sentries were staring at him, but he strode on past them to the edge of the tent enclosure.

It could not be true. Sabina must be alive – she had been alive in his thoughts all through these months.

Castus closed his eyes and tipped back his head. He wanted to shout, to scream, but the air was trapped in his chest and he could not make a sound. Ice water was pouring through him, a torrent of it, unceasing. It would never cease. *Your wife is dead. Dead, and the funeral done.* Never again would he see her. Each new truth struck at him. His throat was clenched, his whole body drawn tight in the lock of grief.

The snow came down, and he felt it settling on his face, each flake melting instantly.

PART ONE

TWO MONTHS LATER

CHAPTER I

March AD *317*

The barbarians were waiting for them on the broad meadow above the Rhine. Valerius Leontius, *Dux Limitis Germaniae* – Commander of the Germanic Frontier – reined in his horse as he saw the figures on the riverbank. His face tightened into an expression of disgust, his flaring eyebrows knotting; this was hardly a task he relished, but it needed to be done.

Behind him, his escort party of soldiers slowed to a halt, the mounted scouts moving forward to screen the flanks. The barbarians must have arrived about an hour before, Leontius estimated; he could see their boats pulled up on the muddy bank between the reeds. They had lit fires on the dry ground beneath a stand of trees, and he could smell smoke and the burnt-earth aroma of their oatmeal porridge.

'Remember,' he said to the tribune who rode beside him, 'no one is to speak to them except me, via the interpreter. Keep the troops back, and make sure there's no contact between them and the barbarians.'

The tribune nodded curtly, almost dismissive. He understood what was to be done.

Leontius was a proud man. He detested this country, as he detested its inhabitants. A flat landscape of shaggy trees, reed beds and shallow meres that reflected the grey sky. This was the frontier of the Roman world, the place where civilisation

23

bled out into barbarism just as the land bled into the sea. To the west lay a green wilderness of branching rivers and salt marshlands, merging into the maze of scrub-covered islands and sandbanks that filled the estuaries along the coast. A place of treachery and deceit, with no fixed boundaries.

The last Roman stronghold was ten miles south at Noviomagus, on the far bank of the River Vahalis. But over to his left, between the trees and the reeds, Leontius could make out the overgrown hillocks of an old fortification. Castra Herculis, it was called. The Fort of Hercules. Once Roman soldiers had garrisoned this place, until the frontier had collapsed during the time of troubles forty years before. Now this was no man's land, an empty waste between the rivers, where roving barbarian bands and Roman patrols each tried to stake their rival claims.

The river up ahead, the Rhine, was the true frontier, and the barbarians waiting for him were Franks, from the tribe of the Chamavi. They had been one of the most savage foes of Rome once, but the emperor Constantine and his father before him had crushed them in battle, most recently only three years before, and now the tribes lived in peace with the empire.

But peace had a cost. And that cost, Leontius thought, was weighing down the leather panniers of the half-dozen mules that waited on the track behind him.

'Let's do this,' he said to the tribune, then waved his hand forward as he kicked his horse into motion.

The barbarians gathered to meet him as he approached. About twenty of them, as far as Leontius could see, all armed with spears and carrying small round shields. Most were poorly dressed, but there were a few veteran warriors among them, their belts adorned with gold and silver trappings. They were big men, with heavy moustaches and thick hair that hung to their shoulders. Many of them, Leontius noticed with irritation, were grinning openly.

'Halt,' Leontius cried, throwing up his hand. His herald and trumpeter moved forward, and a moment later the brassy blare of the horn startled the birds flapping from the thickets. A flock of geese lifted from the river in wild disarray.

The herald cried out the official greeting, in the name of the emperor Constantine, Invincible Augustus, Germanicus Maximus, and of Leontius himself, Commander of the Frontier.

'What are they so amused about?' Leontius hissed through his teeth.

'Excellency,' the interpreter told him, 'they are saying that Rome has brought tribute to their king, and this is good.'

Leontius clenched his fists around the reins, and his horse snorted and champed at the bit. 'Explain to them,' he said, snapping out the words, 'that Rome does not pay tribute to anybody! I have come here to oversee the transfer of our annual *subsidy* to the Chamavi, as agreed in the treaty that their king made when he *surrendered* to the Invincible Augustus Constantine three years ago! Tell them that!'

He could hear the tribune beside him making a whistling sound between his teeth. *Be calm*, he told himself. *Maintain dignity.* He had always had a short temper, and the sight of barbarians gloating openly in his presence grated on his nerves.

'Send the mules forward,' he said. 'Get it over with.'

Like most soldiers, Leontius found the practice of subsidising barbarian tribes deeply dishonourable. But he knew, for all the bold claims of the orators in their imperial panegyrics, all the triumphal parades and exhibitions of captives, that this was the rule along large stretches of the frontier. Barbarians could be crushed in battle, pounded until they were subservient, but short of wiping them out utterly – a lengthy and costly undertaking –

it was often more economical to pay them to remain tranquil. Roman treasure kept kings friendly to Rome in power, and gave them the strength to suppress their own foes. It also, in time, became an addiction: the steady drip of bullion from across the frontier made them slaves in their own land, unable to exist without imperial largesse. It was ignoble, but it worked.

These Chamavi certainly looked ignoble enough, crowding forward as they sighted the mules and their load, letting out loud whoops of triumph. Leontius scanned the country to either side: his small escort of soldiers had spread out to guard the approaches to the site, and a party of them had occupied the old wall of the fortifications to the left. There was always a chance that some other group of warriors would try and seize what they had not earned with their promises.

A chance, too, that the Roman troops themselves might be tempted by greed. If Leontius felt the subsidy payment stick in his craw, he could imagine how much worse it must be for the common soldiers to watch several years' worth of pay passed into the hands of their enemies. There had been irregularities in previous years, subsidies going missing, and that was why Leontius had elected to oversee the transfer himself this year.

Now the mules were unloaded and the heavy leather pannier bags flung down, clanking, onto the trodden grass. Crowding forward, the barbarians gathered around the bags, some of them squatting on their haunches as they ripped open the ties and dumped the contents onto the ground. Silver gleamed in the grey light.

Leontius suppressed a brief smile at the sight of it. The subsidy payments were not in coin, nor in bar silver. Instead the leather sacks held broken fragments, the remains of silver dishes and bowls, chains and cups, all roughly hacked into chunks of a similar size and weight. No barbarian king would gloat over this hoard and pretend that it was booty from a scavenging raid.

But the barbarians appeared unmoved; they had seen the like before. One of them, an old man with straggling iron-grey hair and a stringy moustache, had brought a set of scales, twin cups suspended on chains from the balance yard, and a selection of lead weights. The man squatting beside him scraped at each chunk of silver, tested it between his teeth, then passed it to the old man to be weighed in the balance. The others gathered around them had fallen silent now, watching the operation with close interest.

One of the barbarians remained apart from the others; their leader, Leontius guessed. He was young, his clothes well cut and embroidered with silver thread. Leaning on a spear, he stood with a look of studied indifference. At his feet sat a lean black hound. *How easy it would be*, Leontius thought, *to cut them all down now...*

Even as the notion passed through his mind, he became aware of the soldiers on either flank moving forward. The mounted scouts were almost at the riverbank; if they spurred forward now they could cut the barbarian party off from their boats and their route of escape. Leontius shrugged off his unease. His men were just being dutifully cautious, that was all. Raising himself in his saddle, he glanced in both directions, but beyond the cordon of his own men he saw nothing. Trees, reeds and the drab land stretching away to the flat horizon.

The emperor himself had promoted Leontius to this position. It was a great honour to command the military forces of the Rhine frontier, shabby and scarce though they were. Leontius told himself that, but wished all the same that he was elsewhere. He had fought in Constantine's army all through the campaign in Italy over four years ago, and distinguished himself at the

27

battle of the Milvian Bridge. Now Constantine was far away to the east, in Illyricum, arranging the new treaty with his rival Licinius; there had been great battles, Leontius had heard, great glory. He himself had seen none of it. Here in Germania Secunda, northernmost of the Gallic provinces, there were only the impertinent and conniving provincials to deal with, and uncouth, grasping barbarians like these Chamavi.

The last of the bags was emptied, and the old man with the balance had weighed the remaining few chunks of silver. Others behind him were piling the treasure into wicker baskets, ready to lug back to the boats.

'What are the scouts doing on the flanks?' Leontius said to the tribune beside him. He could see the horsemen moving away from the overgrown fortifications and gathering near the riverbank.

'I'm not sure, excellency,' the officer replied. His face was blank behind the nasal bar of his helmet. 'Maybe they've caught sight of something?'

'Call them back. We're almost done here.'

The tribune nodded, the gilding on his helmet winking in the low light. He turned in the saddle and gestured to one of the soldiers behind him.

Something struck Leontius a blow in the small of his back. For an instant he thought that one of the riders had accidentally shoved him with a spear-butt. Then pain ripped up through his chest and he arced in the saddle, crying out. His head reeled, agony bursting white light through his skull, and he felt hands grappling him as he slipped sideways.

'Treachery!' the tribune shouted. 'Barbarian treachery! Strike them all down!'

Leontius felt himself fall heavily to the ground beside his horse. The blade that had stabbed into his back had ripped free as he toppled, and his body was a pump of blood. His eyes were open, and through the sickening waves of pain that crushed him he saw the troops – his own troops – rushing in from either side, butchering the barbarians where they stood. The mounted scouts rode up from the riverbank, slashing at the fugitives.

He was still trying to speak, trying to shout for help, but his willpower was fading, submerged in pain and terror. Lying on his side, his legs kicking feebly at the ground, he watched the Chamavi leader hacked down by a pair of soldiers. He watched the tribune calmly picking up a fallen barbarian spear. The officer walked back towards him.

'What...?' Leontius managed to say. Blood was soaking the ground all around him. 'What are you...?'

The tribune's face was in shadow, but Leontius heard the sound of his breath as he inhaled. He closed his eyes, helpless. The spear rose, then fell.

Standing over the body of his commanding officer, the tribune twisted the shaft of the spear slightly, making sure the gash in the dead man's neck was clearly visible. The deep stab wound in his back could be concealed.

Down by the river, the last of the barbarians was trapped between a pair of mounted scouts. The riders circled him, baiting him. Then, when he turned to confront one of them, the other drove a javelin between his shoulders. The Chamavi leader's black hound was still bounding around the body of its fallen master, barking and snarling. A soldier stepped up to it, bent his bow, then shot an arrow through the animal's throat. The barking choked off, and there was silence. Only the sound of the distant geese on the river.

The tribune nodded to himself, satisfied. *No survivors.*

CHAPTER II

Sirmium, May AD *317*

She woke with a start of terror, and her whole body was running with sweat. For a moment she lay on the bed, breathing fast, sensing the gloom of her chamber pulsing to the rhythm of her blood. It was a dream, she told herself, a nightmare, but it had gripped her totally: the darkness had taken form, a hot black mist surrounding her and enclosing her. It was in her throat, like smoke or steam, choking off her breath, and she was powerless against it. Illuminated in the darkness she had seen terrible things: her father's corpse swinging from the roof beams, his swollen face leering at her; her brother's severed head bobbing grotesquely on the end of a lance, the dead lips smiling, forming words she could not hear.

Wide-eyed, she stared into the darkness until the familiar dimensions of the room appeared to her. She must have cried out as she woke; one of the slave girls had already risen from her palette on the floor and was crouching over her.

'Domina?' the girl said, shaking off sleep. 'What's wrong?'

'Nothing,' she said abruptly. The girl was Aethiopian, her skin blending with the darkness; it seemed an ill omen, suddenly, and she tried not to flinch from the slave's touch.

'Is it the child, domina? Shall I send for your husband?'

'No! No, of course not. I told you it was *nothing*. Do you

think the Augustus would care to be disturbed for such a trifling matter?'

Sitting up, instinctively moving her palms to cradle her swollen belly, she swung her legs from the bed. Constantine put much faith in dreams; he thought they carried messages from his god. Certainly he must not hear about this one. Besides, the *nobilissima femina* Fausta was a proud woman; she would not want her husband to know that she was a victim of night terrors.

'What's that disgusting smell?' she said, sniffing and then coughing.

'I'm sorry, domina,' the other slave said, hurrying to her side. 'One of the lamps was not properly snuffed – the wick was smouldering.'

That, Fausta thought, would explain her dreams of smoke. *If only it were that simple...*

Her sleeping tunic was soaked with sweat, the linen clinging to her skin. She stood up and started dragging it off over her head; the Aethiopian girl moved to help, and Fausta swatted her away.

'I can do it! Open the shutters and air the room. And bring lights, and water. Something to drink too – my throat's parched.'

She flung the tunic away from her and walked naked to the centre of the room. The Aethiopian – her name was Niobe – swung open the shutters, and cool night air breathed in through the window's bronze grille. The other slave was already bringing a taper and relighting the lamps. In the flickering glow Fausta saw the shapes of the room appearing from darkness, the furniture and the paintings on the walls. She was in her own bedchamber, in the imperial palace of Sirmium, surrounded by her husband's retinue and his loyal soldiers. This was not Rome; it was not Arelate. She was safe here. But nothing in Fausta's twenty-four years of life had given her much belief in safety.

Niobe returned with a basin of water, and Fausta crouched over it and splashed her face, then sat on a stool and let the girl wash her body with a damp cloth. The other slave brought clean linen towels and a cup of white wine, still slightly chilled from the snow-cellar below the palace. Sitting on the stool, sipping wine, Fausta felt herself regaining possession over her mind and body.

There was a large mirror of polished silver in the corner of the room, and Fausta regarded herself in its reflection. No, she was not old yet, even if she felt twice her age. So much she had experienced, in so little time. Pushing her unbound hair back from her shoulders she turned on the stool and drew herself up straight, confronting her image in the silver. The years had been kind to her, and the lamplight was kinder still. Even now, six months pregnant with her second child, there was nothing remaining of the plump frightened girl she had been when she was married. Fausta had put on weight during her last pregnancy, but dieting and exercise had rid her of it. Hopefully she would do the same this time around. Her breasts were still far too big, but otherwise she was pleased with her appearance. She was a mature woman, impressive if not quite beautiful, the wife of the emperor of the western world, mother to his heir.

She was glad, she thought as she turned from the mirror, that she had been sleeping alone that night. The Augustus had come to her bed only infrequently in the months before her pregnancy was announced, at those times of the month when his doctors told him she would be most fertile; he would not have wanted to be with her now, in her gravid state. Matters of the body disgusted him. He seemed to take little pleasure in the act itself; the Christian advisors that surrounded him these days claimed that sex displeased their god in some way. Neither did Fausta enjoy it – Constantine performed in bed as she imagined he must do on the battlefield: promptly, aggressively and with remarkable celerity. Fausta did not care. She had never loved anyone, and never been loved either. The idea that this strange uncomfortable bed-wrestling could be a token of affection was utterly alien to her. Only once had she experienced anything different, and that had been many years ago. Almost another lifetime.

At least the act had yielded results. She had given Constantine a son already, and with luck she would give him a second in three months' time. Surely the gods must love her, if nobody else did... Constantine Junior was just a baby, hardly even a person at all, but he and the child growing in her belly were her security. Surely now he could not tire of her, could not set her aside? Her only rival, her husband's concubine Minervina, had died a year after Constantine captured Rome. It was ironic, Fausta thought, that after all her plots and prayers the woman had succumbed to a winter fever. Natural causes, after all the unnatural ones Fausta had planned.

But she knew that she could never become complacent. Whatever respect and dignity she was given, whatever marks of favour and acceptance, she knew they were only conditional. She had taken her husband's own family name after the birth of her first son: now she was Flavia Maxima Fausta, fully a part of the Flavian dynasty. But she was still the daughter of Maximian, the man who had once been Augustus of the west, the man who had risen in rebellion against Constantine and died a traitor's death with his head in a noose at the residency in Arelate. She was still the sister of Maxentius, the tyrant of Rome, defeated in battle by Constantine, his body dishonoured and mocked. Nobody could forget these things. Constantine himself certainly never would, no matter how many sons Fausta gave him.

She knew all about the perils of power and status, the long terrible drop from prestige into disgrace, failure and ignoble death. The very palace she now called home had belonged to Licinius only a few months before; another man her husband had once called brother, and then defeated and expelled. It was that knowledge which brought the night terrors, the hideous images her sleeping mind could not conceal from her.

Minervina might be dead, but her child still lived, and prospered. Crispus, Constantine's son by his concubine, was only fourteen but had many years advantage over any of Fausta's present or future offspring. Despite Crispus's uncertain parentage, Constantine doted upon him. And now he had been proclaimed Caesar, *princeps iuventutis*, the 'first among youth'. As junior emperor, he was the anointed successor to Constantine's rule. Granted, the treaty agreed with Licinius at Serdica in March had also named Fausta's son and the rival emperor's boy Licinianus as co-Caesars, but they were just infants, too young for the position to mean anything.

Fausta knew little of Crispus; he had spent most of his time in Treveris and Rome, and seemed a quiet and withdrawn child, fond of studying ancient poetry and apparently dominated by his Christian tutors. But she knew the threat he posed to her. If Constantine were to die – the thought itself felt treasonous, ill-omened – then Crispus would succeed to his throne. And what would become of her own children then? If the boy himself did not move against them, his supporters and advisors certainly would. Against them, and against their mother. Her life would be worth nothing. And in this new empire of fathers and sons, what real power did she possess?

Slumping forward on the stool, caressing the smooth firm swelling of her belly, she fought down a shudder. Darkness filled her mind, a shadow of her terrible dreams. These were the thoughts that had oppressed her over this last year. Only very recently had a possible solution to the problem of Crispus presented itself, but it was dangerous. Hideously dangerous.

Enough, she thought. She had dwelled in confused considerations for too long, but now she was awake, resolute. Something needed to be done, and quickly. *Gods below, guide me now; wall me off from fear, and from mercy.* She drank back the last of the wine and dropped the cup onto the floor.

'Domina?' the slave, Niobe, said.

'What hour of the night is it?'

'The night is still timeless, domina. Dawn is far away.'

'No matter. Summon the eunuch, Luxorius.'

The girl stared at her for a moment, surprised. '*Now*, domina?' Then she saw the severity of Fausta's mood, bowed quickly and left the room.

'You'd better find me something to wear,' Fausta told the other slave.

By the time the eunuch arrived, less than an hour later, she was sitting in a high-backed cane chair, dressed in a tunic of rich blue silk, her hair brushed and plaited and arranged with pearls. If Luxorius was surprised to find the emperor's pregnant wife so composed in the middle of the night, he did not show it. The eunuch bowed as he entered the room, then seated himself facing her. He was small, only slightly fleshy, with a round, intelligent face and a dark complexion that betrayed his origins in southern Egypt. His head was shaved perfectly bald.

'Domina,' he said with a smile, 'you keep unorthodox hours!'

Fausta merely smiled. Then she pursed her lips and hooded her eyes, knowing that it gave her an inscrutable air.

'You have a new appointment,' she said.

'The nobilissima femina keeps herself informed.'

'What else do I have to do but keep myself informed?'

Luxorius gave a light shrug. 'Well then,' he said. 'As you doubtless already know, the Caesar Crispus is to be sent west, to Treveris, to take charge of the western provinces in his father's name. Apparently it was felt that the Gauls and the barbarians needed an imperial presence, to remind them of the emperor's majesty. He is to be given a full official and military staff, headed by a Praetorian Prefect, his eminence Junius Bassus. I have been appointed to the staff of the prefect, to act as his *cubicularius*.'

He inclined his head slightly, as if to register that he gave away no secrets. Unlike many eunuchs, his voice was not high and lisping. Fausta guessed that he had been castrated after puberty. An illegal act, and a very dangerous one; few survived the shock or the loss of blood. But Luxorius had been lucky in many ways since.

She nodded. 'No doubt,' she went on, dropping her voice, 'my husband wants his bastard offspring to gain some military experience? He is scarcely a martial figure at present, after all.'

'That I could not say, domina.'

Fausta tutted. 'Don't be coy with me,' she said. 'You know it as well as I do. Is there already some conflict being hatched, so Crispus can win a little glory and be saluted by the troops?'

'If that is the case,' Luxorius said in a careful murmur, 'the information has not been widely shared. It would be a hazardous undertaking...'

'I doubt the boy himself would be exposed to many hazards. You mentioned he has a military staff? Who are his commanders?'

Luxorius frowned, puffing his cheeks in a mime of recollection. 'His eminence Junius Bassus is to have supreme control of the troops in Gaul, the field army, under the Caesar's authority. Of the subordinates, I'm not sure. Most are already in place... But it seems the Dux Limitis Germaniae, commanding the garrisons on the lower Rhine frontier, was killed in somewhat mysterious circumstances two months ago. I believe one Aurelius Castus is to be appointed to replace him. He is currently in charge of the field troops at Aquileia.'

Aurelius Castus. Fausta glanced away for a moment, hoping that Luxorius would not notice her pause. Yes, she knew that name well. Castus had been a Protector in her husband's retinue, then a tribune during the war in Italy. But Fausta knew more about him than his official titles. She remembered that his wife had died quite recently – back in November, was it? At the time the news had saddened her; Fausta had liked Domitia Sabina, even if the woman was flighty and ruled by her emotions, lacking in self-control. She had even considered writing to Castus, although there was a rumour that he was illiterate. Perhaps even summoning him to meet with her – but what consolation could she have offered him? And she was wary of showing favour to any of her husband's officers. Such things made her vulnerable.

Several times in the last eight years Aurelius Castus had been of service to Fausta. In the male-ruled world that surrounded her, he was one of the very few men she felt she could trust. For all that he lacked intellectual qualities, grace or subtlety, he was honest and resolute. He had treated his wife well, while she lived. He was also extremely tenacious, and Fausta could respect that. Of course, there was more to it than that: she had never forgotten the night, years before, when he had been deceived into her bed. Terrifying at the time, sordid in retrospect, and it had only been moments before he had realised her true identity and fled. Even so, no other man save her husband had touched her in that way. And she had never known such passion from Constantine.

Now the thought that Castus would be one of the young Caesar's commanders brought a fresh crab-scuttle of anxiety to the back of her mind. If there was to be fighting on the Rhine, then Flavius Julius Crispus must be the clear victor, not any of his subordinates. Military officers, even good ones, were expendable. Caesars were not.

'You served my brother once, didn't you?' Fausta asked Luxorius, gazing sideways at her own reflection.

'I served the former ruler of Rome. That is no secret,' the eunuch replied. 'As I serve your husband now. Loyally.'

'As you serve *me*.'

'If you say so, domina!' Luxorius stifled a quick smirk.

'And your superior back then – your instructor, I might say – was Valerius Merops, yes? My brother's head chamberlain. One of your countrymen, I believe. And I don't just mean the country of the emasculated.'

'Valerius Merops was also from Egypt, yes.' Luxorius peered at her, obviously wondering where these questions were leading, perhaps half guessing the destination. 'He was an extremely loyal and effective supporter of your brother. A shame he was unable to accommodate himself to the new regime.'

Fausta smiled briefly. A nice euphemism. Merops had died in agony after hours of torture, finally garrotted to death in a dungeon of the Palatine. It was widely believed that, immediately upon the fall of his master Maxentius, he had seized and secreted the ancient Roman imperial regalia. It was never found, and Merops had died with his secrets intact. No matter: Constantine had ordered his goldsmiths and jewellers to create new regalia, more magnificent even than the old set. Emperors were not troubled by such minor inconveniences.

'And what would this Merops have done, would you say,' she asked, 'had he been working for me now? In the matter of my stepson, for example. Might he consider that it is a long road to Treveris?'

The eunuch drew a sharp breath. More in relief, Fausta guessed, that the subject was in the open at last.

'You raise a notion that is... quite possibly treasonous. Domina.'

'And yet? I am the emperor's wife. I have a certain influence, and I could see that anyone who aids me is rewarded. What would your Merops say to that?'

Luxorius took a few moments to think. Not too long though.

'Doubtless he would be most interested. Doubtless he would ask time to consider various options that might become available. It is, as you say, a long road to Treveris. A long and perhaps dangerous road.'

Fausta nodded, then dismissed him with a wave, and Luxorius got up and moved to the door as quietly as he had arrived.

'One more thing.'

The eunuch paused at her words.

'The soldier,' she said. 'Aurelius Castus. It would displease me if he came to any harm.'

Luxorius regarded her with narrowed eyes. He smiled faintly. 'The domina is nothing if not warm-hearted,' he said.

CHAPTER III

Sheets of rain moved across the surface of the lake, hazing the iron-grey water. At the top of the slope, Castus reined in his horse and gazed to the north. On the horizon, he could see the distant mountains appearing for a moment along the far shore and then vanishing once more. The rain beat upon his shoulders, soaked through his cloak and dripped down his back.

'A sight to chill the spirits, is it not?' a voice said. Castus turned to see a mounted man on the road behind him, stocky and well dressed, with the rain dripping down his jowled face and chin-strap beard. Junius Annius Bassus, Praetorian Prefect of Gaul.

'Your eminence,' Castus said, bowing his head slightly. As commander on the Rhine, he was now *vir perfectissimus*, addressed as 'excellency'; but the Praetorian Prefect, as *vir eminentissimus*, still outranked him. Castus found the inflated-sounding titles a tedious annoyance. However grand they might sound in the gilded halls of the imperial palace, they seemed quite absurd here in the rainy frontier province of Raetia. But he knew some men enjoyed them. Bassus clearly did.

The prefect was peering past Castus at the lake and the distant shore. Around him, his cavalry bodyguards and secretaries stood waiting in the rain, miserably silent.

'Once, years ago in the glorious times of our forefathers,' Bassus announced in a ponderous tone, 'all of that lake was a Roman domain! But now our power has receded, and the barbarians have the far shore. The Lentienses, I believe, an Alamannic people... Ah, but if I'm not mistaken you have travelled through that country yourself?'

'Many years ago, eminence.'

'Then I'm sure you remember it well,' Bassus said as he nodded gravely, apparently pleased with his observation. He peered a moment more, then signalled to his followers and jogged his horse into motion.

Castus remained where he was, letting the prefect and his party move on up the road. His horse, the ageing ox-solid grey mare named Dapple that had carried him from one end of Constantine's domains to the other and back, shook her mane and pawed the wet turf. Castus leaned forward and rubbed at her neck.

He had certainly not forgotten that journey through the wild country of the Alamanni: over five years before, in the aching heart of winter, he had carried Constantine's offer of alliance to the court of Licinius in Pannonia. Only Castus himself had survived it. One of the dead had been his best friend Brinno, the son of a Frankish chieftain, who was serving in the Protectores. Brinno had sacrificed himself to allow Castus to escape, and in all the years since then Castus had never met another man he trusted as much, or mourned as deeply. It perplexed him now to think that he was returning to the lands of the Rhine frontier, the home of Brinno's people. What would his friend have thought if he had known that Castus would one day be appointed commander of all that territory? Doubtless he would have been amazed – and amused.

Castus was amazed himself. He had never expected the promotion, or wished for it. *Dux Limitis Germaniae*: that was some other man's role, not his own. Even after years as a tribune, he was not accustomed to high command, to the deference of others, the weighty dignity and protocol of rule. His first inclination had been to refuse the honour. Since Sabina's death, he had lived in a dark half-world, uncertain of his purpose. Grief sat like a cold black stone in his gut, and even when it eased he felt bereft of happiness. He had spent the last three months commanding the troops at Aquileia, his spirits sinking ever lower in the frustrating routine of garrison life, his body settling into middle age. The idea of returning to the frontiers once more was attractive. Perhaps, he considered, this was a challenge he needed – perhaps it was his chance to regain the clarity of mind that Sabina's death had stolen from him.

Still, he knew it would not be a simple assignment. He was not returning to Germania as a mere tribune, but as senior commander of the troops on the lower Rhine, in charge of Rome's defences in the north-west. And he would be commanding in the name of the Caesar Crispus, a boy of only fourteen.

'Such things are not unknown in our history,' Diogenes had told him, back in Aquileia when they first heard of the appointment. 'The deified Gordianus was only thirteen, I believe, when he first assumed the purple – and he was supreme Augustus. As I recall, the deified Severus Alexander was only a year or so older…'

'And what happened to them?' Castus asked. His grasp on Roman history had never been that strong.

Diogenes gave an uncertain shrug. 'Gordianus lost his life in mysterious circumstances, in Persia…' he said. 'And Alexander, of course, was murdered by his senior army commanders. And then, of course, there was Saloninus, the son of the deified Gallienus. He was sent to Gaul as Caesar when he was sixteen, I think.'

'He did well?'

'Ah, not quite. He was also murdered. Again by his own officers.'

'You're not reassuring me.'

'Apologies... But, you see, in this case we have no such worries! His eminence Junius Bassus is hardly likely to revolt against the young Caesar. And the senior military commander... would be *you*.'

Not quite true, Castus knew – there were other regional commanders in the west, already holding their positions, besides the officers of the field army units billeted across the province under Bassus's overall control. Even so, he was far from easy about the arrangement. Crispus had spent the last six months in his father's court, observing the business of imperial rule. But he was still an adolescent, and from the little Castus had seen of him over the years he did not have the makings of a soldier. Would the provincials accept him as their true emperor? Would the barbarian peoples beyond the frontier respect his rule? The youth was not even Constantine's legitimate son, or so the rumours claimed.

Turning away from the lake and the distant mountains, Castus watched the tail of the column climbing the slope behind him. A stream of men, horses, carriages and wagons, and they had been travelling for twenty days since leaving Aquileia in mid July. Castus had his own small official staff and household with him, and a mounted escort. The rest were the Caesar's retinue: three hundred soldiers, slaves and officials. It had been raining solidly ever since the column had crossed the Alpine passes between Clavenna and Curia. The plains of Italy had been bathed in summer sun, but north of the mountains it seemed a different season altogether.

A carriage reached the top of the slope, labouring on the muddy road, and Castus jogged his horse forward and rode along beside it. His orderly Eumolpius was seated beside the driver, more than usually bleak-looking in his waxed rain cape. Castus tapped on the louvred window of the carriage, and a moment later the panel slid open.

'Sabinus,' came an accented voice from within. 'Salute your father!'

The boy's face appeared in the window opening, then his palm. Castus leaned from the saddle, his mouth twitching into a crooked grin as he reached out and rubbed his knuckle against the boy's cheek.

'Not too uncomfortable in there?'

'No, Father,' the boy said, unsmiling.

Castus ran his fingers clumsily through his son's fine black hair. Sabinus took after his mother in appearance: that same dark complexion and smooth oval face. Castus was glad of it; he would not have wished his own lumpen looks on anyone. But it troubled him all the same. The boy's only memories were of Rome, and the luxurious life he had lived there. All his friends were in the city, along with his extended family, now headed by his uncle Latronianus. Since joining Castus at Aquileia, the boy had not been happy. Was it only selfishness, Castus thought, to drag him from all he had known and try to mould him into a soldier's son, away on the far frontier?

He had been in Rome himself back in March. A terrible visit. The city had seemed like a necropolis to him, a place of cold stone and hard bitter sunlight. Sabina had died intestate, and her property was being contested by a plague of lawyers. Castus wanted nothing but his son. In the gardens of the Domitii family mansion on the Esquiline Hill he had walked with Latronianus, the senator's lip curling into a feigned smile as he explained the technicalities of inheritance law, as if he were speaking to a particularly simple child. Sabinus would inherit half his mother's property, and the family would get the rest. But the senator wanted more than that.

'Your boy is a member of our household now,' he had said. 'A true son of the city of Rome. His mother would surely have desired him to stay here, where he feels at home.' Latronianus wanted formally to adopt the boy, and to pay Castus off with a portion of the inheritance funds. Castus had refused, and they had parted with an ill-concealed mutual disgust. Whether it had been wise, whether it had been proper, Castus neither knew nor cared. But he had made his decision, and he must stick to it.

Now the boy stared gloomily at him from the carriage window, before slumping back into his seat. Castus leaned a little closer. Inside the carriage, sitting beside his son, was the boy's nursemaid, the blonde barbarian slave Ganna.

'How much longer until the next stopping place?' she said, her Germanic accent giving the words an accusatory sound. 'He's hungry.'

'Only another two hours to Arbor Felix,' Castus said. 'Maybe three at most, on this road.'

The woman nodded. For a moment she caught his eye, and her expression softened. Castus reminded himself that this journey was taking Ganna back towards her homeland, a place she had not seen since she was captured and enslaved by the Roman army nine years before. But if she felt any eagerness, any anxiety, at the prospect of seeing her own lands again, she gave nothing away.

Rain was dripping in at the carriage window. Castus slid the louvred screen back into place, then raised himself upright in the saddle. As the carriage moved away from him he glanced back down the road at the last few wagons and mounted men climbing the slope. One of the riders drew his attention: a small man with dark skin and a round bald head shining in the rain. Castus had encountered him often enough during the journey – he was an Egyptian eunuch named Luxorius. Cubicularius to the Praetorian Prefect.

'Good day, excellency!' the eunuch said as he drew level with Castus.

Castus nodded to him warily. He did not dislike eunuchs as instinctively as many other men did – he had known a couple that were quite decent – but something about this Luxorius troubled him. A memory, perhaps, that he could not place. And why was the prefect's chamberlain lingering at the rear of the column?

But the eunuch was already moving away between the carts, jogging along on his pony. Castus paused a few moments more, looking once more across the bleak grey surface of the lake; then he turned his horse and rode on into the rain.

It was nearing dusk when they reached Arbor Felix. The fortress stood on a low rocky promontory jutting into the lake, a clutch of stone drum towers rising almost directly from the water's edge. Soldiers of the garrison, Cohors I Herculia Pannoniorum, lined the ramp up to the gateway and cried out acclamations as the Caesar and his retinue passed beneath the massive buttresses and into the cramped circuit of the walls.

Castus found the young emperor an hour later, sitting with his tutor in one of the rooms of the commander's residence, now requisitioned for imperial use. Stamping in from the rainy courtyard, his two bodyguards waiting at the door, Castus passed through the cordon of Protectores. He flung his wet cloak at one of the attendants, then saluted and dropped to one knee. The boy made a lazy gesture of acknowledgement.

'Caesar!' Castus said as he stood up again, in his parade-ground voice. 'You summoned me?'

'Did I?' the boy said, languidly perplexed. 'Oh, perhaps I did...'

Flavius Julius Crispus was slight of build, mild of features, with pimple-spotted cheeks and downy hair on his upper lip. His face had nothing of his father's raw-boned ferocity; he took after his Greek mother, although his curly hair was the colour of dark honey and worn rather long.

'Are the troops settled?' the young emperor said. 'Have they been fed and given dry lodgings?'

'Yes, Caesar,' Castus replied. It was not his duty to attend to such things, but he assumed the questions were an attempt at sounding authoritative. Castus noticed that the youth was holding a gilded sphere, inscribed with tiny images, turning it lightly between his fingers.

'We were just discussing the form of the heavens,' Crispus declared, with greater enthusiasm. 'I'd always thought that they were spherical, like this ball, with our world shaped like a globe inside.' He traced his fingertips over the golden sphere, which Castus now saw was inscribed with the figures of the constellations: bears and hunters, scorpions and magical beasts. 'But Lactantius here tells me that this is not so,' the boy went on. 'What do you think?'

'I know little of the heavens, majesty,' Castus said stiffly. The old man sitting opposite Crispus, the boy's tutor Lactantius, was regarding him with vague distaste. 'But... I have always believed that the world is like a ball, and the constellations revolve around it.'

'Pah, what use is it to ask a soldier about philosophy?' Lactantius exclaimed. 'Perhaps your majesty jests, hmm? Perhaps ask your military thinker to explain how the people

47

on the opposite side of this supposed globe do not fall off? Does their rain fall upwards out of the earth, hmm?'

Castus glared at the man. This Lactantius was a Christian of some sort; according to Diogenes, he had written a book about the unpleasant deaths of various emperors, including Diocletian. As far as Castus was concerned, that was enough to condemn him. Diocletian was a titan, and above criticism.

'Aren't heavy things pulled down towards the earth?' he said, frowning. 'Just as light things rise into the air? So everything pulls towards the centre, like the spokes of a wheel...'

The boy Caesar raised an eyebrow and smiled, clearly entertained by the exchange. For a moment Lactantius tugged at his fleecy beard, then he shrugged.

'An implausible fiction,' he announced. 'Imagine, majesty, the earth spinning like a wheel! A dizzying concept! Scripture tells us quite plainly that heaven is above us and hell beneath our feet – so how could this globular world be suspended with the heavens on all sides? No – it is patently obvious that the earth is a flat plane, with the heavens set above it.'

Castus cleared his throat loudly. He had better things to do than indulge the strange whims of old men. 'Do you require anything more of me, Caesar?'

'No, that will be all,' the boy said. 'You may go.'

Castus tried to keep the sour look from his face until he had got out of the room. His cloak was still wet, and he threw it over his shoulder as he marched back along the colonnade outside. Lamplight fell from the open doorways, and he heard the sound of men singing from the barracks compound, the yelp of dogs, distant laughter.

'Ah, excellency, there you are!' A figure appeared in a darkened doorway; Castus saw the gleam of light on his shaved head. 'His eminence has been waiting for you...'

Castus was baffled for a moment, then understood – the summons had come from Bassus, the Praetorian Prefect, not the Caesar. *Eminence, excellency, majesty...* with all these titles, he thought, it wasn't surprising the messenger had got confused. If men could call each other by their real names, things would be much simpler.

'The Caesar detained me,' he said. 'But I'm here now.'

The eunuch led him through the dark vestibule into a reception room beyond. Junius Bassus was reclining on a couch, peering at a tablet, but he put it aside and stood up promptly as Castus entered and gave his salute.

'I've just had word from the *consularis* governor of Germania Secunda,' the Praetorian Prefect said, pacing across the room. 'He reports that the barbarians on the lower Rhine are becoming threatening. One of the Frankish tribes, I believe. As you know, since the previous Dux Germaniae was killed by the barbarians back in March, the frontier has been without a military commander. I believe you knew Valerius Leontius?'

'He was my senior commander during the Italian campaign,' Castus said. 'A good soldier.' A good man, too, and something close to a friend, although he did not say that to Bassus. He had heard of Leontius's death two months before, and relished the opportunity of avenging it.

'Anyway,' Bassus went on, 'it's imperative that you travel on to Colonia Agrippina without delay and assess the situation.'

Castus nodded, hooking his thumbs into his belt. 'I could move faster by river, dominus.'

'Quite so. I shall despatch an order to the Rhine flotilla to send ships upriver to meet you at... shall we say Argentorate? You can remain with us until we reach Vindonissa, then move on more rapidly from there.'

Bassus might look complacent, but he was obviously capable.

Already Castus was turning the new schedule over in his mind: three days would take him to Vindonissa, three more to the river port at Argentorate. From there, another two or three days downstream by ship and he would be at Colonia Agrippina, the capital of the Rhine provinces.

'Did the governor say anything more about the situation?'

'Unfortunately not. I gather it's more potential than actuality at present, but you'd best be there as soon as you can. All these Frankish tribes have sworn peace with Rome, but they are not a trustworthy people. I've lost count of the times the Augustus has had to beat them into obedient submission.'

Castus cleared his throat. He had fought in several of those campaigns himself. The one against the Bructeri he remembered in particular: he had saved Constantine's life in battle, and won promotion to the Protectores as a result. That was also, he reminded himself, the campaign that had sacked Ganna's village, and led to her enslavement.

'There's something else, before you go,' Bassus said with a confidential air. 'I'd intended to speak of this later, but since you'll be leaving us soon, it must be now.'

He paused, weighing his words. Castus tried not to respond too obviously to the ominous tone. 'Dominus?' he said.

'When you reach Colonia Agrippina, you must ensure that, uh... that your position does not become *compromised*, shall we say.' Once again Bassus paused, pursing his lips so his jowls quivered beneath his beard. 'We have heard disturbing rumours of the attitudes, the behaviour, of some of the provincials. Even some of our own officials in Germania and Belgica. They have a somewhat independent spirit, it seems. They may, perhaps, attempt to influence you unduly. Perhaps thinking you merely a *simple soldier...*' He gave a primping smirk, as if to suggest that he would never think such a thing himself.

50

'Dominus, if there's something I should know...'

Bassus held up a hand, shaking his head. 'No, no – there's nothing more definite I can tell you at this point. Just be wary. And remember: all power descends from the Augustus Constantine. All power is channelled through the Caesar Crispus. There is no other conduit. Crispus rules in the west now, and he must be *seen* to rule. Do I make myself clear?'

Not at all, Castus thought. But the prefect appeared to have made his point.

Outside again, Castus left the commander's residence and crossed the cobbled lane to the *mansio* in the far corner of the fortress. The rain had stopped, finally, and the air smelled of smoke and wet horses. Turning over the prefect's words, he still felt unsure of their meaning. It was warning, perhaps even a threat – but beyond that it was entirely cryptic.

Once again Castus asked himself why he had been chosen for this command. He had earned it, by rank and service, but there was more than that. He had never been known for ostentation or greed – quite the opposite. Was he thought to be immune from the temptation of bribery? Or was it, Castus thought with a start, that there was something he was *supposed* not to notice?

Enough. These thoughts got him nowhere, and he would find out the meaning of the prefect's warning soon enough. Already his mind felt sharper, his body flowing with fresh energy at the thought of escaping this slow imperial procession at last. Free of the need for deference and protocol, he could make his own pace and be his own master.

Leaving his bodyguards in the outer chamber, Castus climbed the lamplit wooden stairway to the suite of upper rooms where his household was lodged for the night. His mind was still filled with considerations of the journey ahead and what he might find in Germania, and he frowned as he saw Ganna sitting outside his son's room. She stood up as he approached.

'He wants you,' she said, motioning with her head towards the door. 'The girl's in there with him.'

The chamber beyond the door was dim, lit only by a clay lamp that glowed gently in the corner. A girl of thirteen knelt beside the bed, mumbling a breathy song, but as Castus entered she fell silent in fright, then backed away on her knees with her head lowered. Castus had bought the round-cheeked, buck-toothed slave to help Ganna look after his son, but she was barely more than a child herself and appeared petrified most of the time. It irritated him; so many people seemed cowed by his presence these days.

Pulling up a stool, Castus exhaled heavily and sat beside the bed. He made an effort to ease his frown and appear less formidable, but his son did not look reassured. Sabinus lay with the blanket pulled up to his chin, his face pale in the lamp's glow.

'Can't sleep?' Castus said, his voice lowering to a gentle rasp. The boy shook his head.

'He's frightened,' Ganna said from behind him.

Castus touched his son's cheek, then ran his palm across his head. He knew that he was too soft on the boy – Ganna had complained about it. The first thing Castus had done when the two of them arrived with him was to dismiss Sabinus's tutor; he learned that the *paedagogus* had flogged him for some failing in his lessons. The boy must be shown discipline, he knew that – but he remembered all too well the terror he had felt for his own father, terror that turned to hatred. He refused to let his son experience that. Perhaps that was just a weakness in him; the boy was unhappy, often moody and tearful, and Castus was all too aware that he knew nothing of children and how they should be raised.

'What's he afraid of?' he said sternly, addressing the two slaves.

'It's the lake,' the boy said quietly, then rolled his eyes towards the shuttered window. 'I heard a man say it was bottomless... and there are barbarians who come across it in boats and cut people to pieces...'

Castus snorted a laugh, but the boy looked genuinely scared. Easy to understand his fear; they had passed several lakes on their journey through northern Italy, but they had been inside Roman territory then. Lake Brigantio was the first frontier that the boy had seen: on the far side was another world. Pointless to try and explain to him that Ganna, his own nurse, was a barbarian; in the boy's mind, those outside the boundaries of civilisation were bloodthirsty savages, less than human. It was what he had been taught, back in Rome.

'Don't worry about that,' Castus said, forcing himself to smile. 'They wouldn't dare come near this fortress, would they? Nobody's crossed this frontier in a very long time! You're safe here, and you'll stay safe. Just sleep now.'

Sabinus nodded bleakly, then closed his eyes and turned his head from Castus's hand. Castus could not help glancing briefly at the shutters himself. The presence of the lake outside, that great expanse of deep cold water in the blackness of the night, did feel ominous.

'When will we go back to Rome?' the boy said in a sleepy mumble.

Castus hid his wince of regret. 'Not for a long while yet,' he said. 'But don't think about that now. Your home's here, with us...'

Sabinus sighed, rolling over into the embrace of the blanket. He was not asleep, but clearly wanted his father to think he was. Castus gazed at him a moment longer, gave the boy's shoulder a clumsy pat, and stood up. As he left the room he heard the two slaves talking in hushed voices, then the boy's quiet, tearful sniff.

Guilt twisted inside him as he returned to his own chamber along the hall. Once again he wondered if he had done the right thing by taking his son from Rome. The idea that the boy could be lost to him, adopted into some stranger's family – worse, into the family of a man like Latronianus – made his heart ache. But how much of it was pride? He did not know.

Another hour had passed before Ganna came to join him. The sound of the door latch startled Castus from the edge of sleep, and he opened his eyes to see her standing beside the bed. In the faint moonlight through the gap in the shutters he watched her shed her rough green tunic. Her back still showed a tracery of old whip scars. Her previous master had been fond of the lash.

'How is he?' Castus asked as she lifted the blanket and slid in beside him.

'Better. Sleeping,' she told him, her long limbs binding close against him on the narrow mattress. From outside came the distant step of a sentry on the rampart walkway.

They had been lovers for nearly four months now, ever since she had left Rome and come to join him in Aquileia. Nothing shameful about that – most men bedded their slaves; it was only unusual that it had taken so long. While Sabina lived, Ganna had been unwilling to come to his bed, and Castus had been unwilling to force her. He had thought often of freeing her, of course. It would have been easily done. But she had made it plain to him that she would not remain in his household, or with him, if he did. She would go home, to Germania.

'If you want that,' she had told him, 'free me now. But if you want me to stay, don't. Somebody has to look after your child.'

It was strange, he thought, almost stubborn of her. As if her pride would only allow her to be with him, and to care for his son, under duress. She said she hated all Romans, but when they were alone together she was passionate, giving everything. Her body was womanly but strong, lean with muscle; sometimes, when they lay together, she would whisper to him in her own language, and he found the strange music of her words not alien and barbaric but intoxicating, arousing.

Lying beside her now, running his big scarred hand lazily through her hair, Castus realised that he cared deeply for this woman. It was madness, he knew: she was a slave, a barbarian and a sworn enemy of the Roman people. But he felt such tenderness for her, even if he understood so little of her mind or her heart.

'What would you do,' he asked her, 'if you went back to Germania?'

'Find my son, of course,' she replied, and shoved at his shoulder. Castus gave a rueful flinch. Too often he forgot that she had a child of her own; she had not seen him in nearly a decade. 'Then,' she said, 'I could die happily, in my own land.'

'Would you marry again?'

She snorted a laugh. 'Who would marry me now? I'm an old woman.'

'You're a dozen years younger than me,' he said, and she laughed again.

'And you're an old man. See,' she said, rubbing her fingers against his temples. 'Your hair's become grey. You are fat!' She prodded him in the belly.

Castus growled deep in his throat, rolling over and pinning her to the bed. Renewed desire stirred inside him.

'If I freed you I could marry you myself,' he said in a breath. Just for a moment he imagined it: her proud scorn in the salons of the mighty. A tempting fantasy. Then he felt the laughter ripple through her body.

'Sometimes,' she said, 'I think you are really as stupid as men say.' But when she kissed the ugly scar on his jaw, he felt her smiling.

'Freedom is not something to give and take,' she whispered. 'You Romans will never understand that.'

CHAPTER IV

'You seem unusually cheerful, dominus,' Diogenes said as he rode beside Castus. 'Does the prospect of fighting entire nations of barbarians really gladden the heart so much?'

'It'd be good to face somebody who isn't fighting under a Roman banner for a change,' Castus said. 'That would gladden me, certainly.'

Diogenes himself looked happier these days; since Castus's promotion, his secretary had gained the new title *princeps officiorum*, chief of his military staff, and all the extra pay and added dignity that went with it. But it was true, Castus thought, that his own spirits felt lifted too. They had left the lake and its gloomy waters behind them now, and were moving through rough wooded country, the road climbing and descending broken ridges and crossing streams swollen to muddy brown torrents by the rains. The morning was clear and bright, and Castus's small party rode at the head of the column.

But it was not just the sunlight and the open road before him, or the prospect of his new command either, that had improved his mood. For nearly a decade, Castus had been in close proximity to the emperor and his court, first as Protector and then tribune. He had followed Constantine loyally, but the relentless round of civil wars, the emperor's grim ambition for total rule, had worn at Castus's nerves. The increasing power and influence of the Christians troubled him too; his own faith was strictly traditional, and the rise of this new cult threatened his sense of the divine order, whatever his emperor might believe. Worse still, the society of the court was haunted by the memory of Sabina. Castus had first encountered her there, and her shade had stood over him in all his official duties.

Now, in this fresh northern light, he felt liberated both from the oppressive confines of court protocol, the emperor's beliefs and ambitions, and the lingering memory of his dead wife. He would not have admitted that to anyone, but he knew in his heart that it was true.

Even so, as the day stretched on he felt the delay chafing at him. Castus travelled with only three light carts and a carriage, but the young Caesar's lumbering retinue snaked back behind him, a column of heavy ox wagons and marching men making slow going on the road. Castus had agreed with Bassus that he would remain with the imperial entourage until Vindonissa, but that was two days onwards.

The road crossed a narrow bridge, then angled to the left and climbed steadily through dense woodland, tangled trees and undergrowth barely cut back from the verges. At the top of the slope Castus paused, turning in the saddle to watch the column behind him with gathering impatience.

'Keep everyone moving,' he told Diogenes. 'I'm going back to speak with the Praetorian Prefect, see if we can pick up the pace and steal a march on them.'

The secretary nodded, signalling to a pair of escort troopers to accompany Castus. A quick glance along the road towards the carriage that held Ganna and his son, then Castus was plunging back down the slope again with the two horsemen cantering behind him.

They slowed after only a few hundred yards, meeting the forward units of the Caesar's retinue and the first of the wagons. Picking their way along the overgrown verge, the three riders traced a path back down the length of the column; Bassus and his own staff were travelling at the rear, and Castus would need to pass the entire mile-long imperial convoy before he could reach the prefect. He was halfway to the bridge when he saw the road opening before him: an expanse of empty rutted mud where there should have been carts and horsemen.

'*Centenarius!*' he shouted back to the commander of the Schola Scutariorum cavalry guard moving slowly up the slope. 'Why is there a gap in the column? Where's the Caesar's carriage?'

The officer wheeled his horse, too slowly for Castus's liking. He pushed back his cap, blank-faced. 'I... I don't know, excellency,' he said. 'They were behind us a moment ago... Maybe some problem on the bridge down there...'

At Castus's warning glance the man's explanation died. 'You're supposed to be guarding him!' Castus growled, raising himself in the saddle.

The commander's face paled, and he gulped visibly. 'Excellency, I...' Then he realised the implication in Castus's words, and his eyes widened in shock.

'After me!' Castus yelled, dragging at his reins and kicking his boots at the flanks of his horse. His own two guards spurred after him, and he heard the Scutarii commander shouting orders to his men to turn about and follow.

Hooves thundered on the muddy gravel, kicking up sprays of dirt. Already Castus could feel the prickling breath up his back, a sure presentiment of danger. At the angle in the road he saw the mill of figures around the stationary wagons, slaves and soldiers paused in confusion as the mounted cavalcade rushed towards them. A man stepped into Castus's path, arms raised.

'Dominus, the way's blocked on the other side of the bridge!' he cried.

But already Castus could see the mass of timber and foliage lying across the road: a fallen tree, or several perhaps, with the rest of the column backed up beyond; a gang of soldiers packed the span of the narrow bridge, trying to shift the blockade.

'Clear the way!' Castus shouted, and the man in the road darted back at the last moment as the riders swept past him. Now came the first trumpet blast, the call of alarm. At the same instant, the unmistakable sound of fighting.

The troops on the bridge fell back to either side, pressing themselves against the railings as Castus and the mounted men following him galloped between them. The fallen tree was large and old, the trunk shaggy with ivy and the branches thick with foliage. Impossible to see what was happening on the far side, although men were already clambering across, while others scrambled back from the other direction in panic. Letting out his reins, clasping his thighs tight against the saddle leather, Castus spurred his horse at the barricade and hoped she would not shy from it.

Three long galloping strides, and the grey mare launched herself at the obstruction. Castus threw himself forward over the mane, sucking in air through his teeth as his muscles clenched. Hooves crashed through foliage and ivy; then the horse was down on the far side, stumbling only slightly. The impact almost threw Castus from the saddle. Breath heaving as he struggled back upright, he hauled on the reins and fought to control the plunging horse.

One glance took in the scene. Already it seemed he was too late. There, fifty yards away among the stationary carts and wagons, stood the imperial carriage with its distinctive purple drapes and gilded trappings. The door of the carriage was open; dead men on the ground around it; the mounted guard either slain or driven off. From the gulleys and thickets on either side of the road poured men in dirt-brown capes, with shields and spears in their hands. Around each of the wagons the fighting swirled, the enemy cutting down slaves and baggage guards as they tried to flee. Castus stared around himself: where were the rest of the troops? Where was Crispus?

Then a javelin whipped past his head, and he kicked the horse into motion. He wore no armour, not even a helmet, and carried no shield. Pulling his cloak around his body, a scant protection, he drew the eagle-hilted *spatha* from his scabbard and roared as he charged.

A knot of spears to his right: the mare jinked and swerved, and Castus slashed his blade between the spearshafts and heard a scream of pain. He had never been a good rider, never liked trying to fight from the saddle. His horse was slow and heavy, but powerful and well trained for war; now she was carrying him into the meshes of fighting around one of the wagons. Struggling to stay upright, Castus let the animal's impetus carry him onwards, blasting aside the first couple of men who opposed him. He lashed his arm back, and felt the spatha's blade shear through flesh.

Gods, was anyone following him? One of the attackers leaped at him from the wagon bed. Castus dodged the clumsy spear-thrust, turned his horse with the pressure of his knees and leaned from the saddle to stab the man through the throat. He felt calmer in his body now, his muscles warming to the familiar dance of combat. Without thinking he cut down two more men, and let his horse kick another to the ground and then mash him beneath her hooves. But his mind was reeling, senses stretched to comprehend what was happening around him.

The attackers were bearded men, their long hair dyed red and shaved at the sides of the skull. Patterned tunics under their dun cloaks, small round shields with spiked bosses. Castus recognised them: Lentienses, one of the fiercer Alamannic tribes from across the frontier. He remembered his son's fears of savage men coming across the lake in boats, and his own reply that such a thing was impossible. At least the two troopers who had followed him down the road were still with him, and the first of the Scutarii were riding into the melee.

Clearing the far end of the wagon, Castus stared along the road towards the Caesar's carriage and dread climbed in his chest. Arrows bristled from the sides of the stationary vehicle. The last mounted guardsman was falling from his horse, a javelin in his side, and now only a pair of soldiers in the white uniforms of the Protectores stood against the attackers. The barbarians had cut the horses from their traces and slain the driver; two of them had clambered up onto the arched roof of the carriage and were stabbing their spears down at the window grilles.

All of this Castus saw in a heartbeat. Then he kicked his horse into a charge, his sword already raised. He could see a figure crouched back against the nearside wheel of the carriage, sheltered by the two Protectores: the Caesar Crispus, a shortsword in his hand, his face shifting from determination to panic.

'*Caesar!*' Castus bellowed as he closed the distance. At the last moment he pulled on the reins, turning the horse around the far side of the carriage. One slicing blow chopped the legs from a man on the roof; the second Alamannic warrior jabbed with his spear, and Castus grabbed at the shaft, pulled, and then drove his blade through the man's belly as he toppled.

Blood up his arm, and on his horse's flank. A face appeared at the carriage window: Lactantius, the old tutor. Castus dragged the sword from the dead warrior's body and let him fall, then nudged the horse onward, circling the carriage at a fast trot. Another barbarian, climbing up the rear of the carriage box, dropped to the ground and fled; Castus let him go.

One of the Protectores was down, injured or dead, but the other was still fighting grimly, hedged about with spears. Castus doubled the rear of the carriage, slashing down from the saddle at one of the warriors before he could raise his shield. From the corner of his eye he could make out the Scutarii forming up across the road. This would be over soon, but the young Caesar was still in danger.

Jumping from the saddle, Castus snatched up a fallen shield and wielded it, smashing the spiked boss at another of the attackers. He caught a spearhead on his sword and turned it, then slid the blade up the shaft, forcing it aside until he could slash at the warrior's unprotected face.

The second Protector cried out as an arrow struck his leg, and sank to one knee. Behind him, Crispus was pressed against the iron rim of the wheel with his sword raised. A flung spear jarred into the carriage box beside him, but he was paralysed and barely flinched. Two Alamanni ran at him, leaping the fallen bodies of his guards.

Bellowing, Castus took four long strides, his sword wheeling. One of the warriors turned, but too late to block the blow; the heavy spatha bit into his neck and almost decapitated him. The second danced back, spear up. Castus feinted with the shield, saw the man flinch from the bloodied boss, then crouched and drove a stabbing blow upwards with all the strength of his arm. The warrior grunted as the blade pierced him below the ribs, then Castus slammed the shield into his face and he fell.

Horsemen all around them now, the centenarius of the Scutarii screaming orders to his riders. Castus turned to the boy crouched against the carriage wheel.

'Caesar! Get back inside!'

'No!' the boy shouted back. 'I want to die on my feet, like a man!'

Plenty of men here to do your dying for you, Castus thought. But just for a moment, in the boy's defiant shout, he had seen a flicker of Constantine's stubborn rage. *His father's son, after all.*

Breathing hard, hefting shield and reddened sword, Castus stood his ground and stared around himself. Most of the attacking warriors had fled before the charging cavalry, and the few that remained were swiftly being cut down. The fight was finished; the emperor's son was safe.

Castus dropped to one knee and checked on the injured Protector. Blood was pooling beneath him; he must have been hit more seriously before the arrow struck. Not much longer for him now. The other was already dead. Figures were clambering from the gloom of the carriage, joining the young Caesar: first a cringing eunuch, then the old tutor, his white hair in crazed disarray.

'Praise be to Almighty God!' the old man cried, raising his palms to the sky. 'We are saved from the fury of the barbarians! Praise to the Risen Christ for the preservation of His servants!'

Castus wiped the blood from his blade as he knelt beside the dying Protector. 'It's the swords of Roman soldiers that saved you, old man,' he said. 'You should be praising Mars for your preservation. And Sol Invictus!'

'Thank you,' another voice said, and Castus turned to see the young Caesar attempting to sheath his sword with quivering hands. 'If you had not come, I...'

Castus opened his mouth to speak, to offer some dutiful words. But Crispus's face had turned grey. A moment later, the boy gasped and sagged against the carriage wheel, then noisily vomited over the spokes.

But now a solid mass of horsemen was coming up the road, Bassus the Praetorian Prefect riding among them. He was managing to appear calm, but his meaty features still quivered with recent terror.

'You arrived at the crucial moment, I see!' the prefect cried as he reined in his horse. He paused to draw a long breath, then gazed around him at the scene of slaughter. The air was sweet with the coppery reek of fresh blood. 'There was another blockade on the road behind us, or we would have got here sooner. Lentienses, I believe. They must have assumed this was a supply convoy, and hoped for good plunder! Few will survive, I suppose, to rue their error...'

Already horsemen were plunging into the thickets on either side of the road, pursuing the fugitives. Castus saw the officer of the Scutarii ordering them on, clearly eager to make up for his earlier failing.

'Eminence, call the men back!' Castus said. 'Order them to keep formation – this might have been a ruse. There could be other attackers...'

Bassus stared at him for a moment with a look of surprised pique. But this was not the moment to observe protocols. The prefect nodded to the trumpeter behind him.

Other attackers... Even as the trumpet notes sounded the recall, Castus felt the spike of ice in his spine. Without another glance he broke into a run. His horse was standing patiently in the road, head down, flanks still heaving. Castus seized the reins and vaulted into the saddle, feeling the ache in his muscles, the first tremors of delayed shock bursting through him. *Not yet, I need more time…*

'One more ride,' he breathed, then kicked at the horse and pulled her head around. The mare responded at once, leaping forward into a canter and then a flat gallop, back up the road towards the barricade and the bridge.

Castus clung to the saddle, his back bent, and felt the sweat tiding down his body. He was primed for the sounds of fighting up ahead, the noise of warriors falling on his own retinue, his own carts, the carriage that held Ganna and his son. The fallen tree was already dragged partway from the road, and Castus galloped around it, the soldiers on the far side falling back as he cleared the hedge of foliage.

On up the road, breathing through clenched teeth, nausea in his gut and a stitch digging at his side, Castus passed the stationary wagons drawn up on the slope, the units of soldiers staring back at him, baffled. By the time he reached the top of the hill his horse was labouring, blowing hard, and he felt every joint in his body jolted out of place.

But there were his carts, his own mounted bodyguard. There was the carriage, Ganna peering from the open door, Diogenes standing beside his horse. Not an enemy in sight.

'What's happening?' Ganna cried as she saw him. Others were riding to meet him, calling out the same question.

'Nothing,' Castus said, reining to a halt, breathless. 'Some trouble down the road. All over now.'

His son was gazing from the carriage window, wide-eyed. Castus remembered that his arm and the flanks of his horse were still spattered with blood, and the sword was naked in his hand. He circled, staring into the trees.

An ambush, he told himself, that was all. A barbarian warband chancing their luck, just as the prefect had said. He drew a long breath and held it. Birds were singing in the trees beside the road, and he ignored the questions, the concern of those around him.

Somehow the barbarians had known just which part of the column to strike, which part to isolate with their barricades. No, Castus thought, this was no simple plundering raid. Such a small group of warriors would never have tried to ambush a heavily armed convoy with cavalry protection. Whoever had directed the attack had known exactly where that one particular carriage would be, and who would be travelling inside it.

CHAPTER V

Heavy sun on the river. The Rhine flowed strong and steady between her green banks, and out in midstream, oars beating slow with the current, the liburnian galley *Bellona* glided smoothly northwards. It was the third day since they had left the port at Argentorate, and the river ran broader and straighter now, no longer looping and curling between massive wooded bluffs and precipices. The country to either side appeared featureless, empty forests unpopulated by man, but Castus knew that there were settlements among the trees. Several times they had passed fortifications, even walled towns, on the left bank, the Roman side. But on the opposite bank he saw nothing but the occasional herd of scrawny short-horned cattle driven down to water on the muddy shore.

'Looks placid enough, don't it?' the navarch said, leaning on the rail of the narrow stern deck. 'Always the same, along this stretch. You never know what might happen, though. Until it does.'

Castus grunted his agreement. He had only spent a few months on the Rhine frontier, many years ago, but he knew the ways of the barbarians. The Franks to the north and the Alamanni to the south had warred with Rome countless times; a generation back they had poured across the frontiers in massive warbands, laying waste to great swathes of Gaul. Successive imperial campaigns had driven them back, and now the diverse tribes lived under treaty of submission. But they were a fractious people, and every few years an enterprising chieftain would lead a party across the river into the Roman domain. This, he thought, was his command now. Dux Limitis Germaniae: Commander of the Germanic Frontier. By the end of the day he would arrive at Colonia and take up his official duties. For now, this river cruise was a relaxing interval of peace.

The navarch, Aelius Senecio, was a scarred old soldier, and Castus had warmed to him at once. He had lost his left hand in a cross-river raid a score of years ago; the stump was fitted with a carved replacement of dark wood. Both Senecio and his crew belonged to Legion XXII Primigenia, based at Mogontiacum. They were legionaries, and the oarsmen could double as fighting soldiers if required; their shields were mounted along the bulwarks and their weapons and armour stowed beneath the rowing benches. But Castus guessed that a long time had passed since they had fought on land: the sweating, muscled oarsmen looked wedded to their craft. Senecio did too: aboard his ship, he was undisputed master, and Castus enjoyed the man's lack of deference to his elevated rank.

Senecio clearly loved his ship too. As *Praepositus Classis Germaniae*, he was acting commander of the whole Rhine fleet, but the *Bellona* was his special pride. His face creased affectionately as he ran his palm along the deck railing, or paced the long central gangway above the tiers of rowing benches. He scowled hotly if any of his crew missed their stroke, or if his eye detected a fault in the ship's immaculate paintwork.

'She's old but strong, the *Bellona*, just like me,' he had told Castus on the first day of their voyage. 'Carausius built her for his fleet. I daresay you've heard of him?'

Castus nodded. He knew the stories of Carausius, the military commander who had seized power in Britain and declared himself emperor. Twenty-five years ago, so he estimated.

'Back then,' the navarch said, 'she was a sea boat, sailing the Germanic Ocean. But when Carausius, may the gods rot him, was brought down the *Bellona* was sent to river duties. Been on the Rhine ever since. You'll have seen bigger boats, I'm sure, but you won't find a better one this side of the Alps.'

True enough, *Bellona* was not a big ship, and had an old-fashioned look. But as a double-banked galley of fifty oars, she was certainly the biggest craft on the Rhine. Her smooth-scrubbed deck ran just over thirty paces, from the warrior-goddess figurehead standing proud above her curving cutwater right back to her upswept stern. With her hull painted blue-green, topsides lined in red and white, a pair of ballistae mounted on the stern deck and a heavier catapult at the bow, she was a fitting flagship for the river flotilla.

The other craft that sailed in her wake could match her for neither size nor elegance. Three wide flat-bottomed barges carried Castus's baggage, horses and the remaining members of his travelling staff. Flanking them were two smaller galleys, sleek thirty-oared vessels with rakish hulls and dragon-head prows.

Braced against one of the two ballistae mounted just forward of the steersman's position, Castus scanned the eastern bank of the river. Still no signs of life. No signs of any trouble either – he had seen no smoke rising from the Roman lands to the west, no troops moving on the riverbank road. The sun was bright off the water, and when he squinted Castus could just make out a single canoe paddling upstream near the Germanic bank, one or two figures sitting upright in the dugout hull, gazing back at him.

Movement from behind him, a flash of green and blonde, and Castus turned and looked back past the steersman and into the shade of the canopy beneath the curved stern post. Ganna appeared, clambering up the ladder and through the hatchway to the deck. The stuffy little triangular cabin below the poop had been set aside for Castus's use, but he preferred to sleep on deck, wrapped in his cloak, with the other men. Now Ganna and Sabinus used the cabin at night, and during the heat of the day.

The crewmen at the stern assiduously ignored the slave woman as she crossed to the heap of personal baggage beside the deck rail. Squatting, Ganna opened one of the chests and brought out a bag of Sabinus's things. Castus tried not to watch her. When he glanced back he saw her poised, head raised, staring at the barbarian riverbank across the water with a look of calm intensity in her grey eyes. They had reached the lands of her own people now, Castus realised. Those were Ganna's own forests, her own distant hills.

'Bructeri, am I right?' Senecio said, once Ganna had returned below deck. 'You can tell from the accent. She looks after your boy all right though?'

'She does,' Castus said, feeling a tightness in his throat.

'Seems that way. Fiercest of the lot, the Bructeri, some say. Cruel too – they poison their arrows. Mind you, they've been quiet enough these last years.'

Castus swallowed thickly, then sucked his teeth. 'What do you know of the trouble in the north?' he asked.

The navarch gave him a guarded look. 'Not much,' he said. 'Maybe since the last dux died there's been some difficulties. He was trying to sort out a problem with the subsidy payments when he died, as I'm sure you know.'

Castus did not. He nodded, not wanting to probe Senecio any further. Doubtless the man knew more, but he was a good soldier, and it was not his place to tell of it.

An assembly of dignitaries waited on the riverbank at Colonia Agrippina. Castus studied them from the deck as the *Bellona* backed her oars and swung slowly with the current. The little group of figures on the timber wharf was still quite distant, and he could make out nothing of their appearance just yet.

Instead, as the ship crossed the stream of the river towards the docks, Castus stared past the waiting figures at the city beyond. It had been many years since he had seen Colonia Agrippina, and much had changed. The city itself was the same, the tiled roofs rising from behind strong walls. Further downstream, the Praetorium, the palace of the governors, stood high upon the bank with its red-pink arches, its tall towers and its central cupola facing defiantly across the river towards the barbarian shore. But the bridge that Castus had seen under construction all those years ago was complete now: massive timber girders supporting a broad roadway, spanning the river on twenty solid stone piers. An impressive bit of engineering: as Castus watched, the central span was rising like a drawbridge, to allow the ships to pass through once they had discharged their passengers. And on the far bank rose the walls and towers of the new bridgehead fortress of Divitia, a Roman foothold in *barbaricum*.

Oars threshed the muddy brown water as the galley manoeuvred her stern closer to the wharf. Castus stood straight, neck held stiff. An hour before, in the cramped little shelter on the poop, he had waited patiently while his orderly Eumolpius unpacked his best military garb, then arrayed him in the embroidered crimson tunic, the white linen arming doublet and gilded muscled cuirass. His heavy red cloak was pinned back from his shoulder and swept up across one arm, and he carried his plumed helmet clasped in the crook of his elbow. He was sweating slightly already; Ganna was quite right that he had gained weight over the last year, and the cuirass constricted his torso uncomfortably.

Castus peered at the assembly on the riverbank. 'Who are they all?' he asked Senecio through tightened lips.

'City councillors, magistrates and priests,' the navarch replied from the side of his mouth. 'The *curator*, and the *defensor*. That's Gaudiosus on the right; he's the tribune commanding the detachment at Divitia. The short man with the nose is Tiberianus, the governor.' The tone of his voice expressed eloquently his feelings about the dignitaries.

Castus nodded. He was remembering the prefect's strange warning, back at Arbor Felix. Were these the people of whom he should be wary? How was he to know? He had a sudden memory of another arrival by ship, years before: the usurper Maximian's *adventus* at the seaport of Massilia. He hoped the memory was not a bad portent.

Shouts from the deck officers and crew as the galley backed up to the docks, her oars sliding smartly inboard as stevedores flung cables across the last gap of churning water. As soon as the gangway was secured, Castus marched up onto the wharf, his small group of staff at his heels. Trumpets sounded a ragged fanfare.

'His excellency Aurelius Castus, *vir perfectissimus*, Dux Limitis Germaniae,' the herald cried. The line of troops drawn up behind the dignitaries raised their hands in salute. Castus lifted his own hand in acknowledgement, then turned to face the assembled civilians.

At the centre of the group was a short man, wrapped in the heavy pleated toga of high office and the insignia of senatorial rank. His hair was clipped short to hide his baldness, and he stood with his chest thrust forward and his head tipped back, so that he appeared to be staring at Castus through his flaring nostrils.

'Claudius Basilius Tiberianus,' the herald declared, '*vir clarissimus*, Consularis Germania Secunda.'

Tiberianus took four slow steps forward, raising his arms, and Castus moved to greet him. They met in a stiff formal embrace. Officially, Castus knew, he and this man were equals: he would have supreme command of the military forces in the province, while the governor controlled the civilian aspects of the administration. In theory their spheres would remain entirely separate, entirely complementary. In practice, things were seldom that easy.

They parted, and Tiberianus took a few steps back, still gazing at Castus down his nose. There was a short awkward pause; Castus realised with dulled surprise that he had no idea what was supposed to happen next. The rest of his staff and his baggage were coming ashore from the barges now. Sweat ran down his back inside his cuirass, soaking into his tunic. He had not expected to feel nervous about this first meeting, but dealings with civilians always made him uneasy.

Great gods, don't let there be speeches. But he knew that he prayed in vain. Already a flustered-looking orator was stepping out from the civilian group, clearing his throat and inflating himself to speak.

'*Truly*,' the orator began, flinging up his hands, '*our mighty emperor, whose preservation is our salvation, has answered our fervent prayers, and shown once again the great love he bears for our western provinces…!*'

Castus tightened his jaw, letting the tide of honeyed phrases wash around him. He looked from one face to the next, studying them, eager not to appear in any way overawed by this assembly of dignitaries. Tiberianus the governor angled his nose even further upwards, his nostrils aimed at the distant horizon. Castus knew how these men must see him: his scarred and brutal face, his muscular neck and heavy shoulders. An uncultured soldier, a peasant risen to high office, skilled only in violence.

'*For was it not in the west that his sun first rose, dazzling the eyes of the faithless foe? Did his divinely ordained rule not take its root in these rich and verdant lands?*'

Scanning along the line of the civilian group, Castus observed the tribune, Gaudiosus. A lanky officer with a bored expression. His troops were garrisoned across the bridge at Divitia fortress and several other strongpoints around the city and along the river. They were legionaries at least, men of Legion I Minervia; the previous garrison, the Divitenses that Castus had fought alongside in the Italian campaign, had been redeployed to the field army. The soldiers that Gaudiosus had brought to form his honour guard looked smart enough, but Castus knew that many of the garrisons on the frontier were composed of raw recruits and time-served veterans, units still bearing the proud titles of their old legions but much reduced in both quality and effective strength.

'*What is it that protects our lands from the unbridled fury of the barbarian? It is not the walls of our towns and cities; neither is it this great river upon whose banks we stand. Rather it is* fear! *The fear of Roman arms, and the swift and mighty retribution that will follow any insult, and lay low their pride with the bodies of their warriors and the hovels of their families!*'

The gathered civilians seemed to take heart from these martial words; Castus saw them stiffen and raise their heads. The governor appeared to be inhaling one enormous breath through his flared nostrils. Irritation itched along Castus's spine; what did these comfortable-looking men know of war and bloodshed? But it pleased him to think that they would take his glowering expression as evidence of his soldierly fervour.

'And not only has the Sacred Wisdom sent his own son to sit in his place, and bestow the light of his majesty once more upon us. He has also sent this son of Mars, this worthy soldier from the embattled plains of Illyricum, to take up the protecting shield of Roman might, and the avenging sword of Roman justice, and restore our lands to peace and security!'

Castus tried to hide his brief smirk. Funny to think of himself as a 'son of Mars'. No doubt his own father would have been most amused. But now the speech of welcome was at an end, and a collective exhalation rose from the assembly. Castus blinked his eyes back into focus. Was something expected of him? Was he – fresh sweat broke on his back – expected to make a speech himself?

It appeared so. Even the governor had ceased his scrutiny of the horizon and was gazing at him expectantly. Castus cleared his throat, and then drew in a long breath.

'I am only a simple soldier, and cannot hope to match your eloquence,' he began, his tone so close to a gruff shout that the front rank of the delegation quailed slightly. 'Our emperor has sent me here with clear instructions to restore the security of this frontier. I intend to fulfil them, and do nothing more.'

He scanned the faces of the assembly once more, judging the effect of his words. 'Let every man do his duty, and attend promptly to my commands and those of the clarissimus Tiberianus, and with the help of the gods your lands and your fine city will be free from all danger.'

More trumpeting, more salutes, but the job was done and Castus felt relief rising through him. No doubt he had offended a few people with his lack of rhetorical nicety and compliments, and the suggestion that he might start giving them orders; well, that was fine. They only needed to look at him to see the truth of his words.

'You must have flown here on the wings of Mercury,' the governor said quietly as they rode together in a jogging two-horse cart. Colonia Agrippina was set back from the river, and they were following the track that crossed the foreshore between the shacks and warehouses to the city gates, the rest of the assembled dignitaries falling into procession behind them. 'We were not expecting you until well after the ides.'

'His eminence the Praetorian Prefect told me of an emergency. I came as fast as I could.'

'Emergency? Hmm.' Tiberianus rolled the words around his mouth, then smiled. 'There was a brief… situation. But the matter is resolved, for the time being at least.'

They were seated very close on the cart's single bench, and the governor's perfume was strong. Castus found that he liked the man less with every passing moment.

'Your precipitous arrival has left us in a stir, I'm afraid – we have no official banquet or meetings prepared. A wing of the Praetorium is available for you and your staff, however. And perhaps you would care to dine with me at my house this evening? A small gathering – only the most important of men. I'm sure they can appraise you of all current matters.'

'It would be an honour,' Castus said, and tightened his lips into a smile.

CHAPTER VI

'Excellency,' Diogenes said, sliding in through the door with a stack of tablets and documents in his arms.

Castus turned from the window. 'Call me that again,' he said, 'and I'll have you sent back to the ranks!'

Diogenes gave an apologetic wince, then set the documents down on the table. They were in one of the reception rooms of the Praetorium on the riverbank, a tall gloomy chamber decorated in a style fashionable about fifty years before. Most of the building was empty, the dusty halls closed and shuttered; Tiberianus preferred his own sumptuous residence in the north-east quarter of the city.

'I've compiled the most recent strength reports for the troops currently stationed on the frontier, dominus,' Diogenes said. 'If you've time, perhaps…?'

'Yes, yes,' Castus told him with a curt wave. It had been a trying day, a day of meetings and negotiations, audiences and administration. Already it was growing dark, the slaves wandering the halls with tapers and lighting the lamps. Castus still had a lingering headache from the night before at the governor's house. He may as well hear the bad news now.

'You have, as you know, three legionary formations under your direct command,' Diogenes said. He consulted one of the tablets. 'These being the remaining men of the Thirtieth at Tricensima and First Minervia here and at Bonna, together with the naval detachment of the Twenty-Second Primigenia. The first two total 4,368 men present with the standards, while the Twenty-Second has 323 men, engaged in river duties...'

Castus listened, nodding, as the secretary went on with his figures. The strength reports were months out of date, and there had been no recent large-scale enlistment. Most likely the force under his command was more depleted still.

'Then there is the Numerus Ursariensis, 216 men, the Numerus Batavorum Exploratorum, 373 men, the Fifth Cohort Valeria Thracum, 239...'

The list continued, but Castus was only paying partial attention. He thought back to the night before, and the dinner at the governor's house. A small gathering indeed, and many of them were not city or provincial officials but landowners, even local merchants. Castus did not believe for a moment the story of his unexpected arrival: clearly Tiberianus had arranged things so that the new dux could be surrounded by his own cronies as soon as possible. He was displeased to note that Gaudiosus, the tribune of the Divitia garrison, was among them. Apparently the governor had already brought him on board.

'Your predecessor,' Tiberianus had said, head tipped well back as the main course was cleared, 'may the gods honour his shade, was not the most active of commanders, I'm afraid to say.'

'Is that so?' Castus had asked, picking his teeth. He was drinking too much, and the wine was going to his head. 'I had heard that his excellency Valerius Leontius died while on an expedition against the Franks. That sounds quite active.'

'Hardly an *expedition*,' said the man beside him on the dining couch. 'He was paying them a subsidy – a bribe, one might say. No, for all their provocation he refused to take proper action against them!'

The governor had introduced this man as Magnius Rufus, one of the wealthiest landowners in the provinces of Germania and Belgica, and former *patronus* of the city of Colonia. He was a big man in late middle age, fleshy but vigorous-looking, with a ready smile and very white teeth. Castus tried to hide his reaction: civilians, he thought, should never dare question the actions of soldiers.

'Forgive me!' Rufus cried, clasping Castus by the shoulder. 'I'm just a plain-speaking Gaul! But I was born in this country, and I know the ways of our barbarian neighbours too well. It's a vain policy, I've always said, to try and appease them, pay them subsidies and expect them to hold to their treaties. They are savages, and they respect only prompt and overwhelming force!'

Castus nodded, narrowing his eyes. He had guessed very early in the evening that this Magnius Rufus was the true host of the dinner, not the governor at all. Rufus had dominated proceedings from the start, often talking over the others at the table. His loud good humour had a slightly threatening air, and even Tiberianus seemed beaten down by it.

'What provocation did the barbarians offer?' Castus asked, turning deliberately to the governor.

'They often try and seize our grain ships on the river,' Tiberianus said. Castus had noticed the governor's eyes flick quickly in Rufus's direction, as if requesting permission to speak. 'As you probably know, most of the grain supply for the frontier garrisons, and for the city of Colonia, comes across the sea from Britain. The Rhine is our transit route, but it's vulnerable. Frequently the barbarians try and impose tolls, or interfere with the river traffic. Last autumn a band of the Chamavi seized a grain freighter that ran aground on a mudbank and pillaged it, killing the crew.'

'And that was after plenty of other mischief!' Magnius Rufus broke in, unable to remain silent any longer. 'And so, you see, our valiant dux Leontius was compelled to act at long last… But he led only a small reprisal raid across the river, at the time of one of the Chamavi religious festivals, and his men burned a grove sacred to one of their hideous gods in the process. There's a rumour,' he said, widening his eyes dramatically, 'that the barbarians cursed him for his impiety! Anyway, six months later he was murdered by them, presumably in revenge, while delivering their subsidy payment.'

Hands fluttered around the table, most of the assembly making warding signs against evil magic. A couple of men dipped their fingers in their wine and flicked droplets onto the mosaic floor as an offering to any spirits in attendance. Castus remained unmoved by the story. He guessed that Leontius had been pressured to act, against his better judgement, and perhaps at a bad time.

'What of the Chamavi?' he said. 'They haven't made any further threats?'

'They've been massing warbands since the start of the summer,' the governor told him. 'Although, they have yet to try and cross the river. They often attempt something at this time of year though – we have stores of grain from our suppliers in Britain, fodder and other stores for the winter, and they do not. Our lands may not yield much in the way of crops, but we have cattle and sheep aplenty. Meat on the hoof.'

'Tell me of their numbers,' Castus said, sipping from his cup. He felt saturated with wine already, and the room was hot and thick with the smells of food, but he forced himself to remain collected and reserved. The tribune, Gaudiosus, leaned forward to speak.

'Each of the petty kings has his own retinue of household warriors,' he said, with a disdainful shrug. 'Maybe a few hundred strong, maybe less. He grants them wealth, arms and plunder, and they serve him to the death. But beyond that are the masses of common warriors who join the warbands. The Chamavi can certainly muster several thousands of them, but their territory extends many miles north. There could well be more than we know.' Castus noticed that the man did not address him correctly, as his superior officer. He narrowed his eyes, and nodded for the man to continue.

'To the west, nearer the river estuary, there are the Salii,' the tribune went on. 'They've been our enemies in the past, but generally nowadays they abide by their treaties.'

Castus knew of the Salii; his old friend Brinno had been the son of one of their chieftains. Brinno, he recalled, had never had anything good to say about the Chamavi, or the provincials of Germania and Belgica either.

'Then upstream from the Chamavi are the Chattuari,' Gaudiosus said. 'There are some other scattered tribes too – Tubantes, Lanciones, Amsivarii – but they are subordinate to the others. Then, furthest south, opposite our city here, are the Bructeri. We call them all Franks, but they have little cohesion. Most of the time they fight among themselves.'

'And long may that continue!' Rufus declared, to much gruff agreement.

The gathering had broken up soon after that, Castus collecting his four guards from the door and marching blearily home through the empty streets to the Praetorium. He had slept badly that night, too many thoughts dancing in his mind on the fumes of the drink. He had remembered his Frankish friend Brinno, keenly and painfully. He had remembered the Praetorian Prefect's strange warning to beware of the provincials. He had thought about Ganna – who had removed herself to a pallet on the floor to escape his mumbling and

82

thrashing – and her longing glances towards the barbarian shore.

Not surprising that he felt so worn down now, so tired and irritable. With a start he realised that Diogenes had almost reached the end of his troop roster.

'… the Sixth Equites Stablesiani, 268 men, the Eleventh Equites Dalmatorum, 212 men, and the Numerus Equitum Sarmatorum, 284 men. That's all of them, dominus.'

'So what's our total strength?'

'Officially, your command should number nearly twelve thousand. However, based on these figures you appear to have about half that.'

Six thousand men. The number, Castus thought, of a single legion of the old establishment. Once upon a time, he knew, the province of Lower Germania had two full legions to defend it, besides auxiliaries. Back then, of course, the troops were commanded by the provincial governors themselves: no doubt Tiberianus recalled those days fondly. It had been Diocletian, in his great wisdom, who had appointed *duces* to the military command, leaving the governors to civilian duties… A thought struck him, something that had passed through his turning mind the night before.

'Have you heard of an emperor called Victorinus?' he asked Diogenes.

'Certainly, dominus. Marcus Piavonius Victorinus, one of the Gallic usurpers. He followed Postumus in the rule of the western provinces, during the time that they broke away from Rome; about fifty years ago, I suppose. Why do you ask?'

'I met a man last night who claimed to be descended from him.' Piavonius Magnius Rufus – yes, that had been the name. The governor, in a particularly obsequious moment, had pointed out the connection. A dangerous connection too: any man descended from an emperor, even the mere grand-nephew of a usurper, had a dubious claim to the purple. Magnius Rufus had laughed it off, of course, but Castus had heard the pride in his voice.

'Funnily enough, Piavonius Victorinus lost his life in this very building.'

'Murdered by his own officers, by any chance?'

'You know the story! Ah… yes.'

Castus glanced around the room, as if he might still see the faint bloodstains in the flickering lamplight. He had heard enough tales of usurpers and their bad ends.

'Would you like me to have this man watched, dominus?' Diogenes said, raising an eyebrow as he reached for a fresh tablet.

Castus shook his head. Diogenes, he remembered, had certain philosophical ideas about government: to him, state power was the sole guarantor of popular freedom. Doubtless he would relish the chance to persecute a wealthy private individual like Magnius Rufus. But Castus had too much work to be involving himself in intrigues just yet. Besides, Rufus was clearly a man of power and influence here.

'He's invited me to visit him at his villa, when I have time,' Castus said, without enthusiasm. 'I'll leave it to you to compose a suitably *busy* schedule.'

Upstairs, in his private chambers, Castus found Ganna already waiting for him. One of the tall arched windows was open, letting in a cool exhalation of night air, and she sat beside it staring into the darkness on the far side of the river.

'Sabbi's already sleeping,' she said as he entered the room. 'He seems happier now, at last.'

'I'm sure he prefers the lodgings,' Castus said through a yawn. He dismissed the other two slaves with a gesture, then slopped wine into a cup. It was unwatered, strong. If he wanted to sleep soundly, he reasoned, he needed more drink to quiet his mind.

Sitting on the couch, Castus looked at the woman beside the window. Only a single lamp burned upon the table, and her figure was half in shadow against the faint moonlight outside.

'You look...' Castus began, then snorted a quick laugh. 'You look like some half-tamed wild animal, still longing for the freedom of the wild!'

He caught the quick movement of her head, and realised how offensive his words had been. *I am tired*, he thought, *and too clumsy to be civil.*

'An animal, you say? It is not my people who are animals. You Romans are the true beasts.'

Castus made a sound in his throat, and drank more wine. He was not in a mood for argument, not tonight. But Ganna felt differently.

'I see the way they look at you,' she said coldly. 'These fine Romans. This governor and all his fat friends. They are wolves! They think you are an animal too, a big stupid bear, and they yap at you and think you will dance for them!'

'Quiet!' Castus snarled into his cup. He knew this mood of hers well; he should dismiss her now, before things got worse.

But Ganna had withdrawn into herself once more; meditative, she brought her knees up and clasped them to her chest as she stared out of the window.

'You said to me some days ago,' she told him, 'that you could free me and then make me your wife.'

'Uh?' Castus said, glancing up. He had not been expecting this.

'Well then, I have a thing to say.' Ganna turned on her seat to face him. 'Free me, marry me, and come with me.'

'To your people? To barbaricum?'

'Yes! Bring Sabbi too. Nobody would harm you, if you were with me. You would be accepted – a great warrior. We could live together, in freedom. Away from these Roman wolves.'

'You forget,' Castus said loudly, unable to keep the anger from his voice, 'that I've seen your country. You think I would want that life? I've marched from one end of the empire to the other in the service of my emperor – my son's lived in Rome itself. Why should we throw that away for your so-called freedom? The freedom of savages!'

He heard the dying echo of his voice, and hated the words he had spoken. Had the views of Rufus and the governor already infected him? But he knew he was trying to deny his impulse: just for a fleeting moment the idea had grabbed at him – it would be so easy – before the hooks of his allegiance had dragged him back. He saw Ganna's face closing against him.

'Very well. I have said my words. I say no more.'

Castus felt his head throbbing, and pinched at the bridge of his nose. He wanted to apologise, but could not bring himself to do it. He could almost laugh – the Dux Limitis Germaniae wanting to apologise to his own slave... Just for a moment the big smirking face of Magnius Rufus appeared to him. Was he really so dissimilar to that man?

'You talk to me of Rome,' Ganna said, her voice tight with suppressed rage. 'You, too, forget. I lived there for eight long years. I know it far better than you! I know the way these civilised Romans behave. I know what foul things they do in their great houses. Your own wife, she behaved no better than a beast—'

'Enough!' Castus shouted, on his feet suddenly. He knew she was hurt and angry, and trying to injure him, but this he could not allow. 'Say nothing of my wife! You are a slave – know your place!'

'My place?' she said, standing up as well. 'What is that?' With a single fierce gesture she pulled the pins from her hair, letting it fall long and blonde over her shoulders. She ripped out the brooch at her shoulder and her tunic dropped to her feet. Naked, she strode to the couch and flung herself down upon it. 'Is this my place? This is the use you have for me? To nurse your son, and fuck on your command?'

'Stop this,' Castus said hoarsely. He bent down, wincing, and snatched up her fallen tunic. Ganna sat up, cross-legged on the mattress.

'You know how your wife died, *excellency*?'

He took two long steps towards her before he managed to halt himself. His fists were clenched, the tunic trailing from his locked fingers.

'She died of a fever,' he said, knowing already that it was a lie.

'She died giving birth to a child that came too soon. The child died too.'

No need for her to say more; Castus knew it all now. He had not been with Sabina for over nine months when she died. 'Whose?' he managed to say.

'Nobody. A man. Not you.'

Turning on his heel, Castus flung the tunic towards the couch. 'Get dressed and get out,' he said. 'Go to your own quarters.'

He did not hear her leave. When he was alone he sank down on the couch, pressing his bunched knuckles to his face. In some way he had known all along, or his fears had whispered the truth to him. Sabina had always been easily tempted. But what a fool he had been. No better than a beast. A dancing bear. His heavy shoulders were locked in misery. Never again, he told himself. Never again would he allow himself to become that vulnerable.

Clumsily pouring more wine, he drank it back quickly, as if he could eclipse the thoughts in his head. A great sigh ran through him, and he hurled the cup and its contents at the far wall. Getting up, he snuffed the lamp with his fingers, barely feeling the flame burn his thumb. Then he staggered through into the sleeping cubicle, hauling off his clothes.

It was several hours later, in the dead of the night, that he woke again with a gasp. His head reeled; then he heard the sound again. The crash of hobnailed boots on the tiled floor of the portico downstairs. Shouts filtered up to him, echoed into indistinction.

By the time the messenger arrived Castus was already on his feet, pulling on his tunic. Lamplight spilled through the opening door. It was a soldier, his cloak thick with dust.

'Dominus!' he said as he entered the room, saluting quickly. 'Message from the commander at Tricensima: The Chamavi and Chattuari have crossed the river in force. They're burning and destroying everything in their path.'

CHAPTER VII

The horsemen were sweating in their mail as they rode through the deserted village. The day was hot, and the air stank of burnt thatch and smoke. Something else too: Castus caught the smell, and for a moment it was pleasant, but then his guts clenched. He had not eaten that morning, and was glad of it.

'These two must have tried to put up a fight,' the cavalry commander said. 'Either that or the barbarians were just making an example of them.'

The bodies had been strung up on the beam of a house and a fire lit beneath them. Flames had burnt away most of the lower limbs and charred the remaining flesh. The horsemen rode by in column, each man glancing grim-faced at the scene.

'What about them?' Castus asked, nodding away to the right between the plundered huts. More bodies lay in the wreckage: women, and what might have been a child. Naked limbs, bloodied and crusted with flies.

Castus knew scenes like this one all too well. He had seen the Roman army do such things to enemy villages often enough; it was the way of war. But these slaughtered villagers had been under his protection.

The cavalry commander made a sound in his throat. 'They'll have taken the rest as slaves, dominus,' he said, kicking his horse into motion again. 'The scouts have picked up the trail ahead – we should be able to catch them. Nothing we can do for these here.'

Castus glanced one more time at the bodies, then followed him.

Ulpius Dexter, Prefect of the Sixth Equites Stablesiani, was tanned and weathered as old saddle-leather, his face lean and corded. Castus had caught up with him and his men earlier that day, and already they had tracked and destroyed two smaller bands of raiders. The Stablesiani were garrison cavalry, one of the units stationed at strongpoints along the supply road that stretched west from Colonia to Tungris, intended to intercept barbarian raiders who managed to cross the Rhine into Roman territory. All of them had moved north as soon as they heard of the invasion; spread out across fifty miles of country, scouts moving ahead of them, they were harrying the raiders northwards along the valley of the Mosa.

'Trouble is,' Dexter said, 'when they split up into small bands like this it's impossible to catch them all. We get a few dozen, maybe, but by the time we've brought enough force against them the main body have escaped over the river with whatever they've taken.'

Castus grunted his agreement. This time, he thought, things might be different. Two days had passed since he first got word of the Chamavi invasion; had the messages he had dictated in the early hours of that morning been received in time, and understood? Had the navarch Senecio managed to turn his ships around before his journey back upriver? In his mind Castus saw the country ahead of him: the long sweep of the Rhine enclosing the open pastures of Toxandria and the broad valley of the Mosa, the wild marshy lands in between. His stratagem needed coordination; he needed his subordinate officers to move quickly and effectively. He had no idea, this early in his command, whether they would do so.

They were an hour further north when they sighted the enemy. The raiders were strung out along an expanse of meadow edged with trees, driving the prisoners and stolen cattle ahead of them; about fifty men with spears and shields, few of them armoured and most burdened with sacks of plunder. As they heard the hooves, the wailing horns, they broke into a run, but already there were armoured horsemen crashing out of the trees and galloping between them, killing the stragglers.

Castus watched the way the cavalrymen operated: the riders split up into groups of four, some with lances and others with bows they shot from the saddle, breaking up the enemy and cutting down any who stood to fight.

'Best method against these pillagers,' Dexter said between breaths as they rode. 'Sometimes they try and defend themselves, but mostly they run. Then it's easy.'

As he skirted the upper slope of the meadow, Castus could see the Chamavi scattering in confusion, the horsemen reaping them at the gallop. On the far side, a group of the barbarians had managed to gather in a defensive ring, shields raised. Among them Castus spotted one prominent figure, a warrior in mail armour and a plumed helmet, with a blue and white shield. As the last fugitives died or threw down their arms, the riders began to circle in on the ring of shields.

Castus had spent many hours on the road, slept poorly or not at all, and his mind and body felt hot and stiff with fatigue. As chief commander, his place was here in the periphery, directing the course of events. He should let the troops under his command do the fighting. He should, but he could not. All the frustration of these last two days boiled up in him now, all the pain of what he had learned about Sabina, the memory of

91

the plundered village, the burnt and mutilated dead, mounting together into a solid black rage.

'They need help down there,' he said, slinging his shield up from the saddle horn and kicking his horse into a canter. One of his bodyguards cried out, but already he was riding fast with Dexter beside him.

His horse crossed the meadow at a gallop, kicking up turf. After two days on horseback Castus was starting to feel welded to the saddle; the aches in his thighs and back had grown familiar now. The rush of the breeze, the motion of the animal beneath him, was invigorating: he could never have imagined this in his years as an infantry soldier.

Already the knot of warriors was retreating towards the thicket of trees on the far side of the meadow. Not a large wood, but dense and tangled with thorny undergrowth. Once they got in there, Castus knew, they might stand a chance of defending themselves against the cavalry. He could hear Dexter bellowing orders to his men to form up, but already the Stablesiani were banding together into a mounted wedge. Castus threw himself in amongst them, and at once he heard the trumpet sounding the charge.

Jostle of horses; clattering lances. A bow strummed behind him; he heard the insect-whine of the arrow beside his ear, and saw one of the Chamavi struck down. Then a sudden rush, hooves battering the turf, and one side of the shield ring rippled and collapsed as the warriors fell back in confusion. A moment of terror, heart-clenching, bowel-roiling, his whole body exploding in sweat, then Castus was into the mesh of the fight and no thought remained. He felt his horse kick; he saw a raised shield and hacked down at it, knocking it aside. A wheeling backhand blow sliced across the warrior's face. Blood sprayed.

A spear struck against his leg, jarring against his greave, and Castus raised his foot and booted another shield away from him. Still his horse was moving forward, snorting and biting as she powered her way between the panicking warriors. The defensive ring was broken on the left, but to the right Castus could see the remaining Chamavi regrouping around their leader, falling back once more towards the woods. He was breathing hard and fast, his chest heaving inside the tight cuirass, his thighs locked to the saddle leather as the fight swirled around him. Somebody hurled a javelin up at him, and he ducked his head and felt the shank clang against his helmet. The impact made him sway in the saddle and he pulled sharply on the reins to right himself; his horse blew angrily and reared forwards.

Then suddenly the last of the raiders was down and the fight had moved on, Dexter wheeling his hand in the air and shouting orders to his men to rally. The surviving barbarians were almost at the woods, retreating in close order with their shields up, harried by the horse archers. A moment more, and they were safe between the trees. Castus glanced back along the valley: a score of raiders dead or wounded, and only one horse down, kicking its legs in the air as the rider scrambled clear.

Dexter rode up; one of the scouts followed him. 'Dominus,' he said. 'The thicket's not too deep, but there's dense scrub blocking our way in. If we go into it, we'll be losing men for sure. I've sent a cordon around the far side, but it looks like they're making a stand in there. We could keep them penned up and wait...'

He raised his eyebrows. Castus took his meaning. The longer they were delayed here, the more time there would be for the other raiding bands to make it back to the river and slip across. He looked at the sky, the tops of the trees, judging the direction of the wind.

'Is this a grove sacred to any local gods, do you know?' he asked with a wry half-smile.

'Not as far as I know, dominus,' Dexter replied, and his face tightened into a grin.

'Burn it.'

Dexter snapped out the orders to his men, then raised his face to the sky. 'Whatever spirits may abide in this place,' he intoned, 'whether god or goddess, I ask forgiveness, and vow to you a suitable sacrifice!'

'Do we have a suitable sacrifice?' Castus asked, frowning.

The cavalry prefect pointed to the few stolen cows that his men had already managed to round up. 'We need fresh meat anyway!'

The flames took quickly in the dry scrub along the edge of the thicket, sending billows of grey smoke back between the trees. Watching the fire crackling through the branches, Castus thought of the story the governor had told him over dinner, about Leontius, his predecessor. Why would anyone burn a sacred grove on purpose? Even foreign and barbaric gods merited respect. But one man with a fire-pot could easily start a blaze in midsummer, as he had just seen.

Already he could hear the shouts of defiance from inside the thicket. Turning his horse, he rode around to the far side, where Dexter was waiting with half of his troopers. The smoke came twining lazily through the trees, carrying the scent of burning.

'The cattle back there had a brand,' he said. 'An *M* and an *R*, joined. Do you know it?'

'Magnius Rufus,' Dexter told him. 'He owns half the grazing stock in the province. Treats this country like his own private estate. Most of the shepherds and drovers in these parts are his slaves and *coloni*.'

'Wealthy man.'

Dexter blew upwards, rolling his eyes and flicking his fingers against his brow. Castus nodded slowly. He had already guessed who the owner of the cattle must be.

Sparks were drifting between the trees now, smaller fires taking hold deeper inside the wood as the smoke thickened into a dense grey fog. The horses stamped and shied at the smell of it, their riders keeping them on a tight rein. Then a burst of shouting, a crashing of undergrowth, and the first fugitives came staggering out of the smoke.

At once the Stablesiani were falling upon them, cutting down any that offered resistance, holding those who surrendered at spearpoint. Dexter rode down the line of the cordon, shouting orders to kill anyone with weapons in his hands. Castus saw a man burst from the bushes only a hundred paces away, a thickset warrior stripped to the waist, his beard split in a howl of rage as he brandished his spear. For a moment he thought of his old friend Brinno, and of Ganna, and a brief swell of sympathy lifted the blackness of his determination. But then he thought of the dead villagers left in the wreckage of their homes, and his heart hardened. The man only managed a few running strides from the edge of the wood before two arrows struck him in the torso, and he reeled and fell.

Behind him came a knot of other warriors; Castus saw the leader's blue and white shield flashing through the smoke. 'Take that one alive!' he roared, and kicked his horse forward into a canter.

The warriors broke from cover, heads down as they blinked the smoke from their eyes. Already they were surrounded, arrows whipping in from all sides. Castus saw the leader struck in the leg. The two men flanking him raised their shields to protect him, but the troopers closed in fast. For a moment

Castus saw only milling horses, the dart and swipe of spears. By the time he reached them the fight was over, the leader lying wounded, cursing through his teeth, his followers slain or kneeling, abject in surrender as the horses circled them.

They left the thicket smouldering behind them and rode on north, with their prisoners and the liberated captives, another ten miles along the valley of the Mosa, following the tracks of men and beasts. Towards nightfall, when it grew too dark to see the smoke trails on the flat horizon, they camped beside a ruined settlement of charcoal burners' huts.

A relief, Castus thought, to be back on his feet once more, to shed helmet and cuirass and stretch his limbs. His whole body felt moulded to the shape of the saddle. He paced the perimeter of the camp, checked the horse lines, then stretched himself on the ground as the men roasted the meat of the sacrificed cow. In the flickering glow of the camp fires he noticed broken walls in the undergrowth, masonry almost obscured by tall weeds and ivy.

'What was this place?' he said.

'A villa, maybe, or a posting station,' Dexter told him, chewing on the fatty half-raw beef. 'This whole country was populated, many years ago. But they farmed the land too hard. Wore out the soil. It's just sandy dirt now, no good for crops, only rough grazing land and wild scrub. It's worse to the west of here, nearer the coast.'

He sucked his teeth, spat out a lump of gristle, then wiped grease from his mouth with the back of his hand. 'No, brother, the gods have not been kind to the province of Germania.'

'Some men still get rich off it,' Castus said. It was easier to talk like this, in the blue twilight with the shapes of men in the shadows around them. No sense of hierarchy out here.

'Aye, some men do. Like Magnius Rufus. Maybe half a dozen like him, besides the grain contractors and the slave-dealers. There are still free people in the towns, in Colonia and Tungris, but most of the rest of the province is just landowners and their slaves. And us, the army, keeping them all safe.'

'They hate the barbarians fiercely enough. Do they feel the threat so badly?'

Dexter grinned, his face in the firelight appearing all hard bones and tight muscle. 'Everyone here does,' he said, flinging a gnawed bone onto the fire. 'Even though they trade with them, use them as labourers, even see them settled in their towns and serving in our army, the people here will always hate and fear the barbarian. They can't forget what happened forty years ago, when the warbands came swarming over the river and put this whole province to the sack. Most of the rest of Gaul, too. You can still see the ruined buildings from that time.'

Castus glanced back again at the overgrown walls behind him. Sparks rose from the fire and spun briefly in the night sky. He had heard the stories of those days often enough, but had never realised how much the people of the north-west carried the memory of it in their blood.

A figure approached from his left, out of the darkness, and Castus tensed instinctively, reaching for his sword. All this talk of ancient destruction had left him on edge. Dexter made a calming gesture.

'Flavius Bappo,' he said, nodding to the man as he joined them beside the fire. 'Frankish, but he serves with us. He's our interpreter.'

The newcomer wore military costume and was short-haired and clean-shaven like any Roman soldier. His slightly protuberant eyes and freckled cheeks gave him a toadlike appearance, but he was smiling as he saluted to Castus.

'Dominus,' Bappo said in a heavy Germanic accent. 'I've questioned the prisoners we took at the wood. That leader, the one with the arrow in his leg, is an important man. Conda, the son of Ragnachar, who is paramount chief of the Chamavi.'

Dexter grinned in satisfaction. 'A good day's hunting!' he declared. 'Ragnachar's other son died in the spring, in the same skirmish that killed Leontius. So Conda's his successor.'

'This Ragnachar,' Castus said. 'He's their king?'

'The Franks have no kings, not really,' Dexter told him. 'We call them kings, but they're elected leaders and their people depose them if they fail in battle. But Ragnachar's held power over the Chamavi for about a decade now. He's a strong warrior. And he loves his son, so they say.'

Castus nodded thoughtfully as he lay down, his head pillowed against his saddlebag. An idea was turning in his mind, but fatigue was blurring his thinking. He could hear Dexter talking to the interpreter – another band of raiders had been sighted to the west, out in Toxandria beyond the Mosa, moving north under cover of darkness. But the voices grew fainter, the words uncoupled into a vague drone, and the whirl of his mind stilled. Castus dropped into a dreamless sleep.

Dawn brought a world of glowing pearl-grey, the landscape obscured by thick ground-mist that hid all but the fleecy shapes of trees. Dexter had got his men up and in the saddle long before first light, and they had already ridden for two hours, across flat marshy country cut up with streams. Now they heard the first sounds of fighting ahead of them, the bellow of massed voices, the bright clink of steel. The mist dulled the thunder of hooves on the dew-damp grass as the riders broke into a canter.

Castus felt the mist on his face; he drank it down like cool water, a balm to aching limbs and harried mind. Anxiety jumped and writhed inside him: somewhere just ahead was the Rhine, the last barrier the raiders must cross to escape the Roman domain. Soon he would discover whether all he had planned had fallen into place.

Riders on the left, appearing wraithlike from the sunshot mist. A draco banner trailed behind one of them, and Castus threw up his hand.

'Who are you?' His shout was a hoarse bark in the damp air. 'Where are the enemy?'

'Aurelius Durio, dominus,' the horseman cried, saluting back as he recognised the commander's own banner. '*Biarchus* of the Numerus Equitum Sarmatorum. Hundred of them just ahead of us, some on stolen horses.'

'Tell your commander to hook around to the left,' Castus called to the man, signalling with a flat palm. 'Push them towards the river, and don't let any slip past you.'

The rider saluted again and turned back into the mist. Beyond him, Castus could make out the shapes of other horsemen, lances glinting as the sun caught their tips.

'Dominus?' Dexter called, raising himself in the saddle. 'You hear that?'

Castus reined his horse to a slow pace, then took off his helmet. Sure enough, distinct through the dulled misty air, came a repeated noise. *Snap... snap... snap...*

'Ballistae, it must be!' Dexter cried, grinning wildly. 'Roman artillery!'

And even as he spoke the mist seemed to roll ahead of them and lift, the open country spreading away to the flat horizon in the morning sun. There was the riverbank – much closer than Castus had imagined – and there, out in midstream, were the unmistakable shapes of Roman warships. Joy punched through him, and he let out a shout of exultation. Castus had known in his heart that the old navarch Senecio would not let him down. Sure enough, there was the *Bellona*, masts and rigging cleared away and the catapult and ballistae on her deck already in action. Other vessels moved beyond her – the two small galleys that had accompanied Castus from Argentorate, and others too.

The misty riverbank was boiling with men. All the retreating raiders had converged on this point, as Castus had known they must: this was where the canoes that had carried them over the Rhine were beached, ready to take them home. Some of the barbarians had already crossed, while others were pushing out into the stream, each canoe packed with bodies, easy targets for the catapults on the galleys. But now there were Roman troops on the riverbank as well, hundreds of fully armed legionaries coming ashore from barges and hacking down any foe that dared approach. Already most of the remaining canoes had been destroyed, and the raiders were trapped.

Deployed in a broad double line, the horsemen began to canter forward across the last distance of open country. Mist streamed in their wake as they closed with the milling horde. Castus rode on their right flank, his standard whipping behind him. Already many of the barbarians were throwing down their weapons, raising their arms in surrender. The legionaries had formed all along the riverbank now, a wall of shields pressing steadily forward. Some of the raiders, bullied by the screams of the chiefs, tried to stand and fight, but Castus could see that their resistance would be brief and futile. All that remained now was submission, or massacre.

He heard Dexter shouting: '*At them! They're breaking!*'

Then the trumpets sounded *charge*, and the moving wall of horsemen let out a single roaring yell as they began to gallop.

CHAPTER VIII

The biarchus of the Numerus Sarmatorum had a smear of drying blood on his face – not his own, Castus guessed – and a ferocious look in his eyes. His bronze scale cuirass glittered in the sun as he rode up to make his report.

'Dominus! We killed over fifty, took about eighty prisoners and liberated thirty-four of their captives.'

Liberated, Castus thought: an odd term. Most of the people taken by the raiders were probably slaves and tenant farmers, now to be returned to their masters.

'What about your own losses?'

The biarchus shrugged. 'Four dead, seven wounded, dominus!'

Castus dismissed him with a nod. Messengers from the other units were bringing their own tallies: the captives must surely number over two hundred. The slain, a great many more. Nobody so far could estimate how many barbarians had slipped away across the river.

'Dominus!' said the centurion commanding the detachment of the Thirtieth Legion. 'We took twenty-eight prisoner and killed around the same. Only minor wounds on our side. Navarch Senecio reports a large mass of Franks gathered on the far bank. About a thousand, he says, women and children among them.'

They must have been waiting to greet their menfolk on their return from the raids. They would be getting a different sort of greeting soon enough. Castus commended the centurion: he had not expected much from the garrison troops of the Thirtieth that had come down the river by barge. They had been a show of force, but that was all that had been required.

Now that the fighting was done, Castus's mood of elation had shifted to a chilled sobriety. He was used to feeling shaken after a fight, sickened even, all the dread suppressed by action now climbing through his body, making his guts heave and his hands tremble. But he had never felt this sense of cold dislocation before, this terrible emptiness.

Beneath him his horse still sweated and trembled after the charge through the mist. Little mist remained now; the meadows along the riverbank steamed. Bodies lay scattered on the turf, the blood looking very bright in the morning sun. Further from the river, the scene resembled a livestock market as the soldiers rounded up stolen cattle and sheep, pigs and even chickens. A slave market too: the surviving Franks were herded together in pens of spearmen, stripped of their weapons, their belts and boots, in many cases even the clothes on their backs. Heaps of seized weapons and plunder lay on the grass. Castus watched dispassionately. He felt only an oily sense of nausea, a vague shame at what he had directed.

For over twenty years he had fought in the wars of empire. He had led men in battle, but this was the first time that he had held supreme command in the field. There was little honour in it, he thought. Several hundred dead, but he doubted if anyone in Rome or even Treveris would even hear of this brief campaign. Did the great men of the empire care who lived or died out here on the forsaken frontier?

'Send word for the interpreter, Bappo,' he said. At once a messenger rode off across the field. The toad-faced man came riding back within moments.

'How's our prince of the Chamavi?'

'He'll live, dominus,' Bappo said, with an insouciant shrug. 'The surgeon took the arrow out, but it split the bone, the femur. He'll walk again, but not for a long time yet.'

Castus gave a satisfied grunt. He slid down from the saddle, rubbed the nose of his horse, and took a drink of well-watered wine that tasted of the goatskin canteen. A soldier brought him breakfast, dry bread and oil with cheese, and he ate standing beside his horse. Then he passed the reins to an orderly and strode towards the river, signalling for his staff to follow him.

There were boats pulled up on the bank, amid the wreckage of smashed Frankish canoes and the corpses that lolled in the shallows. The river here was wide, flowing between flat grasslands threaded with streams and small marshy lakes. As the boat carried him out towards the anchored ships, Castus scanned the far bank. What he had first taken for low trees or bushes were people, he saw now. A multitude of people gathered at the waterside. Their voices carried across to him: a low keening hum of anger, of grief.

Senecio was waiting at the deck rail of the *Bellona* as the boat came alongside.

'I congratulate you on your victory, excellency!' he called.

'Good thing you got here on time,' Castus said with a wry smile, clambering forward as the boat bumped against the hull of the galley and gripping the rungs of the boarding ladder. Fine thing it would be, he thought, to slip and tumble into the river now, in the hour of his triumph...

Three strong pulls and he hauled himself up, Senecio grabbing his arm to help him onto the deck. The standard-bearer came up behind Castus, carrying the long pole with the unwieldy purple banner.

'We pulled all night from Tricensima, dominus,' the navarch said. 'Difficult with the barges – one of them ran aground on a mudbank but we hauled her off. We arrived here at sun-up, just as the first of them started to cross in their canoes.' He gestured with his chin towards the crowd gathering on the far bank. 'Want me to signal *Pinnata* and *Satyra* to throw a few bolts into them?'

Castus shook his head. He arranged his cloak and strode forward along the deck to where it narrowed into a raised gangway. The oarsmen were still at their benches, their tunics dark with sweat, some of them bare-chested. As they caught sight of him they got up, tired but grinning, and began to cheer. Even the men on the lower tier scrambled up from the reeking darkness, raising their arms in salute.

From the southern riverbank, the cheer was returned, the troops thronging the waterside catching sight of the commander's banner streaming from the stern of the warship and lifting their spears and shields as they yelled.

Standing tall on the deck in the hot sun, Castus felt himself lifted by the voices of his men. Just for a moment, he allowed himself to glory in it. Then he turned to the far riverbank, staring across the blue-grey water at the gathered barbarians. On the opposite bank, the men of the Thirtieth Legion were lined up with the cavalry behind them. The two hosts faced each other in the sun, quarter of a mile of strong river current between them.

'Send a messenger,' Castus said, gesturing back over his shoulder. 'I want the interpreter, Flavius Bappo, and the Chamavi prince we captured. I'll need a cut green branch. And request Tribune Dexter to send twenty of his best archers, too.'

104

Then he stepped across to the rail, bracing his palms on the smooth worn wood. The idea that had come to him the night before, whirling in on the edge of sleep, was keen in his mind now. Would it work? Did he even have the authority for it? He did not know, but the day was carrying him forward and he had no better schemes.

It took nearly half an hour for the message to be relayed back across the river and the boats to return, packed with men. The dismounted archers came aboard, most still in their mail and scale, bows already strung and quivers filled with fresh arrows. The men in the boat lifted the injured barbarian captive up to the deck, with Bappo hopping up the ladder after him.

'Navarch,' Castus said, still regarding the horde on the opposite bank. 'Take us across to just beyond bowshot.' Senecio, guessing his intention, had already raised the leafy branch on a pole above the stern. The symbol of parley, but it was best to be careful all the same.

The oarsmen settled at their benches, the voice of the rowing master shouted the rhythm, and the ship moved slowly up against the current to where her anchor lay in the riverbed. The deck crew hauled on the bow hawser, and the narrow hull bucked slightly as the anchor was plucked free and rose, spouting, from the water. The *Bellona* turned slowly in midstream, the oarsmen on one side pulling while the other side backed, and then slid gracefully across the rippling current. The two smaller galleys, *Satyra* and *Pinnata*, slipped across after her and took up their stations, fore and aft in line with the riverbank. On every vessel the ballista crews had their weapons loaded and trained.

From this distance, it was easy to make out the different groups among the barbarians. Many of them were indeed women and children, Castus noticed, but there were numerous warriors among them too: either those who had managed to escape across the river before the galleys arrived, or older men who no longer went out with the raiding bands.

At the centre of the host, under a banner of streamers mounted on a pole, stood a deep-chested man dressed in a scale cuirass, an old Roman cavalry helmet clasped under his arm. His thick yellow hair was greying, and he wore a moustache on his top lip that hung lower than his chin. No mistaking him, Castus thought. Ragnachar, paramount chief of the Chamavi.

'Bappo, to me,' he said, without turning his head. Even at this distance, he felt his gaze locked with the barbarian leader. The only sound now was the slow creak of the oars as the galley held its position. Castus stood as tall and still as he could, his standard-bearer at his back, flanked by a pair of soldiers from the Thirtieth Legion, big men in polished scale armour, with shields and spears.

The interpreter idled up to the rail beside him.

'Tell Ragnachar, King of the Chamavi,' Castus said, in a stern voice loud enough to carry over the water, 'that I am Aurelius Castus, Dux Limitis Germaniae, and I command here by order of the Caesar Flavius Crispus and his father, the Invincible Augustus Constantine.' Most of them would not understand his words, but they would guess the meaning from his tone.

Bappo cried out the address, the string of names and titles almost incomprehensible in the Germanic tongue. The barbarian host remained silent, watching and waiting.

'Tell him that his warriors have broken the treaty with Rome by invading our province. My troops have slain hundreds, and taken hundreds more captive. These prisoners will be sold as slaves.'

This time a great cry and a wail went up from the crowd on

the bank as Bappo yelled out the translation. Castus saw many of the barbarian warriors surge forwards into the shallows, brandishing their weapons. Women raised hands to their faces and tugged at their unbound hair. Ragnachar remained still, his posture betraying nothing.

'They ask,' the translator said, 'why they have a treaty with Rome, when the Romans attack their people and steal the tribute payments they promised? They mean the subsidies, dominus.'

'I know what they mean,' Castus said under his breath. He noted the detail about the stolen payments.

'Boats coming out,' said Senecio. Castus had already spotted them: half a dozen canoes edging from the bank, warriors crouched over the paddles. He heard the navarch's orders to his ballista crews. 'Any of them get close, drill them. Don't wait for my signal.'

He looked to Castus, who inhaled sharply and nodded. The sun was hot, and he fought the urge to wipe the sweat from his face. He could reveal no sign of weakness now.

'Show them the prisoner,' Castus said quietly.

He had ordered the injured captive, Conda, to be concealed beneath the awning at the stern of the ship, with archers placed on either side of him, arrows nocked to their bows. Now he was carried forth, supported by soldiers. He was a much younger man than Castus had thought, barely more than twenty. His beard was downy gold, his sweating face twisted with shame and the agony of his wound.

A groan went through the assembled barbarians as they saw their chieftain's son displayed on the deck of the *Bellona*. But Castus was still watching Ragnachar. He saw the chief flinch visibly as he recognised the figure on the ship, then take two staggering steps forward into the water, raising both arms towards his son as if he could reach out and touch him.

Just for a moment, Castus wondered how he would feel in this barbarian chieftain's position. If it were his own son, his Sabinus, displayed like a trophy by an enemy leader. For two long heartbeats he felt a strange affinity for the enemy chief's distress. Then he drew in a breath, held it, and exhaled. No mercy now. Only severity.

'Tell the chieftain Ragnachar,' he cried, his voice rasping in his throat, 'that his son was captured with arms in his hands. His life should be forfeit. But tell him this: I will return his son to him, if he gives me in exchange all the prisoners his raiders have captured, and fifty other hostages. Youths aged between fourteen and eighteen, sons of the most noble families of the Chamavi and Chattuari.'

Shouts came back across the water at once, many of the other warriors protesting loudly. Castus glanced to the interpreter.

'They say,' Bappo told him, with a slight smile, 'that you have hostages already. The men you have taken can be your hostages...'

'They are captives of war,' Castus said curtly. 'To accept their submission I need hostages willingly surrendered. Tell them these youths will be well treated, as guests of the Roman Empire, so long as the Chamavi and Chattuari keep the peace on the frontier.'

Now, he thought, *let's see how much power this Ragnachar holds over his people.*

'Dominus,' Senecio mused from behind him, tight-lipped. 'It's not my place, I know, but surely it can't be wise to return the chief's son?'

'He won't be fit enough to fight for many months,' Castus said from the corner of his mouth, not turning his head. 'Besides, I'm told these Franks elect their chiefs. If we just keep Ragnachar's boy, the others could depose him and make war in revenge. This way, there's far more of them with something to lose.'

He heard the navarch's dry chuckle. 'Oh, the wily Ulysses!'

Bappo was still conducting a long-distance debate with the warriors on the riverbank, growing increasingly heated as he yelled and they yelled back.

'Silence,' Castus ordered. A few last shouts came across from the barbarian throng. 'Tell the chief,' he said, 'that his people have until noon to surrender the hostages and send them across the river. If this is not done, I will put his son to death right here in front of him.'

He signalled to one of his bodyguards, who drew his sword and held it up, the blade flashing. Ragnachar stood in the water, staring for a long moment, then threw back his head and shouted.

'He says,' Bappo told Castus, 'that he wants your sworn oath that the hostages will not be harmed.'

'My oath,' Castus called back over the water, 'as a soldier and a Roman. On all the gods, I swear that the hostages will not be harmed, if Ragnachar and his people do not trouble this province again.'

Bappo cried out the translation, and Castus watched the barbarian chieftain stagger back from the water and disappear into the mass of his people, covering his face with both hands.

'Now,' Castus said, and glanced up at the sun, still only halfway to its zenith in the eastern horizon. 'We have a few hours to wait, I think.'

The rowing master called the stroke, and the galley swung back out into midstream once more, to anchor in her previous station. One of the navarch's slaves brought a folding stool and set it on the deck behind the steersman's position, and Castus seated himself, trying not to let his agitation show. Would he really execute the young captive in cold blood? He did not know, and hoped he would not have to test his own resolve. Sitting stiffly, he took a cup of wine and sipped gratefully. His throat felt tight and sour from the words he had spoken.

'Don't you mind negotiating with your own people like that?' he asked Bappo.

The interpreter blew out his cheeks, then shrugged. 'They aren't my people, dominus,' he said. 'I'm of the Tubantes; they're Chamavi. You Romans think all Franks are the same!'

Castus shrugged. True enough. He remembered Brinno telling him once about the different tribes and their conflicts.

The sun climbed higher; the oarsmen sweated on the exposed deck as they studied the barbarian shore. They could rig the canopies and give the men some shade, Castus considered, but with the enemy still gathered on the riverbank the *Bellona* needed to remain cleared for action, ready to move, or fight if required.

A movement caught his eye: somebody waving a bunched cloak from the galley anchored downstream. Castus frowned – he knew the signal. *Enemy in sight.* A moment later, they all heard the shouts across the water.

Senecio ran forward at once, scrambling up onto the triangular platform behind the figurehead. Castus remained standing, peering into the long reach of the river downstream. Where the blue water met the blue sky, a line of shapes winked into view.

'What is it?' he demanded as Senecio returned.

'We have company, dominus,' the navarch said. 'Frankish war boats, fully manned and armed, and coming this way.'

There were six of them, much bigger craft than the Chamavi canoes. Between raised prow and stern, each boat was packed with men, pulling hard on the oars to drive against the river current.

'Salii,' Senecio said. 'Their territory lies just downstream from here.' The galley crew had already rushed to their stations, the oarsmen to their benches and the artillery crews to their ballistae, swinging the weapons round to face this new threat. On deck the archers were crouched behind the shields mounted on the railings, arrows ready.

'Friends or foes?' Castus asked.

'Could be either. They're split up into different groups, no overall leader. Some are worse then others. They're sea raiders and brigands, mostly.'

Shading his eyes, Castus could see a figure standing proudly at the prow of the leading boat. A tall man, dressed in red with his cloak thrown back and his arms folded. The boats kept on coming, oblivious to the Roman artillery trained upon them, sliding up the river channel between the ships and the far riverbank. Only then did the regular pulse of their oars slacken.

'Bappo, find out who they are,' Castus said. He walked to the rail and stood braced, staring at the figure in the lead boat as the interpreter shouted his message. Something about his appearance stirred a memory, almost an intuition. It was not the leader who answered, but one of the warriors in the second boat.

'They're Salii, as the navarch says,' Bappo reported. 'They've come to see why we are on the river in such force.'

'Tell them we can go where we choose,' Castus said. 'This river belongs to us. It's they who must explain themselves.'

Again the cries went back and forth. Castus could see some of the boats throwing out anchors to keep them steady in the current. He could see the warriors aboard the boats more clearly, too: twenty or thirty in each vessel, well-muscled men with hair to their shoulders and thick moustaches, all of them bristling with weapons, their round shields laid ready beside them. Some of them were calling out to the mass of Chamavi on the riverbank, making abusive gestures and raising mocking laughter.

'Enough of this,' Castus said. 'We're not here to listen to barbarian banter. Tell them that one boat can approach, and their leading man can come aboard.'

He glanced at Senecio, who nodded grimly. A single boatload of warriors could pose little threat to the *Bellona*, but Castus noticed the tension of the men on deck, the gathering anticipation. The Franks had been their enemies for too long to be trusted.

The men in the leading boat seemed to expect the summons; they bent to their oars at once, bringing the vessel smoothly around and across the water towards the bigger Roman galley. The Franks at the rowing benches gazed back over their shoulders as the two vessels met, their gazes mingling hostility and a kind of fascination. Then their oars slid inboard, the swept prow of the boat nosing against the hull of the galley, and the leader in the red tunic stepped up nimbly onto the stem post and across the narrowing gap of water, climbing in over the rail and onto the galley's deck.

Castus narrowed his eyes, certain that his intuition had been correct but scarcely able to believe it. The Salian leader was a young man, about thirty, and as heavily armed as his men. He wore a Roman spatha on one hip and a long knife on the other, with an axe stuck through his belt. His brooch and buckles glittered with gold and gemstones. He walked proudly down the gangway, oblivious to the oarsmen staring up at him from the tiers of benches to either side.

'His name is Bonitus,' Bappo said. 'War chief of the northriver Salii.'

A Roman name, Castus thought with interest. He nodded, waiting until the young warrior reached the poop deck. 'Tell him that I am Aurelius Castus, and I command this frontier in the name of the emperor. If he comes as a friend of Rome, he is welcome.'

Bappo started to speak, but the chief cut him off, speaking in accented Latin. 'All my people are friends of Rome,' he said. But there was a note of defiance in his voice still. 'Now I see why you are here!' he went on, gesturing to the mass of Chamavi on the riverbank, and the bound captive seated on the deck. The prisoner glared back at him; clearly these two had met before.

But in the man's voice, in his stance and attitude, Castus recognised the truth of his intuition. For a moment he remained silent, studying the warrior before him, until he was sure.

'I knew one of your people once,' he said. 'Brinno, son of Baudulfus.'

Bonitus blinked, visibly startled. His lips tightened, and Castus noticed that he had reached instinctively for the hilt of his sword.

'Brinno was my brother,' he said, frowning. 'He died fighting for your emperor.'

'I was with him at the time,' Castus said. 'He fell in battle, in the lands of the Alamanni. He was a true friend, and a brave warrior.'

Bonitus stared at him, his fingers still brushing his sword hilt, his face flickering between surprise, suspicious disbelief and an obvious desire to know more. Castus was aware of the silence around them, the baffled looks passing between his officers and men. Though there was little physical resemblance between Bonitus and Brinno, something in his stance, the attitude, was strikingly similar. But where Brinno had been

113

eager, carefree and open, his brother was cold and reserved, with a sense of darkness held tightly within him. Castus held the Frankish chief's gaze, compelling him to believe what he had said.

'My brother was much older than me,' the Frankish chief said warily. 'I did not know him as I should. But he was well treated by the Romans. He was given much honour, even though he came as a captive, like this one here.' He flicked his hand at the bound Chamavi prisoner, with a sneer of mild contempt.

Castus remembered the story Brinno had told him, long before: how the Salii had been defeated by Constantius, father of Constantine, and Brinno himself taken as a hostage to Treveris. Only when his father had proved loyal to Rome had the young man been admitted to the Protectores, the emperor's own bodyguard.

'The empire treats its friends well,' he told Bonitus.

The Frank gave a derisive snort. 'Heh! You think, really? Twenty years my father kept his promise of friendship with your emperors. Even before that, he respected your ways – he even gave to me a Roman name! I keep his promise still. But our lands are poor and threatened always by the sea. Our enemies press on us. In your provinces there are many better lands, where no people live. When I send messengers to your governor, asking that my people may cross the river and settle these lands, what does he say?'

Castus sucked his cheek, trying not to betray a reaction. 'I know nothing of this,' he said.

'Your governor Tiberianus sends away the messengers! He tells us to stay on our side of the river. He says that if we cross over, Rome will be our enemy and we will have war. How is this for friends, heh?'

Castus nodded slowly. He saw now why these war boats and their heavily armed crews had come up the river to meet him.

'The clarissimus Tiberianus does not command the troops on this river,' he told Bonitus, all too aware of the others all around him, listening intently. 'I will report what you have said to the Praetorian Prefect in Treveris, and to the new Caesar, Flavius Crispus.'

Bonitus grunted and nodded curtly. He was still studying Castus, assessing him. He seemed to come to a decision, throwing back his shoulders.

'If you were truly a friend of my brother,' he said, 'then you and I also should be friends.'

'Let it be so,' Castus said. He hesitated for a moment, anxious not to make some awkward gesture. Then he stepped forward and stretched out his hand.

The Frankish chief clasped his palm, a sudden fierce pressure. It was enough; both men stepped away again. Bonitus turned abruptly and strode down the gangway, calling out to his crew. With a brief glance back, he stepped up onto the rail and dropped down into his own boat as the Frankish oarsmen bent over their oars once more.

It was less than an hour until noon, and finally the mass of Chamavi on the far bank had opened, lanes forming to allow the little knots of figures down to the boats. Castus watched, squinting into the glare off the water. Mothers hugged children, fathers stood aloof, gazing fiercely at the Roman ships. Then the first of the boats put out into the stream, loaded with its human cargo.

Back and forth the boats went, and the men on the ships tracked them. Downstream, the six Salian vessels had anchored out of range of the Roman artillery but still within sight, their crews watching what was happening. Castus sent a message for Dexter to check each hostage as they landed, and establish his identity if possible. Only the sons of warriors and chiefs could be accepted. Noon drifted past, and another hour was gone before Castus saw the banner waving from the Roman shore.

'Release the prisoner,' he said. 'Put him in a boat and carry him across to his people.'

The young barbarian shouted in pain and relief as his bonds were severed. His face was still blanched with distress, but when he glanced back Castus saw the ferocious hatred in his eyes. Then the young man dipped his head and the soldiers wrestled him over the rail into the waiting boat, none too gently.

Already the horde on the northern bank was beginning to break up, fading back into the flat landscape. Ragnachar remained beneath his banner, his household warriors around him, until the boat drew into the shallows and the young captive was passed into the arms of the men who ran out to carry him to dry land. Castus watched the distant scene: the father reunited with the son. Ragnachar bent down and embraced the young man, then smacked him hard across the face and turned away.

'A good day's work, dominus,' Senecio said, and wiped his face with a rag. 'Usually it's emperors who do that sort of thing.'

Castus caught the angle of his words and looked up quickly. Senecio would not meet his eye.

'I have a mandate to protect the frontier,' he said. 'I'm doing that.'

But the navarch's comment stirred apprehension in his gut. He had said and done nothing, he was sure, that exceeded his authority. He had made no new treaties, only reconfirmed old ones. And he had acted in the name of the emperor. Still, he recalled Bassus's instruction, the strange warning the prefect had given him many days before. *All power descends from the*

Augustus Constantine. All power is channelled through the Caesar Crispus. There is no other conduit.

Pacing along the gangway to the forecastle deck, he watched the last of the barbarian throng drifting away from the riverbank. Downstream, the six Salian boats were already under way, oars beating slowly. Castus stared at the flat horizon where the sinuous river met the sky; he could still make out the figure of the Frankish chief, Bonitus, standing at the prow of the lead boat. Just for a moment, he caught the raised palm, the gesture of salute.

'What do you make of him?' Castus asked Senecio.

The navarch squinted into the glare of sun at the six boats as they moved around the bend in the river.

'There's not a Frank alive I'd trust,' he said. 'But that one… He'd be a loyal ally, I think. Or a very fierce enemy.'

PART TWO

CHAPTER IX

Treveris, September AD *317*

As the blade descended towards his neck he tried not to flinch. Keen steel rasped up his nape, and he kept his head straight and his eyes closed. Luxorius had nerved himself against most fears, but sharp metal still made him queasy. In the deepest recesses of his pained memories, he knew all too well what blades had done to him.

'The dominus will be attending the festivities today?' the barber said through his nose, running the razor over the smooth dome of the eunuch's skull. His tone was not especially respectful; palace barbers were slaves, but thought highly of themselves, and few men cared to be polite to eunuchs anyway, whatever their station.

'The birthday of the young Caesar?' the *tonsor* went on. 'Just fifteen years old! Who would imagine such a young man holding all that power, eh?'

Luxorius made the slightest of noises against his closed lips, but it was enough to make the barber pause, wipe his blade, clear his throat and then get on with his work. Everyone knew that eunuchs reported all they heard to their superiors, after all. Best to keep one's views on the powerful to oneself.

Inhaling slowly, Luxorius felt the blade stroke across his temples. He was glad that the hair on his face had never had a chance to grow; the thought of a razor playing around his mouth was enough to make him squirm. But he was scrupulous about his appearance, and always made sure that his head was perfectly shaved. Especially, he considered, before imperial celebrations.

The barber stepped back with a stifled grunt of relief, swung his body this way and that to check his work, and then wiped the razor again. Luxorius took a dampened cloth from one of the attending slaves, wiping his head and neck, then submitted to a few dabs of the scent the barber called *saffron dew*. When all was done he stood up, shook out his tunic, and arranged his cloak around his shoulders.

It was still early, the sky growing paler but the sun not yet up. As the eunuch paced out into the colonnades of the palace enclosure he felt the cold in the air, the tightening grip of autumn. Soon would come the first teasing threat of winter. He pulled a woollen cap down over his ears and tried not to shiver. This would be the fourth northern winter he had endured, and each one seemed colder than the last. Surely he would never adapt to these uncivilised temperatures.

In his blood, Luxorius carried the memory of the far south, the desert lands. He had been born in Coptos on the banks of the Nile, in the Egyptian Thebaid. The years of his distant youth he recalled now only in scattered images: the serrated shadows of palm leaves, the dusty mud-brick walls of the old town, the slow silty water of the great river and the cool chambers of his parents' house. Shortly before his fifteenth birthday, the Caesar Galerius had marched south along the Nile valley to crush the uprising in the Thebaid; Coptos was one of the rebel strongholds, and the emperor had made an example of it. When the town fell, Galerius ordered the walls torn down, the houses razed to the ground, the entire adult population slaughtered and the children sold into slavery.

Luxorius had been a handsome youth, or so the slavers who bought him at auction said. They paid a good price for him, but they knew that good-looking young eunuchs could be many times more valuable. Castration was illegal within the empire, though there were places just across the frontier, in the country of the Nobadae, where the operation was performed.

Little of what followed remained with Luxorius now. He remembered the dirty flyblown village, the mud hut with a blanket across the door. Inside, the old man with the creased face and bad teeth, waiting with his wire garrotte and the curved knife laid in a basin of vinegar. Beyond that was only blood, agony and shame.

It had taken a year for Luxorius to recover fully from the operation. The slavers had taken him north, to the great market of Alexandria, where they sold him again, for a vast profit, to a merchant from Cyrenaica. And from there, many years later and after much education, he had reached Rome. The Rome of Maxentius, who had defeated and humiliated Galerius, destroyer of Coptos and murderer of his family; Luxorius had been only too happy to take up service in the imperial palace.

And now Maxentius was long dead, his memory damned. Galerius too was gone, and Luxorius was a slave no more, the free servant of a new master. Or, perhaps, a new mistress.

Fausta's instructions to him back in Sirmium had seemed simple enough. Luxorius prided himself on an ability to make things happen: the ambush of the young Caesar's carriage on the road through Raetia had been a feat of organisation, with not a few attendant hazards, but Luxorius had arranged it all, negotiating through middle-men with the barbarian brigands and passing them the information, and the calculated misinformation, needed to spur them into action. It would have been a success, too – if the new Dux Germaniae had not arrived so promptly on the scene the boy would have been slain, the brigands gone and Luxorius's work would have been complete.

After that, opportunities had been far slimmer. Crispus had been well guarded for the rest of the journey, and since his arrival in Treveris a month before he had been surrounded by the court retinue and immune to chance accidents. Luxorius had pondered poison, even straightforward assassination, but the result would have been too obvious, the chain of culprits too easy to trace. Those members of the imperial retinue Luxorius had so far encountered seemed depressingly immune to intrigue and disloyalty. And, meanwhile, there had been *developments*.

Only two days before, the news had arrived by express courier from distant Sirmium: the emperor's wife had given birth to a second son, to be named Constantius. A reason for glad rejoicing throughout the entire world, one would think – unless one was prone to devious thoughts. Who else now but Fausta, mother of the emperor's youngest heirs, would want to strike at the golden Caesar Crispus?

No, the eunuch thought as he neared the great audience hall; no, he would have to go about his task far more subtly from now on.

The first pale autumn sun was flickering across the palace pediments as he crossed the chilly courtyard and entered the vestibule of the audience hall. A crowd was already gathered before the tall doors; their hushed voices mingled and echoed into a roar of sound under the coffered ceiling. All of them were imperial officials, waiting to greet the young Caesar, and Luxorius made his way between them, smiling and nodding to right and left.

As head chamberlain to the Praetorian Prefect, Luxorius occupied a reasonably superior position in the offices of the palace, although the hierarchies were rigidly maintained and there were many above him. But there were plenty of his own station, and a small contingent of eunuchs who constituted their own private subspecies. Luxorius attempted to make himself agreeable to everyone, but it amused him to observe the jealousy and ambition, the gossip and the spite that ran like fissures through each tight little circle of officials.

Interlocking spheres, Luxorius thought as he stood with hands linked before him, trying not to shiver in the cold draughts sweeping across the mosaic floor. The society of the palace was made up of them. His own duties were routine enough, overseeing the Praetorian Prefect's personal household, but they brought him into contact with a wide spectrum of other officials. With a certain diligence, he had managed to expand his circuit of connections beyond that of the eunuchs and the prefect's own staff.

'Grace and peace to you, brother,' a man said, stepping up beside him.

Luxorius smiled as he touched the monogram amulet around his neck: the Greek letters X and P conjoined, Christ's sigil. 'Grace and peace,' he said. 'May the Lord's name be forever praised.'

The newcomer was Arsacius, master of letters to the young Caesar. An exalted position, but he allowed the eunuch to embrace him lightly and kiss him on the cheek.

Luxorius had joined the Christian faith only the year before. Not through any particular religious convictions, but rather from expediency. Both the emperor Constantine and his son were *believers*, as were Prefect Bassus, and several other highly placed men. But most people, more scrupulous or less ambitious, still held back from it, uncertain of its virtues or legitimacy. Christianity was becoming, Luxorius thought, a sort of elite club in the higher circles of the administration, and membership brought certain rewards of access. Unlike in the east, or in Rome and North Africa, the new religion had so far made very little progress here in the north-west, but even the provincials of Gaul were beginning to notice its potential benefits: the congregation in Treveris had almost doubled, just in the month since the new Caesar's arrival.

'Is there any more word about events in the north, brother?' Luxorius asked, keeping his voice low, his expression pleasant.

'Only yesterday, yes,' Arsacius said, and the eunuch heard the smile in the man's voice. 'A letter from the governor of Germania Secunda. He's received a delegation of prominent citizens very concerned at the actions of our new dux, it seems.'

'Oh? But surely defeating the barbarians and driving them back across the river is precisely his purpose?'

'So one would think!' Arsacius said. 'However,' he went on, dropping his voice even further, 'many seem to feel that our commander did not punish the barbarians sufficiently. They even claim that he favours them in some way, and has promised to allow barbarian immigrants to cross the border and settle within our territory.'

'Has he?' Luxorius asked.

'I doubt he knows exactly what he has or has not done!' the other man replied, chuckling. 'He seems, I would say, a rather unsophisticated sort of officer. But he has asked to send us a delegation of ambassadors from some barbarian people or other. I seem to remember he was selected personally for the position by his eminence the prefect... Could he have been intended to annoy the provincials, do you think?'

'I really couldn't say!' Luxorius said, widening his eyes. 'But surely the settlement of barbarians within the empire has a certain provenance?' Sometimes he found it helpful to feign ignorance; it was expected of a eunuch, when discussing matters of state.

'Indeed so,' the master of letters said, with a condescending chuckle. 'It was done by the emperor's father, and by Probus I think. The great Marcus Aurelius too. But those were defeated men, prisoners. The concern now is that large bodies of free immigrants will be permitted to settle on Roman land, in their own communities. Something which many of our provincials hold in abhorrence... Although it would bring in greater tax revenues, no doubt, and provide a source of first-class military recruits that would ease the burden of conscription...'

But now a stir ran through the assembled crowd of officials, and both men fell silent. The tall inlaid doors of the audience hall were opening, and a moment later the blare of trumpets came from within. The senior members of the imperial staff paced forward through the portals and into the hall, followed by the others, all in order of precedence.

Entering the hall, Luxorius felt his breath catch slightly, as it always did. The room was so vast, so cavernous, so gloriously decorated in shimmering coloured marble and gold, that it was hard not to feel humbled by it. He kept his head down, pacing quickly to his place in the front rank of the prefect's gathered *officium*.

For several moments the assembly waited in near silence, the vast hall filling with the slow susurration of their breath, the scrape and tap of shoes on marble, the rustle of embroidered clothing. Luxorius thought about what the master of letters had told him; he already knew, as everyone in the palace knew, of the actions of Aurelius Castus against the invading barbarians. Almost all had applauded it, publicly at least. But all knew that the young Caesar needed a war, a public demonstration of military aptitude. He would not win the title of Germanicus Maximus by sitting in the palace in Treveris reading poetry.

If Castus's actions had calmed the situation on the frontier, then Crispus was unlikely to get his first taste of battle any time soon. Why then, the eunuch wondered, had Bassus decided to send the dux on ahead? Why not wait until the Caesar himself could take the field and at least appear to trounce the barbarians in person? Could it be, he thought, that his chief was playing a different game altogether? One thing was clear: if Luxorius were to arrange another strike against the boy Caesar, it would need to happen far from the security of the palace. Some kind of military expedition might present just the opportunity he needed.

His thoughts were interrupted by another brassy yell of trumpets. All eyes turned to the far end of the chamber, where the soaring apse and high podium were obscured by drapes of purple silk. With a waft of incense, the drapes were drawn aside; up on the podium, in a high-backed chair of gilded wood, the Caesar sat flanked by his guards and slaves.

As one, the assembly raised their arms and cried out the salute. '*Long life!*' Then they sank to their knees on the cold marble.

Standing again as the first of the orators began his birthday panegyric, Luxorius studied the young man on the throne. He appeared immaculate, his spotty cheeks smoothed with cosmetics, his curly hair lightly gilded and adorned with a jewelled band, his tunic blindingly white. Only as the ringing echo of the salutes faded did Crispus's mask slip; he smiled, almost shy, then grinned widely.

The eunuch felt no animosity towards this young man. In fact, he could almost like him. But the vicious twists of his own

128

life had left him immune to sympathy for others. Looking at him now, Luxorius was sure of one thing. The Caesar Crispus was marked for death. The only question was how long it would be before he met his fate.

CHAPTER X

'Turn her! Turn her – *right*... harder right! Use your knees. Good – firmer with the reins, steady now... *Right*, I said!'

The voice of the instructor carried across the dusty sand to where Castus stood watching in the shade of the wooden portico. The man was jogging beside the pony as it trotted in circuits around the oval practice ground. Mounted on the pony's back, Castus's son Sabinus clung tightly to the saddle with a look of intense concentration on his face. As the boy finally managed to draw the pony around the tight curve at the far end of the circuit, Castus felt pride glowing through him.

'He's coming on,' the old man beside him said. 'Still keeps grabbing at the saddle horns, mind. But he's not so scared as he was.'

Castus nodded, grunting his assent. Tagmatius was a retired legion drillmaster; Castus had enlisted him to supervise his son's riding lessons and teach him to use a light wooden practice sword in the rudiments of the *armatura* weapons drill. The hunched, gruff-voiced *campidoctor* was gentle enough when he needed to be; Sabinus was terrified of him all the same.

And now, Castus thought, *the boy has two of us here making him nervous.* He tried not to stare too intently, tried to smile a little and let his pride show. But he was on edge himself, eager for his son to succeed and to prove himself, for the boy's

130

own sake. This was the first time Castus had been to the old cavalry practice ground outside the city walls to watch how the lessons were going.

The pony trotted on up the track, towards the far end of the circuit again. It was a small shaggy beast, no bigger than a mule, but Sabinus looked unnervingly precarious in the saddle. He had appeared even less confident a while earlier, as the old drill instructor prompted him through his sword exercises. But it was necessary, Castus knew: all a part of his education. He had explained that to the boy. He would learn to ride and to handle weapons, just as he learned his Latin and Greek letters and arithmetic with his new paedagogus. He would get the sort of education that his father had been denied; Castus himself had been functionally illiterate until he was in his early thirties, and still felt uncomfortable with reading and writing.

He could train the boy, he could give him the best food and lodgings, the most attentive slaves, but he could not make him happy. Castus knew that his son still pined for Rome, still missed his mother grievously. Only when he was with Ganna did he awaken to life and pleasure. Castus knew that there was little he could do about that, and the knowledge ached in his bones.

'Whoa, draw her in now!' the slave cried, scuffing to a halt. 'Use the bit – pressure with the knees...'

Sabinus was leaning well back in his miniature saddle, pulling the reins almost to his chest. The pony might be small, but she was temperamental; she tossed her head, champed the bit, then blew out and came to a sudden stop. The boy jerked up straight in the saddle, beamed for a moment in satisfaction, then tumbled forward over the pony's neck to land in the dust.

Castus moved at once, the staff he had been leaning on falling from his hands as he reached out, as if he could somehow catch his son as he fell. But already the instructor was pulling the boy up from the dust, scrubbing at his limbs. Sabinus was trying bravely not to cry.

They rode together back into the city, sitting side by side in a rattling open carriage. Castus pulled the hem of his cloak around the boy's shoulders.

'I'm sorry I fell off. I didn't mean to,' Sabinus said.

'Don't worry!' Castus told him, grinning. 'I've fallen off more horses than you've ever seen! Everyone needs to take a fall sometimes.' His scarred jaw made his grin crooked, and the boy glanced up at him with a wary smile.

The carriage passed through the gloomy arch of the gate and entered the city. A pair of mounted soldiers of Castus's bodyguard rode ahead and behind the carriage, and the old campidoctor Tagmatius sat on the facing seat. Colonia Agrippina was an ancient settlement, laid out on the familiar Roman grid, but away from the temples and bigger townhouses near the Praetorium on the riverbank the buildings were small and mean-looking. Few rose more than two storeys, with façades of bare brick, wood and pitted plaster. The streets were lined with timber porticos floored with raised plank walkways, and the thoroughfares between them were black with mud and dung. Narrow dank-looking alleys, fogged with charcoal smoke and strung with laundry, split the blocks of houses to either side.

'What have you been learning with your tutor today then?' Castus asked, scooping a heavy arm around his son's shoulders.

'About when Aeneus ran away from Carthage,' Sabinus said.

'Did he now?' Castus said. He knew nothing about it – history, he assumed. But the idea that his son, *his own son*, was learning of these things made him blush with a pride so warm it was almost embarrassing. 'And do you like reading about that, hmm?'

'It's a bit boring,' the boy said, hunching his shoulders. 'I prefer the book about the talking farm animals.'

They rode on into the city; Castus kept his head straight and only moved his eyes as he scanned the passing streets. The population of Colonia was a strange mixture. More than half were the usual Gallic townspeople, dressed in their plain woollens and hooded cloaks. But among them were more exotic figures, some of them traders from distant parts of the empire. There were barbarians too, from across the river, tall bearded men standing in baffled unease at the street junctions, or gathered at the dark mouths of the wine shops. They were allowed to enter Roman territory without their weapons, provided they left again before darkness fell. There were plenty of beggars, too, huddled around the porticos with their greasy tin bowls, their crutches, their exposed wounds. Castus wished he could shield his son's eyes from the misery, but it was better he saw it all.

'Defender of the province!' somebody shouted from the portico, raising his hand in salute. A couple of other voices repeated the acclaim. Castus kept his back straight, not turning in his seat. The carriage slowed as the crowds grew thicker, and more people cried out, saluting him. He was surprised; he had not been back in the city for long after a lengthy tour of the frontier defences. Had the news of his defeat of the raiders really gained him such popularity?

'The gods preserve you, commander!' a woman called from a street corner. Others just stood and gazed at him as he passed, blank-faced. Castus was, he had to admit, quite prominent in his embroidered cloak and cap, with his gold brooch and the eagle-hilted sword clasped at his side.

'Dominus! Dominus...' a voice cried, a ragged figure limping from the crowd. He grabbed at the side of the carriage, grinning up at Castus with crooked teeth. 'A few coins for a shave, dominus? For an old soldier?'

'Old drunk, you mean,' the drillmaster growled, raising his stick. 'I know you!'

But Castus was already reaching into his belt pouch. The man was hobbling along beside the carriage, still clinging to the side; Castus found a couple of *nummi* and tossed them to him.

'Blessings on you, dominus!' the old soldier cried, snatching the coins from the air with surprising dexterity. 'May the gods preserve you for us!' He stumbled, dropping back as the carriage moved onwards. 'Take care,' he called. 'Take care they don't do for you, like they did for Leontius!'

'What?' Castus grunted, turning sharply in his seat. He had recognised the name at once: his predecessor, the former commander. He wanted to call out, seeing the limping old veteran still staring after him as the crowd swirled across the street behind the carriage.

'Ignore him. He's a notorious idiot, that one,' Tagmatius said with a scowl.

The carriage jolted across the uneven cobbles at a junction, and the old soldier was lost in the crowd. Castus turned again to face forward, trying to ease his frown.

'There's Ganna!' Sabinus said suddenly, starting forward on the seat and pointing, as if he were about to call out to her.

'Be still!' Castus said abruptly, seizing the boy's arm and dragging it down. 'Don't point,' he said, softening his voice. Sabinus looked startled, and slumped back onto the seat.

The boy had sharp eyes; Castus himself would not have spotted the slave woman. She was standing under one of the porticos along the street to the right; her head was half covered with her shawl but it was clearly her. Two men stood with her, long-haired and bearded. Barbarians, from across the river. Her own people. Then the carriage had moved on past the junction and she was gone.

There was nothing unusual about seeing her there, Castus told himself. Ganna was not confined to their quarters; she often went out into the city. He blinked, fighting the urge to order the driver to halt the carriage. Something about the woman's posture, her attitude, had been wrong. It took him a moment to realise what it had been: the slump of her shoulders, the way she had touched her face as she spoke to the two tribesmen. She had been weeping, Castus was sure of it.

Striding back into his private meeting chamber in the Praetorium, Castus tossed his cloak to one of the attendants and crossed to the table, sitting back against it. Diogenes glanced up from his work, but saw the look on Castus's face and did not speak.

Seeing Ganna in the street had been a surprise, but Castus knew he needed to put that out of his mind for now. He had quite enough worries. Barely a day had passed since his return from the inspection tour of the frontier garrisons, but already he had learned of the private communications the governor had been sending to Prefect Bassus and the office of the Caesar. The people of Colonia might be hailing him as a saviour, but Castus knew that there were others in the province who resented his handling of the Frankish barbarians. They resented the fifty high-born hostages he had billeted at Tungris, at Juliacum and here in the city, and they disliked the idea that Castus would forward the pleas of the Salii directly to the Caesar, bypassing the civilian channels. And now there was this new cause for concern.

The sentry appeared at the door, ushering Tagmatius into the room.

'You wanted to speak further to me, dominus?' the retired drillmaster said.

Castus gestured for him to approach, and to take a seat. 'This is about your son?'

Castus shook his head briskly, waving away the question. He remained propped against the table.

'That man in the street back there,' he said. 'He mentioned something about my predecessor. *Take care they don't do for you, like they did for Leontius.* What did he mean by it?'

Tagmatius sucked at his teeth. 'Like I said, the man's a drunken fool. He was with the old Minervia once, but got invalided out after a cart ran over his foot. Since then he's just prattled about the town, talking nonsense…'

'Nevertheless, he meant something by what he said.' *And you know more than you're letting on,* Castus thought. He had always been able to read a man's intent in his expression, and with Tagmatius it was easy enough to see that he was hiding something.

Pushing himself away from the table, Castus dragged over a stool and sat facing the old man. 'You're out of the army now,' he said. 'You're not under my orders. So I'm not asking you as your superior officer – I'm asking you man to man. How did Leontius die?'

Tagmatius took his time answering. Eumolpius appeared bearing a tray with two cups of wine, and the old man brightened visibly. He took a drink, chewed his lips, then peered up into the far corner of the room. 'It was back in the spring,' he said. 'Dux Leontius had gone up to the frontier to supervise the subsidy payment to the barbarians. There'd been some problems with it before, which is why he went in person…'

'Where was this?'

'Place called Castra Herculis, I believe. Abandoned fort, up by the Rhine north of Noviomagus. We've used it as a place to meet the barbarians for decades. Anyway, Leontius went up there to hand over the silver, and he never came back. The story was the barbarians tried something, or there was an argument. A fight broke out, and Leontius died. Along with a fair few barbarians too. That was the last time we sent a subsidy to them.'

'You don't believe it?'

Tagmatius gave a guarded smile. 'There were rumours,' he said. 'Nobody knows for sure, except them that were there. But Leontius wasn't popular. The men didn't care for him – thought he was a bit stiff, a bit pompous. But he argued with the governor, too, and with some of the local big men. You know the ones I mean.'

Castus nodded, glancing away to conceal his unease. He had heard tales before of unpopular officers being secretly murdered by their own soldiers – they ran through the army like a vein, and always had done. Back in Italy, several of his men had attempted to do the same to him. And if there was a shipment of silver thrown into the situation too, he could well believe it.

'Who were the troops that went to the meeting with him? Who commanded them?'

'That I couldn't say,' Tagmatius replied. 'I've been out of the army a long old while!'

Castus glanced at Diogenes, who nodded. There should be a record somewhere of the unit that had accompanied Leontius that day.

When the old man had left, Castus fell to pacing heavy steps from one side of the room to the other and back. 'What do you make of it?' he asked Diogenes.

'Could be it happened as they said,' the secretary suggested, raising his eyebrows. 'Or the troops killed him to steal the silver for themselves. But if that were the case, they would have been discovered by now. Mutinous soldiers are not good at keeping secrets.'

'So?'

'So perhaps they were taking orders from somebody else. In which case...'

In which case I need to know who, and why.

Castus nodded, then forced himself to stop pacing and sit down again. Nothing to be gained by worrying at the problem. He thought over what he knew of the senior officers under his command, the ones he had met during his tour of the river garrisons. Not one of them he would particularly trust. Tribune Gaudiosus, across the bridge at Divitia fortress, was idle and vain and apparently very close to the governor. The prefect of the fortress of Tricensima to the north was old, timid and vague. The tribune commanding the *numerus* of scouts at Noviomagus may have been a decent leader, but had appeared sullen and almost insubordinate. The men they commanded had not been much better: half of them were barbarian recruits, barely a step away from the tribesmen they were supposed to be guarding against. The rest were too old, or too young, and all were too inexperienced.

The junior officers had been better, some of them: Dexter in particular, and some of the other commanders of the strongpoints along the road to Tungris. But this had always been the problem with the new frontier-defence system: the able officers, and the best of the troops, were promoted to the field army units, and the borders manned by the rejects and the time-served veterans, bulked up with irregulars. Half of the garrison at Tricensima were made up of men from the old Praetorian Guard of Maxentius: they had been good soldiers, once, but defeat on the field of the Milvian Bridge five years before had broken their pride and their sense of discipline. Now they were just serving out their time, resenting their new home and the emperor who had sent them there.

'Some messages came for you, dominus, while you were away,' Diogenes said in a rather speculative tone. 'Perhaps you'd care to hear them now?'

'Hmm?' Castus said, breaking from his stream of thought. 'Yes – read them to me.' He knew that Diogenes had taken to opening and reading his messages, and trusted him to do it; ever since that terrible day in the camp in Thracia, when the news of Sabina's death had come as such a shock, Castus preferred to give his secretary time to digest the importance of any fresh information.

'The first letter comes from Rome,' Diogenes said. 'From the senator Latronianus.'

Castus jerked upright, his face tightening into a snarl. He had heard nothing from Sabina's cousin since he was last in Rome, six months before, and had hoped he was rid of the man for good. 'What does he want?'

'It appears that at last the complex administration of your late wife's inheritance has been decided.'

'They've been discussing this for nearly *a year*?'

'Well, yes. It appears the lawyers of Rome have had much employment from the Domitii family. As you know, your wife died intestate and by the Orphitian legislation her inheritance should pass to her offspring – your son, of course. However, much of her patrimony came from her father, and after his execution it was seized by the tyrant Maxentius.'

Castus gave an irritated rumble. He remembered hearing a great deal about that from Latronianus himself. 'What of it?'

'Also, it seems that Honoratus had made provision in his own will that a portion of the inheritance was only to pass to his daughter's husband – her first husband, at the time. Now, however, that means... you. Congratulations, brother: you seem to have become a very wealthy man.'

'How much?' Castus asked, after a heavy pause.

Diogenes dipped his head over the tablet. 'Townhouses in Rome and Fidenae, three *insulae* in Rome, estates in Africa and Campania totalling eight hundred *iugera* of arable land, a villa on the coast of Dalmatia and two in Africa with all associated lands, rents and slaves... the list goes on.'

Castus barked a laugh. His head was reeling slightly; it was hilarious, unreal. 'Tell him he can keep it,' he said. 'The bastard just wants to bribe me. He still hopes I'll give my son up for adoption by his cursed family...'

'Yes, he does lack an heir himself... But could I suggest that you keep the villa in Dalmatia? A very pleasant part of the world, so I hear...'

Standing up, Castus paced once more to the far wall. 'All right,' he said. 'Ignore it for now. What about the other message?'

'This one' – Diogenes picked up the second tablet – 'comes from Piavonius Magnius Rufus. He repeats his invitation to stay at his villa. In fact, he is holding a banquet on the kalends of October and desires that you attend as guest of honour. Apparently he wishes to *express the great admiration felt by all the citizens of the province for your recent prompt action against the barbarians...*'

'Does he indeed?' Castus said in a low breath. He snorted a laugh, remembering that Rufus had once described himself as a 'plain-speaking Gaul'. But Castus had suspected for some time that the landowner held the key to a great deal in the Rhine provinces. He also knew that he could only ignore his invitations for so long. He needed some idea of what had happened to his predecessor, and what Bassus had meant by his strange warning about the provincials. Magnius Rufus was possibly a dangerous man, but Castus had never been shy of confrontation. And if he wanted answers he would need to get them from the man himself.

'Tell him I accept,' he told Diogenes. 'Put it politely though – you know how.'

Diogenes gave the slightest of knowing smiles, then picked up a fresh tablet.

It was late that evening when Ganna came to his room. Castus was sitting alone, wrapped in thought, and she stood behind him and began to massage the bunched muscles of his shoulders. For a while he said nothing, closing his eyes and enjoying the familiar pressure of her hands.

'I saw you earlier today,' he told her. 'In the city. You were talking with two men.' The rhythm of her hands stalled for a moment, then resumed.

'They were of my people,' she said quietly. 'From across the river.'

'What was it they told you?'

Again she stopped, and he heard her sniff. 'They told me that my son lives. My brother has taken him into his household. He is a great man, now, my brother. The high chief's bodyguard.'

Castus turned in his seat, looking up at her. He took her hand. 'You want to go back to them?' he asked.

Ganna dipped her head, unable to answer for a few heartbeats. When she spoke, he heard the break in her voice. 'I don't know. They told me they could take me away, across the river by boat. But I refused. I didn't want to leave… what I have here.'

Standing up, Castus took the woman in his arms. Her back was stiff and hard, her whole body tense, but he could feel the shudders running through her. 'I meant what I said,' he told her. 'I would give you freedom any time you wished for it.'

'Even if I left you?'

'Even then.'

She pressed her face against his neck. 'What would Sabbi do if I went away?' she said, her voice muffled. 'He would have nobody.'

Only me, Castus thought. But the idea gave him no pleasure. He thought again of Latronianus's offer: how much better it would be, how much easier, if he sent Sabinus back to Rome, back to the place he knew and felt comfortable. Then Ganna could go back to her people with a clear heart. *And then*, Castus thought, *I would be alone here*. All that remained of the life that he had tried to build would be gone. The only thing left to him would be the stark demands of duty.

Ganna stepped away from him. 'Come to bed now,' she said. 'We will speak of this another time.'

CHAPTER XI

The villa of Magnius Rufus was four miles south of the town of Juliacum, set in a shallow valley on the banks of a stream. Quite different, Castus thought as he rode towards the villa, to the abandoned country only twenty miles north. The gravelled track he had been following from Juliacum was lined with trees, breaking in places to wide views across the valley, and the wooded slopes on the far side were bright with the colours of autumn.

'How soon until we reach Rufus's land?' he asked Dexter. The tribune was riding beside him, with two mounted bodyguards.

Dexter laughed. 'We're in it already,' he said. 'His estate boundary's right outside Juliacum – all of this country's his for miles in every direction. Everything you can see.'

Castus whistled between his teeth, glancing around with renewed interest. Rufus's estate was truly vast, and he knew that the landowner possessed several like it. By contrast, the lands offered by Latronianus as part of Sabina's inheritance seemed paltry. Now, as he looked between the trees along the road, he saw the fields and orchards lining the valley, the plantations on the low hills surrounding it. There were slave labourers, too, working in the fields; many of them had blond or reddish hair, and although they were all clean-shaven Castus recognised them as Franks. Prisoners of war, like the ones he had captured himself just over a month before. Some of the slaves paused to watch as the horsemen rode by, staring up from their work with hostile eyes, until the overseers closed in with their sticks raised.

'Does Rufus always keep his slaves chained when they're working?'

'Not all of them,' Dexter said with a wry tone. 'Only the ones that try and run away. I believe he thinks of it as a deterrent to the others...'

The sound of hooves came from along the road, and Castus instinctively tightened his grip on the reins. Four riders appeared from the shadows beneath the trees, all of them wearing grey tunics and the conical felt caps of freedmen. Castus noticed at once that they were armed – with hunting spears, but each carried a sword at his side too. Whether they were ex-slaves or free citizens, it was illegal to keep armed men on a private estate, but Castus decided to say nothing of it for now.

'Excellency!' the lead rider cried, throwing up his hand in a military salute. The other men handled their horses well, and had a lean and experienced look. Ex-soldiers, Castus guessed. 'The dominus is waiting for you at the villa,' the rider went on. 'He's instructed us to accompany you for the last mile.'

'A friendly ambush, luckily,' Dexter said under his breath as the four riders turned their horses and formed a vanguard ahead of them. They set off at a quicker pace, the two bodyguards bringing up the rear.

The road passed through a tunnel of trees, then burst from shadow into full sunlight. Castus blinked, and saw the villa on the far side of the valley. It was an impressive sight: the red-tiled roofs glowing in the afternoon sun; the white pillars of the front portico standing proudly above terraced gardens that dropped to the river. As they descended the track Castus saw that the stream had been dammed here to create a series of artificial lakes and pools; he assumed they were ornamental, but as the riders crossed the low wooden bridge between the larger two pools he glanced down and saw the flicker of plump red-backed fish close to the surface. Something else caught his eye as he looked up towards the villa; off to the left, beyond the humped roofs of the bath annexe, was a much cruder-looking structure of grey stone. It closely resembled the military watchtowers that stood along the frontier roads of the empire.

Before he could study it more closely, a figure appeared on the lower garden terrace. One of the riders blew a curved horn to announce their arrival.

'The hunters return!' Dexter said quietly. 'And it seems that we are the catch...'

Magnius Rufus raised both arms as the riders climbed the slope towards him, greeting them as if he were saluting the rising sun. He was dressed in a tunic and cape of spotless white embroidered with gold.

'Friends!' he called as Castus and Dexter dismounted in the gravelled courtyard outside the stables. 'Friends, you grace my house with your presence!'

Castus had not forgotten how much he disliked Magnius Rufus. Distrusted him too, more importantly. But seeing him now, displayed before his own palatial residence at the heart of his expansive estate, Castus had to admit that he was an impressive figure. Rufus came striding down the path from the terrace. He was beaming broadly, his teeth gleaming in his muscular face, and Castus once again experienced that sense of chilled malevolence from the man. Standing stiffly, he allowed Rufus to embrace him.

'Come, follow me, excellency,' the landowner declared,

taking Castus by the arm. 'A brief look over the house, then a bath – I've had the water heated for you. No doubt you're aching after the ride from Colonia?'

Castus had to agree. He had left the city at daybreak, and ridden over thirty miles. Climbing the steps from the courtyard to the front portico, he paused to admire the view across the valley. The sun was low in the western sky, and the trees opposite were glowing with colour, gold and fiery copper.

'Splendid, is it not?' Rufus said, spreading his arms as if to encompass the scene and display it to his guest. It was, after all, his possession.

They moved along the broad shadowed portico and in through the main doors to the central hall of the house. A huge open space, gloomy under its high ceiling, the floor flagged with marble and the walls set with objects on plinths. A tall water clock dripped quietly in the far corner. Beside it, Castus noticed a life-sized statue in black marble, a lumpy-looking heroic nude figure. The head had been removed at some point, and replaced with a slightly lighter-coloured portrait of Magnius Rufus himself.

'Who's this?' Dexter asked, pointing at another bust that stood on the opposite side of the hall.

'Ah, my illustrious ancestor!' Rufus said. He paused to dip his eyes and touch his forehead in reverence. 'The emperor Victorinus. A usurper, of course… but a great man nonetheless, I hope we can agree. He did marvellous things for the western provinces, back in the time of troubles.'

'Did you ever meet him?' Castus asked, exchanging a quick glance with Dexter.

'Me? Oh no… He was treacherously murdered before I was born. I am only forty-five years old, you know!'

Castus shrugged, nodding politely. He would have given Rufus a decade on that at least. But the landowner's expression of intense self-satisfaction had not altered. He gestured, leading the two men through to the rear portico and along to the door of the bath annexe.

'You'll find fresh towels in there, oils, and a very capable masseur!' Rufus said, bowed once, and then left them.

The masseur was capable indeed, but Castus was wary of talking too much in his presence; it was only half an hour later, as he and Dexter reclined in the wide sunken pool of the warm bath, that he asked the cavalry officer what he made of their host.

Dexter smirked, propping his lean muscled arms along the rim of the bath and glancing over his shoulder before answering. 'He's a distillation of all the worst aspects of the Gallic landowning class,' he said. 'But you've got to allow, he lives well by it.'

'He does,' Castus agreed, gazing up at the vaulted ceiling above them. Painted boats bobbed on a painted sea, the naked figures of fishermen hauling in extravagant catches. The warm water poured into the bath through a bronze spout shaped like a gaping lion's mouth, and flowed away again down a channel. The villa could not compare to the splendours of the houses Castus had seen in Rome – nowhere in the world, he thought, could do that. Nor was it as palatial as the imperial quarter in Treveris, or even the Praetorium in Colonia. It was a country house, that was all, but set in such a landscape, and so close to the disputed frontier of the empire, it seemed an oasis of civilised calm and refinement.

However, Castus had not forgotten that other building he had seen as he rode up towards the villa. He was just about to mention it to Dexter when a familiar voice boomed from the changing room. Moments later, Magnius Rufus strode through the archway, flinging off his robe.

'I hope you don't mind if I join you?' he said, stepping down into the pool with a hefty sigh of satisfaction. No reply seemed necessary; Castus and Dexter shifted to opposing ends to give their host room. With slight amusement, Castus noticed that the naked Rufus did not particularly resemble the heroic statue he had seen in the hall. He was a big man, but heavily belted with fat. The water rose considerably as he settled himself.

'We should have wine, maybe?' Rufus said. 'Water for the outside, wine for the inside, isn't that the way?'

'Later, perhaps,' Castus said. He knew that there were things Rufus wanted to tell him, things that he would need a clear head to judge. He also knew that Rufus was the sort of man who liked to talk, and who expected to have people listen and agree with him. Many years as a soldier had proved to Castus the benefits of remaining silent, expressing few opinions, leaving it to others to expose their intentions. He had been planning to draw Rufus out slowly, hold back and let the man reveal what he would; now he was here, he felt unwilling to remain so reserved.

'I notice you have a fortified tower at the end of your house,' he said.

'Ah, yes,' Rufus replied, his smile dropping just for a moment. 'A sad necessity! When I first bought this villa, you know, it was all but a ruin. The barbarians sacked the place during the time of troubles. Luckily the owners had already fled. But I was determined that such a fate should not befall my property, so I ordered the tower built. It's a meagre sort of fortification, perhaps, but it serves as a lookout and a redoubt, should the barbarians once more ravage this country.'

'You have your own private militia too, it seems.'

Rufus shrugged, the water slopping around his shoulders, then spread his hands and grinned. 'Illegal, I know! But there are only a few dozen of them. I use them as overseers on my land, mostly. Sometimes laws that are made in imperial capitals do not account for the demands of frontier life!'

Castus inclined his head, as if conceding the point. 'But my army is short of men,' he said in a level tone. 'We need recruits. If I have to, I'll order a general conscription, and you'll have to provide your share.'

Rufus pursed his lips towards the ceiling, shifting so the water slopped against the lip of the pool. 'We have much to discuss, you and I,' he said in a more confidential tone. 'At some... later stage of the evening.' He glanced at Dexter, who was managing to appear totally disinterested. 'Yes, *much* to discuss... but some of my other guests have already arrived, I think, and all will be eager to greet you, I'm sure!'

There were more guests, in fact, than Castus had been anticipating. As he walked out onto the front portico, freshly dressed in a clean tunic, breeches and soft shoes of red leather with smooth unstudded soles, he found them all waiting for him. A mass of civilians, it seemed at first, with a greater mass of slaves and attendants behind them, all turning to him as he appeared from the doorway.

'His excellency the Commander of the Frontier! Defender of our province!' Magnius Rufus declared, throwing out a meaty hand, and at once the whole assembly clapped and cried out their greetings.

'You've emerged just in time for our evening entertainment,' the landowner said, and then guided Castus through the crowd, introducing the other guests. No doubt, Castus thought, he was enjoying appearing in control here. He kept his expression neutral, wary in this company, responding with the barest of nods to each new greeting.

'My good friend Fabianus – my neighbour, in fact,' Rufus said, introducing a lean-faced man, thin-lipped and narrow-eyed, who smiled like a snake. 'Fabianus and I have known each other a long time! And this is Julius Dulcitius, one of our most prominent import merchants – you must speak to him about the grain supply from Britain…'

Rufus was steering Castus steadily through the crowd towards the balustrade, where several cane chairs had been placed, as if they might sit and admire the view. The valley and the fishponds had fallen into evening shadow, but the autumn colours still blazed along the crest of the hill.

On the steps below the portico was a party of musicians; beyond them, on the upper garden terrace, several of Rufus's grey-clad mercenaries were stationed around the perimeter of a grassy area. As Castus seated himself, the musicians began to play: tambourines fizzed and tapped, flutes whined and a bagpiper set up a rhythmic honk and skirl. All along the portico the guests gathered between the pillars, some seating themselves on the balustrade, all gazing down at the scene below them.

At first it appeared that the procession of young men walking out onto the garden terrace were performers of some kind; there would be a play, perhaps, or a dance. Then Castus noticed their costume: heavy brass helmets and shoulder-guards of ornate and antique appearance, shields and weapons.

'Friends,' Rufus called, 'in honour of our guest and his recent exploits against our enemies, I thought it only fitting to present for your entertainment a display of martial prowess!'

The twelve gladiators stood in line before the portico, raising their weapons in salute. Castus studied their faces: none were professional fighters, but they had a look of grim determination. They were slaves, he guessed. Frankish prisoners like the ones

150

he had seen working in the fields. Only one of the men, slim as a leather strap and with almost white-blond hair, looked like he knew how to fight. He had the eyes of a killer.

'Do you like the equipment?' Rufus asked, leaning close to breathe in his ear. 'I bought it from the gladiatorial school in Lugdunum...'

The rhythm of the music picked up as the first four men moved out to face each other. They would fight in pairs, Castus realised: a light-armed and heavy-armed man working together against matched opponents. He stood up, wanting to put some space between himself and Rufus, and feigned an interest in the show. He had seen gladiatorial bouts often enough, and he could appreciate the skill of the better fighters, but he seldom understood why civilians were so enthusiastic about them. It was supposed to promote manly virtue, so he had heard. Or to harden the spirits.

In the evening light the two pairs circled, one man at a time darting forward to test his opponents. They looked serious enough, Castus thought; he wondered what incentive Rufus had given them to fight like this, or what punishment he had threatened if they did not.

The clash of steel snapped him back to full attention. One of the fighters – a 'fisherman', armed with a net and trident – was trying to goad the man opposite into attacking. His opponent, the white-blond man, had cast aside his helmet. He closed with the netman, fast and dangerous, his crooked shortsword held low in a fighting grip. All along the balustrade the guests were watching, rapt. Some of the men were pointing and commenting to their neighbours, making rapid assessments of the fighters' chances.

Beyond the men was a group of women; Castus had not seen them before, and assumed they were the wives of the male guests. They must have been waiting in one of the other rooms of the villa when he was introduced to everyone. They seemed as attracted to the violence on the terrace below them as their husbands. But he noticed that one of the women had drawn back; she took a step, then another, then turned and walked silently into the house. Just for a moment, Castus glimpsed her face. His breath caught; there was a quick hard jolt in his chest, and the noise of the fighting seemed for a heartbeat to fade into silence. Then the woman was gone.

Down on the terrace, the netman had taken a wound to the thigh. His partner was protecting him as he backed away, but the blond-haired fighter was pressing his attack, jabbing and feinting with his crooked blade. Over the sob and howl of the pipes, the rattle of tambourines, Castus heard the rasping panicked breaths of the injured man. The crowd of spectators were leaning out over the balustrade now, sensing a kill.

Easing himself backwards, Castus edged away until he was out of sight of Rufus and the other guests, then strode into the house behind him. The hall was dark, deep in shadow, but lamps in the adjacent rooms threw oddly angled light through the connecting doors. The sound of the music and the fighting outside grew fainter as he moved through the rooms of the house. Slaves passed him, carrying lamps. A group of four lugged a heavy dining couch between them. All ignored him.

He found her in the last room that opened off the portico. A library, it looked like, with cases of scrolls, tablets and bound codices displayed on shelves around the walls. The woman was standing with her back to the door as Castus entered, one hand raised to run a finger along the labels below the shelves. He shuffled his feet, then cleared his throat, and she turned in surprise. Instantly she appeared flustered, as if he had disturbed her in some private moment.

'You don't care for watching the gladiators, domina?' Castus said.

'No,' she replied, glancing back nervously at the shelves. 'No, I... it seems too cruel. They're just slaves, not trained men. He promises them gold, you know, if they draw blood. Freedom for any that kill.'

Castus nodded. He had guessed as much. The sounds from the front portico drifted on the evening air, the sob and the wail of the pipes, the clash of arms. A few of the spectators were shouting encouragement to their favourites now.

'I knew you at once,' Castus said, lowering his voice as he crossed the tiled floor. 'I could barely believe it.'

'They were all talking about you, and I recognised your name, but... it's not an uncommon name. I didn't know if it was really you. Then when I saw you, I thought you'd probably have forgotten me. Dux Limitis Germaniae... How grand you've become!'

They were close together now, in the growing dimness beside the library shelves. Castus found he could not take his eyes from her. How long since he had last seen this woman – eleven years, or was it twelve? Back in the legion fortress of Eboracum in Britain, during the Pictish war. She had been only seventeen then, barely more than a child, but she had stayed in his memory ever since. The years had not changed her much: her face had grown more round, her hair was a lighter brown than he remembered, but she had the same curve to her lips, as if she were about to smile or speak, the same aquiline nose. The same cool intelligence in her eyes.

'Marcellina,' he said. He noticed her glance at the scar that disfigured his cheek. The years had marked him more deeply. 'How did you come to be here? You were going to Londinium when I saw you last. To marry your cousin, wasn't it?'

'You have a good memory,' she said with a quick smile, then dropped her gaze again. 'I did go there, yes. But the engagement to my cousin didn't last. There were complications. Then my brother fell sick, and his tutor ran off with most of our savings. He died, my brother.'

'Sorry to hear that,' Castus said. He remembered the boy, filled with grief and youthful disdain as he sat with his tutor in the townhouse in Eboracum.

'But I was lucky, I suppose,' Marcellina said. 'I was introduced to a merchant from Gaul, and then married to him. Dulcitius brought me here six years ago. So, you see, I'm now a respectable Roman matron! We have two children as well, both girls. They'll be eight and ten years old this autumn.'

Castus nodded, digesting it all. Dulcitius, he remembered, was the grain importer he had met on the portico earlier. It pained him to think of Marcellina married to such an unimpressive man – but who was he to judge? And how their situations had changed: when they met last he had been a junior centurion, promoted from the ranks, illiterate and inexperienced. A man his comrades called *Knucklehead*. Marcellina had been the daughter of a Roman equestrian, an envoy and former frontier commander. Castus now held the rank that her father had once possessed.

The realisation brought a spike of unease; Castus remembered how her father had died, choking on poison in a stone-lined pit beneath a Pictish fortress. He remembered Marcellina herself, a terrified fugitive in the ruins of her father's villa. She had killed one of her attackers with a mattock; she had almost killed Castus himself.

Looking at her now, he knew that she was remembering those same scenes. Those, and what followed: their flight to the walls of Eboracum, their strange and tender last meeting

154

on the night of Saturnalia. The attraction between them had been obvious, and the years had not dulled it. Back then, he had been far beneath her in rank and station, but now?

'It's good to see you again,' she said, and took his hand. The distance between them seemed to narrow, although neither had moved.

A sudden shout came from outside, then a chorus of raised voices. Castus guessed that the pale-haired fighter had scored his kill. The music still pulsed and whined. He felt the pressure of her hand, and could find nothing to say.

CHAPTER XII

The meal was laid out in the largest of the dining rooms,
the doors at one end folded back to provide a view over
the valley as the sunset dyed the distant woodlands. There
were three semi-circular couches, each set for seven guests,
with small round tables between them. In the space between
the couches, slaves waited with dishes and flasks. Musicians
played a quiet melody on flutes and a lyre. Castus was glad
that the bagpiper had not joined them.

He was placed at the end of the central couch, the position
of honour, from which he could address the others if he desired,
and at which he was served first from every new dish. Rufus
reclined at the opposing end; the other five men around
the couch were all local landowners or merchants. Castus
noticed Marcellina as soon as he entered the room; she was
on the left-hand couch, which was occupied solely by women.
Dexter had been placed with another group of men reclining
opposite.

'You see, excellency,' said Rufus's thin-faced friend Fabianus
as they picked through the appetisers, 'although we live on
the edge of a barbarian wilderness, we maintain the ancestral
customs of Rome.'

'Quite so!' Rufus broke in. 'In fact, I'd wager our ways are
closer to those of our illustrious forebears than many who call

themselves Roman these days! Here in the Gallic provinces, we preserve the blood of great Caesar himself.'

'The first Caesar, that is,' said Fabianus's neighbour, with a smile. 'Not our current boy emperor!'

Castus frowned at the man, holding his gaze until he looked away, abashed. But now the first of the main dishes was carried in: smoked eel on a bed of mashed herbs and pickled cabbage. As the slaves screened him from the others around the table, Castus risked a glance across the room. Marcellina met his eye at once, then quickly dropped her gaze. It was maddening to be so close to her – only half a dozen paces separated the couches – and unable to speak, unable even to look at her without the danger of discovery. Castus knew that, for all their professed virtue, these provincials of Gaul were gossips as keen and malicious as any other civilians.

'I'm proud to confess, friends,' Rufus was saying, 'that everything you will eat tonight, excepting only the eel, comes from my own estates. The carp were bred in my own pools; the boar hunted in my own forest reserves. And later you will get to taste my cherries!'

Maddening too, Castus thought, to have to recline right next to Marcellina's plump husband, who smelled of garlic and spoke with his mouth full. Stammering slightly, he was informing Castus of the threats to his trade on the Rhine.

'Our freight-carrying ships from Britain, excellency, have an average capacity of ten thousand *modii*. Now, as you know, your troops garrisoned along the river require grain in the region of forty thousand five hundred modii per month to sustain them. A little they can produce themselves, obviously, but during the summer and autumn months – do you see? – we need to bring nearly fifty shiploads of grain across the sea from Britain and up the Rhine, carrying the produce of nearly three thousand iugera of arable land, to fill the military granaries…'

As the man went on with his explanation, Castus inclined his head and glanced to his right. He saw Marcellina nodding as she listened to the woman beside her. A moment later she similarly inclined her head. Their gaze lingered for a heartbeat, then two.

'And so, as I say, the barbarian threat to our river commerce, besides disrupting trade, also disrupts your own ability to counter it…'

More dishes came and went: fish and flesh, smouldering in their sauces. The food was heavy and rich, and Castus tried not to fill his belly, nor drink too hard. He noticed that Dexter, at the far table, was being similarly abstemious. Some of the other guests were quite clearly not.

'Have you actually met this boy Crispus, excellency?' asked a man at the centre of the couch, his face shining with meat juice. 'Is it true he's only fifteen?'

'I've met the *most noble Caesar*, yes,' Castus told him, with an emphasis that made the man gulp thickly and glance down at his dinner.

The slaves were bringing glasses of amber wine now, lightly sweetened with honey. A huge dish of plump dark cherries stood on the table.

'All of them Christians!' the drunken guest was saying. 'The Caesar, and the prefect too! Most of his court I'll bet… How is the empire to survive with that impiety at its heart?'

'Friends!' Rufus cried loudly, raising himself from the couch. The musicians fell silent at a gesture. 'Friends, join me now in a toast to our most honoured guest, his excellency Aurelius Castus! Three times long life!'

He lifted his glass as all around the hall the other guests

lifted theirs, crying out the acclamation, '*Vivat! Vivat! Vivat!*' and the sound rolled out across the portico and into the night.

'Walk with me a while, excellency,' Rufus said, once the last of those guests who would not be staying at the villa had departed. 'The evening air's quite the tonic after a heavy meal, I find – and I can show you that tower you were so interested in!'

From the portico Castus could see the line of torches moving away up the track along the valley. Those who left had estates close by, or houses in Juliacum. Marcellina had gone, with her husband; Dulcitius had bid him a fulsome farewell, but she had not spoken. Castus knew they had a villa just to the west of Juliacum, and a house in Colonia. Doubtless, Dulcitius had said, they would meet again soon. For a moment, as she turned to go, Marcellina had glanced back at Castus. Had he imagined the promise in her eyes? Surely he had – she was a married woman now. She had her own family, her own life, and he was not a part of it.

Shrugging off the lingering sensation of regret, he followed Rufus along the portico. Slaves brought them cloaks, for there was a damp autumnal chill to the evening. They descended the steps to the garden terrace, where the gladiators had fought earlier, then climbed the path to the southern end of the villa. Another figure joined them in the half-darkness: Rufus's thin-faced neighbour Fabianus.

'A substantial structure, as you can see,' Rufus said, gesturing at the blockhouse built onto the end of the villa. Castus gazed up at it, appraising. The tower was several storeys high, with a low tiled roof and slit windows on the upper floors. A ladder gave access to the raised door, and there was a wooden walkway built around the topmost storey.

'Perhaps tomorrow you could see inside, if you'd like?'

Castus shook his head. He knew that looking at the tower was just a pretext for this evening stroll; Rufus wanted to talk, and Castus was content to let him.

'Let's walk a little further then,' Rufus suggested. 'There's an *exedra* down by the lower fishpond. A fine place to sit.'

They descended the path from the tower. As they walked, Castus became aware of the shapes of men moving in the gardens around them. Rufus's armed retainers, he realised. For the first time he felt the prickle of anxiety, a suggestion of threat rising in his mind. Dexter had remained back at the house, and Castus carried no weapon with him. He wondered whether Rufus and Fabianus might be armed. Their cloaks could conceal a knife or even a sword with ease. He guarded his feelings, giving away no signs of apprehension.

'Anyone who knows about our recent history here,' Rufus was saying as they walked, 'must surely understand our desire for security. The Rhine is only two days' march from this place – on the other side are the savages who have devastated our province repeatedly within living memory. So you cannot blame us for looking to our own defences...'

'I was sent here to protect this province,' Castus said. 'It's my job to do so.'

'Of course! And you've already proved that you can take action... But can you act in your own best interests?'

Castus frowned, letting the silence stretch. They had arrived at the fishpond, and Rufus led them into the wooden structure that stood upon its bank, a round rustic pagoda, like a temple to some local sylvan deity. There were benches inside – Castus imagined Rufus coming here to gaze proudly upon his plump carp. The waters of the pool spread away into the darkness, lightly hazed with mist.

'How did my predecessor, Valerius Leontius, die?' he said. Rufus and Fabianus had taken a bench, but Castus remained standing.

'As we told you,' Rufus replied. 'He was killed by the barbarians. Some argument – a sordid business. I don't rightly know! But he was... *inflexible*. He failed, I think, to correctly grasp the situation here.'

'And what is the *situation* here, would you say?'

Fabianus got up and strolled to the wooden pillars, gazing out at the pool. The mood had shifted noticeably. This whole evening, Castus knew – the bath, the entertainments and the meal – had been intended to make him malleable. Now they were trying to intimidate him. He kept his composure, trying not to shudder as the cold air leaked through his cloak.

'I'm told,' Rufus said in a musing tone, 'that you met with the leader of these barbarians who wish to settle in our province. That you gave him... verbal assurances that his demands would be passed directly to the office of the Caesar at Treveris.'

'Requests, not demands. Yes, I did. Such things are the business of imperial government. The Caesar himself and his prefect will decide what's to be done.'

'Ah, the Caesar, yes. A boy, sent to rule over men! It might almost be taken as an insult... And the prefect is Bassus – another Christian. But I can tell you, my friend, we here on the frontier will not lightly surrender our lands to our ancestral enemies!'

'As I understand it, the lands in question are deserted. Nobody farms them or occupies them.'

'No, no, no!' Rufus cried with sudden emphasis, getting to his feet and raising a finger. 'They are the pastures we use for grazing our herds! The forests we use for timber and for hunting! You wish to fill them with barbarians? These people are thieves and brigands – they know nothing of our culture or civilisation. Bring them within our frontiers and they will wander at will, taking whatever they can find.'

Fabianus mumbled something about inviting wolves into the sheepfold; Castus ignored him. Rufus's words were seditious, certainly, and the tone was aggressive, but Castus fought to remain calm. He would not give in to anger. Not yet.

'Then again,' Rufus said, 'I also hear you have a barbarian concubine? I hope that familiarity does not lead you to underestimate their danger? It would not do, surely, for the commander of our frontier to be thought a… *barbarian lover?*'

Castus drew himself up stiffly, and threw his cloak back from his shoulder. He exhaled. 'That's no business of yours, citizen.'

'Forgive me, excellency, I spoke in haste!' Rufus said, grinning. 'I meant no criticism. Like all men, I ride my slaves from time to time, women and boys alike. It's a master's prerogative. But one should not form attachments with them, of course…'

At the periphery of his vision, Castus could make out the figures of men stationed on the path and along the bank of the pool. Six, perhaps; maybe more. He still doubted this was more than a performance, but the threat was overt now.

'If you have something you want to say to me,' he told Rufus, 'say it now.'

Rufus sucked his cheeks, frowning. Fabianus had returned to stand beside him.

'It was a shame about Leontius,' the landowner said. 'He could have become a very wealthy man. He chose otherwise.'

'He chose to do his duty,' Castus replied. He thought of the wealth that Latronianus had offered him, and almost wanted to laugh. He was far beyond any temptations that Rufus could provide.

162

'You know,' the landowner went on, gazing into the night, 'the north was proud once. We raised our own emperors here – now we call them usurpers, of course, but in their time they were glorious. Constantine himself was one of them, originally. Now he's gone to the east, perhaps never to return – but he's not the sole ruler of the Roman Empire! What would happen, do you think, if someone here – Governor Tiberianus, shall we say – were to make a bid for power? Such things have happened before.'

'And been crushed before,' Castus said. He knew very well that Magnius Rufus had no intention of supporting Tiberianus. He was talking about himself.

'If any such usurper declared himself,' Castus continued, 'it would be my duty to oppose them. And I wouldn't hesitate to destroy any attempt to usurp imperial authority, with all the troops under my command.'

'Indeed,' Rufus said. He paused a moment. 'But do you think your troops would obey you, if you did?'

They returned to the villa in heavy silence, Castus making an effort to ignore the armed men that still dogged their steps. On the lighted portico he found Dexter waiting for him. The tribune raised an eyebrow, questioning; Castus shook his head curtly.

'I bid you goodnight, excellency,' Rufus said, smiling broadly as if nothing had happened. 'Perhaps you might think over what we've discussed, and tomorrow we can speak again?'

Not if I can help it, Castus thought. He had already decided on an early start the next day. Dexter led him through the house and up the stairs to the adjoining rooms set aside for their use. The tribune had already stationed the two guards in the corridor outside, unarmoured but with swords at their sides. Castus nodded his approval; clearly Dexter had guessed something of what had been said that evening.

In his room, Castus threw off the borrowed cloak, then sat on the edge of the bed and pulled off his shoes. There was a small window, opening onto the tiled roof of the front portico; he checked the latch, and made sure it was secured from the inside. Then he barred the door to the corridor, stripped off his tunic and breeches and extinguished the lamp on the side table. Before he lay down, he fetched his scabbarded sword and laid it beside him on the mattress.

Staring into the darkness, he thought over the conversation beside the pool. He was angry, and his anger was turning to a hard aggressive energy. Rufus's sly, arrogant words had been openly treasonous; Castus had the urge to move against him at once. He could order Dexter's men to seize the landowner, drag him in chains to Treveris to face trial. What evidence did he have? A few words, spoken after a dinner party... Men had been executed for less. But Rufus was wealthy enough to have bought influence even in Treveris; doubtless there were men in the imperial council who would speak for him. Tiberianus too; Castus could only overrule the governor by declaring martial law. Was the threat that serious?

With a start, he recalled the landowner's closing words. If Rufus really had conspired in the murder of Leontius, then he had followers in the army as well. Castus could not even trust the men under his own command to support him.

Another thought struck him, starting icy sweat on his brow: was Ganna safe? Rufus knew about her, and would not hesitate to harm her if he could, as a warning if nothing else. Could anybody here be trusted?

Enough, Castus told himself. He must take no hasty action now. Fatigue was clouding his mind, the sense of rage seeping from him gradually. He remembered his talk with Marcellina earlier that evening in the library. At once the thought of her calmed his mind. Clearly she had no love for Magnius Rufus. He could rely on her. But would he ever be able to speak intimately with her again?

Raising his head, he thumped the bolster, then lay down again and rolled onto his side, pulling the quilted blanket across him. The image of Marcellina lingered in his mind as he slid into sleep.

He was awake. For a moment he felt disorientated, the darkness pressing in around him. Then he felt the cold breeze across the side of his face, the air disturbed by movement. A single heartbeat, and he flung himself up and off the bed, snatching for his sword.

The knife came down hard into the bolster, striking the frame of the bed beneath. Already Castus was across the room, but before he could draw the sword from its scabbard the figure beside the bed whirled, dragging the knife free, and sprang at him. Ripped horsehair sprayed in the moonlight through the open shutters.

Castus tried to cry out, but the sound choked within him as the attacker collided with his chest and slammed him back against the wall. With his free hand Castus punched at the man's face. He could see the gleam of the knife, lifted to strike.

The attacker was grappling him, and seemed almost invisible in the darkness. When Castus grabbed for his wrist his fingers slipped off something cold and wet. Fear bloomed in his chest: he was fighting a demon, some inhuman thing out of the night... But it was a man: a man stripped to his loincloth, his body thickly coated in black grease. Castus locked his fingers around the man's throat, squeezing tight. The knife flickered, and he dodged it just in time; the blade stabbed at the wall beside him, gouging the plaster.

A thud from the door, the bar jumping in its socket. Voices from the corridor outside. Castus heaved against his enemy, but the man had a wiry strength. Teeth glinted in his blackened face.

Shoving himself back against the wall, Castus brought his knee up hard into the man's crotch, then swung his head forward. His skull butted against the bridge of the attacker's nose, and the man let out a yelp of pain. Castus forced his arm out straight, pushing against the man's windpipe and driving him back, then chopped a hand down against his wrist.

The knife fell to the floor, the blade ringing. Another blow against the door, and the wood shuddered in its frame. The attacker was staggering, off balance, and Castus drove two more hard punches at his head. The man dropped, scrabbling on the floor for the knife; Castus kicked it clear, and he jumped back into the far corner of the room.

They stared at each other. In the scrap of moonlight through the open window Castus made out the pale hair beneath the grease. The man snarled, feral. Then the door exploded inwards, the bar shattering.

With one swift movement the pale-haired man was on his feet and leaping for the window. He dived through it, like a man diving into water; Castus heard the crack of tiles on the portico roof outside. In the doorway, Dexter stood with drawn sword, the two soldiers crowding in behind him. But by the time Castus reached the window and hurled himself against the sill, the man was gone. Only a smear of black grease was left on the sloping tiles below.

Down the stairs, there were slaves running through the halls with lamps. Castus strode quickly out to the portico, carrying his sword, with Dexter and his soldiers coming after him. The light of the lamps had dazzled his eyes, and the ground outside the portico was lost in total darkness.

'You're safe, thank the gods!' Rufus cried, coming out of the house in his sleeping tunic. His armed retainers were filling the portico now, waving their burning torches out into the night. 'I can only apologise, excellency! One of my own slaves,' he went on, shaking his head and grimacing. 'I gave him his freedom only this evening! You see, this is how barbarians repay you... Doubtless he wished to avenge your recent slaughter of his people!'

Castus turned away from him, unable to bear the sight of the man. The energy of combat was still racing in his blood, tremors of delayed shock running through him. He felt suddenly sick, and fought it down. How much more, he wondered, had Rufus promised the man who had attacked him? As he stared angrily at the torches waving in the dark, intended to dazzle his eyes rather than illuminate anything, he understood that the hired slave had not been ordered to kill him: the window shutters had been rigged to open from the outside, but the knife blow that should have struck him had fallen a moment too late. This had been a warning, a goad. And he could expect more of the same.

CHAPTER XIII

From the tall windows of the Praetorium Castus gazed out at the river, the water moving smooth and dark as cold oil. On the far side the pastures that ran down to the bank were white with hoar frost, the bare trees beyond massing to the horizon. Winter had come early to the frontier, whirling in on an icy northern wind. People said that some years the Rhine froze. Castus could well believe it; he had seen the ice-covered Danube once. He stared at the water.

'Where was it?' he asked, turning from the window.

'In the stable of the riding school, dominus,' Tagmatius told him. The old drill instructor stood at attention, his eyes bleary and blinking. 'Must have taken at least one man to hold her, another to do the cutting. They just left her there in the stall. Lot of blood.'

'My son saw this?'

Tagmatius shook his head. 'I checked the stable before he went in, luckily. Can't have happened long before, though. First light, probably. The optio there reckoned they'd got a slaughterman to do it.'

Castus frowned, nodding. Doubtless his son had been intended to find the dead pony. This was his warning – it had taken two months to come. Anger uncoiled in his chest, and he clasped his fists at the small of his back.

'How many people had access to the stables last night?'

'Quite a few. Slaves and such. There's a sentry on the gate but plenty come and go. The optio said he'll have the slaves whipped and questioned, but I doubt he'll find much.'

Castus rubbed his jaw. The killing of a pony was not a matter for the army; he could inform the city aedile, but he doubted that the official would discover much.

'It's not right!' the drillmaster said, his face reddening. 'Killing poor beasts and scaring children!'

'Let me know if you hear anything more,' Castus said. 'And have the pony disposed of somewhere in private. Nobody must know of this, understand?'

Tagmatius nodded grimly. Castus waited until the man had gone, then turned back to the window. His mind seethed with frustration. Enemies surrounded him, but he had no way of determining who they were. Magnius Rufus, certainly; the governor, most probably. But beyond them were others, a great many others: the whole province and the frontier were riven with treachery and deceit, civilian and military alike. *Gods below, these are the people I'm supposed to be protecting...*

No, he would tell nobody about the dead pony, just as he had kept quiet about the feigned attack at Rufus's villa. Doubtless the governor had spies among his staff, and Rufus too, and he could not allow them to discover that he had been affected by this. Whatever remained of his authority rested on the projection of confidence. He must appear in control, invulnerable. *The mask of command.*

Already Castus had dictated a report to the Praetorian Prefect about Magnius Rufus, and the essentials of what the landowner had said at the villa. Diogenes had taken it down, and Castus had given it personally to one of the *agentes in rebus* attached to his staff, a confidential messenger of proven loyalty. He was covering his back; if word of Rufus's intentions leaked out, Castus himself did not want to appear complicit. And if Bassus himself decided to act, so be it.

The subterfuge was not to his tastes. Always before Castus had favoured the direct approach, attack as the best defence, a straight assault against any foe, with sword in hand. But here, in this land where friends and enemies appeared the same, where loyalty and treason seemed to merge and flow like the branching rivers at the mouth of the Rhine, he was blind to what faced him, and he could not act clearly.

Diogenes had already searched through the records left by the murdered officer, Leontius; any that might have related to the delivery of the subsidies, or mentioned the troops that had accompanied him on his last journey to the river, had been lost or destroyed. All Castus had to guide him were suspicions and doubts.

Staring at the cold water sliding past beneath the bridge outside, he felt the weight of responsibility heavy on his shoulders. He knew what he had to do, and he had been delaying it too long.

Two hours later, Ganna stood alone in the centre of the large room. She was wearing her simple green dress, a shawl around her shoulders and her blonde hair hanging loose. In her grey eyes was a look of resignation mingled with defiance. Castus could barely meet her gaze; how had she already guessed what he was intending?

'I have decided,' he announced stiffly, the words souring his mouth, 'to send my son Sabinus back to Rome. He will be happier there, surrounded by familiar things, and he will get a better education in the capital than here on the frontier.'

And he'll be a lot safer, he thought. Ganna said nothing, but Castus could see the slight twitch of her cheek.

'As a sign of gratitude for the care you have given my son,' he said, urging the words out, 'I am giving you your freedom. My secretary Diogenes is drawing up a document of manumission as we speak. You won't gain full Roman citizenship, as you were a captive taken in war, but your freed status will give you certain legal protections.' His throat tightened, and he stifled a cough. 'You can remain here as part of my household if you wish, but you are free to return to your own country if not.'

There was a long silence. Castus forced himself to look at her. That face he knew so well, now closed against him.

'I don't want to leave,' she said. 'But if you do this, you know I must.'

He nodded. He wanted to tell her of his reasons, of the threat to her if she remained with him, the threat to them all. But he was steeled to his task now, and there could be no turning back. He remembered the old maxim his first commander had taught him. *Never try to hold what you cannot defend.*

'A convoy of merchants leaves for Bructeri territory early tomorrow morning,' he said. 'You can go with them.'

He saw her throat tighten, and she sniffed. So soon – but it had to be done quickly, before his resolve slackened.

'Do it then,' she told him. 'If you're going to do it, get it done.'

'There's no need...' he started to say.

'Do it! There must be witnesses. I know how you Romans love everything to be correct.'

Castus barked a command, and at once the sentry and two of the clerks appeared in the doorway. A moment later, Diogenes and Eumolpius joined them.

Ganna remained motionless as he approached her.

'It is my wish,' he declared, 'that this slave, Ganna of the Bructeri, be freed.'

He took a breath, wanting to hold back, not to go through with it. He saw the challenge in her eyes. Raising his hand, he swung it at her face; at the last moment he pulled the blow, and his fingers brushed her cheek in a rough caress.

'Do it properly!' she hissed. 'I need to feel it.'

Again he swung his hand, and his open palm slapped across her cheek. Her head jerked, and she closed her eyes as the colour rose to her face.

'With these blows I liberate you from the power of my hand,' he said, reciting the words in a deadened voice. 'And from the violence of slavery.'

He raised his left hand, and slapped her other cheek. The print of his palm bloomed pink on her skin. The men at the far end of the room nodded, signifying that they had witnessed the act of manumission. Diogenes cleared his throat.

'I now declare that you are a free woman,' Castus said.

Then he stepped forward and threw his arms around her, pulling her into his embrace. Ganna pressed herself against his shoulder, and he could hear her choking back tears.

The next morning, an hour after dawn, they stood together on the bridge in the cold grey mist. The merchant caravan – two wagons and a train of mules – waited on the roadway. Behind him, Castus could hear his bodyguards stamping and blowing on their cupped hands.

Dropping to her knees on the mud of the road, Ganna embraced Sabinus. The boy clung to her, his fingers knotting around the rough weave of her cloak, and Castus heard her whispering to him. The boy nodded, gulping as he cried. Castus stared at the river, hardly daring to breathe.

Standing up, Ganna brushed at the mud on her tunic.

'You'll send me word that you're safe?' Castus said.

Ganna looked at him, her face reddened by the cold, strands of hair escaping from under her shawl as she shook her head. 'No words,' she told him.

Then she turned and climbed up onto the tail of the cart, carrying the sack that contained all her possessions. Castus heard the cry of the drover, and the head of the convoy lurched into motion. Before the cart could move he strode up to the tailgate, passing her a small bundle wrapped in thick cloth.

'Take it,' he said. Ganna held it in her hand, feeling the weight of metal. The jewelled handle of a dagger jutted from inside the cloth. She did not need to ask what else it contained. For a moment she appeared offended, and he thought she would hurl the gifts back at him. Then her brow creased, and she thrust the wrapped weapon and the purse of gold into her bag. Castus stepped closer. He untied the thong around his wrist, with the blue bead amulet she had given him many years before. Taking her hand, he knotted the leather cord around her wrist.

'For protection,' he said. 'You need it more than me now.'

Then he drew her close and kissed her. For a moment she embraced him, returning the kiss. Then the cart jolted beneath her and pulled them apart.

Sabinus gave a cry, dashing forward, and Castus just managed to catch the boy before he ran out into the road. Holding his son close, one spread hand pressed over his chest, Castus watched the cart rolling away across the wide spans of the bridge. The ironbound wheels rumbled across the wooden planks of the roadway, and Ganna stared back at him until she was almost at the far side of the river. Then she pulled her shawl across her face. The convoy moved on through the gates of Divitia fort, following the straight road that would take them out through the far side, past the sentries and the customs officials, and into the wild country of barbaricum beyond.

Already Castus felt the loss of her, the churning sadness threatening to overwhelm him. He went to his horse, rubbed at her nose and felt her breath hot against his fingers. Mounting, he lifted Sabinus up to sit across the saddle in front of him, supported in the crook of his left arm. The boy was quiet as they rode back into the city. The dirty shacks that lined the street up from the gate looked black and grey in the morning chill, and the beggars stared with pallid faces as the dux rode by with his mounted guard. Castus remembered what Ganna had offered him months before: just for a moment he imagined them riding off together, into the forests of Germania. A new life, far from the sordid intrigues of the Roman world. His face twisted into a sour smile: the fantasy had no weight. He was a soldier; the army had made him and shaped him, and he belonged to the empire.

Sabinus twisted in the saddle, burrowing his face into the fold of Castus's cloak. He had been quite sincere about sending the boy back to Rome. Now, in the bone-chilling cold of the morning, with Ganna gone from his life for ever and the grief of their parting pooling in his chest, he was not so sure. Sabinus was still sniffing quietly, his fingers and nose pink with cold. A year ago he had lost his mother, and now he had lost the woman who had raised him since he was a baby. Castus tightened his hold on the boy, the bunched muscle of his bicep like a shield that would hold the dangers of the world at bay.

Cold earth, cold hands. Under a sky the colour of spit, thirty men laboured with mattock and spade, hacking trenches into the hard ruddy soil. Another thirty hefted great baulks of timber from the wagons on the road, driving them into place to form the palisade. Castus sat on his horse and watched them working; the men were soldiers, and their stacked shields bore the trident and twin dolphin emblem of the Thirtieth Legion. Building fortifications had always been a job for the legions, and Castus knew the work all too well.

At the centre of the ringwork of trenches and palisade stood a stone watchtower, begun decades before but never completed. With the fortifications around it, the tower would form a stronghold on the road between Colonia and Tungris. Castus was reminded of the defensive tower that Magnius Rufus had recently built next to his villa; he guessed the landowner had used this one as a model.

Dismounting, he walked up the slope over the rutted ground to the gap in the palisade. This was only one of the dozen or so new and repaired fortifications he had inspected over the last three months. Watchtowers and *burgi* were going up along the west bank of the Rhine from Colonia to Noviomagus, and down the Mosa to Traiectum. When all were complete, the frontier districts would be held in a web of garrisoned posts and forts; any hostile force crossing the river would be detected quickly, and trapped in a killing ground fifty miles deep and wide. That was the theory – but the work would take time, and manpower was short.

As he marched towards the wooden ladder that rose to the tower doorway, Castus overheard the centurion commanding the legionaries giving orders to his men. A Pannonian accent, much like his own. The man paused as he noticed his commander watching him, then saluted.

'You're a long way from home, brother,' Castus said.

Beneath his fur cap, the centurion's bearded face flickered into a smile. 'You too, excellency.'

'You were with the Guard?'

The centurion glanced away, his shoulders rising. 'Long time ago,' he said. 'Fifth Cohort.'

Castus nodded. There were plenty of ex-Praetorians with the Thirtieth. Their posting to the frontier was a form of punishment: most would serve their time and then settle here. Few would see their old homes on the Danube again.

'Before that?' Castus asked.

The centurion brightened visibly. 'Thirteenth Gemina,' he said. 'Up at Carnuntum. Better days, I'd say.'

Castus could only agree. The Danubian soldiers that had joined Maxentius's Praetorian Guard had lived well in Rome, and fought well at the battle of the Milvian Bridge. But that was a disgraceful memory now. Castus wondered whether this centurion had been there, fighting among his enemies. Probably so. Would time ever mend the divisions between them?

He turned to go, but the centurion stepped towards him. 'You reckon they'll attack again, dominus?' he asked. 'All this, I mean.' He gestured at the trenches and palisade.

'I don't reckon anything,' Castus told him. 'But if you want peace...'

'... *prepare for war!*' The centurion grinned. It was an old maxim.

The ladder groaned beneath his weight as Castus climbed. He edged past the two sentries in the doorway, then climbed another ladder from the dingy chamber inside up to the second floor lookout.

Wind blasted at him as he stepped out onto the walkway. Moving around the circuit of the tower, boards creaking, Castus gazed at the landscape in each direction. The tower stood on a low ridge, a wide marshy river valley to the west. Clutches of trees stood black against the grey sky. The subtle undulations of the ground could hide a lot, but the land around the tower had been well cleared; nobody could approach this place undetected. It was a good landscape for war.

He left the tower and rejoined the horsemen on the road.

Castus was travelling with only a small escort: his four bodyguards, his standard-bearer, his orderly Eumolpius and four pack mules. He could cover more ground, and cover it faster, this way. But they had been on the road for many days in this hard season and all of them, Castus knew, were eager to return to the comforts of Colonia.

It was late afternoon, and they were still several miles from Juliacum, when the sky to the south darkened dramatically. The wind rose, driving freezing rain before the storm, and the riders pulled their cloaks tighter as they kicked their horses into a trot. Ahead of them was a group of other mounted men, with some slaves on foot. Castus swung out into the road to give them a wide berth; he knew the boundary of Magnius Rufus's estate lay close by, and he had no wish to encounter any of the landowner's people.

'Excellency!' a voice cried. Castus reined in his horse and glanced back. The leading rider had pushed his hood away from his face and Castus recognised Dulcitius, the grain merchant. Marcellina's husband.

'We thought when we saw you coming that you might be brigands,' the merchant said. 'They do prey upon travellers on this road... But then we saw your banner. This is a happy meeting!'

Castus had heard stories about the brigands, escaped slaves and rebel peasants turned to thievery and ambush – *bagaudae*, the locals called them. They had been a force in Gaul decades before. But he had assumed they were a myth these days; nobody he had met had ever encountered one in reality.

'It seems we'll have sleet,' Dulcitius said, squinting through the rain as he gestured at the approaching darkness. 'You'll be soaked and frozen before you reach Juliacum! My villa lies just over there, along the track you can see – will you join me and shelter until the storm passes?'

Castus looked back at his small retinue. Eumolpius sat hunched in the saddle, teeth clenched to stop them chattering. The five troopers looked staunch enough, but he could see the spark of hope in their eyes at the offer of shelter.

'Let's go then,' he said, and swung his arm.

The villa stood at the end of a track lined with poplars. It was a single-storey building, with a portico at the front flanked by outbuildings around a yard. A modest place, Castus thought. In the shelter of the gateway the men dismounted, and Dulcitius ordered his slaves to take the horses and mules to the stable. Sleet was coming down already, slanting with the wind, and the group of men huddled in their cloaks as they jogged across the yard.

'Your men can rest in the side chamber there,' Dulcitius said. 'I will have hot food sent to them. But perhaps, excellency, you would care to follow me?'

He led the way into the main house, Castus behind him trying to stamp the mud from his boots. Outside, the yard was almost obscured by grey sleet, turning now to hail. They passed through the doors and into the reception room, where braziers stood warming the air. Castus felt the steam rising from his sodden cloak.

'Wine, perhaps? And would you like me to have the baths heated?'

'A drink, yes, but no bath,' Castus said. He felt uncomfortable here. 'We won't stay long. As soon as the storm's passed, we'll be on our way.'

Dulcitius was fussing around the room, giving whispered instructions to his household slaves. Castus paced awkwardly; he was beginning to regret coming here. A slave approached, with an apologetic expression and a pair of house slippers in his hand; Castus waved him away with a frown. He could smell food cooking, and a lingering feminine perfume that quickened his pulse. Perhaps he should leave now, before the merchant got any further ideas of hospitality? Before Marcellina made an appearance... The noise of the sleet was loud on the tiled roof overhead, and somewhere he could hear water dripping.

Female voices from the next chamber, and a moment later three figures appeared in the doorway. Dulcitius returned, followed by a slave bearing a tray with cups of wine. 'Ah, there you are!' he declared. 'Excellency, may I present my daughters, Julia Dulcitia and Julia Maiana? I believe you've already met my wife...'

Marcellina stared at him, visibly surprised. She looked tired, pallid, with dark rings under her eyes, but she managed a tense smile. The two girls stood watching him, perplexed. The older one was tall and gangly, with very wide eyes. The younger had a round face and a pert, questioning expression.

'Greet his excellency!' Dulcitius told his daughters. Both girls bowed slightly, touching their foreheads with their fingertips.

Castus took one of the cups of wine. He was trying not to meet Marcellina's eye. Her strained nervousness was easy to read, and Dulcitius still seemed agitated. Too agitated, perhaps: he was still talking, stammering something about the weather, but he was clearly on the edge of panic. Not just the surprise of an unexpected guest, Castus knew. He felt his sense of uneasiness tightening into apprehension.

'How did you get that?' the younger girl said, touching her jaw. She was gazing at him, her head angled to one side.

'Eh? Oh... in a battle,' Castus told her, his hand instinctively rising to cover his scar. 'A cavalry spear...'

'Did it hurt a lot?'

'Girls!' Marcellina said promptly. 'Don't ask rude questions. Go back to your chambers now.' She trapped Castus's glance and held it for a heartbeat.

'Now, won't you sit, excellency,' Dulcitius said. 'A long ride today, I expect!'

Castus made a sound in his throat, then lowered himself into one of the chairs. Marcellina had crossed to a small cabinet with doors of ornate brass grillwork that stood against the far wall. Castus followed her movements from the corner of his eye. Her husband was saying something about the bad weather damaging the winter crops as she opened the cabinet, crouching before it.

'My wife feels the cold and damp badly,' Dulcitius said. 'She has southern blood, you know!' Castus recalled that Marcellina's father had been from Spain. But she had grown up in north Britain: it was not the weather that was causing her distress. She was still crouched by the cabinet, and he tried to make out what she was doing.

'I remembered that verse by Ovidius you were asking about when we last met,' Marcellina said, with a rather false smile. The cabinet was stacked with scrolls, Castus noticed. She straightened up holding one of them, a slim tube capped with ivory bosses. 'Here – I found a copy. Why don't you take it with you?'

She crossed the room again and passed the scroll to Castus with a flicker of her left eyelid. There was a dark smudge on her finger, he noticed. Trying not to let his confusion show, he took the scroll and held it clumsily, rubbing his thumb over the ivory. There was no way he would want to read verse, especially at a time like this...

'Oh yes,' he said. 'I remember now.'

'You'd better take a look and check it's the right one.'

Castus felt a breath up his spine. He cleared his throat, glanced down at the scroll and unrolled the first leaf.

Scratched in charcoal, tight against the roller, a single word: *FLEE*.

'I never would have guessed you were an admirer of poetry, excellency,' Dulcitius was saying. 'My wife's very fond of reading – unnaturally so, some might suggest! Yes, her collection there's quite extensive...'

Castus rolled the scroll tight again and tucked it inside his tunic.

'Seems to be the right one,' he said, feeling the thickness in his voice. Dulcitius appeared to have noticed nothing. Raising his head, Castus peered at the ceiling. The roar of the sleet had not eased. He could hear it crashing against the paving of the portico outside.

Marcellina was staring at him, hollow-faced. He caught her slight nod.

Drawing a deep breath, he stirred himself and stood up, trying not to appear hurried. He paced to the door and edged it open to glance outside. 'Looks like it's clearing up,' he said. 'I thank you for the shelter, but I think we really ought to move on. I want to be at Juliacum before dusk.'

Dulcitius was on his feet, hands fretting at the front of his tunic. 'Oh no, please, do stay longer. It's only another few miles into town – there's plenty of time! I've told the kitchen slaves to prepare a meal...'

Castus narrowed his eyes at the man. He forced himself to smile. 'Your kindness does you credit,' he said. 'But my decision is made.' He looked back at Marcellina, nodding his farewell. 'Thanks for the verses,' he said.

They rode hard through the driving sleet, heads down in their cloaks. Where the track from the house met the main highway Castus signalled a halt; he glanced left and right, but there were no signs of other travellers. A hundred paces towards the town, a copse of trees stood near the road, the bare branches thrashing in the wind.

'Over there,' he called above the noise of the storm. 'And be on your guard.'

As they neared the trees Castus could tell that there was nobody waiting. But it was the only good spot for an ambush along this road. He guessed that Dulcitius must have sent his message as soon as they arrived at the house; doubtless whoever had intended to waylay them had been close by, but not yet in position. He led his small troop of men off the verge and into the cover of the trees, their horses forging through the dripping brambles and scrub.

Dismounting, Castus scanned the road. Still nobody in sight. Rain spattered over his shoulders, pouring icy water down the back of his neck. The men with him remained silent; he had told them nothing since leaving the house, but all seemed aware of what was happening and needed no orders from him. Good soldiers. He jerked a thumb at his head, and each man took his helmet from the leather bag on his saddle horn and put it on over his wet cap.

They did not have long to wait. The sleet had slackened to a cold flurrying rain as the group of riders appeared on the road, moving fast from the east. Twelve of them, all dressed in short waterproof capes with hoods drawn up. Some carried spears, and all had scarves tied across their lower faces. They did a good impression of being brigands, at least.

Castus let them pass, a palm raised to hold his men in silent readiness. The group of riders reached the turning to Dulcitius's villa and halted, peering down at the rutted surface of the road, reading the marks of the horses. One pointed away to the left; another stared at the trees, but appeared to see nothing unusual. Slowly, careful not to make any sudden movement, Castus swung himself up into the saddle and nudged Dapple forward out of the copse.

He was up on the road before any of the riders noticed his appearance. Drawing his cloak tight around his body to free his right arm, Castus unsheathed his sword.

'Looking for somebody?' he shouted down the road.

The riders drew closer together, readying their spears. They were mounted on small ponies: good for cross-country hacking, but no match for a trained warhorse. No time for delay now: Castus glanced back to see the first pair of his soldiers joining him on the road. Then he raised his sword and signalled the charge.

Immediately his opponents scattered in panic. Two of them had drawn bows from under their cloaks, but their aim was poor; Castus had closed half the distance when the first arrow snicked past him. Rain was in his face, the noise of the hooves loud on the wet gravel of the road. For three heartbeats he felt only the sting of the wind, the punch of blood in his head, then his charge carried him crashing between the enemy riders.

He caught the first of them as he tried to turn his pony. Dapple rammed into the other animal, pitching the rider from the saddle. Castus was already aiming a straight-arm stab at the next man's face. The man flinched, and Castus flicked his hand down into a slash that opened his forearm.

A pony reared, screaming as its rider tried to control it. The two mounted soldiers were in among the enemy now, yelling as they struck. Castus dragged back on the reins, letting Dapple rear and kick, then smashed his sword down onto another rider's head. The blade chopped through the man's hood, and blood sprayed up pink in the rain.

Half of them were down already, dead or injured. Two more were cantering away from the road across the fields. Castus was shouting, ordering his men to catch the fugitives, to get them alive. He saw one of his soldiers dodge a spear-thrust, then slash a rider from the saddle with a backhand cut. Muddy water splashed and spattered around them.

Soldiers ahead of him, circling. Castus saw one of the enemy riders canter closer and aim a javelin; he threw himself forward against the horse's neck and felt the missile dart past him. As he straightened, a gust of wind flung the rider's hood back from his head. White-blond hair was plastered against the man's skull, and as the scarf covering his face dropped Castus saw the expression of hate, the killer's eyes. He yelled, urging his horse towards the enemy.

The rider turned, his pony rearing. As he galloped clear he struck downwards with his second javelin, stabbing it into the back of one of his injured comrades lying on the road. Then he kicked wildly at the pony's flanks, hauling at the reins to send the animal plunging over the roadside ditch and into the open ground beyond.

The skirmish was over. One of Castus's men was kneeling in the mud beside the only fallen enemy who remained alive. He shook his head. Blood soaked the road, filling the ruts and the puddles. The suddenness of the attack had been effective; none of the soldiers were injured.

Four of the attackers had escaped, fleeing in different directions. Castus stared after the white-blond man. The ground between them was broken with ditches and clogged with low scrub, too hazardous to cross at a gallop. Castus drew on the reins, pulling his horse to a halt. The man slowed, glaring back at him.

'Run to your master!' Castus bellowed through the rain. 'Tell him if he tries anything like this again, I'll come and find him myself. And I'll *kill him*!'

He was smiling grimly as he rode back onto the road. Magnius Rufus had covered his tracks well. But if he wanted a war, Castus thought, then he would get one.

PART THREE

CHAPTER XIV

Treveris, March AD 318

Anyone might think, Luxorius mused to himself as he paced along the broad corridor of the palace, that the population of Treveris would have had enough of imperial celebrations by now. Enough of games, enough of parades, certainly enough of panegyric speeches. But apparently they had not. Only days before it had been the birthday of the Augustus Constantine, and today it was the first anniversary of Crispus's promotion to Caesar; once again the city had been alive with festivity since dawn, the streets garlanded, the area around the palace loud with shouts of acclaim and the braying of trumpets, the crowds in the circus roaring their approval of their young master.

But it was no surprise that the city loved shows so much. There was food from the sacrifices and the public banquets, free entertainment and a good excuse for drunkenness and excess. There was money, too, distributed as donatives to the soldiers and the city officials: new-minted gold coins, stamped with the head of Crispus and the motto *Princeps Iuventutis*. 'First Among Youth'. No surprise either, Luxorius thought, that so many people were drawn to the great city, to swell the numbers of the urban mob. A horde of open mouths and open hands, while the surrounding countryside emptied, the villages decayed and the land was swallowed up by the vast slave-farmed estates of the wealthy.

It was not his concern. The eunuch felt little connection, and even less love, for this grey northern land. Let all of Gaul sink into the sea: he would not care. As he moved along the corridor, his soft leather soles padding quietly on the polished marble tiles, he could hear the sounds of singing and chanting drifting in through the tall windows on either side. Now evening was falling, the official celebrations were complete, but the city would not be quiet for many hours to come. There was something disgusting, yet also awe-inspiring, about the passions of the mob.

At the end of the corridor he passed through a painted vestibule, between a pair of Protectores standing guard in full scale armour with shields and spears, then approached the tall doors at the far side. He stood for a moment, conscious of the silence, before the doors opened and he advanced into the chamber beyond. The door slave was a eunuch like himself; for a moment their gaze met and lingered, loaded with mutual contempt.

'Detained by the celebrations, I expect, Luxorius?' the Praetorian Prefect said. Bassus was reclining on a couch, his heavy beard-covered jowls sunk almost to his chest, his shaven top lip gleaming slightly. The air smelled of incense, perfume and stale sweat.

'I'm afraid not,' the eunuch replied, with an agreeable smile. 'Administration, eminence – the burden of us all.'

There were four other men in the room, seated on high-backed chairs. Cervianus was the head of the Caesar's Corps of Notaries, while the red-faced Hypatius, *comes rei militaris*, commanded the main force of the field army. The chief secretary of Bassus's officium was present, and also Cupitus, Controller of the Sacred Revenues for the Prefecture of Gaul. All but the first were Christians. Slaves stood in silent attendance.

'Sit,' Bassus directed, and the eunuch took a chair near his superior's couch. This was an informal gathering, but an important one. Officially, Caesar Crispus was advised by his *consistorium*, headed by his prefect. In practice, Bassus opted to discuss affairs with a much smaller group, his own confidants, and make up his mind before taking any new proposal before the full council of state. It allowed him greater freedom; besides, in the consistorium all but the emperor had to remain standing, and Bassus preferred to deliberate in comfort. Luxorius assumed he himself was valued for his impartiality.

'So, what's the latest word from the provinces?' Bassus asked.

'All seems well at present,' the chief notary said, dipping his eyes only briefly to the inscribed wax tablet in his lap. 'The provincials are pleased that the Caesar has most generously remitted their last year's tax arrears. They praise him with their every breath!'

'Good,' said Bassus. 'That's the purpose of provincials. How are our finances bearing the loss?'

'A few squeezes here and there,' Cupitus said with a sigh. He appeared, Luxorius thought, like a man who could benefit from some squeezes himself. 'But nothing the treasury can't smooth away.'

'Well done. Hopefully it won't be necessary to extend any further bribes. A small amount of largesse now, and we reap a much greater reward in future taxes paid in full. Does the frontier remain tranquil?'

'Indeed, eminence,' the notary said. 'The tribes of the Franks and Alamanni are all abiding with their treaties. The Franks in particular, it seems, are showing signs of accommodation. The salutary blow recently dealt them by our Dux Germaniae seems to have convinced them of the merits of a deeper cooperation with Rome.'

'Ah yes, our bull-headed commander on the Rhine,' Bassus said with a flicker of amusement. 'He has been, perhaps, a little *too* efficient!'

Polite smiles from the assembled dignitaries. Luxorius had realised long before that the commander's diplomatic initiatives had taken Bassus by surprise. The prefect had only wanted the barbarians subdued until a future date, not rendered entirely subservient. But if the commander had exceeded his mandate, he had done so unwittingly, and Bassus could not fault him for it directly without exposing his own duplicity. The young Caesar needed a war; a tranquil frontier would not provide one. So much of our policy, Luxorius thought, is about managing and manipulating threat. But he smiled along with the others all the same.

'And what of the attitudes of the provincial notables?' the prefect asked. 'Have there been any further complaints about the actions of his excellency Aurelius Castus?'

'A few, eminence,' the chief secretary said with a worried frown. 'As you know, both the governor and several of the more prominent citizens have stated their displeasure at the commander's, ah, *high-handed* attitudes and enactments. He recently dismissed the tribune commanding the fort at Novaesium, on a charge of incompetence and corruption, and appointed the chief centurion of the garrison in his place. The dismissed officer has a number of friends in the province, and has made an official complaint and request for reinstatement.'

'Ignore it,' Bassus said. 'His friends can always be placated. I sent Castus up there to clean the place out. A labour of Hercules! Seems he's succeeding a little too well in that also...'

'There are also the reports from the dux himself,' the chief notary said. 'They chiefly concern the planned imperial tour of the frontier cities next month. His excellency has suggested that the Caesar meets with the chiefs of the Salian Franks to answer their pleas for resettlement within our borders. He proposes the town of Noviomagus as a suitable venue.'

'Yes,' Bassus said, tapping his fingers against his thigh. 'This… requires some thought, I believe. How long has it been since an emperor met directly with the barbarians?'

'Over three years, eminence,' the secretary said. 'Since the most blessed Augustus Constantine accepted the surrender of the combined Frankish tribes.'

'Would it demonstrate greater strength for the Caesar Crispus to meet with these chiefs at Noviomagus, then?' Bassus was speaking quietly, as if turning the ideas in his mind. 'Or should we instead summon them to appear before his majesty at Colonia, say, or even here at Treveris?'

'The chiefs apparently refuse to travel so far, eminence,' the secretary broke in. 'They fear being murdered by our provincials, apparently…'

Bassus grunted. Clearly he already knew this, and had spent quite a long time considering it. 'Even so,' he said. 'They could be compelled. We must not appear too ready to respect their qualms. Besides, the decision has already been taken – would the barbarians be more tractable if they were confronted by the Caesar in person, rather than by his subordinates?'

There was a long silence. Bassus was studying his fingernails, not glancing up as he waited for the views of the assembly.

'Might it be dangerous, eminence, for the Caesar to travel so close to the frontier?' Cupitus said. His eyes flicked back and forth, as if seeking support from the others.

'A strong force of my field troops would accompany him,' said Hypatius, the military man. 'He would be in no danger, I assure you.'

'And yet, if the barbarians are... displeased by the answer?'

The two men glared at each other. No love there, Luxorius knew.

The eunuch sat forward a little in his chair, trying for the right mixture of candour and cool reserve. He did not wish to appear too eager. 'It seems to me, domini,' he said, ignoring the mutters of distaste from the other men present, 'that our purposes could well be served by having the Caesar travel to meet the barbarians in person. After all, we wish these Salii to remain as our allies in any further conflicts with their Frankish brethren.'

'So what?' Hypatius broke in, with a dismissive gesture. 'One group of barbarians is much the same as another.'

'Allow my cubicularius to speak,' Bassus commanded, and then nodded to Luxorius to continue. Luxorius permitted himself a moment of silent satisfaction. He knew that the prefect wanted him to frame the view that he, Bassus himself, wished to present. But he also knew that it would serve his own purpose. Nearly a year had passed since Fausta had given him his mission to strike down the young Caesar; a year, and nothing to show but one botched attempt back in Raetia. Now there was the real possibility that Crispus would once more leave the safety of the palace and journey into the wilder country of the frontier. It would be difficult, but the opportunity was there, and tantalising.

'What better illustration could there be of the sublime confidence of the most blessed Caesar,' he said, 'than to appear himself, in person, on the very frontier? Would the barbarians not be overawed by the spectacle of their ruler surrounded by the glittering array of his army and court? Their displeasure at his judgements would be mollified by the very fact of his presence! A magnanimous gesture, and a demonstration of power...'

A more lengthy silence followed his words, the men of the assembly unsure whether to agree, or to continue with their objections. Bassus remained apparently unmoved. Watching the prefect, Luxorius knew that there was nothing beneath his smooth and urbane exterior. After a year spent in his presence, Luxorius knew the truth: Bassus might be the supreme functionary of the Caesar's court, the power behind the throne of the western empire, but he was a hollow man, with neither beliefs nor aspirations beyond the maintenance of his power and prestige. He was not even aware of his own duplicity. Striking at Crispus would accord with Luxorius's outstanding commitment to Fausta, but the thought of pricking Bassus's pompous self-regard and complacence was even more attractive.

'An agreeable suggestion,' the prefect said at last. 'I believe we must give it our fullest consideration.' Everyone present knew what that meant: no further discussion was required.

'There is another matter, concerning the Dux Germaniae,' the chief notary said, consulting his tablet. 'I refer to his claims that several prominent landowners have expressed themselves treasonously, and even conspired against him. Our own agents in the *officia* of both the dux and the governor can find no corroborating evidence. I confess I don't know what to do about it… What does your eminence suggest?'

'I've thought it over,' Bassus said. 'Our commander is an unsubtle sort, and perhaps gives and takes offence too freely. I have ordered him to desist from any further direct dealings with the men in question, and to take no further action unless to safeguard the dignity of his office. We know that some of these landowners are over-mighty, but they must be kept compliant to our wishes.'

'Very wise, eminence,' the notary said.

'Meanwhile, order your people to continue their investigations. Keep me informed of any progress.'

The notary nodded, and Luxorius noticed the prefect's secretary scratching a memorandum of it himself. As it happened, he had recently become friendly with the secretary, who was very keen on discussions of a religious nature. No doubt, the eunuch thought, he would soon learn of what the investigations had uncovered.

Bassus gave a satisfied sigh, and gestured for the slaves to bring refreshment. The evening's work was done, it seemed. In his mind, Luxorius was already composing the carefully worded message he would send to Fausta.

'Now,' Bassus said, 'you really must try these preserved cherries. A gift from one of those landowners you mentioned. Steeped in honey and wine. The flavour is quite exquisite!'

CHAPTER XV

In the streets of Colonia Agrippina the crowds were roaring. The route from the south gate to the forum was garlanded and lined with the flags of the city *collegia* and images of the gods, and the noise of horns and flutes competed with the cheers of the multitude. People had climbed up onto the roofs of the porticos and larger houses, precarious on the wet tiles as they gazed down at the imperial procession passing below. In the midst of it all, Caesar Crispus rode in an open carriage, keeping his head straight and his gaze fixed on the road ahead, with a skinny yellow dog seated beside him.

From the steps of the basilica, Castus could hear the noise as the procession approached. It had rained two hours before, but now the sky was clear and the spring sun made the city shine as if it had been scrubbed in honour of the Caesar's arrival. On all sides of the forum the dignitaries of the city were drawn up in order of precedence, all of them in their stiff heavy robes. Castus could see Magnius Rufus in the front row, his proud face composed in a suitably reverent expression. Behind him was his snakelike neighbour, Fabianus, and behind them Dulcitius. Castus tightened his jaw, and tried to resist the urge to stare. Instead he fixed his gaze on the Christian bishop, Euphrates, standing in uncomfortable proximity to the more traditional priests and the representatives of the

197

Jews of the city, all waiting to greet their young master.

The governor was beside Castus on the steps. Tiberianus had cooperated fully enough with him in the planning of this imperial adventus, but the mood of hostility still lingered between them. All winter Castus had endured it, but nothing more had happened to suggest open conflict. Rufus and his friends had made no further attempts at intimidation. The weather had been wet but mild, the river had not frozen and the barbarians had remained quiet. The impression of calm, Castus thought, was almost too much of a good thing.

With a blast of trumpets the first troops of the imperial entourage came swinging into the paved expanse of the forum. Castus picked out their shield blazons and could not hide his delighted smile as he saw the red sun-wheel on yellow, the emblem of II Britannica, the legion he had commanded himself for many years. He had believed they were still in the east, with Constantine. The men of the Second deployed along the left of the forum; opposite them were troops carrying blue shields with the image of the war god, emblem of the Martenses, the field detachment of Legion I Martia. Together they formed a broad avenue of shields and bristling spears.

The procession moved down the avenue between the lines of soldiers, first the Horse Guards in their glistening armour, their banners flying, and then the Caesar in his carriage. Many of the dignitaries sank to their knees as he passed, and then the carriage drew to a halt before the steps of the basilica. Crispus dismounted, then climbed the steps with his Protectores forming a cordon around him. Tiberianus approached, dropping on one knee on the lower step to perform the *adoratio*, kissing the hem of the young emperor's gold-embroidered purple cloak. Once the governor had moved back, Castus did the same. Crispus stood in the sunlight, and the massed cheers of the crowd filled the forum. The mood of grandeur and ritual was punctured only by the yellow dog, which was happily pissing against the wall of the basilica.

'As in heaven, so it is on earth,' a voice said as the cheers died away. Castus turned and saw the old tutor, Lactantius, standing beside him. 'The light of the father shines through the son!'

'I thought it was Constantine who likened himself to Christ,' Castus said in a low voice. 'Wouldn't that make Crispus the grandson?'

The old man glanced at him, his mossy grey eyebrows rising in surprise. For a moment he appeared baffled, as if he had been tricked into some error.

'I believe your grasp of theology is as weak as your philosophy,' Lactantius said, composing himself with a dry smirk. 'Your idolatry has blinded you! If only you learned to see with the eyes of faith, God's truth would be revealed to you.'

'There's my god,' Castus said, flinging up a hand towards the bright morning sun. 'The light of the world. He warms my face, and I don't need *magic eyes* to see him either.'

Lactantius let out a piqued gasp, then turned abruptly and followed Crispus into the basilica.

It was only an hour later, rocking on his heels as the sonorous voice of the orator filled the huge hall, that Castus began to wonder about the appearance of the Second Legion. He had seen only a few of the old faces he recognised in the ranks, but had learned from one of the Protectores that the legion had spent the winter at Mediolanum, and had arrived at Treveris only a few days before, in company with several other new field army detachments. Bringing troops over the Alpine passes while the snow was still on the peaks was a determined undertaking; was such a reinforcement routine, or was there something planned? Unease flickered in the back of his mind, while the orator continued his praises.

'*... longed-for hope of a new age, marked out for the helm of the world! Already your blessed father has schooled you in all the sciences of empire, which youth and tender years now firmly grasp. For us you arise like a new sun from the east – we feel the glow of divine light, the splendour of the world revealed anew...!*'

Did emperors always, Castus wondered, have to endure these sorts of platitudes wherever they went? Around him the dignitaries of the imperial retinue stood in respectful silence, stifling their coughs as the incense swirled between them. Up on the throne Crispus sat stiff and immobile, his face an impassive mask.

'*At the first word of your approach, great Caesar, the savage foe slinks back beyond the Rhine. Those who once took the cities of our province by siege now besiege only you, with pleas for peace and mercy! As the Tiber is crowned by bridges, so fortifications now subjugate the northern flood, and the barbarians themselves refashion the shackles of their ancient servitude...!*'

Castus made a sound in his throat, and the men to either side of him glanced in his direction. He was glad there were no emissaries of the barbarians present, to hear their slavery declared so publicly. He supposed these panegyrics were all a form of theatre, not intended to represent reality. Even so, it seemed a dangerous sort of hubris.

Now the orator was speaking of ripe wheat growing golden in open fields, grapes swelling on the vine and honey dripping from oaken boughs... Castus angled his head and scanned the crowds filling the rear of the basilica. He picked out Magnius Rufus, and a small group of women near the back. Was

Marcellina here? He had seen nothing of her since his brief visit to her husband's house in the winter. He put the thought from his mind; the oration was finally drawing to a close, and soon enough he would have to present himself to the young emperor, and try to guess what strategy the wisdom of his counsellors had devised.

'Is it really true that the sword of Julius Caesar is kept in a temple here in the city?' Crispus asked. 'I'd very much like to see it!'

'Supposedly, majesty,' Castus said. 'But I think the original was lost when the city fell to the barbarians back in the days of Probus.' He had seen the so-called 'Sword of Caesar' months before, shortly after his arrival in the city. It was kept in the temple called the Altar of the Ubi, and the custodians had exhibited it with reverent awe. The undistinguished lump of rusty corrosion had probably never been a weapon. But perhaps Castus should have allowed the young man to retain his illusions?

'Too bad,' Crispus said with a shrug. 'I should have liked to touch something once held by the Immortal Julius. Although,' he added with a reverent glance at the ceiling, 'he was just a man, of course...'

Released from his imperial duties, Crispus was back to his youthful self, spreading his gangling limbs across a couch in the private dining room of the Praetorium, while the dog lay at his feet with its pink tongue dangling. A new wing of the building had been opened and freshly cleaned to accommodate him and his retinue, although his stay would be brief.

'How far is it to Noviomagus,' Crispus asked, 'where I'll be meeting the barbarian kings?'

'Five days' march, majesty,' the Praetorian Prefect replied.

'Two by river,' Castus said. 'I've ordered the flagship of the Rhine flotilla down from Mogontiacum.'

'Excellent!' Crispus declared. 'The troops can march at first light tomorrow, and I shall follow them by water three days later.'

Already, Castus had noticed, the young man was showing signs of growing into his role. Eight months had passed since he left the young Caesar on the road, shortly after the ambush in Raetia. He had been a child then, but his experiences of rule in Treveris had given him a brisk sense of his own authority. All the same, Castus also noticed that Prefect Bassus seldom left the young Caesar's side. Clearly Crispus was not yet trusted to act for himself, whatever he liked to think.

'This might be a good moment, majesty,' Bassus said, 'to go over our policy with regards to these barbarians, and their... *requests*.'

'I thought we'd already discussed that?' Crispus said. His voice cracked and warbled. 'But maybe we should ask the commander here? Aurelius Castus – you've met these barbarians. What do you think of the situation, as a soldier, a fighting man?'

Castus noticed the prefect glancing in his direction with a clouded expression. Crispus too was staring at him, eagerness in his eyes. He remembered the last time he had seen the youth, in the bloody chaos following the ambush; did the Caesar regard him differently now? He swallowed heavily, looked at his feet. 'I believe some of them can be trusted,' he said. 'That is – I think their request for resettlement should be seriously considered... Barbarians serve well in our armies, both on the frontier and with the field troops. We need manpower, and the Franks could provide it.'

'You see!' Crispus said, grinning widely at Bassus. 'I told you it was a good idea! If our commander thinks...'

'What the commander *thinks*,' Bassus said ponderously, 'is not a matter of imperial policy, majesty. I must remind you

202

that the consistorium have reached certain conclusions on the issue. Only a limited broadening of territorial rights can be considered...'

Castus began to speak, and then stifled his words. He told himself that it was not his concern; he had made no promises to Bonitus and his people, and the other Frankish chiefs were strangers to him. But he had looked forward to the outraged reaction of Rufus and his cabal of landowners.

Crispus was nodding, slightly crestfallen now. It was sobering to notice, Castus thought, how much Bassus controlled the youth. He remembered other emperors he had encountered: Diocletian, stern and unsmiling, the personification of power; Galerius, hearty and overbearing, with his thin twanging voice; Maximian's tempestuous authority. Then Constantine, this youth's father, with his ranging moods, his coldly focused ferocity, his threatening jollity. All of them were their own men. Hard to imagine this fifteen-year-old lad living up to that. Could Crispus ever truly be a leader...?

A sudden commotion from the next room disturbed his thoughts: a child's cry. He tensed quickly, seeing the Protectores at the doorway reaching for their swords. Crispus's yellow dog lurched upright, snarling, and the young man calmed it with an outstretched hand.

'Dominus,' Castus said. 'I forgot to mention... my son...'

He turned to see the boy stepping through the doorway, clutching his wooden practice sword to his chest. Slaves and eunuchs clustered behind him, and two Protectores flanked him, trying to hide their smiles.

'We tried to take his weapon from him, dominus,' one of them said. 'He wouldn't hand it over!'

Castus gestured, and Sabinus ran to him. With a protective hand on his son's shoulder Castus presented him to the Caesar.

Crispus had sat up straight on the couch, making a slightly absurd attempt to appear more imperatorial.

'This is my son, Aurelius Sabinus, majesty. He asked to meet you, if he could.'

'A fine warrior in the making, I see,' Crispus said, and waved the boy closer. Castus urged his son to approach, and Sabinus took a few steps forward. Now he was in the room, surrounded by strange adults, his resolve had deserted him.

'Give me your sword,' Crispus said, stretching out his hand. Sabinus, awestruck and trembling, glanced nervously back at his father, then held the weapon out, hilt extended. Crispus took it, raising an eyebrow. 'A proper weapon,' he said, running his palm along the splintered wooden blade. 'I may not get to handle the sword of Julius Caesar, friends, but this will do!'

He raised the wooden sword, and his attendants laughed dutifully. Even Bassus mimed a chuckle. Castus stood behind his son, laying his palms on the boy's shoulders. Perhaps, he thought, this young man would not make such a bad emperor after all.

The town of Noviomagus stood on the banks of the Vahalis, a river which branched from the Rhine a hundred miles upstream from the sea. Flat marshland surrounded it on both sides of the river. Once, in the distant days of Rome's glory, legions were based at this place. The ruins of their fortresses still showed as grassy hummocks, but the only permanent fortification now was a palisaded entrenchment on a low rise near the riverbank, home to a numerus of Batavian *exploratores*. Below the fort was a civilian settlement, a ragged place of shacks and wooden huts, populated mainly by Frankish settlers and a few merchants from Belgica and the provinces of Germania. Now, very temporarily, it was the centre of imperial administration in Gaul.

The troops of the field army detachments had arrived the day before, nearly two thousand marching legionaries of the Second Britannica, Lanciarii and Martenses, together with half as many horsemen of the Scutarii and Promoti. With them had come the bulk of the Caesar's retinue, the wagons and carriages that transported his staff and slaves, and the officials of the essential ministries of state. It was early evening by the time the *Bellona* and her escort of smaller vessels rounded the bend in the river and came to anchor in midstream. The soldiers lined the bank and cried out the imperial salutes as the Caesar was rowed ashore in a barge. The white imperial pavilion already stood waiting for him, at the heart of the newly entrenched camp.

Castus came ashore in the next boat. The two-day voyage downriver had been pleasant enough, the young Caesar ordering the ships close in to the left bank several times, so he could inspect the forts and watchtowers as they passed. Castus had pointed out the new constructions, and told the young man what he knew of the various peoples who inhabited the far side of the river. The Praetorian Prefect, Bassus, had kept out of the way, apparently content that his charge could not wreck the western empire while seated on the deck of a river galley.

In the last glow of the evening sun, Castus went up to the fort and got the report from the officer commanding the numerus. The tribune was a sullen man, who appeared to resent his posting, but his report was adequately detailed. The delegations of the Salian Franks were assembled on the north bank of the Vahalis and the chiefs would cross with their retinues early the next day; in the meantime, the river would be guarded by Roman shipping and patrol boats. As he left the fort, Castus gazed across the dark river at the glow of fires on the far bank, the rising smoke trails. He felt a stir of unease; the Franks would not be getting what they wanted from the new emperor. Would they be content with the minor concessions Bassus was allowing them? If not, what would they do? He looked down at the Roman encampment, the regular tent lines inside the fortified enclosure, the pavilions of the emperor and his retinue, and for the first time in his life the sight of Roman troops in the field did not gladden his heart.

After passing the report to Bassus and his clerks, Castus decided not to return to his own tent straight away. Two days on the confined deck of a liburnian galley had left him restless, and he knew he would sleep little. With only a pair of bodyguards accompanying him he walked down from the camp towards the riverbank. It was almost fully dark by now, but he could still make out the small patrol boats rowing slowly against the current, keeping the cordon of the river closed. The air smelled of mud and wet sedge, and a light rain was falling, misting the glow of the fires on the far bank. Castus walked in silence for half an hour, consumed in thought.

He was just turning back for the camp when he heard a shout from away to his left, the cry of a sentry in the darkness. His two bodyguards reached at once for their swords. A lone figure came out of the gloom, stumbling on the damp turf, arms raised.

'Who's there?' the sentry cried again. 'Identify yourself!'

'Please, no need for alarm!' a voice said. 'I... I was walking by the river and I got lost in the darkness...'

Castus remained still, watching the figure as it approached. He thought he recognised the voice, but for a few long moments he could see little of the face or form. A torch flared suddenly, bursting colours across his vision, and when he held up his hand, blinking against the glare, he saw the gleaming shaved head of the prefect's eunuch secretary, the Egyptian, Luxorius.

'Dangerous place to go wandering by yourself,' Castus said.

The eunuch smiled, still keeping his hands raised. 'I'm afraid nightfall caught me unawares!' Luxorius said. 'Perhaps, excellency, I could follow you back to the camp?'

Castus grunted, gesturing for the eunuch to follow him. He remembered noticing something familiar about the Egyptian when he saw him last, during the journey from Aquileia. Now, in the slanting light of the torch, he realised what it was. Many years ago, in Rome, he had encountered another Egyptian eunuch, the chamberlain of the usurper Maxentius. Merops – that had been his name. What had happened to him? The resemblance was striking. But the thought of those days in Rome brought another half-forgotten face to his mind: the notary Nigrinus, who had disappeared at that same time. Somehow in the tangle of memory the two had become intertwined.

Castus shook his head, clearing the fog of recollection. This eunuch of Bassus's surely had no connection to either Merops or Nigrinus. But a lingering intuition sparked in his mind all the same. It did little to dispel his sense of unease.

All that night he lay half awake, listening to the light patter of rain on tent leather, the distant roaring of the barbarians around their feasting fires, alert for the first cry of alarm or attack. But the night passed quietly on the Roman shore. By first light the next day the troops were assembled, the ranks of armed men forming a huge hollow square on all sides of the podium of stacked turf where the Caesar would sit enthroned to receive the barbarian chiefs.

Castus took his position to the left of the podium, dressed in his burnished armour and embroidered cloak, his plumed helmet held in the crook of his arm. Standing stiffly at attention, he sucked down the fresh morning air, dispelling the after-images of fragmented dreams that still flickered across his dulled mind.

His breakfast of bread, oil and watered wine churned in his guts, and he belched quietly.

Trumpets split the air as the Caesar mounted the podium, flanked by his Protectores, with Bassus clambering after him. Crispus seated himself on a high-backed chair of gilded oak, a cushion of gold-encrusted purple beneath him and a long purple draco banner snapping and coiling above his head. Mounted troops of the Schola Scutariorum formed up in a tight block behind the podium. Castus caught the sweet reek of horseshit, mingling with the scent of trampled grass.

Looking along the ranks of the assembled troops, it was impossible not to feel a sense of pride at the awesome display of Roman military might. Castus smiled to himself, his spirits slightly restored. Yes, he thought, this was where he belonged. Although he would rather have been in the ranks himself, instead of his position of prominence beside the tribunal.

The first of the barbarian chiefs had already crossed the river, and steadily they were assembling on the bank. When all had reached the Roman shore they advanced, escorted by troops, into the centre of the hollow square to face the emperor on his raised throne. Castus watched them; if any were awed by the military display, they did not show it. The Franks walked proudly, heads high, not deigning to stare at the soldiers surrounding them on all sides. Castus saw Bonitus among them, and the similarity to his brother Brinno seemed even more striking now.

Gathering in a great mass, as if contemptuous of the regular formation of the Roman troops, the barbarians parted to let their chiefs through to the front. There were six of them, all powerful-looking men with thick moustaches. Out of respect, they had been permitted to carry their swords. Now they drew the weapons, holding them hilt-first towards the figure of the boy-emperor, points directed at their throats. With one rumbling voice they called out the imperial salutation.

'Who's that in the front?' Castus said from the corner of his mouth. He had an interpreter beside him, Bappo, the frog-faced Frankish recruit of the Equites Stablesiani, who had joined the retinue on its journey north.

'Gaiso,' the interpreter said quietly. 'War chief of the eastern Salii. Big man.'

'True enough,' Castus said. The Frankish leader was massively built, his silvered mail stretched over his broad chest and bulbous belly. Gaiso threw back his head, raised one hand, and began roaring out his address. The official interpreter, a pale and undistinguished man, struggled to keep up with the translation.

'What's he really saying?' Castus said in a harsh whisper.

'He's talking about his ancestors,' Bappo hissed back.

'What about them?'

'Oh, all their brave deeds. Mainly while they were fighting you! He says that his grandfather led a Frankish army as far as Spain, and his great-uncle travelled as far as the Euxine Sea and stole a Roman fleet to sail all the way home through the Pillars of Hercules, sacking every city he passed.'

'Is that true?' Castus asked, frowning.

'... decades of friendship with the Roman people,' the official translator was saying, 'after learning to put aside worthless war and accept the superior benefits of peace...'

'Oh, it's true!' Bappo said. 'And now he's saying how his father fought the emperor Constantine's father.'

'He sounds quite pleased with himself.'

'Ah, my people are great talkers!'

Sure enough, Gaiso's story was growing with the telling, the burly chief growing red in the face and smacking his lips as he related the details of his people's long struggles against the empire. Castus could see men in the ranks beginning to shuffle and mutter; many of the Roman troops understood the Frankish tongue.

'... and now he comes to you, eager to pledge his undying allegiance to the Roman state,' the translator said, with a weak smile, 'and to beg that you accept his loyalty and extend the protection of Roman power over his people...'

The chieftain's voice boomed on, filling the air with the strange snarls and guttural vowels of the Germanic language. Castus found himself thinking of Ganna, and the words she had whispered to him when they lay together. He quelled the memory at once.

Gaiso let out a great bellow of laughter. Whatever the nature of the chief's joke, it was lost on the translator, although Castus could see many of the other Franks smirking happily. Behind him he could hear Bappo stifling his mirth, too.

'What did he say?'

'Ah, a joke,' Bappo said. 'Something about a cow and a calf, I didn't quite catch it all...'

Castus grunted deep in his throat. He felt his shoulders tightening, his brow growing hot.

After Gaiso came another chief – Flaochadus, the interpreter explained – and then several more, all with their lengthy and rambling addresses. The sun was high overhead, now, and the square of armoured men and horses seemed to trap and condense the heat. Castus flicked a glance to his left, up at Crispus seated on his throne. The youth sat rigidly, with an expression of extreme discomfort. Beside him stood Bassus, his heavy face closed and inscrutable.

Finally it was the turn of Bonitus. He paused for a moment, then strode briskly forward, well clear of the mass of other barbarians. With his thumbs hooked in his belt he gazed defiantly at the boy on the throne.

'Caesar,' he said, loudly and in clear Latin, 'we have not before met, but I see in you the figure of your father.'

A stir ran through the officials gathered around the tribunal. Clearly many of them had not expected to encounter barbarians who spoke their language; they craned forward, staring, perplexed and dismayed.

'Twenty years ago,' Bonitus went on, his accent giving the words an aggressive bite, 'my own father, Baudulfus, swore allegiance to Rome. Even before then, though he fought against you, he respected your ways and your culture. With my father I have battled against the enemies of your people beyond the frontier – even against our kinsmen of the Chamavi and Chattuari, when they threatened you. My brother served in the Protectores of your father Constantine, and fell in battle with Rome's foes.'

Just for a moment, Bonitus glared at Castus, caught his gaze and held it. One heartbeat, then two.

'Now,' Bonitus declared, raising his hand towards Castus, 'with this man as your commander on the frontier, I am happy to be a friend of Rome. With your father as emperor, and you as Caesar, I and my people are happy to serve you. The laws of Rome are pleasing to us – even your taxes we can endure. But our lands are poor, our harvests bad, and enemies press upon us from the north and east. Give us leave to cross into your domain and we will serve you better, farm your lands, make soldiers for your armies. If you agree, this is good. If not – so be it.'

For a moment more Bonitus stared up at the podium, then with a curt gesture he turned and marched back into the throng of men behind him. At once a muffled hum of voices rose around the tribunal, officials whispering together in swift debate. All fell quiet again as Junius Bassus, Praetorian Prefect of Gaul, moved to stand beside the throne.

The prefect stood in silence for a long time. Castus heard the sounds of gulls crying along the river, where the patrol boats still churned the waters with their oars. Bassus gave a snort, clearing his throat.

'The Caesar has listened to your words,' Bassus declared, in a surprisingly loud and confident voice. 'And he is glad to receive your friendship and loyal acclaim. He has also heard your requests.'

Another lengthy silence. Castus felt his mood darkening once more.

'The Caesar understands your concerns. He sympathises with the plight of all those who dwell outside our peace. But as the first duty of any father is to protect his own family, so the first duty of a ruler is to preserve the safety and security of his borders. In token of your alliance, we will therefore permit the Salian people to cross the Rhine and dwell within the ancient lands of the Batavi, westwards from here and north of the Mosa. But we cannot permit any further erosion of our province, nor the arrival of so many foreign peoples upon our soil.'

The translator passed the words to the assembled barbarians and at once there was an outcry of raised voices. Castus was still watching Bonitus: the young chief stood silently, scowling. Gaiso was waving his fist in the air, shouting.

'They say...' the translator stammered, 'that the Batavian lands are all salt marsh and bad pasture... they are forsaken lands, and of no use to either Rome or themselves... They say you are repaying their allegiance with worthless mud and water!'

The ranks of soldiers had tightened, although Castus had

heard no order given. Horses stamped and blew, shaking their harness. Up on the tribunal Bassus stood impassive, but his mouth was closed in a tight bud of disapproval.

'The Caesar's will has been proclaimed!' a herald cried.

Slowly the angry uproar died down, the Frankish chiefs and their retinues muttering and casting fierce stares towards the podium. Castus drew in breath – if anything was going to happen, it would happen now. He blinked, and saw Bonitus staring back at him. The Frankish chief shook his head slowly, then looked away.

For a few long moments it appeared that the Franks would be content to return to their boats. Then two figures came pushing between them. Warriors, both of them; Gaiso's men, Castus thought. They strode to the front of the throng and kept walking, advancing on the tribunal. Castus's breath caught as he saw what they were holding.

'What are they doing?' somebody gasped.

At once the Protectores had moved to screen the young emperor, raising shields and drawing swords. The two Frankish warriors, both in mail and heavily moustached, came to a halt ten paces away. One of them grunted a few words, then they flung what they were carrying down on the turf before the tribunal, before turning to stride back and join their chiefs.

Two severed heads rolled on the grass.

'What's the meaning of this?' Bassus exclaimed, glancing around at the officials and the guards. Castus had taken a step forward, hand on his sword hilt. He peered at the heads: fresh blood still bright; they had died only moments before. But neither of them looked Roman.

'They said, dominus,' the interpreter was saying, visibly shocked, 'that these are the two that took Roman gold to kill the Caesar in his tent tonight!'

213

Gaiso let out a grunt of disdain. Then the entire Frankish group turned as one and retreated, their pride intact, to the waiting boats.

'Somebody get that mess out of my sight,' Bassus said.

CHAPTER XVI

'It would appear,' the governor said, 'that our dealings with the Franks back in the spring achieved the best result possible. Would you not agree?'

Castus made a sound in his throat. 'Best of a bad few choices,' he said. *And no thanks to you.* Tiberianus tipped his head back; he was contriving to lounge on a very low couch and stare down his nose at the same time. Castus peered intently at the man's nostril hairs until he looked away, abashed.

They were in the sumptuous reception room of the governor's Colonia townhouse, midsummer sunlight slanting in through the open doors from the portico. The floor mosaic was almost concealed beneath a thick rug of Persian design; the wine that Castus had been offered came in a glass goblet held in a mesh of filigree gold.

Despite the intense and mutual dislike between them, Castus and the governor were obliged by protocol to meet once a month or so and exchange pleasantries. Castus had kept himself busy with his official duties for the last month, however, and this was the first time he and Tiberianus had met since the affair at Noviomagus.

'It seems to me,' the governor said, getting up abruptly and pacing back and forth on his rug, 'that we have three options in regard to our barbarian neighbours. Either we give them

215

silver, we give them land, or we fight them. It surprises me that you seem so… loath, shall we say, to attack them. One would think that the battlefield was your native place, no? Scenes of gore and slaughter your meat and drink? Perhaps the delights of peace, of noble high office, have dulled your appetites?'

Castus refused to rise to the provocation. He had grown accustomed to the governor's displays of arrogance, his insults both veiled and naked. This was the man, he thought, who conspired to have me send Ganna away, who conspired to threaten me by terrorising my son… But he had no proof of that, of course. Nothing but the certainty of his intuition. He did not care. He knew that he was invulnerable to the governor's scorn; he had made himself that way. *Let them hate me, so long as they fear me.*

Some emperor had said that, Castus remembered – one of the bad ones, probably. He had often wondered why so many of Rome's rulers in ancient times had seemed so passionate in their cruelty, so very tyrannical. Now he thought he knew. Power offered these temptations. So many times he had wished death or savage injury upon Tiberianus, upon Magnius Rufus, upon all their cabal of corrupted minds. Without the bonds of discipline and duty, would he have given way to his impulses? He remembered a story he had read in one of the books Diogenes gave him, back when he was practising his letters. The emperor Severus, the Divine Severus, had ridden his horse over the corpse of a fallen rival, making the animal kick and trample the body, in full view of his assembled troops. It was a display of rage. Castus knew all about that now, but he hoped he would never descend to such things. Did the gods not strike down their enemies? Were they not wrathful, vengeful, merciless? Severus might have become a god, and was doubtless a great and mighty emperor, but still he had been a man, with all the mortal failings.

'Talking of recent events,' Tiberianus went on, 'did you ever discover if there was any truth to the story of the barbarians paid to attack the Sacred Majesty?'

'No,' Castus told him. 'The notaries investigated, but they found nothing. Could be the Franks were just making a statement. You didn't hear anything yourself?'

The governor puffed his cheeks, then made a tutting sound and shook his head. 'Perhaps some kind of a threat, then? You never can tell, with these savage types.'

Castus shrugged. He knew that if the governor's spies had plumbed the depths of that mystery, Tiberianus would tell him nothing about it. No confidences passed between them.

'Before you go,' Tiberianus said – Castus had made no movement to leave – 'I wondered whether you might be considering giving your troops some exercise across the river? They do get so restless in the summer months, before the harvest comes in. I'm thinking of that unfortunate episode at Novaesium...'

Castus knew what he meant. Earlier that month a small party of barbarians had crossed the Rhine in a boat and tried to steal a couple of cows. It was a minor affair: mounted troops from the nearest fort had intercepted them, and few of the raiders had survived to return home.

'I consider that matter dealt with,' Castus said.

'Yes, I know, but it does create a certain apprehension among the population. I've been forced to mention it in my report to the Praetorian Prefect. I thought perhaps a swift reprisal expedition might be in order? Against the Bructeri, for example. Burn a few huts, round up some captives...'

Castus raised an eyebrow, and said nothing.

'The truth is, I'm intending to give a display of wild beasts at the opening of the Games of Apollo next month, and some barbarian prisoners would make ideal prey. The Sacred Augustus Constantine gave a similar show at Treveris, of course, many years ago.'

'Use slaves, if you must,' Castus told him.

The governor angled a long and searching glare down his nose. 'That simply *wouldn't* be the same.'

Seething, Castus marched back along the street from the governor's residence towards the Praetorium. Now that he was no longer in the man's presence, he thought back over Tiberianus's words; they had been intended as jibes, but was there any truth in them? Perhaps, Castus considered, he really had become less attuned to war in recent years? Once he would have believed that attacking and destroying the barbarians was the only honourable option. Was it only age that had made him more cautious in his thinking, or had something else changed him?

It was only a short distance back to the Praetorium, so a carriage or horses had not seemed necessary: four of his bodyguards were accompanying him, and there was no risk of trouble. But Castus had forgotten that today was the local festival of Fortuna; the goddess was extremely popular among the poor and unemployed of the city, who all hoped for luck's rewards, and the streets around her temple were thronged with people in a state of wild excitement. Already the two guards that preceded him were shoving between the bodies that blocked the route, calling out to them to clear a path.

'Wait,' Castus ordered, seeing another tumultuous horde coming from the direction of the forum to besiege the temple precinct. He glanced down a side street, wondering if it might be quicker to make a detour around the area rather than continue to push through the mob. No doubt Tiberianus would find it highly amusing if he heard that Castus had been forced into some undignified shoving match with the city's rabble. He was just about to give the order to change route when he saw a covered litter waiting in the lee of the temple wall, the bearers standing idle around it. As he watched, he saw the thick drape screening the interior drawn aside and a woman's shawled head appear in the opening.

'Over there,' he said at once, and his bodyguards fell into step around him as he crossed the street. Had he recognised the woman in the litter? He was not sure, but that did not matter; his duty was clear.

'Your way's blocked by the mob, domina,' he said as he approached. The two bearers and the slave that went before them stepped aside, lowering their heads – all three were Franks by the look of it. The drapes opened a little more, and the passenger leaned from the litter and drew her shawl back.

'So it seems,' Marcellina said. She betrayed only a flicker of recognition, a slight widening of the eyes and a suppressed smile. Almost as if, Castus thought, she had waited here on purpose, to try and meet him... 'But please, don't concern yourself,' she said. 'The crowd will clear soon, and I've got letters to write.'

Castus glanced into the litter and saw the tablets and stylus laid on a small writing block cradled between the cushions.

'All the same,' he said, conscious of the four bodyguards standing behind him, the slaves waiting all around, 'I'd be honoured to accompany you back to your house.'

Marcellina thought for a moment, then nodded and slid her tablets beneath the cushions. She lay back, and the bearers heaved on their poles and lifted the litter between them. Castus fell into step beside her, the bodyguards forming a cordon ahead and behind. He had already guessed that there was little chance in this meeting; Marcellina had been waiting at a spot she knew he must pass.

Along the side lane they turned into a parallel street, wider and less congested. Castus had no idea where Marcellina's husband's house might be, but there was a slave to lead them and he was content to accompany her. For a while they made their way in silence, the noise of the streets swelling and then fading around them as they passed into an area of larger residences.

'I'd hoped to see you before this,' Marcellina said, holding the drapes part-closed and speaking through the gap. 'But I'm so seldom in the city, and it's difficult...'

'I wanted to see you too,' Castus replied, speaking barely above a whisper. 'To thank you – your warning back at the house last winter—'

'It was nothing,' she said quickly. She moved a little closer to the drapes, dropping her voice. 'Please don't blame my husband too much for what happened. I know you must, but... He's my husband and I'm very fond of him. But he's weak, and stronger men have him in their power.'

Castus grunted, nodding. He had guessed as much. Everywhere the strong and resolute imposed themselves upon the fainthearted. It was the way of the world. 'These others,' he said quickly, glancing through the drapes, 'do they try to influence you as well? Do they... I don't know... threaten you?'

'No! They care nothing for me – why should they? And they don't know of any connection between us. Nor must they. I'm careful to appear very wifely and unassuming, you see.'

Castus coughed a laugh. He knew well that there was more spirit and courage in this woman than in Magnius Rufus and all his friends. He had seen that, back in Britain, long ago. But he had seen how the years had changed her, the very many years of domestic life and disappointed expectations wearing away at her soul. For all her fine clothes and houses, her children and her literature collection, marriage to Julius Dulcitius must bring few pleasures.

They were passing the north side of the forum now. The sound of riotous singing from an alleyway, and a burst of laughter: a knot of revellers swung out across the street, but with one glance at the armed bodyguards escorting the litter they fell back.

'It was Saturnalia when you came to see me in Eboracum,' Castus said.

'I remember!' Marcellina replied, and grinned broadly. He was glad to see it. 'I was bolder then... You mustn't think,' she went on, 'that my life is too drab. Compared to what might have happened, it's a blessing from the gods. I grieve every day for what I lost back in Britain – my family, my home, my hopes, everything! – but I'm content. Please believe that.'

Castus nodded, unable to meet her searching eye. She sounded unconvinced herself. Abruptly the slave leading the litter gestured to the left, and the bearers swung into a narrow alley that ended at the large brick portal of a townhouse.

'This is Dulcitius's house,' Marcellina said. 'Will you...?'

'No, thank you,' Castus said quickly. 'I have business at the Praetorium. I only wanted to see you safely home.'

'One moment,' she said, drawing a tablet and stylus from beneath the cushions as the slaves lowered the litter down between them. She scratched quickly; then, as the litter bumped to the ground, she nudged the tablet and let it fall to the cobbles.

'Thank you for your escort, excellency,' Marcellina said, climbing out and pulling her shawl around her head. She bowed demurely and then walked towards the house.

Castus watched her as she passed through the portal. With a swift movement he stooped and picked up the fallen tablet. As he straightened again he caught the eye of one of his bodyguards, who stifled a leer and glanced away, whistling silently to himself. Sticking the tablet beneath his belt, Castus signalled to his men and set off once more towards the Praetorium. With every step he felt the tablet burning against his side.

Five words, so rapidly scratched into the wax that it had taken him a good few frowning moments to decipher them.

I must see you. Soon.

Castus slumped at the end of the couch in his private chamber, staring at the tablet lying on the table beside him. For so long now – ever since their reintroduction in the library of Rufus's villa the previous autumn – the thought of Marcellina had been itching in Castus's mind. Not an unpleasant itch, but it troubled him deeply. Since Sabina's death he had promised himself that he would involve himself no more with women – free Roman women, anyway. Part of the pleasure of his relationship with Ganna, he had to admit, was its impossibility. He had offered to marry her, had wanted to do it, but knew that she would never accept. Her rules had been different to his own, different to those of civilised society. But with Marcellina he was opening himself to vulnerability once more, to the possibility of loss, of disgrace and of weakness. She was a married woman anyway. He should put this from his mind.

With a decisive cough he leaned forward, snatched up the tablet and rubbed at the wax with his thumb until the words were gone. But when he reclined again he picked up the scroll she had given him at the house months before. He had erased her word of warning from that, too, and then made a few attempts at reading the verses. Ovidius, the poet was called. *Metamorphoses.* He wondered if that too was supposed to be a message of some kind. Transformations in life, in fortunes. Idly he ran his fingers over the smooth ivory boss of the scroll, staring at the ceiling.

A sudden crash from the next room broke him from his reveries. A man's shout, and a scratching of boot-studs on floor tiles. Castus was on his feet already as the door burst open and a figure was propelled, stumbling, into the chamber.

'Sorry, dominus!' the sentry cried, following close behind the intruder. 'This beggar's been demanding to see you for all this last hour – we threatened to have him flogged... Shall I beat him now?' He plucked a stick from his belt and raised it, sneering.

'Please, excellency,' the man crouching on the floor gasped, raising his hands. 'Hear me out, I'm no beggar. I'm no beggar!'

He certainly looked like a beggar. Filthy, with matted hair and ragged beard, he wore only a sleeveless tunic smeared with mud and what looked like pitch. There was a badly healed scar on his upper arm. A sword cut; Castus could see that at once.

'Leave him,' he told the sentry, and the soldier lowered his stick and stepped back with a disappointed shrug. The intruder stood upright. He was slightly bow-legged and, beneath the dirt and the straggle of beard, his face was broad and tanned.

The raised voices had drawn others from the next room: a pair of military clerks and Diogenes, with a startled expression and a stylus tucked behind his ear. Castus studied the man a moment more, then sat on his stool and braced his chin on his fist.

'Speak,' he said.

'My name's Dolens, dominus. I'm a mariner by trade, from Dubris in Britain. Twelve days ago we sailed – five ships, with stores for the Germania garrisons, crossing the Narrow Sea to the Rhine. We were near the river mouth, maybe ten or fifteen miles south, when we saw a host of boats coming out from the land, all of them packed with armed men.'

'Coming out from the land where?' Castus demanded.

'We couldn't tell at first, dominus,' the sailor said. 'It was dawn, low sun to the east and the coast's so flat there… We tried to steer away, but we had a westerly wind and they were rowing hard against it. They came up with us and boarded on both sides. Some of us tried to fight, but there were too many of them…' He twitched his shoulder up, exhibiting his scar.

'And then?'

'Well, dominus, they seized all five ships and towed them back into the islands between the estuaries to the south there. They had even more boats and men hidden in there, up the little creeks. Looked like we were headed for one of the bigger islands, but I managed to jump overboard and swim ashore. Ten days I've been wandering, dominus… They hunted me at first, but I gave them the slip quick enough, and came here as fast as I could…'

The man's voice choked off in a rasp. His chest was heaving, and Castus could see how weary he was, how much it was costing him to speak. He gestured to one of the slaves to bring him something to drink, and another stool.

Once the man was seated, and had sucked down three cups of water, he appeared more composed. Castus rubbed his cheek, pondering. Within the month the first grain ships would be coming across from Britain, bringing vital food supplies for the troops on the Rhine. This was bad news indeed.

He said nothing for a while, studying the man carefully. He had always been skilled at reading expressions, and noticing the truths that men tried to hide. Now he watched the sailor's eyes, alert for any sign of mistrust or duplicity. There was none.

'Who were they, these men who attacked you?'

'Barbarians, dominus!' Dolens cried, wiping his mouth. 'Big hairy men! Swords and axes, spears and javelins. Beards all over them...'

'Franks?'

The sailor shrugged, raising his palms. 'I wouldn't know to tell the difference,' he said.

Castus turned away. He pictured the configuration of the Rhine mouth and the coastline to the south of it: a vague place, even to the best navigators. A mess of rivers and islands, sandbanks, forests and dunes. Most people avoided it. But it was the westernmost limit of the old Batavian lands – the very place that Bassus had recently granted to the Salii. Sour anger churned inside him. Surely this could not have happened? Surely the Salian chiefs had not repaid their worthless gift by turning to piracy? If they had, the entire supply route to the Rhine was under threat.

'What were the ships carrying?' he asked.

'Horse fodder, ropes and tar and sailcloth, blankets and woollens. A small cargo of luxury stuff – preserved food, brassware, wine...'

Castus held up his hand, before the sailor could reel off the entire cargo manifest. He needed time to think, but if the attack had happened over ten days before then he needed to act quickly.

'Could you make any estimate of their numbers?'

Dolens screwed up his mouth, frowning. 'I saw between ten and twenty boats,' he said. 'Each with about thirty or forty men aboard. They had more than that though – up the creeks and around the islands, I mean.'

Anything between a few hundred men and a thousand, Castus calculated. A large band, and if they had based themselves on one of the estuary islands they could have fortified it against attacks from upriver. Rooting them out of any stronghold there would require a considerable force.

'Take this man to the baths, have his wounds dressed and give him food and a bed,' he said. 'Dolens – you're not to leave the building. I'll need to speak more to you later.' He gestured, dismissing him, and the sailor bowed and departed.

Once he was gone Castus got up and began pacing. His blood was quickening, and he tried to breathe slowly and deeply. As the others filed from the room he motioned for Diogenes to join him. For a long while he paced in silence, the secretary waiting patiently and tapping his pursed lips with the stylus.

'What do you think?' Castus said. 'Is this Gaiso and his people?'

'He would be the obvious choice,' Diogenes said. 'But it seems strange nonetheless... He would surely know that word of this would reach us, eventually, and we would act...'

'Yes,' Castus said. 'Strange. And don't the Franks prefer moustaches to beards? But we have to consider it.' His mind was clearing now, moving faster – there was almost something mentally nourishing in this kind of thought, this sort of rapid decision-making.

'We'll need men,' he said. 'We'll need ships. We'll need supplies for ten days in the field.'

'But if this is the Franks, we have no idea how many of them might oppose us.'

'True. Make that supplies for twenty days. Alert all of our frontier garrison commanders to double their patrols and keep their men in combat readiness. Send a message to Senecio at Mogontiacum – I'll need the *Bellona*, about four lighter galleys and transports to carry the troops. What day is it now?'

'*Dies Mercurii*,' Diogenes said. 'Six days to the kalends of July... Which troops would you send?'

'That's the problem,' Castus said with a hefty shrug. 'If I draw men from the frontier garrisons I'll leave the river defences weakened. Besides – there's none of them I'd trust for this. I need experienced soldiers, veterans … Where are the Second Legion based now?'

'Still near Treveris, I think. They could be here in six or seven days. But they're field army troops…'

Castus nodded curtly. 'Then I'll need a message to the Praetorian Prefect, sent by our fastest rider. Explain the situation and politely request half a cohort, or four centuries if he can spare them, of the Second. I'll need them here in five days.'

Diogenes raised an eyebrow, then made a note on his tablet.

'Another message to the governor of Britannia – tell him to hold back all further shipments via the Rhine. If necessary send them through the ports on the Gallic coast, and we can bring them overland by wagon.'

'Prudent,' Diogenes muttered as he wrote.

'And I want a message sent to Bonitus as well.'

'The Frankish chief? Is that… wise?'

'The gods alone know that,' Castus said, rubbing his brow as he thought. 'But I have to assume that he's not involved in this, or things are worse than we know. Tell him these raiders are a threat both to the empire and to his people – I need his warriors to join our expedition. They have boats, and they might know those waterways; without them we'll be blundering about in the marshes like drunks in the dark. We'll meet him and his men at Noviomagus, tell him… You think he can read Latin, or has somebody who can?'

'Maybe better to send a verbal message,' Diogenes said. 'I can go myself if you want.'

Castus hid his brief smile. 'Courageous,' he said. 'But no – I need you here. Send two of my clerks to Traiectum and find

Bappo, the interpreter with the Sixth Stablesiani. Give him the order to take the message and read it to Bonitus himself if necessary.'

'Bappo... message... Noviomagus... Franks,' Diogenes mumbled, scratching quickly. He raised his head. 'Who are you proposing to lead the expedition?'

Castus paused in his pacing. He had given that no thought. It seemed obvious. 'I'll lead it myself,' he said. 'There's nobody else I'd trust with it – Senecio's able, but he's a naval commander. Dexter's a cavalryman. As for the others – Gaudiosus I wouldn't trust out of my sight, the prefect at Tricensima's an old woman... No, this is mine.'

'Well, delegation never was one of your strengths!' Diogenes said with a wry smile.

'Would you have me send another man to do what I will not?'

Diogenes sighed, closed the tablet and stood up. Castus was grinning as the secretary turned to go. He was embarking on a sudden and dangerous expedition, against an unknown enemy in an unknown and treacherous country. He had no accurate idea of the force arrayed against him, or which of his supposed allies he could trust. He had only a matter of days to prepare his men and take them to war. But his heart was full and his mind clear, for the first time in months.

He laughed to himself, gazing out of the window at the fast-flowing Rhine. Evening was coming on, and already the slaves were lighting the lamps. Tomorrow his work would begin. Tiberianus would get his captives, with any luck. Not in time for the Games of Apollo, but soon enough.

Either that, or he would be rid of Castus for ever.

CHAPTER XVII

Six days. Each of them a tightening ligature of stress and anxiety. Castus had stormed and stamped, sweated and sworn, sleeping only at brief intervals. He had despatched messengers to all the frontier posts, to Treveris and to the flotilla base, to Bassus at the imperial court and to the Franks beyond the Rhine. His chambers in the Praetorium had been a chaos of men coming and going, documents written and sealed, still more documents that required attention. Steadily all that was needed for the expedition had accumulated: men and ships and stores. But with every passing day Castus had felt the pressure growing greater. The sailor Dolens had told him that around thirty men had been captured with the ships; most were slaves, but not all. How many of them still lived? And there was always the terrible fear that the raiders would disperse with their plunder and be impossible to track down, or that further convoys would come across the sea and fall into their hands.

At least, in all that time, he had seen nothing of the governor; Tiberianus had doubtless sensed the storm of military activity consuming the Praetorium, and very wisely kept clear. The islands of the sea coast were nominally part of his province, but few governors in the last four decades had assumed any responsibility over them. What happened there was a business for the military. However, Castus had seen nothing of Marcellina either, of course, and little of his son.

Now, on the afternoon of the sixth day, he stood on the river wharf just upstream of the bridge of Colonia. It seemed, finally, that all was ready. The thought gave him a great sense of satisfaction, but a lingering worry remained. For the first time he was in sole charge of a military expedition. No senior officer stood above him to direct and guide his actions. He was the last link in the chain of command. Granted, this was no major expedition, there was no enormous baggage train, no complex route of march. His men had only to pull downstream with the current and let the river guide them, and somewhere in that maze of water and mud before the rivers spilled into the sea they would find their enemy. But still Castus felt the jump of nervous tension in the pit of his belly, the certainty that he had overlooked something, neglected some crucial consideration, had been too simplistic in his thinking somehow. The expedition was a risk, a throw of the dice; the thought gave him a strange anxious thrill. There was a reason, he thought, that gambling had been prohibited under the emperors for so many years, and why that prohibition was so commonly flouted.

Out in midstream the *Bellona* hung at anchor, stationary in the current. To either side of her were the smaller vessels, the thirty-oared single-banked galleys *Pinnata* and *Satyra*, and the two smaller eighteen-oared scout craft *Lucusta* and *Murena*. The crews were still busy aboard each ship, checking the stores and the rigging, and smearing mutton fat on the watertight leather sleeves of *Bellona*'s lower bank of oars. The crews were all legionaries, and each ship had shields mounted along the deck rails: bright green with the twin Capricorn emblem of Legion XXII Primigenia.

Closer, moored along the jetties that lined the wharf, were the four big barges that would carry the rest of the troops. Flat-bottomed, blunt-prowed, each had a single huge mast and eight oars, with canopies raised over the stores piled amidships. The barges had been the last vessels to arrive, and Castus was more than glad to see them. At least, he thought, there would be no shortage of drinking water, until they reached the sea estuaries where the salt bled into the rivers.

'I wish I was coming with you,' Diogenes said, gazing across the river at the ships. It was a fine sight, in the lowering sun. 'You're sure you won't reconsider?'

'No,' Castus told him. 'I want you here, running my office. I need you to look after my household, too – I don't have time to think about appointing a procurator. Besides,' he said, turning with a weary smile and clapping the wiry man on the shoulder, 'we both know your soldiering days are done!'

'Oh, I don't know,' Diogenes said, with a look of dismay that made Castus regret his words. 'I'm only a year or two older than you! No man likes to consider himself redundant…'

'Nothing of the sort,' Castus said, forcing another smile and tightening his grip. 'I need a man here I can trust, and there's nobody better than you. I'll need you to keep an eye on what the governor's up to as well,' he said in a lower voice.

Diogenes shrugged, nodding, clearly not very reassured. Castus hid the twitch of irritation as he marched back across the riverbank and up the track that led to the city gate. Nervous energy was flowing through him, battling with tiredness, and he lacked the willpower to be diplomatic at a time like this. If Diogenes wanted to be a soldier he should learn to take orders…

'Excellency!' a voice cried, and Castus snapped out of his daze of annoyance to see a familiar figure waiting for him on the track. His spirits rose at once, and he returned the centurion's salute. He had met Modestus the day before, when the detachment of the Second Legion had arrived from Treveris, but the troops were exhausted after their two-day forced march and there was no time then for more than a greeting. Now he embraced him warmly.

Stepping back, Castus grinned with genuine pleasure. He had known Modestus since his time at Eboracum, when he had been the worst idler and drunk in his command. Since then the blunt-faced soldier had risen in rank and in quality. He was still a junior centurion – another officer, Vetranio, had been appointed to command the detachment – but he was an experienced fighter, hard as any Castus had known, his weapons and armour bright and his belt gleaming with proud decorations.

'Praepositus Vetranio sent me down to report that the men are all ready to embark,' Modestus said smartly. 'Soon as that gang of greasy-fingered fish-fiddlers clear out the way, anyway…' He jabbed his thumb towards the men of the Primigenia, still busy aboard their ships. There was already a mutual disdain between the two legions: the Second considered that they were real soldiers, field army troops, while the Twenty-Second regarded the river and its ships as their own domain. Castus hoped that they would learn to get on. The ships were small and they would be packed together during the two-day journey down to Noviomagus; a narrow river galley was not the place for disputes. With any luck, once they reached the Frankish territories they would bond together well enough.

'Any more word on who we're facing?' Modestus said, falling into step beside Castus as they walked together towards the gate.

Castus shook his head. 'Barbarians, that's all we know. Pirates.'

'Ah well,' Modestus said, baring his teeth, 'they'll bleed just the same when the iron goes in, whatever they call themselves.'

'Is Felix still with you?' Valerius Felix had joined the legion before the Italian campaign and had accompanied Castus on a desperate mission into Rome; he was a wiry, oddly angled little man, probably a former criminal, although he had never said much about his past. Castus suspected that his unconventional skills would come in useful.

'He's my optio!' Modestus said. 'Seems pleased enough to be serving under you again, too, although he don't give much away, as you know.'

Castus nodded, and they parted as they reached the gate. 'Tell Vetranio to bring the men down in two hours,' Castus said. 'We'll get them aboard before sunset and make a few miles downstream before dark. No time to waste now.'

Back in the Praetorium he checked the last few details with his clerks, dictated a final message to Bassus reporting on his plans and preparations, and sent one of the agentes in rebus riding off with it towards Treveris. He wanted to sleep, but he could not rest now until the whole expedition was afloat. Even then, he doubted that he would get much time for sleep in the coming days. Propping himself on the side of the table, he scrubbed at his brow and yawned heavily, feeling the muscles of his neck stretch. Then he picked up his helmet, slung on his sword and went downstairs.

He found his son in the courtyard of the private wing, engrossed in a ball game with two of the slave children. The boy's nurse, Bissula, the plain-looking girl Castus had brought in to fill Ganna's place, stood beneath the portico and clapped every successful catch. Castus joined her for a moment, watching Sabinus as he tossed the ball with his right hand and caught with his left. He was good, dextrous. Sometimes he even spun on his heel to reverse hands, laughing as he confounded his opponents and sent them scrambling after his throws.

'Father!' the boy cried, noticing him at last. The ball thudded into the gravel at his feet, and Sabinus ran to the portico. Castus scooped the boy up in his arms and lifted him, feeling his growing weight, the kick of life in him. For a moment Sabinus clung to him, then he writhed free and dropped to the ground, dragging at Castus's hand.

'Come and play,' the boy said. 'It's quite easy, but these slaves are no good...'

'Not now, lad,' Castus said, drawing the boy back and squatting down beside him. 'When I come back there'll be time for games.'

His son knew what was happening, of course. Castus had taken the boy down to the riverbank the day before to look at the ships, during a brief interval in the rigours of preparation.

'Are you going to find the barbarians and cut off all their heads?' Sabinus said, sticking out his bottom lip.

Castus frowned. 'Who's been saying that?' He aimed a savage glance around the courtyard, but the slaves were miming ignorance. No point in hiding these things, he considered. 'Don't you worry about anything of that sort,' he said, scruffing at the boy's fine black hair.

'When will you come back?' Sabinus asked, a tremor of distress in his voice. He was trying not to appear concerned, Castus could tell.

'Not for a few days,' he said, as warmly as he was able. 'Maybe ten, or even more. But, like I say, don't worry. Keep on with your lessons, and look after everything here for me... How's the new pony shaping up?'

'Not as good as the old one,' the boy said, his face dropping further. 'I fell off twice yesterday, and Tagmatius was angry.'

'Was he now? Well – he's very pleased with your progress. He told me so...'

'Will you promise to come back?' the boy broke in, with a look of anguish.

Castus embraced him again, feeling his body trembling. 'Of course I promise,' he said. For a few long heartbeats he held the boy tightly, feeling the weight of the words crashing through him. His son had been abandoned too many times.

'Any way I can, I'll come back to you. I promise.' His voice caught as he spoke, and he closed his eyes for a moment. Then he released the boy and stood up.

'Now,' he said. 'What do we say?'

Sabinus blinked at him, then raised his hand in an oath-taking gesture. 'I'll do what is ordered, and at every command I'll be ready,' the boy recited.

'*We*. We will do what we are ordered...'

'Yes.'

'Good boy.' He stooped down again, kissed his son on both cheeks, then squeezed his shoulders. 'Back to your game,' he said, with a squinting half-smile.

By the time he returned to the riverbank the sun was low and the troops were assembled, the full detachment of the Second and half the strength of the Primigenia. Castus had drawn a small detachment of Nervian archers from one of the less undermanned frontier posts, only forty men but enough to provide some missile support for the galleys. They, too, waited in a semblance of rank.

A procession of priests advanced from the city gate, leading the sacrificial animals. Castus stood to one side while the ritual was conducted, the beasts felled one by one. Smoke wreathed the altar and drifted along the riverbank, threading between the ranks of soldiers, and incense wafted in the evening air as the priests cried out their prayers to Jupiter, Mars and Sol Invictus, asking that good fortune and victory attend the expedition. The omens were good; Castus released a long-held breath.

With his helmet clasped beneath one arm, one hand on the eagle hilt of his spatha, he mounted a podium of piled crates and stood facing his men. The sun filled his eyes, and he squinted. They seemed so few, assembled here together – should he have waited for reinforcements? No time for those thoughts now. He could not help noticing the differences between the units. The Second had been issued new red tunics when they arrived at Treveris, and while few wore armour they presented a bold, uniform, soldierly appearance. The men of the Twenty-Second, by contrast, were still dressed in their shabby work tunics of blue-grey and off-white. Most wore greasy-looking woollen caps, and some even had straw sun hats on their heads. The Nervians looked more like barbarians than Romans. Never mind – they were scant, fewer than four hundred with their officers, but they were his own, and he was ready to put his trust in them.

'Fellow soldiers,' he bellowed, his voice reaching far out across the river. 'All of you know what lies ahead of us. The Rhine, our frontier, our supply route, is threatened by a pack of barbarians who think they can turn pirate and raid our shipping without paying the price. We're going down there to teach them otherwise.'

A stir of eagerness ran through the troops. Castus could sense their enthusiasm: a good sign. Behind him, a crowd of civilians had come from the city to line the muddy riverbank and watch the expedition depart. From the corner of his eye, Castus could see Tiberianus with his entourage, waiting to give his official farewell. He ignored them.

'I know there are differences between you,' Castus yelled. He saw the smirks, the glances exchanged between the units. 'But you need to work together. This won't be your usual duty. Some of you men of the Second might have to pull an oar now and again. You Primigenia men might have to get off your benches and heft shield and spear. But I've chosen you all for this, and I know you can do it. The Twenty-Second Legion have guarded this riverbank against the enemy for nearly three hundred years. And the Second have fought in this land more than once, as I know well.'

He paused, allowing his words to fade across the river. Birds were circling the masts of the anchored ships. Already Castus could see the cables hauling taut on the bridge, lifting the central section upwards to allow the flotilla to pass.

'Work together; follow the orders of your officers. And when we meet the enemy, stick every mother's son of them! I can ask no more of you.'

He drew his sword and raised it above his head, holding it so the low sun flashed off the blade.

'Britannica, Primigenia, Nervii... *are you ready for war?*'

'READY!' the massed cry came back at once.

Twice more he called out the traditional question, and twice more they answered.

Then he swung his arm down, and gave the order for the embarkation to begin.

By the evening of the following day the ships had reached Tricensima. It had been an easy voyage so far, the sun warm but the air cooled by a breeze from the south that filled the big sails and carried the ships northwards with only the lightest pressure of the oars. Castus had remained on deck the whole time. The passing landscape he knew well from his last voyage:

237

the flat green country, the sinuous bends of the river and the occasional forts and watchtowers on the bank were familiar to him now. Instead he watched the ships, and the men aboard them. Twice he had them go through practice drills on deck, the rowers dragging their long oars inboard and taking up their weapons, the marines of the Second Legion joining them at the rails and bulwarks. The ships had drawn closer alongside, and the troops had practised leaping across from one vessel to the next. It had gone well: only two men had been injured, one with a javelin in the thigh and the other with a broken leg from tumbling between the oars. So far, Castus thought, so good.

As the convoy of nine vessels came round the last bend in the river, Castus saw the walls and towers of Tricensima fortress rise from the green land on the western bank. Once this place had been home to a full legion. Now the old walls had been demolished and the settlement had contracted within a new fortification, smaller but far stronger than what had been here before. But there was no messenger waiting at the river wharf, no signal from the towers of the fortress; Castus had hoped for word from the north, a response to his despatch to Bonitus and the Franks.

'Bad sign, you think?' Senecio asked as they sent the wounded men ashore.

'Could be,' Castus replied. He wanted to keep his thoughts to himself for now. Everything would be clearer once they reached the territories of the Salian Franks. Not for the first time, he worried that his message to Bonitus had been a mistake; if the Salii had been responsible for raiding the shipping lanes, then he had merely warned them of his approach and given them time to muster against him. But still he wanted to trust Bonitus, if only because of his old friendship with the man's brother. A hazardous risk to take, even so.

The troops disembarked, and Castus had them exercise on the broad meadow between the river and the fortress. He wanted to push on down the river without delay, every passing moment chafed at his nerves, but he needed the men in good fighting shape. Their enthusiasm, at least, remained undiminished. They passed the night ashore and got under way at first light, the river rolling steadily across the flatlands and bearing them on northwards and westwards.

And by the evening of the next day, with the sun turning the water to an expanse of beaten gold, they met the Franks.

'Like something out of Homer,' Senecio muttered as he stared from the bows.

'Eh?' Castus said.

'*Something out of Homer*. With all the ships. That's what my old centurion used to say, years ago. Never quite knew what he meant by it...'

Castus frowned. There were certainly plenty of boats ahead of them. They were still several miles east of Noviomagus, at the point where the Rhine and Vahalis divided; the broad sweep of river appeared full of vessels. But as he squinted into the glare, Castus could make out that there were only about ten of the larger ones, the oared war boats. About the same number of smaller boats, and even canoes. All of them drawing steadily on their oars and paddles to keep them in position against the river's current.

'They must have come up the Rhine and gathered here to wait for us,' Senecio said. He thumped his wooden hand on the rail beside him. 'If they're hostile, we've got a fight coming.'

'Signal *Lucusta* and *Murena* to move up ahead of us,' Castus ordered, pacing back down the gangway towards the stern. 'Have them intercept any of the Frankish boats that try and

239

approach.' He was thinking of the story that the sailor, Dolens, had told: the barbarian vessels were small, but several of them could surround any of his ships and board from all sides. '*Satyra* and *Pinnata* to take position on our flanks,' he went on. 'Keep the troop barges behind us. We move slowly, light pressure on the oars. All marines and archers to battle quarters, all catapults and ballistae spanned but not loaded.' The last thing they needed was for some itchy-fingered artilleryman to loose his weapon by mistake.

The deck of the *Bellona* rumbled beneath him as the men moved to their positions, Modestus and his twenty soldiers of the Second Legion assembling along the gangway, the archers gathering at the bows. Castus heard the slow ratcheting clack of the catapult winches, the steady splash of oars as the two light scout galleys pulled ahead of the bigger ships.

'They're moving,' Senecio said, shading his eyes with his wooden hand. Sure enough, the mass of Frankish boats had surged forward, their sharp prows raising white water from the river's current. 'What's the order, dominus? Full pressure and break through them, or back oars?'

'Wait,' Castus said quietly, his mouth almost too dry to force out the word. His chest was tight, and he forced himself to breathe.

One boat was drawing ahead of the others, and the scout galley *Lucusta* was already angling across the stream to cut it off. It was not one of the larger vessels, but there was a crowd of men in the bows. One of them was waving something; Castus blinked sweat from his eyes.

'Green branch, dominus!' the bow-officer called, over the heads of the marines.

Castus felt the tension burst from his chest as he exhaled. A moment later he could make out the tuft of foliage, the sign of parley; another moment and he recognised the man holding it: the frog-faced interpreter, Bappo.

'Keep watching those other boats,' he said tightly, trying not to make his relief too obvious. 'It still might be a ruse.'

But now he could hear the interpreter crying out greetings. As he paced across the deck to the rail, Castus felt the anxiety lifting from him like mist from a dawn meadow.

'Tell the chiefs to come aboard,' he yelled across the river, cupping his hands to his mouth. He saw Bappo wave back, then the boat backed oars and turned.

'My compliments, dominus,' Senecio said. 'Looks like you've got your army!'

CHAPTER XVIII

They came aboard over the bows, climbing up from the prow of one of the war boats, Bonitus first and then Gaiso, then the third chief – Flaochadus, Castus remembered. Modestus and his men were still assembled along the gangway, and they parted to form an avenue as the barbarian leaders marched up to the stern deck where Castus awaited them.

'We were expecting you,' Bonitus announced, seating himself on one of the stools and taking a cup of wine. 'We heard of this trouble on the coast, and guessed you would come.'

Bappo crouched beside the other two chiefs, translating. They presented quite a contrast: Gaiso massive and barrel-chested, Flaochadus lean as a starved dog, with a thin moustache and bloodshot eyes.

'They weren't your own people, then, these raiders?' Castus asked.

Bonitus gave a taut smile and shook his head. 'They're men from the north, from the top of the ocean,' he said, jerking his thumb. 'Chauci and Reudigni. You would call them *Saxons*.'

Castus heard Senecio's grunt of surprise. 'Haven't seen Saxons in our waters for many a long year,' the flotilla commander said. He leaned closer to mumble to Castus. 'You think the Franks are bad – the Saxons are worse by far. Savages, they are. Cursed by all the gods.'

'They have the same problems as us,' Bonitus said. 'They lose their lands to the sea, and look around for better places. But these are a raiding group, only, come down for the summer to make prey of your ships and our villages alike. Their leader is called Hroda, and he has about a thousand spears.'

'So why haven't you attacked them yourself yet?' Senecio growled.

Bonitus made a shrugging gesture. 'We wait for you!' he said. 'It's your land, after all – no?'

'They have five of our cargo ships and about thirty captives,' Castus told him. 'What have they taken from you?'

'Prisoners and cattle,' the chief said. 'About one hundred of our people.'

'They take them as slaves?'

'Mostly.' Bonitus smiled coldly. 'The Saxons have an odd custom, from the ancient days. Before they are putting to sea, they cut the throat of a captive across the prow of each ship. A sacrifice to Hludana, goddess of storms, to spare them from her wrath. They prefer to keep slaves who speak the Germanic tongue, so your people are in more danger, I'd say!'

Castus fought down a shudder. The thought of human sacrifice revolted all civilised men. He knew that some of the wilder Germanic tribes still practised it, but the idea that it might be carried out by these raiders within the borders of the empire filled him with dark fury.

'It's my intention that they'll have no opportunity of putting to sea,' he said. 'As soon as I can get my ships down into the islands and find their lair, I intend to slaughter every last one of them.'

'Difficult,' Bonitus said quietly. 'The islands are a treacherous place. Few know the waterways there – they say that land and sea change places with the moon. Others say that the whole place is cursed, haunted by ghosts. The land of the dead.'

He was still smiling as he spoke, but Castus caught the tension in his words. He guessed that the unwillingness of the Franks to attack these intruders was not just diplomatic.

'Will you join with us?' he said.

'Under your command?'

'Under my command.'

Bonitus paused, considering. Castus heard Bappo swiftly translating his question to the other chiefs. Gaiso sat up straight on his stool, inhaling, then grunted.

'We will,' Bonitus said. 'But we order our own warriors, not you.'

'Agreed.'

'Then we make a pact of iron.' Bonitus stood up and drew his broad spatha, held it in his right hand and placed his left hand flat upon the blade. Gaiso and Flaochadus did the same. Stepping closer, Castus laid his palm on the sword.

'By Woden and Teiva, we are one in this thing,' Bonitus said, and Castus met his eye and nodded. The other chiefs mumbled their agreement. Then they all stepped back as Bonitus swung the sword up to the sky.

'Now,' the chief said. 'We go to Noviomagus, yes? We must feast and drink, and *plan our attack...*'

Night had fallen by the time the enlarged flotilla reached Noviomagus, and the ships and boats moored in mid-river. It had been an awkward voyage for the last few miles as the Roman vessels tried to hold formation while the Frankish boats moved around them, rowing alongside, dropping back and then darting ahead, the crews on both sides regarding each other across the darkening water with mutual suspicion. At least, Castus thought, the divisions in his own command had been fully sealed. Surrounded by barbarians, the men of the two legions, and even the Nervian contingent, were brothers once more.

Castus sent a boat to the south bank to inform the tribune of the fort of what was happening. He could already see the fires burning in the Frankish encampment opposite, the same ground they had occupied before the meeting with Caesar Crispus back in the spring.

'Keep all the men aboard ship tonight,' he told Senecio. 'Double sentries fore and aft. Don't let any of those boats get too close.'

'Of course, dominus,' the older man said curtly.

Castus peered at his face in the gloom, then smiled. 'Sorry,' he said. 'I'm trying to teach you your business. You know all this better than me!'

'No need for an apology,' Senecio said. 'It's tough holding the command. You think you need to do everything, check everything... You can trust me and the ships. Just watch out for yourself.'

Castus nodded, thumped his fist against the other man's shoulder, then clambered over the rail and into the waiting boat. He was taking Modestus, with twenty legionaries of the Second as a bodyguard, together with Bappo the interpreter and his orderly, Eumolpius. It seemed a small and vulnerable party as the boats passed across the dark river towards the fires on the northern bank. Once on dry land, the troops formed up around Castus and they marched through the clamorous throng of the Frankish encampment to meet the chiefs beside the largest of the fires.

Smoke hung in the air, filled with the sweet smell of roasting pork. There were four large pigs already spitted and turning over the flames, and all around the fire men sat on benches made of fallen logs. As Castus joined them Gaiso passed him a cup made from a curling animal horn. Castus raised it to his mouth and sipped. Good wine – he was relieved.

'Eat!' Gaiso declared, gesturing at the roasting meat. 'Make strong!'

Castus could only agree; living on campaign rations for the last two days had been an unexpected privation. He had grown soft in his tastes during his time at Colonia, accustomed to the pleasures of a privileged table. Now women were moving around the circle of men sitting by the fire, offering wooden platters with roasted pork and chunks of gritty bread soaked in fat. Another woman refilled Castus's drinking horn – he had not realised it was empty. The wine was strong, and he felt it already going to his head. Chewing a chunk of pork – half blackened and half raw – he reminded himself to hold back on the drinking and feasting, whatever the barbarians might be doing.

But the fast-flowing wine and the heavy food were swiftly melting the suspicions between the two groups. Some of Castus's men were still standing back, leaning on their spears, but most had joined the Frankish warriors in their meal. He noticed the soldiers' eyes following the serving women, saw their smiles in the wavering firelight. Several of the Franks were already drunk, rolling and roaring with laugher. The heat of the flames, the smoke and the smells of the meat filled the air, embracing but oppressive.

'Roman!' Gaiso called, raising his drinking horn. 'I you brothers yes!'

Castus raised his own cup in reply, managing a half-smile.

'If he asks you to wrestle,' Bonitus said quietly, joining him on the log, 'you must refuse.'

'You think he'd beat me?'

Bonitus gave him an appraising glance. 'Maybe not,' he said. 'But if you win his pride is hurt, and he always tries to fight again. If he wins, he thinks you weaker than him. Understand?'

Castus nodded. He noticed that Bonitus himself seemed completely sober. On the far side of the fire the skinny chief, Flaochadus, was entwined with a buxom blonde woman.

'His wife,' Bonitus said, hiding a scowl. 'Always she wants to take him home before wars. Sometimes he allows it.'

'They must be in love,' Castus said, with a snort of laughter.

Bonitus's expression darkened and he shook his head in disgust. He dropped his voice to a rasping whisper. 'She is *very perverted*,' he said.

Together they stared across the fire at the large woman sitting in her husband's lap, tugging at his hair and stroking his face quite openly. Even Flaochadus's own warriors seemed to find it hilarious. Castus wondered at the ease with which these barbarians mocked their own leaders. Glancing around the fire, he watched his own men eating and drinking, calling loudly to their barbarian hosts, waving their hands as they tried to tell stories or explain things. Even Modestus was glowing with drink and good humour. *Gods help me if I have to order them to fight these men...*

'Tell me,' Bonitus said, leaning back on the log bench, 'how my brother died.'

Castus felt a lurch in his gut, a chill across his brow. 'You already know,' he said. 'Brinno was killed fighting, in Alamanni country.'

'But you were there,' the Frank said with sudden intensity, leaning closer. 'Tell me everything. For many years I have wanted to know.'

And so Castus told him, hesitantly at first but then in full, remembering as he spoke that there was no shame in it, nothing to hide. He told Bonitus of the despatch party sent through the wilderness of the Agri Decumates in the dead of winter, the Burgundii warband that had ambushed them in camp and then tracked them through the forests. He told him of the battle at the stream, the ruined town in the frozen white mist, then the final dash to the river the following morning. Castus and Brinno had been the last survivors of the party, and Brinno had given his life to allow Castus to escape. Even then, Castus had almost died when he fell through the ice of the frozen Danube.

When he had told the tale, Bonitus sat for a while in thought, frowning and nodding.

'Your brother died a hero's death,' Castus told him. 'He saved my life, and allowed our mission to succeed...' He paused, aware that he was treading upon ground that had long lain undisturbed. 'I could not go back for him,' he said, almost stammering the words. 'I could not go back and find his body. I'm sorry.'

'You had no choice,' Bonitus said. 'These things are done in war. It is good for me to know that you saw him in his last moments. He died fighting for you, his friend. He did not die alone.' He gripped Castus by the shoulder. 'The gods will not punish you for neglecting his body.'

Castus nodded, obscurely relieved. He had been unaware that the memory of that day had so haunted him. He was used to suppressing thoughts of shame and dishonour; what was done was done. He had never expected that Bonitus's acceptance would mean so much to him.

A bellow cut through the fog of voices around the fire. Gaiso was on his feet again, flourishing his drinking horn. He emptied it of wine, and beckoned to a serving woman with a heavy clay jug. The warriors around the fire raised a cheer.

'Ha!' Bonitus said. 'Now we have enough of Roman piss, he says. Time for some real warrior drinking!'

The jug went around the fire, dark liquid slopped into every cup and horn. Castus caught the smell of it. A moment later, a smiling woman had filled his horn to the brim with odorous Frankish beer. Gaiso was still standing, still shouting, and now all the others were getting to their feet as well.

'A toast,' Bonitus said, and stood up with Castus.

The yells were easy enough to translate. *Romans and Salii! Victory! Death to the Saxons!*

Sudden silence, as each man raised his arm and sucked down the strong dark drink. Then a roar of voices raised in a fierce cheer. Castus belched heavily, then sank down onto the bench again. It was going to be a long night.

Dawn was grey and clammy damp, the dew heavy on the grass and the smoking remains of the feasting fires reeked of burnt bones and wet ash. Castus dragged a blanket around his shoulders and struggled to his feet, feeling the kick of blood in his swollen head. All around him there were bodies sprawled under blankets and furs, Romans and Franks almost indistinguishable. He bent down and nudged one sleeping figure, shifting the blanket aside. Eumolpius was lying with his mouth wide open, snoring. A few paces away a soldier's boots protruded from under another heap of coverings. A woman's blonde hair spilled from the other side of the blanket.

'Excellency!' a clipped voice said. Castus blinked, his head reeling, and focused his eyes on the group of soldiers approaching from the river. The optio leading them stamped to a halt and saluted. 'The praepositus Senecio asks when you might be ready to embark, excellency,' he said. Castus peered at him, trying to read his expression, but the man's face was a careful blank.

'Right now,' Castus said as he began to walk, stepping between the bodies. What madness had possessed him to drink so much? To fall asleep in the middle of a barbarian encampment? He grabbed at his cloak, checking that he still had his gold brooch, then at his belt. Nothing was missing. Even so – it had been foolhardy. But the sudden relaxation, after so many days of tense responsibility, had overcome him. He cursed his own weakness.

'Excellency? Are you quite well?'

'What? Course I am... Mind your own...'

Castus belched heavily, tasting beer, then fought down a swell of nausea. The optio and his party of soldiers were looking elsewhere.

'Rouse up the rest of our lot,' he ordered one of the soldiers. 'Get them on their feet and back to the ships, quick as you can. Make a bit of noise about it, see if we can stir our allies too.'

Down by the river, there were already plenty of men on their feet, both Romans and barbarians. Out across the pale waters, Castus saw the welcome shape of the *Bellona*, still at anchor in midstream, the four smaller galleys stationed around her. Had he dreamt that Senecio had sailed away without him? He could barely remember. He had a sudden recollection of a scene from the night before: Modestus and one of Gaiso's warriors locked in an arm wrestle. He grinned, then caught himself and straightened his face.

Several of the men by the river had stripped off and were splashing in the water, plunging themselves beneath the surface. Castus glanced again at the ship, judging the distance, then unpinned his cloak and threw it to the optio.

'Take my gear back to the *Bellona* in the boat,' he said. 'And if you see me drowning, pull me out.'

He dropped to sit on the muddy turf, pulling off his boots and leg wrappings, then shedding breeches, tunic and loincloth. Standing up, he drew in a chestful of air then strode naked down into the river. The water was colder than he expected, and he gasped. The current pushed at his shins, then his thighs, then he threw himself forward into a splashing dive.

Submerged, he felt the water cleansing his head at once. He swam three strong strokes beneath the surface, then came up for air. Shaking the water from his eyes, he checked the position of the ship again and then struck out towards it, flinging his arms forward in a powerful front crawl. The current tugged at his body, but he fought against it, keeping himself on course.

One of the smaller galleys passed close by him, the oarsmen cheering from their benches as they saw him in the water. Castus ducked his head beneath the surface again. Another memory came to him, and he almost missed his stroke: something Bonitus had told him... for a few lunging strokes Castus felt his mind totally emptied, the memory gone. Then it returned, a flicker: Bonitus had said something about the death of the previous dux, Valerius Leontius. What was it? For a few more rapid heartbeats Castus followed the thread of the memory, but the words were lost to him.

When he raised his head again he saw the hull of the *Bellona* much closer than he had expected, the oars shipped and Senecio waiting at the rail gazing down at him. Four more strokes, and his reaching hand grabbed at the rope ladder dangling from the stern. Shivering as he emerged from the water, Castus hauled his heavy body up the rungs and clambered onto the deck, to be met by two grinning oarsmen with rough woollen towels and dry clothes.

'Excellency,' said Senecio, with a smart and sober salute. 'I trust your negotiations went well last night? What's our *plan of attack*?'

'Oh, it's a splendid plan,' Castus said as he scrubbed the towel over his scalp. 'We sail down the river, find the Saxons and kill every last fucker of them.'

Senecio inclined his head, trying not to smile. 'A plan worthy of our emperor himself!' he said.

Castus slumped down onto a stool as the naval commander strutted off along the gangway. Now that he was aboard again his headache had returned, and the rocking motions of the ship in the river's current were making him queasy. Senecio had not seemed too outraged to see his senior officer in such a state; Castus guessed that the balance of power between them had shifted. He trusted the older man's judgement implicitly, but he knew that Senecio had felt his own shipboard authority slightly challenged by his presence. He sighed heavily, and pulled on his tunic.

The night's debauchery had not been limited to the Frankish camp, unfortunately. Many of the men aboard the moored ships had got hold of drink, either from the Franks or from the settlement of Noviomagus, and there were plenty of sore heads and bleary expressions in the pale light of morning. Castus was attempting to eat a breakfast of stale bread and cheese when a boat came alongside and Vetranio, the senior centurion commanding the legion detachment, came aboard.

'Excellency!' the centurion cried. Castus returned his salute with a tired wave. Vetranio was about his own age, but Castus did not know him well; the man had been promoted to the Second after Castus had quit the command. He was a good soldier, solid and determined, but a stickler for correct discipline.

'May I report that the Franks appear to be embarking, excellency,' Vetranio said.

'You may,' Castus told him with a pained glance across the river. Despite the excesses of the night before, his barbarian allies were piling into their boats, setting to their oars with loud shouts and cries of laughter.

'We're ready to up anchors and move when you give the order. But I'm afraid to report that several of our men are still in a state of drunkenness. One of them, I'm sorry to say, is Centurion Modestus. Do you want him punished?'

Castus swallowed sourly. Vetranio's gaze was locked somewhere above his head, the centurion being very careful not to notice his commander's wretched condition. 'No, not for now,' Castus said. 'We'll attend to that when we return.'

'As you wish, dominus,' Vetranio said. He glanced across the water at the riotous Franks. 'Although I must say... we may be allies with these barbarians, but we surely shouldn't emulate their behaviour!'

'Quite so,' Castus replied, feeling the blood rush to his face. He dismissed the man, then slumped back on the stool. Vetranio's words were insulting, but true nonetheless. *My first independent command, and already I've let things slip...* Always in his younger years Castus had been disciplined, attentive to his duties. He had never been a heavy drinker, never let his guard slacken. He would have to be more careful from now on.

Standing up with effort, trying not to groan, he crossed to the rail and watched the Franks as they rowed out from the riverbank. Last aboard was Flaochadus, his own warriors carrying him down to the river, to the sound of cheers from the other boats. *Disgraceful*, Castus thought. But he could not help a wry grin. *His wife must have exhausted him...* The idea brought a tug of longing. Castus had not been with a woman for months, ever since Ganna left. He had known long periods of celibacy while he was in the ranks, of course, and even while he was married to Sabina. But now he longed for female company. *I have grown soft with luxury...* He caught himself thinking of Marcellina: where was she now? Still at Colonia, or back at her husband's villa? For a few moments the warmth of longing filled him, then he cleared his mind. There was no time for that – not now; perhaps not ever.

His mood sank even lower as the flotilla assembled under a sky of sullen grey cloud and moved off westwards, downstream. The Roman ships kept their formation, holding the centre of the river, while the Frankish boats veered and chased around them. Only the ten larger vessels were accompanying them, Castus noticed; the smaller boats and canoes had dropped away. Sitting at the stern of the *Bellona*, he studied these Frankish war boats more closely: each held between twenty and forty men, tight packed on the oar benches, but they were sleek and graceful-looking, with sharp hulls rising at each end to jutting prow and stern posts. With the oarsmen pulling hard the boats seemed almost to rise out of the water, skimming the river's surface.

After a few miles, the river straightened and broadened, and one of the larger boats pulled up parallel to the *Bellona*. Castus could see Bonitus waving from the prow.

'I believe they're challenging us to a race, dominus,' Senecio said. 'Shall I give the order? We've got a good long reach ahead.'

'Why not,' Castus told him. He drew in a long breath, feeling the last shreds of his headache fading. 'Signal the other ships to keep their formation, then let's show these barbarians what a Roman galley can do!'

Senecio snapped out his commands as he paced down the gangway and at once a stir of enthusiasm ran through the crew of the flagship, the oarsmen forgetting their fatigue and their lingering hangovers. Cries from the bow-officer and helmsman, the tramp of the marines as they filed back down to the stern at Senecio's command – their weight would lift the bows a little, and give the current more to push against – then the rowing master called out his order and the two banks of oars, fully manned, swung and dipped into the new pace.

At once a volley of shouts came from the Frankish boat, the crew throwing themselves forward and hauling in unison; the sharp keel seemed to lift even further as the vessel shot forward. The *Bellona* was twice the size, and twice the weight; but she had nearly twice the number of oars as well. Castus watched as the double tier of Roman oarsmen urged the ship forwards, the long galley steadily picking up speed. From the lower deck he could hear the banging of the wooden mallet that set the rowing pace, but the oarsmen were each watching the man ahead of them, all the way back to the rowing master at the aftermost larboard oar. When he glanced to his left Castus saw the flat green riverbanks rolling past more rapidly; the sultry air was stirred to a warm fresh breeze. Above him, the long purple draco standard mounted over the stern lifted its tail and began to writhe, the head letting out a whistling moan as the breeze passed through its gilded jaws.

The men in the Frankish boat were shouting in time with their strokes. Castus could hear their bellowing chant over the sound of the oars – *Huor-gah! Huor-gah!* The sharp prow of their vessel carved a wave of white water. But still the *Bellona* was gathering speed, her old timbers groaning as they took the stress, her oars flashing like huge white-tipped wings as they beat at the water. The Roman oarsmen neither shouted nor sang; beside the mallet's thud, the only sounds were the collective grunts and the massed sigh of exhaled breath as they drove the ship forwards.

Castus ran along the gangway to the bows. Leaping, he caught hold of the figurehead and stood with one foot braced on the wooden anchor fluke. Beneath him, the spur that ran forward from the keel was bursting the surface of the river and sending spray up over the bows as the ship pulled ahead of the barbarian boat.

The sense of speed and momentum was exhilarating, the rhythm of the oars thundering through every fibre of the ship, the banks of oarsmen moving fast and in unison, a machine of muscle and wood powering the galley through the water. Stretching up, Castus raised his fist in the air and yelled with triumphant laughter. If only his son could be here to witness this...

But the Franks had not given up yet. Castus could hear Bonitus's hoarse shout as he ordered his warriors to even greater exertion. Once more the gap between the two vessels began to close.

Swinging himself from the bow, Castus descended the ladder to the lower deck. A narrow passage ran between the benches of the lower oarsmen, beneath the gangway overhead, and Castus made his way aft, reaching up to steady himself on the deck timbers and the massive taut bracing cable that stretched the length of the ship. It was gloomy and hot, extremely cramped, and he could smell the black ooze of the bilges beneath him: the effluvia of anchor cables, river mud and the close-packed humanity. To either side the lower oarsmen sweated on their benches, swinging forward and back, most of them stripped to their loincloths. Castus clambered to the far end of the passage, where the *pitulus* sat with his time-beating mallet, then mounted the aft ladder to the stern deck.

'Looking strong down there?' Senecio cried. His lips were drawn back from his teeth, his arms folded tight.

'Looking very strong,' Castus said. He flung a glance toward the rival boat, and although they were still level he could see that the Franks were tiring, the rhythm of the oars losing its disciplined regularity. He knew they were on the verge of surrender.

'Boatswain reports we're taking in water at the bows,' Senecio said. 'But a last burst of speed up to that next bend and we'll have them in our wake, I think.'

'Do it,' Castus told him. He clasped the rail and stared across the water. A moment later he heard the order – *double time* – and the steady beat of the mallet grew faster. Once again the galley gave a heave and then surged forward.

'Easy,' Senecio said with quiet satisfaction.

Cries of dismay from the Frankish boat; Castus stared at them, grinning, and a few moments later he saw the oars rise in clattering confusion, the hull slowing abruptly and swinging around with the current. Bonitus stood up from the prow once more, raising his palm in a token of submission.

'Trail oars!' Senecio called. 'Ease the way off her steadily now.'

But word of the triumph had already passed through the ship, down into the gloom of the lower tiers. The oarsmen sat up on their benches and began to cheer, the marines and archers crouched on the stern deck joining them. Castus clapped Senecio on the shoulder, both men grinning broadly as the *Bellona* cruised on across the last stretch of river with the oar-blades gliding in the water.

If only, Castus thought, *all our victories were so easily won.*

CHAPTER XIX

'Salt,' the bow-officer said, raising his head from the bucket he had drawn up over the side. 'Faint, but you can taste it.'

'I knew it,' Senecio said, nodding. 'You can feel the rise of the river. We're into the tidal reaches, dominus.'

Castus grunted, glancing at the distant riverbanks along the horizon in the lowering evening light. All that day they had been threading their course steadily westwards as the water broadened on either side of the flotilla. The stretch they were moored in now was easily half a mile across.

'The old ship feels it too,' Senecio said, tapping the rail with his wooden hand. 'She tastes it! Longs for the open ocean, no doubt...'

'With any luck we won't be going anywhere near the open ocean,' Castus said. In the growing darkness the river was flat and grey as a sheet of iron; the low country beyond the banks looked much the same. They were far from civilisation now. He had seen no sign of human habitation since leaving Noviomagus. For the last few hours there had been no sign of animal life either. And now ahead of them were the islands of the great estuary, tangled scrub and banks of reeds. A haunted place, Bonitus had called it. *The land of the dead.*

'Did people really live here once?' Castus asked. The silence of the river was almost unnerving.

'Aye, long time ago,' Senecio said. 'This was the old Batavian land. There were towns here, and roads. Canals and dykes to hold back the floodwaters. But it's all peat ground, see, and they dug out the peat beds for fuel and building. The land sank.'

'Is that possible?'

'That's what they say, dominus. When the sea broke through the dunes along the coast it flooded right across here. Now all that land's salt marshes. You can dig a well wherever you like and all you'll find is brackish water. No good for man nor beast. All that grows here is scrub, reeds and those nasty-looking stunted trees.'

Castus tightened his shoulders, suppressing a shiver, then turned and made his way aft. They would remain moored here at the head of the estuary for the night – there was plenty of open water ahead, but the tidal reaches were treacherous with shoals and mudflats, masses of rotting driftwood and submerged obstacles that could rip up the hulls of the ships. They would need daylight, and caution, to move further into the marshy maze of islands.

All that night the ships lay at anchor in the tideway, none showing any lights but all with sentries stationed fore and aft, staring into the blackness. Castus slept badly, down in the little triangular cabin beneath the poop, starting awake at every sound: the lapping of the water under the stern, the slow creak and tick of the timbers, the soft shuffling of the watchman on the boards above his head. Once he bolted from his bunk and raised his head up the ladder, only to be told in a hushed voice that the noise had been a floating tree scraping along the side of the hull. Finally, as his eyes began to detect the palest seep of light, he threw on his cloak and went on deck.

The estuary looked beautiful in the dawn. The water was luminous grey, and between the clouds the sky was glowing faintly, the sun not yet risen. Everything was soft and still, except a flight of geese winging silently upstream. Castus stood for a while, blinking the sleep from his head, taking it all in.

He found Valerius Felix in the shelter behind the helmsman's post. The wiry little optio had taken over command of the *Bellona*'s marine complement after Modestus's debilitating hangover on leaving Noviomagus. Castus was glad to see him: Modestus was a firm enough man – when he was sober – but Felix had a steely tenacity and a quick intuitive cunning that Castus had relied on before. He was also the only Roman soldier Castus had ever met who actually came from the city of Rome itself; he spoke with the oddly gnarled and nasal accent of the common people of the Eternal City. The optio nodded a greeting as Castus joined him.

'Anything?' Castus said.

'Not a thing but geese and eels since midnight, dominus.'

'Eels?'

'Them things,' Felix said, pointing over the side. Castus looked down in time to see a quick ripple in the water. 'Nasty slimy creatures they are. Suck out your eyes. Place is swarming with them.'

Castus remembered the eels that Magnius Rufus had served at his villa the previous autumn. Maybe they had come from this very estuary?

'I forgot, you don't like ships,' he said.

Felix tightened his lips. 'Don't mind ships. Rivers are all right. You know where you are with a river, at least. Water goes this way and that way, land's over there. It's the sea I can't abide. Deep water all around you. Monsters. Makes me shiver.'

'You'd never swim in the sea then?'

'Wouldn't want to give them the opportunity, dominus. The monsters, I mean.'

Castus laughed quietly to himself. Even so, the quiet and the pale light gave the scene around them an unearthly look. Beautiful, yes, but strangely threatening.

'You believe the stories about this place?' Castus asked after a pause. 'The ghosts…?'

Felix shrugged, then shook his head. 'No, but some do. Some of the men, too, though they act brave enough. They've been quaking in their boots all night. This is a forsaken place, whichever way you look at it. Not a place for men.'

The sun was up now, though still concealed by cloud, and the air was getting warmer already. It would be another close, sultry day. Castus saw a boat approaching: one of the Frankish vessels, with Bonitus standing at the prow.

'Guard on deck!' Felix called, and his men clambered blearily up from between the rowing benches, shrugging off their blankets and readying their shields and spears. Bappo the interpreter crawled yawning from the shelter of the stern canopy. By the time they had assembled the Frankish boat was alongside.

'Come down,' Bonitus called, beckoning to Castus with a grin. 'I see your men are not ready to receive guests!'

Castus jutted his jaw, wanting to refuse. But he had never been aboard one of the barbarian vessels, and might never get another chance. Pulling his cloak around him, he stepped carefully over the rail of the galley and lowered himself towards the prow of the Frankish boat. Bonitus reached up and took his boot heel, guiding it to the step cut into the stem post, then grabbed him as he swung himself inboard. A quick leap and a stagger, and Castus found himself standing up in the raked bows, thirty warriors turning on their benches to stare at him.

The boat rocked as he steadied himself; the keel was only a couple of feet beneath the rowing benches, and with the surface of the river so alarmingly close Castus felt as though the whole thing would capsize with any sudden movement. Bonitus moved casually though, a pair of the forward oarsmen shuffling back to clear the benches for them to sit.

'You've eaten?' Bonitus asked. 'We have dried pork, and beer?'

'No, thank you,' Castus said. The thought made his stomach clench. He glanced back at the warriors seated behind them; most of them were ignoring him now, talking among themselves in low grumbling voices, but Castus was aware of the arsenal of weapons lying beside the benches: spears and axes, shields mounted along the wales. They were still only a long leap from the side of the *Bellona*, and Felix had the rail of the galley lined with armed men. The water lapped and eddied between the hulls of the two vessels.

'So, today we find the Saxons, yes?' Bonitus said, smacking his fist lightly into his palm. 'You have some plan?'

'Sort of,' Castus said. He had been turning ideas in his mind all through the night, and the day before. But he knew how hard it was going to be to find the raiders and attack them before they could slip away to sea.

'We'll need to spread out to cover a wider area. Keep the troop barges in the main channels, lookouts at the mastheads and send the lighter boats scouting the creeks and islands to either side. There's a danger that the scouts may be ambushed, or cut off by a bigger force, so we'll need to move fast once anyone locates the enemy.' He paused for a moment, thinking. 'How far is it between here and the open sea?'

'Thirty miles, maybe forty. About the same distance to the Scaldis estuary to the south. At least a day to search half that, I'm thinking.'

Castus made a sound in his throat. He'd suspected as much. And doubtless the Saxons had charted these waterways well already; they were on home ground here. They could have spies posted all along the banks, concealed in the reeds and thickets. Perhaps they had already been alerted to the flotilla's arrival... No, unless the Saxons came to them, they would have to search slowly and carefully and hope they flushed out their prey before they became prey themselves.

'The sailor who brought word of them, Dolens, told me that he thought they were taking the captured ships into the southern part of the islands,' Castus said. 'That's down towards the Scaldis. We're in the north-east now, so I intend to work steadily southwards, with a few ships detached to watch the coast.'

'That would be wise,' Bonitus said. 'They may have boats coming and going from the sea.'

Castus dropped his voice to a rumble. 'How much can I trust Gaiso and Flaochadus?' he asked.

Bonitus pondered briefly. 'Flaochadus will follow the strongest party, always. His will is weak. Gaiso is more difficult. If all is well he follows you, but if he thinks you are not giving him respect, or you are failing in your task, he will turn on you.'

'That's what I thought. I want to send your boats out ahead of us – they can manoeuvre better in the tideways. If I send Gaiso and his people to the far right flank, and all my communication with him passes through you, can I trust him to keep his position?'

Bonitus considered for a moment. 'I think so,' he said. 'But don't leave him out there too long. He may take offence!'

Castus nodded, rising carefully and making his way up to the prow. Climbing back out of the boat looked harder than climbing in. 'Another thing,' he said, lowering his voice as he turned back to Bonitus. 'The other night, during the feast, you told me something… about Leontius, the man who commanded here before me. What was it again?'

Bonitus's face closed as he glanced up at the nearby galley, and he gave an evasive shrug. 'Heh, I don't remember!' he said. 'Much drink, much foolish talk!'

Castus stared at him for a moment, but he knew he would get no more out of the Frankish chief now. Perhaps there would be a better time. 'Tell your people,' he said. 'We raise anchor and move in one hour.'

The oarsmen lightly eased the boat back across to the side of the *Bellona*, and Castus called to Felix to help him back up on deck.

All that day they scoured the waterways of the river country. Castus sent the *Lucusta* and two of the Frankish boats west down the main channel of the Vahalis to the sea coast, to scout the inlets for signs of the enemy. The rest of the flotilla kept together, moving steadily southwards between the islands and mudbanks. The Roman ships had dropped their yards to the deck, and had a lookout clinging at each bare masthead, checking that no vessel moved too far from the group, and scanning the country in all directions. They moved slowly, their oars barely rippling the sluggish waters, the smaller craft probing ahead with rods and lead line to find the deeper channels.

It was an unsettling landscape, flat and greyish-green, threaded with grey-brown water. The air was heavy with the smell of the sea. At times the ships moved out into open estuaries, rolling with the chop of the incoming tide. At others the islands closed in to form narrow culverts, hedged with tall banks of reeds and thick scrub, or creaking bulwarks of tangled driftwood. As the tide dropped it left exposed sandbanks and stretches of mud, covered with scuttling crabs and shrieking gulls. Wide flatlands lay between some of the islands, covered with what looked like lush green grass, but the few men who tried to walk upon them sank at once to their waists in black muddy ooze.

And hour after hour there was no sign of their prey. Barely any sign of humanity at all. Around noon they came across a clutch of collapsing huts, clearly unoccupied for years. Some abandoned fish-traps clogged the nearest tideway, and once they passed the wreck of a boat, black-green with moss and barnacles.

'Ever feel like you're being watched?' Senecio said as he stood with Castus on the stern deck of the *Bellona*.

'I've been feeling it since dawn,' Castus replied. He was eating lentil porridge and raw onion, washed down with vinegar wine. 'Surely we should have seen something by now? A smoke trail on the horizon, even...'

'And they could be all around us,' Senecio said, glowering at the nearest island. 'Just waiting for the right moment to attack...'

At least they would be prepared for that. The *Bellona* had only her lower bank of oars working; the upper-tier men had armed themselves and stood ready at their benches, with the marines of the Second and the archers. But the long slow day was sapping their morale. Castus could feel it. The gods only knew how the crews of the smaller ships were faring.

'Reckon we're close to the Scaldis estuary now,' Senecio said, several hours later. 'We should find a safe anchorage before dusk. Deep water, good holding ground. Bring the flotilla together. We'll have to spend another night aboard ship.'

Castus nodded, and moments later he saw the man at the masthead waving the signal to the other vessels. A whole day, he thought, and nothing to show for it. Had the Saxons really

265

left this place and returned to their distant homes at the top of the ocean, the far north? He doubted it – no chief would assemble such a strong warband and bring it all this way just to capture a few ships loaded with stores. No, they were here somewhere, and soon enough he would discover them.

They found their anchorage an hour later: a wide channel between bushy islands, clear of sandbanks even at low tide. Dusk was falling as the last ships joined them, the *Lucusta* and her two Frankish consorts, reporting no sightings along the sea coast. The vessels anchored in formation, the *Bellona* at the centre in midstream. Castus had ordered silence, but as he paced the deck in the gathering darkness he could hear loud voices and gusting laughter from the Frankish ships moored across the channel. The barbarians had brought drink with them, and would not rest easily without it.

He would take the last watch of the night, he decided, and clambered down into his cramped cabin to rest. After the day's frustrations he expected sleep to be elusive, but there was little to think about now, few considerations chasing through his mind. With a single heavy sigh he slipped into unconsciousness, deep and profoundly dreamless.

'Dominus,' a hushed voice was saying. Castus felt somebody shaking his foot. He opened his eyes to total blackness, and for three heartbeats could not remember where he was. Then he made out the faint moonlight through the cabin scuttle, the vague shape of his orderly beside the bed. 'Dominus,' Eumolpius said again. 'Change of watch.'

Yawning, Castus swung himself upright and groped in the darkness for his cloak and belts. He felt as though he had slept only half an hour, not two-thirds of the night. Stumbling, cursing, he hauled himself up the ladder onto the deck. Breathing deeply, he tried to clear his mind of the last traces of sleep. The moon was half full, but covered by cloud, and only a slight misty radiance lit the estuary. Castus shuddered, pulling his cloak tight around him, although the air was softly damp and still.

'At least our Frankish friends have gone to sleep at last,' Felix said, his cloaked form appearing out of the gloom. 'They were getting quite rowdy out there.'

'Hopefully they haven't *all* gone to sleep,' Castus replied. He peered out across the waters of the channel, but most of the other vessels were lost in the darkness and he could only make out the shadowy form of the *Satyra* moored just ahead, and two of the troopships a short way astern. Felix passed him a cup of vinegar wine and he drank slowly, listening in to the silence of the surrounding land. The deck creaked, somewhere a marsh bird cried and the water lapped at the hull beneath him, splashing quietly.

Three hours until sunrise. Castus leaned back against the starboard ballista mount, sipped his wine and waited. *Where are you?* he thought, scanning the black emptiness of the estuary, as if he could force the enemy to reveal themselves by willpower alone. He waited, as the night seemed to grow darker and the damp air chilled him through his cloak.

Then, in the first misty grey of dawn, sliding out from the land with only the barest whisper of oars, came the silent keels of the enemy.

The cry of a sentry on a distant boat startled Castus from his watchful trance. At once there were more shouts, and a moment later the bray of a trumpet somewhere in the grey mist. Castus threw off his cloak, stepping to the rail as the men on deck stumbled up from their blankets and grabbed their shields and weapons.

'What's happening?' Senecio said, clambering up the ladder. Castus was still peering into the darkness, unsure. It was happening quickly, he knew that: there were shouts from all around now, the clash and yell of combat somewhere off to the left. Impossible to determine the distance and exact direction. A trumpet sounded beside him, oars and boots and shields battering the deck. The *Bellona* rolled with the motion, and Castus felt her turning slowly with the current.

'Anchor cable's cut!' one of the sentries shouted. 'We're drifting!'

'Hands to the oars,' Senecio cried at once.

No enemy craft had come close enough to cut their cable, surely? Castus stood with feet braced, his sword in his hand. Already he could see the shapes of the nearest vessels, the deck of the galley *Pinnata* swarming with figures. Where had they come from?

'Men in the water!' somebody called. 'They're all around us!'

The voice choked off as a figure vaulted across the rail, hurling a knife to strike the sentry in the throat. Immediately the soldiers closed in; three spears struck the intruder through the chest, and he fell back into the water. But there were more of them, long-haired bearded men, stripped to their loincloths, grabbing at the shipped oars and swinging themselves up the hull, scrambling onto the deck with long knives between their clenched teeth.

'Repel boarders!' Senecio was yelling. Castus took a step back, glancing around. As he turned he saw a man dragging himself up over the stern, his hand clasping the deck railing. He had a brief glimpse of a face glaring up at him, a snarl of teeth between the dripping strands of hair, then he stamped forward, swinging his blade in an overarm cut that chopped through the man's wrist and bit into the wood of the rail beneath. The man screamed, then vanished into the black water. The severed hand dropped onto the deck.

Now, with the mist thinning and the first sun glowing through the clouds, it was possible to make out what was happening. The swimmers must have come out under cover of darkness, trying to kill the sentries on the smaller vessels and disable the larger ones, while the main Saxon force approached under oars. Already the *Pinnata* and two of the Frankish boats were locked in bloody combat, their drowsy crews trying to beat back the attackers appearing from the water all around them. Further downstream, the black shapes of the Saxon vessels had closed with Bonitus's boats, and were circling the *Satyra*. At least some of the Romans had reacted promptly: Castus saw the scout galley *Lucusta* already under oars, the few archers and the light ballista on the narrow foredeck returning the Saxon missiles. They must have cut their own cable to have moved so fast.

Oars clashed and boomed below the deck of the *Bellona*, and a moment later the lower-tier blades splashed into the water on both sides, the voice of the rowing master and the beat of the mallet urging the oarsmen to their strokes. At least now, Castus thought, they would not drift into shoal water and run aground. He had remained standing on the stern while the marines drove the intruders from the deck; all of the men who had climbed aboard were dead or had retreated, and the men of the Primigenia were slinging the bloodied corpses over the side. The dawn estuary echoed with the sounds of battle, the cries of rage and pain, the thud of shields. But it still felt dreamlike, a combat of ghosts.

'All boarders repelled, dominus,' Felix reported, tipping his helmet back. 'The men are up and ready, artillery spanned and loaded. They won't catch us out like that again.'

'What's the damage?'

'One dead, six injured. Reckon we got about ten or eleven of them.'

'Make that twelve,' Castus said, thinking of the man at the stern. The severed hand was still lying on the deck in a spatter of blood; he booted it over the side.

A gang of crewmen were heaving the spare anchors up from the hold; others were busy with the new cable. Eumolpius appeared with the padded linen vest Castus usually wore beneath his cuirass. Castus put it on, and his orderly tightened the straps beneath his arms and buckled his belts and baldric over the top. It would provide some protection against missiles at least; Castus was a strong swimmer, but wearing any heavier armour in a naval battle seemed unwise.

All along the rail there were soldiers, legionaries of the Second and Twenty-Second standing together across the rowing benches with locked shields. Behind them, on the gangway, were the archers and javelin men. The *Bellona* was a floating fortress now. It was time to take the fight to the enemy.

CHAPTER XX

Away in the offing the crew of the *Pinnata* appeared to have won their struggle against the boarders. Blood streaked the hull of the galley, but Castus could see more injured and dead aboard than able men. And now the Saxon longboats were closing in on the *Bellona* and the anchored troopships beyond. The heavy beat of oars, the hoarse chant of the barbarian warriors, sounded loud on the waters. These Saxons boats were bigger than the Frankish vessels, broader in the beam, and their tall stem posts were carved into the shapes of savage beasts. Standing up in the lead boat was a bare-chested muscular man with matted hair and beard. He raised his shield and spear above his head, letting out a deep roaring war cry that carried across the dawn estuary. One of the ballistae spat, but the bolt went wide. The Saxons were coming on fast, their oars bursting spray from the water.

'Surely they're not going to ram us?' Senecio muttered through his teeth.

Arrows flickered around the bare-chested chief at the prow, but he did not flinch as the vessels closed. Castus could hear the rapid ratcheting clack as the ballista crew next to him reloaded. His gaze was fixed on the approaching boat.

A flat *thwack* from the ballista, and Castus watched the bolt sail over the head of the Saxon chief and arc down into the stern of the boat, killing two oarsmen instantly and pinning a third to the thwarts. But the ballista crew could not depress their weapon any further, and now the Saxons let out a cheer and threw themselves into a last driving stroke that would bring their boat crashing against the oar bank of the galley.

'Portside – ship oars!' Senecio screamed. 'Prepare to fend them off!'

With a thunderous clatter the oars ran inboard, the *Bellona* swinging round in the water as the far bank kept rowing; but the Saxon boat was already alongside, the chief tensed in the prow ready to spring.

'Javelin,' Castus said, reaching back. Felix passed him the weapon, and Castus jumped up onto the deck rail. A moment to swing his arm and take aim, then he flung the javelin with all his strength. The Saxon chief noticed him and raised his shield – too late. The barbed iron head struck him below the shoulder, the long weighted shank plunging down through his chest. His body buckled, then he toppled sideways into the water. Every man on the Roman deck roared as he fell.

Now the oars were slamming out again from the galley's hull, the wooden blades battering against the Saxon boat. Castus saw one of the barbarians smashed down by an oar-blade, another knocked sideways into the water. But the rest were scrambling forwards, ready to leap, hurling grappling hooks across to catch on the galley's rail and between the oar benches. Many of the soldiers of the Twenty-Second had armed themselves with *falxes*, hooked scythe blades mounted on long handles; as the Saxons hauled their grappling lines taut, the falx blades swung and sheared through them.

A smell of burning tar and smoke, and a moment later Castus saw the two men with a heavy earthenware fire-pot slung between them. They heaved, and the pot flew from its rope cradle and spun, trailing smoke, to shatter on the Saxon deck. Screams from the warriors packed behind the beast-carved prow as burning coals, pitch and tow sprayed along the length of their vessel. The men on the *Bellona* cheered again as the longboat yawed away from them, the warriors desperately trying to quench the blaze. Smoke eddied across the deck, and the air smelled of blood and burning.

'Starboard!' somebody shouted. 'Another boat!'

Castus turned just in time to see the second Saxon vessel begin its ramming assault on the opposite bank of oars. The barbarians gave a last powerful heave, and the sharp prow of their boat came rushing in against the galley's side, the shallow hull riding up over the oars that were still in the water. The *Bellona* rolled wildly with the pressure on her beam, and the crack of breaking oar-shafts and the screams of men came from the lower benches. More grappling hooks came arcing across, and the deck heeled further as the barbarians hauled on the ropes and the marines tumbled back across the gangway to face the new threat. Already the attackers in the second boat were flinging themselves at the galley, some jumping down onto the oars pinned beneath their keel, while others clambered over the beast- prow and leaped the gap between the hulls.

'Drive them back!' Castus shouted, snatching up a fallen shield as he pushed his way through the chaos of men clogging the gangway. The first Saxon on the Roman deck had already been cut down by a scything falx blow; the second and third were right behind him, striking overarm with their spears. More of the attackers were scrambling up the side, clambering over the wrecked stumps of the oars.

Castus banged his shield rim down onto the rail, breaking a Saxon's arm. He punched a second man with the boss, driving him back into the threshing water. The deck was heeling so steeply that he had trouble standing upright; with one foot braced against the rail he sliced down with his sword, cleaving through two of the grappling ropes. A ballista bolt spat past him; the artillery crews had swung their weapons around to shoot along the deck at the mass of attacking Saxons.

One of the attackers, a bearded giant with long braided locks whipping around his head, took a running jump from the prow of the Saxon boat, straight across onto the Roman deck, battering down two defenders as he landed. With a plunging blow of his spear he slew another man. Castus swung his shield, climbing between the rowing benches and along the tilting deck. Many of the Romans had already retreated to the far side of the ship, across the barricade of the lowered yard, trying to use their weight to level the deck as they flung darts and javelins at the boarders. The big Saxon with the braids was roaring defiance, holding his position, oblivious to the missile storm, dead and injured men all around him as his comrades came scrambling across in support.

Castus hauled himself up the tilt of the deck, studded boots grating on the planking. He got his shield up, then took two running steps and launched himself at the Saxon. The spearhead slammed against his shield and he heaved it aside; before he could strike, his boots skidded on a slick of blood and he slipped to fall on his back. The Saxon towered above him, lifting the spear to stab downwards. Castus kicked out wildly, catching the warrior behind the knee and knocking him sprawling back onto the rowing benches. Spears and javelins rattled above him, iron blades slicing through the air. Then he was back on his feet, scrambling for balance as the Saxon reared up again and flung the spear at his head. Castus dodged, then brought his sword down in a wheeling overhand cut that smashed past his enemy's shield and chopped down through his collarbone, hacking deep into the Saxon's torso like a butcher's cleaver cutting meat.

Blood sprayed as he dragged the blade free, showering the warriors at the ship's rail. For a heartbeat the big Saxon remained swaying on his knees, then he toppled. With a yell of triumph the Roman marines surged back across the gangway, driving into the attackers with shield boss, falx and spear. The Saxons still clinging to the *Bellona*'s rail fell back; faced with the wall of battering shields and striking blades, many flung themselves down into the water as the remaining grappling ropes were cut loose behind them. Those left aboard the boat were heaving at their oars, trying to back away from the galley while the archers and ballista crews picked them off one by one.

As the Saxon boat fell away from the starboard beam, the galley rolled back onto an even keel. Castus climbed across the gangway to the other side; the first boat was still there, wallowing only a few paces away, where it had been driven back by the ramming oars. The men aboard had managed to extinguish the fire and were massing again for a renewed assault. But, as Castus watched, one of the big blunt-ended troop barges came rowing up behind the longboat, heavy sweeps pushing it fast through the water, Modestus and his men crowding the foredeck with bows, darts and javelins. Modestus yelled the command, and the Romans flung a storm of missiles into the Saxons crowding the oar benches. Many found a mark; a moment later the heavy timbers of the barge's bows crashed against the Saxon hull. Wood creaked, and the boat rose and began to capsize as the warriors flung themselves into the water to be speared and shot by the Romans on the barge.

With half her starboard lower-tier oars broken or mangled, the *Bellona* was drifting with the tide, circling slowly in a wrack of shattered hulls and floating corpses.

'New oars, boys!' Senecio was shouting. 'Get them up and shipped. Let's get some way on her!'

Castus steadied himself against the mast, breathing heavily. His right arm was red to the shoulder, but he felt only bruises. There were injured men coming up from below deck, carried by their comrades, and their blood joined the streams of it flowing along the seams of the deck planking and pooling between the benches. Down in the hold, the crew had manhandled the spare oars from their stowage along the keel, swinging and wrestling them into the vacant spaces along the rowing banks.

From the bow, Castus gazed forward across the estuary. Over near the far shore, the Frankish boats had managed to turn and attack the Saxons. One of them – Gaiso's boat – had forced her bows in over the beam of an enemy vessel. As Castus watched, the huge Frankish chief led his men storming forward, leaping over the prow and onto the Saxon deck, his axe slashing down. But some of the other Franks had fared worse: Castus could see two capsized hulls, another sinking wreck, and a lot of men still struggling in the water. His own vessels seemed all intact; only the *Pinnata* and the flagship had been attacked directly. In the centre of the estuary, four or five Saxon boats had fought their way clear. Oars beating, they were turning to flee.

'Navarch,' Castus called. 'How soon can we get under way?'

'Soon enough, dominus,' Senecio yelled hoarsely from the open scuttle.

Castus thumped his fist against the deck rail, staring at the retreating enemy. He could see *Lucusta* and *Satyra* already moving after them; the Saxons would not get away so easily.

'First time I've fought a ship on both sides!' Senecio said, climbing up to join Castus at the bow.

'It's not over yet,' Castus said, pointing. Away to the right, between the *Bellona* and the north shore of the estuary, the battered *Pinnata* had run aground on a sandbank. Two of the Saxon longboats were closing in on her, the rowers pulling hard with a hoarse, determined chant. The few able men left aboard the galley had no chance of fighting both of them off.

'Gods below,' Senecio said under his breath, then ran back down the gangway, yelling commands to the deck crew and oarsmen. Behind him, Castus could hear the men cranking back the arms of the heavy stone-throwing catapult at the bow. He remained where he was, watching the two black hulls closing on the stricken galley.

'Oars out! Pull on the command!'

A volley of splashes as both banks of oars struck the water. The rowing master gave a shout, the first bang of the mallet came from below deck, and with a long creak and a heave the wallowing motion of the *Bellona* shifted into a smooth forward glide.

'Shoot as soon as you get the range,' Castus told the catapult crew. Felix had come forward and joined him at the bow, with half a dozen Nervian archers.

The rhythm of the mallet quickened, the oars crashing down into the water, pulling and then rising to swing in unison. Steadily the speed of the galley increased. Glancing down over the bow, Castus saw the placid water of the estuary already foaming around the keel spur.

A *thwack* from the catapult, then a distant thud as the stone struck the side of a longboat. The archers were craning forward now, aiming at the Saxons on the oar benches.

'Target practice!' said one of the Nervians, then loosed his arrow.

Still the galley gathered speed, the gap of water between her bow and the Saxon boats closing rapidly. The Saxons had begun to take evasive action, abandoning their prey and swinging around for the open estuary. Castus felt the motion of the oars change as the helmsman altered course; spray spattered up from the bow. One of the longboats was moving too slowly; the *Bellona* crossed her wake, then turned again to cut her off. The rhythm of the oars increased to ramming speed.

'Brace yourselves,' he said, then crouched low behind the deck rail. He could see the Saxons still pulling frantically at their oars, trying to turn again, some of them standing up to hurl javelins at the ship bearing down on them. Too late: two more driving sweeps of the oars and the *Bellona* rammed the side of the longboat. The spur lifted and broke the enemy keel, then the heavy bows smashed through the hull. Castus felt the shock through the deck timbers beneath him, but the galley barely slackened speed. Shattered wreckage grated along the hull to either side of him, and he heard men screaming in the water as the archers at the rail shot down at them. A moment later and they were swept beneath the threshing oars.

One of the Saxons had managed to leap up and cling to the galley's anchor davit; Felix raised his javelin, leaned across the rail, and stabbed the man through his neck.

The other Saxon boat was too far away to catch, the crew labouring hard at their oars as they made for the open estuary. Castus straightened from his crouch and gazed back along the blood-slicked deck. All across the reach of the estuary there were boats capsized or burning, and the *Bellona*'s long curving wake was foaming with broken wreckage and bodies. Smoke drifted across the calm grey surface of the water.

'Report,' Castus said.

'Thirty-six dead, excellency,' Vetranio told him, 'nearly half of them aboard the *Pinnata*. Forty-two injured, twelve critically. The Franks lost about the same; one of their boats was destroyed and two capsized, but they reckon they can repair the damage. All of our ships are safe, except *Pinnata* lost half her oars. Enemy casualties... impossible to say, dominus.'

Castus nodded. He was sitting on a stool behind the helmsman, watching the crew dragging up buckets of water to wash and scrub down the deck. The twelve dead aboard the *Bellona* had already been sewn up in their blankets and dropped over the side: an ignominious end for a soldier, but there was no dry land for a burial or wood for a pyre. One of the dead had been the frog-faced interpreter, Bappo; he had been struck by an axe and bled to death in the scuppers. Castus had never liked the man, but his loss was bitter. Now the Romans would have to rely on Bonitus to negotiate between them and their Frankish allies.

A glance up at the sky: solid cloud covered the sun. The air had a damp sticky feel, with an odd tugging breeze. Still early morning, only a couple of hours since the battle. Senecio was muttering about thunder.

'*Satyra*'s coming in, dominus!' the sentry cried. Castus stood up at once and strode to the rail. Two of his galleys and some of the Frankish boats had gone in pursuit of the retreating Saxons; with any luck, they had tracked the enemy to their hiding place.

The oars slid inboard as the smaller galley came alongside, the optio of the Twenty-Second who commanded her hopping nimbly across to the flagship and climbing in over the rail. He approached Castus and made his salute.

279

'Ten miles down the estuary, excellency,' the optio said, flinging his arm out to the westwards. 'There's a narrow channel opening between a small island and the larger one over there. Must be another channel at the far end – two of the Frankish boats went to look. I sent one of my boys up the mast and he says he saw longboats pulled up on the shore of the bigger island, some kind of stockade in the scrub above too. But they've staked the channel – the Saxons were pretty careful going in. *Lucusta*'s still up there keeping watch.'

'Good man,' Castus said, clapping the optio on the shoulder. He clenched his back teeth in a satisfied snarl. Now at least he had the enemy's location, and if they moved quickly enough there would be no chance of the Saxons slipping away. The position sounded strong, and a frontal assault could be costly. There was always the possibility that the pirates would start slaughtering their prisoners if they were attacked. He needed to see the place for himself before he could make any plans.

'Navarch,' he called. 'Signal all ships: up anchor and form around the flagship. *Satyra* can lead the way.'

Standing before the helm, he watched with gathering anticipation as the oarsmen ran to their benches. Cries echoed across the anchorage from the other ships of the flotilla. He knew the men were weary, many of the younger and less experienced of them still shocked after the sudden combat at dawn. Soon they would be tested hard once more, but at least now none could be in any doubt about what they were facing.

Two hours later, and ten miles to the west, Castus clung precariously to the masthead of the *Bellona*, one foot in a loop of rope, trying not to glance down at the narrow strip of the galley's deck thirty feet below him. He had never liked heights and this height seemed particularly exposed, with the vast sweep of flat land and water all around him and the huge sky above.

With one arm hugging the mast tightly he peered across the low reed-grown island to the strip of water beyond, and the larger island on the far side. There was dark dense foliage beyond the belt of mudflats and marsh. Then, as he squinted into the metallic light, he picked out the black shapes of the Saxon boats pulled up on the muddy beach above the channel between the islands, the strip of cleared shore beyond them and then the ragged line of a fortification meshed so cleverly into the surrounding scrub it was almost invisible. Turning his head, he saw watchers at the mastheads of the other Roman ships. With great care he raised his arm, gesturing to the men on deck to lower him down. The loop of rope juddered, then began to drop.

Back on deck after his awkward descent of the mast, Castus ordered the signal hoisted to call all the commanders to the flagship. The men were still at their benches, rowing slow and steady to keep the ship motionless against the ebbing tide. Senecio was relieving them by shifts to eat their midday meal; Castus glanced up, and saw that the boats were already approaching.

'You all know of the enemy position,' he said, once the commanders, both Roman and Frankish, were assembled on the deck before him. 'There are two entrances to the channel – the one further west's wider, but shallower. Both are staked, so we'll need to go slow and probe ahead. Beyond that there's a space of open water in front of the enemy encampment. We need to act fast, before we lose the tide; I want Bonitus and Gaiso with their boats, and *Pinnata* in support, to move west and enter the far entrance to the channel.'

The two Frankish chiefs nodded; Gaiso in particular appeared satisfied that he would not be under direct Roman command.

'The main assault will go up the channel nearest to us here,' Castus went on. '*Lucusta* and *Murena* will take the lead, with Flaochadus's two boats. They'll sound the passage, and clear any obstructions they can. *Bellona* will be following close behind, and we'll ram through anything left. Behind us will be two of the troopships, under the command of Centurion Modestus. As soon as we're in the open water, the galleys will support the troopships with their artillery while we get the men ashore as fast as we can.'

He paused, glancing between the faces. All looked grimly resolute. Vetranio alone had a questioning look.

'At the same time,' Castus said, 'I want the third force, under Vetranio's command, with two troopships and *Satyra* in support, to land on the large island a mile to the east and march inland to attack the enemy position from the rear.'

Vetranio stiffened, nodding briefly.

'It won't be easy. The ground's marshy, and there could be thick scrub and flooded ditches blocking your route. When you're in position, signal with a fire arrow. We'll do the same: that's the signal for the general attack. Questions?'

There were none, but Castus could read the uneasiness in the men's eyes. He knew that dividing his force like this would be a risk; if any group was delayed, the Saxons could defeat the others one by one.

'Then let the gods be with us,' he said. 'We move at once.'

As the commanders returned to their ships he sat alone on the stern deck, trying not to think of the possibilities. He had laid his scheme, and now he must stick to it. A headache throbbed on and off, and the pressure of the air seemed to have increased. Sipping water, he stared across at the nearest troopship, watching Modestus preparing his men for the assault. The rasping sound of whetstones on blades sounded clearly in the thick damp air.

'Excellency, you should eat,' Eumolpius said, appearing at his elbow with a wooden platter of bread and cheese and a flask of vinegar wine. Castus was not at all hungry, but he took the

food and forced himself to eat. Chewing methodically, he felt
the sweat trickling down his back and gathering around his
waistband. He was still wearing his padded linen vest, stained
with blood from the morning's fighting.

Time slowed; the small flotilla of vessels unmoving on the
slowly ebbing tide. A dull roll of thunder came from the south.
Castus wondered whether a storm would give added heart to
the Saxons, or frighten them with the wrath of their gods. He
cast a quick glance towards the sun, hoping for a gleam of light
that he could use to offer a prayer to Sol Invictus, but the sky
was still closed above him.

'The signal!' the man at the masthead cried, pointing away
to the south.

'That's Vetranio,' Senecio said. 'Nothing yet from the Franks.
We wait, I suppose?'

'We wait.'

But for how long? Castus got up and began to pace. He
could not leave Vetranio and his men unsupported; if Bonitus
and Gaiso had not reached the far channel entrance yet, there
was little more time for them to do so.

'Signal the scout galleys to move forward,' he said, after
waiting as long as he could bear. 'We'll get under way as soon
as they reach the channel mouth.'

Senecio gave the order, and moments later the two eighteen-
oared galleys began to cut across the estuary, their oars bursting
spray from the water. Castus watched them as they headed
in towards the channel, with Flaochadus and his two boats
trailing behind them. Then the navarch nodded to the rowing
master, the mallet began to beat and the double-banked oars of
the flagship began to rise and fall. Castus eased out a breath,
and felt the energy of the coming battle rising through him,
eclipsing all dread.

CHAPTER XXI

For the first few hundred paces, perhaps the first half-mile, the channel appeared no different to the maze of estuary waterways the flotilla had navigated for the past two days. Mudflats edged the shore, with tall stands of head-high reed beyond. Still the same eerie quiet, only the creak of oars and the grunt of the men on the rowing benches breaking the stillness. Castus stood at the bow and watched the vessels ahead: the two Roman scout galleys and the Frankish boats, moving steadily up the channel with the wash of their oars stirring the dull grey waters. All the Roman ships had unstepped their mast; they were in fighting trim now, the ballista crews alert and scanning the banks for movement.

A cry came from the left-hand Frankish boat, the hull yawing and the oars thrashing in disarray; they had struck one of the submerged stakes that lined the channel. Castus watched them back oars and reverse their course, angling to the right. The boat did not appear damaged, but now all of them were moving much more slowly, probing ahead for further traps. He felt the tension in his body, the muscles of his shoulders and neck taut. Everything in him wanted to give the order to power ahead at full speed.

Now one of the scout galleys had come to a stop, oars barely moving in the water. A man signalled from the stern: more stakes, or some sort of barrage blocking the channel. There must be a way through it, an open passage, but it could take time to locate.

'Dominus,' Senecio said, and pointed towards the inland horizon. Castus looked up and saw dirty grey smoke trails rising above the shaggy scrub. He stood up in the bows, head raised, but there was no sound of fighting. Too far away. But the detachment he sent inland had surely been discovered; unless he could bring up his main force in support they would be annihilated.

'Force the passage,' he told Senecio. 'Signal the other ships to follow right behind us.'

'You're sure?' the old navarch asked, frowning. 'The bow timbers are already weak. If we run hard against those stakes...'

'Fuck the stakes!' Castus snarled. 'Don't question my orders!' He felt a fury coming over him, a savage desire to drive this struggle to its crisis. Behind him he heard Senecio calling out the orders, but his gaze was locked on the distant smoke trails, the vessels halted in the channel ahead. Shouts from the rowing master, and a moment later he felt the lurch as the *Bellona* began to gather speed in the water.

Flinging a glance back, Castus saw the two heavy troop barges following in the flagship's wake, their long sweeps working hard to keep pace. Forward again, he saw the scout galley *Lucusta* still shoving against the submerged obstructions, the oarsmen heaving as they tried to break through. Marsh birds burst from cover on the southern shore, and when Castus glanced that way he saw movement among the reeds, half-naked men scrambling down to the water and wading out into the shallows to fling spears at the vessels caught among the stakes.

Three more powerful strokes sent the *Bellona* bursting forward along the channel. Castus felt the shock as the hull scraped against a submerged stake, the yells of the men on the benches as their oars clipped more of them. Then came the order: *Lift oars! Brace yourselves!* Castus grabbed the rail as the prow of the galley crashed against a mass of timber lashed together into a barrage. The impact made the whole ship shudder, and his feet went from under him. For a moment the galley seemed to hang motionless, as if caught in some vast clinging web. Castus scrambled to his feet as the surface of the channel exploded into foam, the lashed stakes ripping free from the muddy bed of the channel. Another powerful heave of the oars, and the bows of the galley broke through the barrier.

A javelin struck the bulwark only a foot from where Castus was standing. He had been so distracted that he had forgotten the enemy thronging the nearest bank, standing up from the reed thickets. He dodged backwards as another missile arced overhead. But now he could hear the massed cheering from the men in the troopships behind him, as the galley surged on through the last wreckage of the stakes and into the open water beyond. The ballistae at the stern were snapping, the archers lining the gangways pelting the banks with arrows.

Ahead was a wide pool of open water, narrowing towards the far channel. Reeds and marshy scrub lined the north shore, but to the south there was a sloping beach of sand and hard mud. And the area above the beach was filled with men. Some of the Saxons had managed to get their boats in the water already; Castus heard a crack as the heavy catapult released its shot. The stone ball soared across the water, falling to smash the beast figurehead of one vessel and kill the man at the prow. A direct hit; the artillery crew cheered. *Murena* rammed the side of a second vessel. The ballista crews were shooting as fast as they could load and aim. Tearing himself away from the rail, Castus ran back down the gangway between the lines of archers.

'Bring her round,' he yelled to the helmsman. The two troop barges were already forging through the shattered remains of the staked barrier and angling in towards the shore, their bows packed with armed men.

The stern of the *Bellona* swung, and Castus hung across the rail and shouted to the nearest barge. He snatched up his shield and slung it on his back, lifting his sword scabbard clear of his legs. As the gap between the two vessels narrowed he clambered across the rail, clung on for a moment, and then leaped.

Hands gripped him as his foot came down on the mud-slippery bulwark, hauling him aboard. The barge was already surging forward again, two men at each oar standing and leaning into their stroke. Castus pushed his way into the tight mass of soldiers packing the bow.

Modestus grinned as he saluted. 'Come to get a closer look?'

'Thought you might need some help!' It was hard to speak, the pressure in his chest was so great. The men around him were primed, tensed for attack, every one of them clutching spear or javelin, shields readied. Castus was glad to see that some of them carried entrenching tools: axes and mattocks. They would need them to break through the stockades of the enemy encampment.

The water hissed by along the barge's low freeboard. Above it, Castus could hear the sounds of combat from the shore. There were figures running from the distance, streaming along the shore towards the Saxon encampment: Frankish warriors in bright tunics, bellowing their battle cries. Bonitus and Gaiso must have grounded their boats further up the channel and waded ashore.

'Come on, y'buggers, *pull*!' Modestus shouted. 'Are we going to let those Frankish scum kill everyone before we get our boots on dry land?'

A chorus of angry yells. One of the men slipped overboard and plunged into the muddy brown water. The rest crouched, ready to leap at the command.

Water slapped across the prow, then the keel grated on sand. With a thunder of boots on timbers, a crash of foam, the first wave of attackers vaulted over the bows of the barge and into the shallows, wading up onto the beach. Modestus was with them, crying out the commands to assemble in formation. Already the troops were striking down men on the shore.

Castus waited, holding back the second wave of men until the first had struggled up onto the sand. Then he drew his sword and leaped across the bow into the churning water with thirty armed men behind him.

The Saxons were charging down against them, every man with spear and shield, a short fighting knife and a sheaf of light javelins. The faster of them managed to catch the Romans in the shallows, cutting them down before they could stumble out of the water. But they were too few to stem the surge, and all dropped to javelin, dart or ballista bolt. The waters lapping the beach were muddy-red with blood. Modestus had his men formed into a wedge attack column; Castus, with Felix beside him, did the same. Now the second barge was ashore, the men disembarked and forming up. Spears and javelins flickered around them, but the troops did not flinch.

'Hornblower!' Castus shouted. 'Sound the charge!'

As soon as the first note sounded the columns powered forward. Castus got his head down and threw his shoulder into the hollow of his shield. All around him was the clatter of other shields locking together, the thud of breath and the stamp of wet boots. Something caught at his feet as he ran and he stumbled forward, almost falling, and then staggered back upright. A body appeared ahead of him, a Saxon warrior with raised spear; he slammed into the man with all his weight, battering him down with the shield and then aiming a low stab to strike him as he fell sprawling.

More Saxons crashed against them, and the shields drove them back. Castus was barely conscious of it; the fury carried him onward. A blade struck his shield rim, skidded across it and sliced his upper arm. Roaring, Castus hacked the attacker's legs from under him. Pain flickered up the side of his neck, and he could feel blood running hot down his arm. Screaming men on all sides, the close air exploding into a thunder of battering shields and colliding bodies.

He needed space and distance. Needed to see what was happening. With a conscious effort of will he halted and allowed the column of men to push on past him. He was breathing hard, gulping air, and his left bicep was cut badly. His shield sagged, and when he tried to lift it he felt the hot tug of pain in his elbow and shoulder. The last ranks of the attack wedge passed him, and Castus braced himself on his grounded shield and stared around him.

The sudden charge up the beach had taken the Saxons by surprise. So many of them had poured down from their encampment to try and slaughter the Romans in the shallows that they were hampered by their own numbers, and now they were fleeing in confusion. Most were running straight back towards the openings in the stockade fence; the rest were trying to defend their boats pulled up on the shore. But the Franks had got there first, and a ferocious barbarian combat was swirling around the beached black hulls: Frank against Saxon, spear and knife against axe and broadsword.

Turning, Castus saw that the *Bellona* and the other galleys had beached, and their crews were leaping ashore over the bows. The green shields with the twin Capricorn blazon of the Twenty-Second Legion formed a disciplined wall, bristling with spears and falx blades. Aboard the ships the archers and artillery were still shooting, lofting missiles high over the fighters on the beach to rain down on the mass of men struggling to get back inside the stockade.

Between the lapping shore and the belt of inland scrub, the muddy sand was carpeted with bodies. A pair of Franks came running past, each of them swinging a severed Saxon head in his teeth by the braided hair. Castus stared at them. Eumolpius was beside him, prising his hand from the shield and lifting his arm. Castus winced as the pain shot through him. The orderly muttered something under his breath as he ripped the cloth of Castus's tunic away from the wound. He had a flask over his shoulder, vinegar wine, and he poured it to wash away the blood before binding the wound. Castus stood with teeth clenched. When he glanced down he saw the gash in his bicep, deep through the flesh into muscle. Fresh blood welled from the wound, and a wave of nausea passed briefly through him, bringing cold sweat to his brow. A handspan to the right, and the blow could have sliced his neck, his face, his eyes…

'Give me that,' he said, sticking his sword in the sand and taking the flask to drink deeply. His throat was parched, and the wine was glorious. There were other wounded men staggering back from the battle, limping on their spears, some of them crawling. A short distance away Castus saw a man of the Second Legion dragging himself down the beach on his shield; his tunic and the hollow of the shield were drenched with blood, and the man's face was white with pain.

'See to him,' he told Eumolpius. 'Give him wine if he'll take it.'

The orderly nodded, finished binding Castus's arm into a sling, then hurried away.

The fight on the beach was done, the area around the boats had been cleared, but the enemy were still holding out inside their stockade. Castus could smell the burning now, and saw the smoke beginning to billow through the scrub thickets above the beach. Vetranio and his men must have fired the bushes on the far side of the camp. Screams came from inside the stockade, and Castus remembered the prisoners held by the Saxons. The realisation jolted him into motion; wincing as he slung his shield across his shoulder by its strap, he pulled his sword free, took a deep breath and strode on up the beach.

Frenzied motion around the stockade: some of Modestus's men had formed a tortoise of their shields and moved up against the lattice of stakes and spiked branches, covering the men who worked with axe and mattock to break a way through. The warriors inside stabbed out with their spears through the gaps in the fence, or hurled javelins over the top. Castus saw Gaiso and his Franks a few paces to the right, slamming at one of the gates in the barrier, hacking with their axes at the mesh of woven branches.

'Felix,' Castus shouted, and the wiry optio turned at once. 'Form your men up to support Modestus as soon as they have a breach – push your way through it if you have to.'

But Modestus was already pulling his men back, screaming at them to assemble in a tight block of shields. Felix brought his men up behind them, and at a word of command they charged. The mass of shields struck the stockade where the axes had weakened it; a heave, boots grinding in the dirt, and the wall gave before them. The attack party shoved through the breach, their cheers booming from inside the carapace of locked shields. Then they were inside, and storming into the compound beyond.

Castus ran to follow them, his slung shield banging against his injured arm. But he felt no more pain, his body numbed to all feeling. His bloodied fingers found the shield grip, then he was heaving himself up and through the gap in the stockade with sword in hand.

Inside was a smoky twilight gloom, filled with running figures. The Saxon encampment was a wide cleared area, confused with huts of reeds and woven branches and shelters made of sail canvas. The stockade wall at the far side was blazing fiercely, and the breeze drove the smoke and burning debris across the compound. Several of the huts were already on fire. The ground was heaped with bodies, wounded and dead.

Castus slowed to a stride, beginning to feel the pulse of pain through his upper arm again. Here and there he could see figures locked in combat: a few of the Saxons were still putting up a fight. But mostly he just saw carnage. Gaiso's Franks had breached the compound gate at the same time as the Romans broke in, and now they were slaughtering with abandon. Squinting into the eddying smoke, Castus saw a woman lying dead outside a burning hut, her throat gashed across. He saw severed heads mounted on stakes: Saxons, or their luckless prisoners – it was impossible to tell.

A figure came running towards him, a short round-faced man in a filthy tunic, a rope halter swinging from his neck. He threw himself down on his knees before Castus, raising his hands.

'You're the commander here?' the little man said. 'Dominus – thank you! I am the master of the *Europa* of Dubris... Over twenty days we've been captives of these savages! Gods be praised you came when you did, before they could murder us all!'

He fell forward, clasping Castus by the ankle. It almost looked as though he was about to kiss his boots. Dismayed, Castus stepped back and managed to disentangle himself.

'Find your people,' he told the shipmaster. 'Get them down to the shore safely, as many as you can gather. And the other prisoners too. Go!'

The fire was spreading through the camp, but now Castus could hear the centurions shouting orders to their men, pulling them back into a disciplined formation. They would need to clear out what stores and plunder they could before the flames consumed everything. The Franks, though, were still busy seizing whatever they could find, killing any Saxons they rooted out of the huts.

Castus felt the strength ebbing from him, weariness pouring in, his mind fogging. After all the days of preparation, the long voyage downriver and through the islands, the planning for the battle, all was done. He should feel jubilant, he knew, but instead he was merely tired. He wanted to slump down and sit on the muddy ground, but he forced himself to remain standing, to wipe his sword and slip it back into his scabbard, to keep his head up and his senses alert. He was still the commander here.

Vetranio came striding out of the smoke, a band of his own troops behind him. 'Excellency,' he said, saluting. His face was seamed with blood. 'All enemy defenders cleared from the rear of the camp – a lot of them slipped away but we captured a hundred or so.'

He glanced around at the chaos between the burning huts, the bodies on the ground and the whooping Frankish warriors. 'If we could restrain our savage allies, dominus,' he said with a grimace of disgust, 'we might take a lot more captives and end this thing.'

But there was little chance of that. A gang of the barbarians had gathered around the massive figure of their chief, Gaiso. The chief saw Castus and grinned, lifting what looked like a muddy brown lump suspended by ropes from his fist.

'Victory, Roman!' Gaiso said. 'This – *Hroda*!'

The Saxon leader, Castus remembered. And now he recognised the object the chief was displaying to him. A human head, roughly hacked, partly burned and plastered in mud. Castus glanced away. The death of such an enemy meant nothing to him now.

Gaiso turned and roared to his men, then hurled the severed head into the air to fall among them.

The flames of the burning camp lit the night sky. The fires had spread on the breeze, rushing through the dry scrub and the reeds along the margins of the water. Another low boom of thunder came from the south, and the flicker of lightning showed through the fire-haze. All evening the storm had been getting closer.

Castus stood watching the fires from the deck of the *Bellona*, anchored in the channel half a mile from the Saxon camp. His upper arm and shoulder were bound tight with fresh linen, the wound in his bicep cleaned and stitched. Breathing deeply, he smelled the smoke and the dampness of the approaching storm. The men would get wet tonight, but they did not seem to care. Over on the near bank of the channel, the only area of dry clear ground, Romans and Franks were camped together. The sound of their songs and laughter drifted across to Castus as he stood on the deck. They had found plenty of wine among the plunder taken from the Saxon camp; the men had done well, and deserved their leisure.

Over fifty had died in the day's fighting. As many again badly injured. But the pirates had been wiped out, hundreds of them slain and the rest either taken captive or scattered to the surrounding marshes and creeks. Castus would send patrols out the next day to try and round up the stragglers. Half the Saxon boats had been destroyed, burnt or sunk, the rest captured. Thirty Roman prisoners had been liberated – most of them slave sailors from the merchant ships – and over a hundred Frankish civilians too. The ships themselves had been recovered, all five of them beached in a tidal creek near the camp with most of their cargoes still aboard.

The operation had been a success. Castus told himself that, as he had done several times before. The day after tomorrow he could assemble his flotilla once more, load his prisoners aboard the captured boats and make his way back through the islands to the Vahalis. Then the long haul back up the river to Colonia, and no doubt a triumphant welcome. Everything had gone as he had planned it. But still the risks he had taken were unnerving. How easily things could have gone otherwise. His victory was the work of chance, as much as discipline and preparation.

No more thinking. Soon he would be back in the Praetorium at Colonia, fed and rested. He would see his son again – having returned, just as he had promised, with only a fresh scar to show for it all. He smiled as he imagined telling Sabinus all about what had happened – he had never been good at telling stories, but in his mind he heard the boy's eager questions, the wonder and anticipation in his voice.

And then there was Marcellina. Castus had avoided thinking about her for the last few days. Now he recalled the note she had dropped for him in the street outside her husband's house. *I must see you. Soon.* The thought of her brought a warm stir of longing, mingled with unease. Something close to nausea but not unpleasant. He was nervous, he realised. After all these months of telling himself that he would never become involved with a free woman again, he felt his resolve weakening. But how would it ever happen?

A voice from along the deck, a sentry's challenge – '*Princeps*'. Castus stiffened at once, his right hand going to his sword hilt. Always the chance that Saxon fugitives would try swimming out to the Roman ships to wreak some last vengeance. Then, from the dark water to starboard, the watchword called back in a Germanic accent – '*Iuventutis!*' – and the lap of oars. Castus peered down from the rail and saw the shape of the Frankish boat drawing up alongside the galley, Bonitus standing at the prow.

'I disturb you?' the Salian chief said.

'No,' Castus replied quickly. 'I was... thinking. Come aboard.'

Bonitus stepped nimbly up over the stern of the galley and onto the deck. The boat shoved away behind him, the few men at the oars pulling silently. The sentries on the gangway went back to their posts, mumbling and all too sober.

Eumolpius had already fetched an extra stool from the shelter below the stern. Now both men sat, Castus tightening his jaw as the linen bindings pulled at his wound. Bonitus sniffed, gazing for a moment at the distant blaze.

'So, our fight is done,' he said. 'Soon we go our ways.'

Castus nodded. 'Our people worked well together.' He would have preferred to have kept the Frankish contingent back from the storming of the camp, but he could not deny that their numbers had been vital.

'Salii help the Romans, eh?' Bonitus said. 'Honour our treaty.'

'Against a common enemy,' Castus reminded him. 'The Saxons threatened us both.'

'Even so. Easy for us to leave things to you. But – we helped. So now maybe Romans think again of our desires?'

Castus frowned uncomfortably, clearing his throat. 'I cannot change the decision of the emperor, you know that.'

Bonitus gave a dissatisfied grunt, slapping his thigh. 'The decision of the fat man who speaks for the boy emperor!'

'I cannot change that,' Castus went on, stressing the words. 'But... give it time. I'll make it clear in my report that you served us well. That could help you, in the future.'

'Help? Hmm. Words cannot help when my people are hungry. Words cannot bring us good lands to farm.'

Castus raised a palm, nodding. If he had his way, it would be different. But he had so little power in these things – surely Bonitus could understand that?

'Be patient,' he said, though the words had a sour taste. He understood now that Bonitus had come to him as an emissary for all three of the Salian chiefs. Though he felt a connection of trust with Bonitus himself, he was still very wary of Gaiso in particular. He needed to tread carefully here. To offend the pride of these barbarians would be unwise.

'Ach, *patience...*' Bonitus said. He cleared his throat and spat quickly over the rail. Then he clapped his hands together. 'I remembered,' he said, with a changed tone, 'what I told to you, that night of the feasting. About the interpreter.'

'Bappo?' Castus asked. He remembered they had spoken about the death of Leontius, but how was the interpreter involved? He felt suddenly very alert, very awake.

Bonitus was nodding. 'That man who served you, yes, before he died. When he came to us with your message, he stayed several days. He drank with us, and we talked. He told of the death of the last commander, this man *Leontius.*'

Castus grunted, urging him to say more.

'For a time I thought to keep this to myself. Not to make problems. But now… we are brothers in combat, you and me. This man Bappo told me that Leontius was killed by his own men. By Romans. They went to give silver to the Chamavi, and they killed him then.'

Castus was sitting very upright. He had already guessed that to be true, but he needed to know more. 'He heard this from somebody?'

'No. He saw it. He was *there*.'

For a moment Castus could not speak. His body prickled with sweat as he realised the implications. Bappo had been the interpreter for Dexter's Stablesiani cavalry unit. If he had been present when Leontius was murdered… Nodding, digesting the meaning, Castus resolved to think no more of this for now. He would wait until he returned to Colonia, then call Dexter in on some pretext, and discover what he knew.

'He said also,' Bonitus went on, 'that you have many foes among the Romans. The governor; others too. Maybe some of them want to…' He made a slicing motion in the air with a flat palm. 'You also, like this.'

'I know that much,' Castus said. He had a sudden memory of Ganna's words to him, the previous autumn. *They think you are an animal… they yap at you and think you will dance for them…*

'Why do you fight for these rich men?' Bonitus asked. 'Why follow their commands, if they kill your soldiers and plot against you? They are unworthy!'

Castus shrugged. 'We don't choose our masters,' he said.

'Hah! And this is your *civilisation*! I am glad I am no Roman. We Franks are free men.'

'So you say,' Castus muttered quietly.

A heavy boom of thunder came from overhead, like an iron

drum rolling down steps. Both men glanced up, and lightning flashed through the smoky clouds. A moment later, the first drops of rain exploded off the deck of the galley.

Bonitus stood up, pulling his cloak across his head. The sentries on the gangway were already drawing up their hoods as they huddled into their capes. The sound of the rain drumming on the deck planks and beating on the water quickly became a loud steady hiss.

'You should sleep,' Bonitus said, oblivious to the rainwater streaming down his face. 'You look very tired, my friend.'

Then he turned, gesturing to his boat, and stepped out across the rail. Castus watched him go, then stumbled back into the shelter of the awning and down the ladder to the warm gloom of the stern cabin. For a long time he lay awake on his bunk, listening to the heavy percussion of the rain on the planking over his head. Everything was done, he told himself. He had no more worries now, and soon he would return home. But still the truth of what Bonitus had told him revolved in his mind, until finally fatigue overwhelmed him, and without another thought he tumbled into sleep.

CHAPTER XXII

The news reached them three days later, as they camped at the mouth of the Vahalis. Late evening, the sun low in the west and a breeze chopping at the grey waters of the estuary, Castus was seated outside his tent when the messenger found him, stripped to the waist as Eumolpius clipped his hair and shaved him of the thick stubble he had grown over the last few days; he wanted to make an early start the next morning.

'Dominus!' the messenger cried, saluting. 'Centurion Modestus reports that the Franks are looking ugly.'

'No change there,' Castus muttered, trying not to move his mouth as the orderly plied the razor across his cheeks.

'They're sounding ugly too, dominus. The centurion asks that you come and see for yourself.'

Castus gave an irritated grunt. He waited until Eumolpius had finished with the razor then stood up, wiped his chin with a rough towel and pulled on his tunic. He was buckling his belts as he strode towards the perimeter. Already he felt the warm prickling sensation at the nape of his neck, the premonition of trouble.

His men were camped on a stretch of open ground sloping to the estuary shore, a ditch and crude palisade of sharpened branches on three sides enclosing the tent lines. The fourth side was open to the river, and the muddy beach where the lighter galleys were hauled up stern-first out of the water. The *Bellona*, the troop barges and the recaptured merchantmen were moored just offshore. The Franks had their own camp, in the open a few hundred paces to the east along the shore; all day there had been smaller boats and canoes coming downriver to join them – to greet the warriors on their return from the expedition and escort them home, Castus had assumed. He had been looking forward to getting clear of his troublesome barbarian allies. Now, as he approached the eastern perimeter of his small encampment, he knew that things would not be so easy.

Already he could hear the noise: angry shouts and the rattle of spearshafts on shield rims. He knew the sounds all too well. He had grown used to the boisterous racket of the Franks, but this was something different. This was a belligerent noise, aggressive. The preparation for battle.

Modestus was waiting for him beside the palisade. He said nothing as Castus joined him, just raising an eyebrow and gesturing out across the ditch towards the barbarian camp.

'What's happening?' Castus demanded. A tremor ran up his spine, quickly suppressed, and his scalp was itching fiercely.

'No idea, excellency. One of those boats came down the river less than an hour ago, and they've been shouting and banging their weapons about ever since.'

Most of the Franks had gathered near the waterside, thronging around their beached vessels. Now, as Castus watched, several large bands began moving towards the Roman encampment, shouting and brandishing their shields. Castus could see no leaders among them; the barbarians seemed animated by a mutual grievance. The captives they had liberated from the Saxons had joined them, swelling their numbers.

'Call in the piquets and sentries,' Castus ordered. 'Stand the men to arms – all of them. Do it quickly, but quietly. No horns or signals.'

Modestus saluted and jogged away to the tent lines. Now Vetranio was striding up to join Castus at the palisade, a look of vexed confusion on his face. 'What's happening?' he called.

'Reckon we're about to find out,' Castus told him. A small group of Franks was approaching on foot, led by a man in a hooded cloak. Castus could not see his face, but he knew him by his stalking stride. He raised a palm, gesturing to the soldiers along the camp perimeter to lower their weapons.

'Bonitus,' he called.

The Salian chief strode forward alone as his companions dropped back. As he reached the ditch he halted and threw back his hood. His expression was grave, anger flickering across his brow. The low sun stretched his shadow out behind him.

'News from up the river,' Bonitus said, low and urgent. 'I come to warn you, Roman. Once only I say this.'

'Speak,' Castus demanded. He folded his arms, Vetranio and several of the soldiers gathering to flank him.

Bonitus drew in a long breath, staring back at Castus. 'Your governor has murdered the hostages of the Chamavi and Chattuari,' he said. 'All of them. In the arena at Colonia – he threw them to the beasts.'

For a moment Castus could not speak. Shock reeled through his head, and he clamped his jaw tight.

'Now,' Bonitus went on, 'the Chamavi king has sent the call for war to all the Frankish people. Already his warriors assemble. Bructeri, too, and Lanciones. Thousands are coming down the Vahalis in boats – to find *you*.'

Castus forced the words from his mouth. 'And the Salii will join with them?' A terrible hollow dread was opening inside him.

'We have a pact!' Vetranio broke in. 'The pact of iron – your people and ours!'

Bonitus turned to him, his voice loaded with contempt. 'This pact was against Saxons. Now Saxons are defeated. Our pact is ended.'

Vetranio choked out a gasp. 'These barbarians have a lawyer's conception of honour!'

'You gave your oath to the Chamavi,' Bonitus said to Castus, slow and quiet. 'You said their hostages would be treated well. Not harmed. Now this crime is upon you. You and all your men. We always knew Romans could never be trusted!'

Castus remained silent, struggling to think clearly. Tiberianus could barely have waited before summoning the hostages to Colonia; the Games of Apollo had begun only four days after the expedition departed. Had the governor intended this? The madness, the stupidity of it was stunning.

'But you,' he managed to say. 'Your people – you too will fight us?'

Bonitus shrugged one shoulder. 'As for me,' he said, 'I stand back from this. For the sake of my brother, who called you his friend. But if you attack us, then we are enemies. I come only to tell you – leave this place now. I try to hold the others back as long as I can. But leave, before you meet your death.'

For a heartbeat his expression shifted – was it sympathy that Castus saw there, or just disappointment and disdain? Then the Salian chief threw his hood back over his head, turned and stalked back to join his men. Beyond them, the other Franks were beginning to assemble just out of bowshot of the Roman lines.

'Excellency?' Vetranio said. 'What are your orders?'

Castus was still stunned by the news. He felt blinded, weakened. How had this happened? What vengeful god, what

evil fate had decreed this? Moments before he had been on the
cusp of total success, and now everything had been snatched
from him. Images tumbled through the fog of his mind: the
hostages – little more than boys, youths – torn to shreds by the
beasts in the arena. Massed hordes of barbarians, united by
fury, ready to pour across the Rhine. Tiberianus must have been
planning this for months, he realised, waiting only until Castus
was out of the way... What a fool he had been to leave Colonia!
But behind Tiberianus, no doubt, was Magnius Rufus. Castus
could almost see the man's glinting smile. And in Colonia itself
was his son, his Sabinus... Marcellina: where was she? Safe
behind the city's walls, or out in the country on her husband's
estate? He could do nothing to protect either of them now. It
was already too late. Panic thrashed at the edges of his mind.

'Dominus!' Vetranio said. 'Your orders?'

Gazing around him, Castus saw the tent lines emptying,
the troops assembling in their units. Such pitifully few men.
And beyond the meagre fortifications of the camp a vast empty
country, hostile, filled with the enemy. He looked at the faces
of the men surrounding him, seeing the fear and confusion in
their eyes. All were waiting for his word, his order.

'They don't outnumber us, not yet,' Vetranio was saying.
'We could try and hold out here...'

'Hold out for what?' Castus heard another centurion say.
'There's no reinforcement coming. Everyone in Colonia must
think we're dead men already... And there're thousands of
Chamavi coming down the river.'

'It could be a trick!' Vetranio said, angry desperation in his
voice. 'These bastard barbarians, they're all liars... I knew we
should never have trusted them!'

Think, Castus told himself. The fog in his mind was starting
to clear, his despair and shock shifting to rage. He felt the

blood moving hot and fast in his body, the strength returning to his limbs.

'We can't hold out here,' he said. *Never try to hold what you cannot defend.* 'Send word to Senecio – tell him to get the galleys in the water. Bring the troop barges close inshore. All the men are to fall back to the ships, the Twenty-Second to begin with, while the Second hold the perimeter. When the ships are manned and ready the last men fall back by sections, in a defensive cordon. Abandon everything we can't carry – and move fast. And sound the horns and trumpets – let them know we're ready for them. Go!'

Messengers were already spilling away from him. Breathing hard, Castus strode down the slope towards the water with Vetranio at his back. He could hear the centurions and optios crying out their orders, the trumpet notes wailing in the evening air. As he passed the last line of tents Eumolpius came jogging up beside him with his helmet and linen vest. Castus tore his left arm free of the sling, gasping as pain lanced from his wounded bicep, then struggled into the armour without breaking stride.

'We're too late!' Vetranio cried, pointing. 'The bastards are already inside the perimeter!'

Castus judged the scene with a single glance: the Frankish boats rowing in across the shallows, the warriors already scrambling overboard and gathering on the muddy shore. Gaiso was leading them, roaring threats at the thin screen of Roman oarsmen and marines that opposed him. Only a few paces away, the crews of the galleys were still heaving their vessels off the beach. The low sun glittered off the water, dying the estuary ruddy gold.

'You, Roman!' Gaiso yelled as he saw Castus approaching him. He was wading up through the shallows, carrying no shield but with a short throwing spear gripped in his right hand, point downwards. His mouth and moustache were flecked with spit as he shouted. 'You kill all hostage! Soon you feel wrath of Franks! Chamavi, Chattuari, Bructeri, Salii – all! Soon you die!'

The cordon of troops around the landing place contracted as the soldiers drew closer, shield to shield. Felix moved forward to take charge of them and stood at the centre of the line. Behind them, Nervian archers waited anxiously, bows strung and arrows nocked. Castus pushed his way between them and confronted the Frankish chief, Vetranio at his shoulder. Where was an interpreter when he needed one?

'The hostages are no concern of ours!' he said, anger clipping his words. 'Go back to your own lands and people in peace, or you'll be the ones feeling our wrath!'

He had no idea if Gaiso understood what he had said. His sword was still in its scabbard, his shield arm useless. The chief took a few more steps, out of the lapping water and up onto the muddy beach. He lifted his spear back over his shoulder. Behind him, his warriors waited, tensed in expectation.

'Romans!' the chieftain cried. 'Always enemy!'

Castus saw the flex of his arm, the spear canted back; he took a step to one side, drawing his sword in a wide slash as the chieftain hurled the spear. His blade cut air, the missile darting past him, and Castus heard Vetranio's cry from behind him. A glance over his shoulder: the spear had caught Vetranio in the chest, piercing him straight through his body.

Already Gaiso was dragging the sword from his scabbard. He never got the blade clear; six bows thrummed, and a dozen darts and javelins arced down from the Roman ranks. The chief's battle cry broke to a scream of pain as the arrows struck him. For a moment he remained standing, swaying on his feet. Then a last javelin lanced through his hip, and Gaiso flung up his arm, turned slightly, and fell dead into the muddy water.

Nothing for it now.

'Attack!' Castus yelled. 'Drive them off the beach!'

With a ragged yell the soldiers stormed forward, shields together and Felix in the lead, smashing the Franks back into the water. The archers were shooting fast, bundles of arrows clasped against every bow stave, lofting missiles over the combat in the shallows and down into the enemy boats. The artillery on the galleys were shooting too, now, darting bolts across the water. Men who had fought side by side as brothers only days before were now slaughtering each other.

Castus knelt for a moment beside Vetranio. The man was already dead, blood on his lips, his hands still clasped around the shaft of the spear jutting from his chest. Standing, Castus saw Senecio running along the beach.

'Dominus,' the old navarch gasped, fighting for breath. 'The ships are ready, we're just getting the anchors up now... But we need more time! Most of the crews are still ashore...'

'You'll have all the time you need,' Castus told him. 'You're in charge of the embarkation – make sure everyone gets aboard. Take all of our injured and dead, too, and the liberated prisoners from the ships. I'll remain ashore until everything's done.'

The fight at the riverbank was already over, the last of the Franks falling back to their boats and rowing clear, leaving their dead lolling in the water. Felix was shouting orders, forming his men up again on the beach. He seemed to have taken few casualties. *First bout to us*, Castus thought grimly.

But he could hear the clamour beyond the eastern perimeter, the thunder of spears striking shields, the shouts of defiance. With one of their leaders down, the Salii might hang back a while longer, but now they were fired by revenge their attack would not be long in coming. Along the palisade the legionaries of the Second were assembled in readiness, Modestus pacing along behind them growling threats and encouragement.

'Claudius Modestus,' Castus called as he jogged towards him. 'Vetranio's dead. You're now senior centurion in command of the detachment.'

Modestus stared for a moment, wide-eyed. Then he saluted with a grin.

Across the tattered palisade and the crude ditch, the throng of barbarians was growing. The defences might hold them back for a short time, but they had the numbers to make a concerted rush. Behind him, Castus could hear the men of the Twenty-Second hurrying down to the shore, abandoning their tents and baggage and their smoking cooking fires. Again the cloud of despair rose in his mind; even if he got his men clear of this place, what could he do? He needed to get back to Colonia, organise some sort of defence, find his son and Marcellina... But the best he could pray for was a few more hours of life.

He shook his head, trying to muster his thoughts. He needed to be firm now. The men around him were relying on his judgement utterly. A flush of pride ran through him – and fear as well. If he failed here, all was lost.

Scanning the barbarian front line, he picked out Bonitus, standing slightly apart from the others with his own band of household warriors around him. The Salian chief did not glance in his direction, but Castus knew that Bonitus was aware of him. He seemed to radiate a strange stillness, a calm that could erupt at any moment. But for now his inaction was holding the angrier of his fellow warriors back.

'Dominus,' a messenger called, panting up behind him. 'All the ships are manned and ready. Troop barges coming in now.'

'Good,' Castus said curtly. *Thank the gods.* 'Modestus – on my command we fall back to the centre of the encampment by

308

units and form a shield perimeter. Then retreat slowly to the beach. Understand?'

'Yes, dominus!' At once Modestus was stalking away, snarling out orders. Castus watched him, then looked back at the Franks. Already they were massing forward, the veterans among them moving to the front to form attack wedges.

Waiting, counting heartbeats. Modestus had moved around the perimeter now.

'Hornblower,' Castus called. 'Give the signal!'

The brass notes rang out, and with a single movement the men at the palisade hefted their shields and ran back towards the centre of the enclosure. Before the Franks could react they had formed up again, a solid buttress of shields and levelled spears. Then the barbarians let out a vast yell, and began to surge forwards.

'Back, back!' Modestus was shouting. 'Shields up, eyes to the front! Slow and steady now, boys!'

Castus took his position at the centre of the formation, beside the trumpeters and standard-bearer, as slowly the mass of Roman troops retreated. Two shuffling steps back, then a pause to dress the lines, then two more steps. A steady collective grunt of breath; the low mutter of commands. All the while the shields held tight, every man facing out towards the enemy.

Now the Franks were swarming across the abandoned fortifications, heaving aside the palisade, yelling and brandishing their spears. Castus watched them from between the ranks of his legionaries. They poured into the camp, whooping and screaming, slashing wildly at the leather of the tents as if they were slaying the men who had sheltered within them. Others kicked at the cooking fires, or stabbed at the discarded bedrolls. Castus saw the chieftain Flaochadus proudly raising a camp stool above his head like a battle trophy. There was no sign of Bonitus.

'Few more paces, boys!' Modestus cried. 'Look at the bastards! They don't dare face us now...'

Sure enough, the Franks were hanging back from the retreating formation. Some yelled and waved their spears, a few lobbed javelins or loosed slingshot to jab and rattle against the buttress of shields. But Flaochadus was not going to lead an attack, and without another commander the barbarians lacked cohesion. For a moment Castus wondered whether a sudden rush could scatter them. But no – barely a hundred legionaries held his formation, and the Franks outnumbered them now.

Mud beneath his boots; the smell of the estuary filling the air. Castus ordered one last trumpet signal, and the formation broke as the men piled back towards the waiting barges, splashing through the shallows and scrambling aboard. There was a smaller boat waiting to take him out to the flagship but Castus remained standing on the beach, staring back at the Frankish horde as they poured down the slope after the retreating soldiers. When the last of his men was safely afloat, he paced backward to the boat and swung himself aboard. A spatter of flung spears and slingshot struck the mud and the water, then the keel grated and lifted as the oarsmen pushed off from the beach.

CHAPTER XXIII

Leaning on the rear ballista mounting of the *Bellona*, Castus stared back over the stern. In the fading light he could see the waterway to the east, where the estuary narrowed into the mouth of the Vahalis, teeming with vessels. The Frankish boats had been joined by the captured Saxon longboats, now fully manned and armed, and a host of smaller craft. They had made no move to attack, yet, but they seemed determined to stop the Roman flotilla from moving up the river.

'Like something out of Homer, eh?' he said.

Senecio, beside him, snorted a mirthless laugh.

The deck of the flagship was crowded with marines and archers, while the oarsmen pulled slowly against the incoming tide to keep the *Bellona* stationary in midstream. The smaller galleys and the troop barges were positioned on either flank, their prows facing the river mouth.

'What do you think?' Castus asked. 'Could we break through them?'

Senecio gave an appraising sigh. 'Possibly. With the tide behind us and a scrap of this south wind we could certainly try. But we wouldn't get through them without losses. Then we've got a long pull up the river, and if your barbarian friend's right we could be meeting opposition all the way. Hard work. Especially dragging these behind us.'

He jerked his thumb over his shoulder. Off to the right, the five big merchant ships they had recaptured from the Saxons were still at anchor. Only one of them – the *Europa* of Dubris – still had her sails. The Saxons had taken the sailcloth from the others, and it had been burnt in the wreck of their camp. They would have to be towed by the galleys. Castus stared across at the *Europa*; all the wounded men were aboard, and most of the civilian crews of the ships. Her hold was packed with two hundred Saxon prisoners.

'What cargo are the other four carrying?'

'Fodder, timber, naval stores, woollens,' Senecio said with a shrug. 'We tried to lighten them, and they've only got skeleton crews aboard, but even so...'

Castus nodded. Hauling the ships would slow down his galleys, however lightly they were laden.

'What other options do we have?' he asked quietly. The deck rocked beneath him with the motion of the tide.

'We could run south, back the way we came,' Senecio told him. 'If they don't pick us off in the islands we could make the estuary of the Scaldis. Two days upriver and we abandon ship and march across country. Eight days, maybe nine, to Colonia.'

'Too long.'

Senecio had a calculating look on his face. Clearly he had another plan in mind. Castus waited.

'Or,' the navarch said, 'we could row out westwards against the tide. Out of the estuary and into the open sea. The barbarians might think we were making for the British coast, but once we've got enough sea room we could turn and get the wind behind us, run north-east up the coast to the mouth of the Rhine. Not an easy passage, especially in the dark. But the *Europa*'s got a pilot aboard who knows that landfall well enough. He could tell us the sea marks.'

'Then what? Haul up the Rhine straight through Frankish territory?'

'They wouldn't be expecting us...' Senecio said, obviously still pondering his plan even as he spoke. 'We could slip around behind them, keep to the midstream and row by night. It's still a risk, dominus, I can't claim otherwise. But it'd take us where we need to be.'

Castus chewed at his lip, frowning into the gathering darkness. If the Franks saw them running out towards the open sea, would they follow? And then how would he keep his ships together out in deep water by night? He raised his head and looked at the sky. A low moon, shredded by moving cloud. The breeze was freshening from the south.

'Could the ships make it?'

'The smaller galleys were built for coastal work as well as rivers. The barges too. As for the old *Bellona* – she took a battering when we ran through those stakes. I'd prefer to get her out of the water, caulk her seams, try and get to those leaks around her bow... But she'll swim, for now.'

Castus nodded. He felt a swelling tension in his shoulders and back, a cold flush across his brow. His throat was tight and dry. Yet he had done well to get this far, to get his men aboard the ships without losses. Some god had granted him a reprieve. But how long would it last? Again that terrible ache of despair, the sense of control spilling from his hands, events rushing away from him. He shuddered, then clenched his jaw. *As far as anyone at Colonia knows, we're all dead men already.*

'Let's do it.'

An hour later, full dark, the wind picking up and the incoming tide flowing strongly. Creak and plash of oars as the galleys pulled hard for the west. Behind them, four big hulls were

313

anchored abreast across the estuary; as Castus peered into the darkness over the stern of the flagship he saw the boats leaving, the last men pausing to chop through the anchor cables. Then the first tongues of flame licked up from the decks, dancing brightly in the breeze. The ships swung, loose from their moorings, the fires in their holds burning more fiercely now as the current carried them, drifting and turning, up towards the armada of Frankish boats blocking the river mouth.

The flames cast a glow high into the sky, illuminating the dark estuary and casting the faces of the men sweating at the oars into stark relief. Ahead of them, the *Europa* was reaching down the channel with the south wind on her beam. A stout and weatherly ship, Castus thought; she would continue across the sea to the British coast, carrying the wounded men and the civilians to safety. For the rest of them, a harder night lay ahead.

Making his way to the helmsman's post, Castus felt the ship already beginning to roll with the motion of the waves. Every man aboard had a sailor's healthy dread of the open sea at night. The lighter galleys especially would have a wet time of it. But every ship had a covered lantern at her masthead, and orders to light it once they had cleared the land. Hopefully that would enable them to stay together. The *Europa*'s pilot had said there was an old fort and a lighthouse at the mouth of the Rhine, abandoned long ago but still a good sea mark if they reached it by dawn. Beyond that, Castus thought, they were in the hands of the gods now.

Night filled the estuary, eclipsing the distant shores. To the east the fires of the burning ships still lit the sky, and no Frankish boats had tried to pass them. Sacrificing the ships had been Castus's idea. He would account for the losses; escape was the more pressing consideration. Beneath him, he could hear the timbers of the old galley beginning to creak and wail, the incoming waves dashing around her prow and foaming over the oar-blades. The air was thick with the smell of salt water.

Quietly, steadily, the small flotilla slipped along the estuary. Castus remained standing beside the helmsman; he knew he should rest while he had the chance, but if the oarsmen could not sleep then neither would he. A figure came along the gangway, stumbling with the unfamiliar motion of the deck.

'Dominus,' Felix said, and Castus saw his twisted smile in the faint moonlight. 'Why is it, I ask myself, that whenever you're in command I find myself out at sea someplace?'

'Sorry!' Castus said with a grin. 'Such is fate though, eh?'

Felix shrugged, unconsoled. 'Just don't let me puke into the wind,' he muttered.

Another two hours into the night, and the first deep sea swells lifted the ship, the waves rolling in against her beam and sending windblown spray across the deck. The *Bellona* shuddered and rolled, but the oarsmen kept on hauling, grunting with the effort now, cursing between clenched teeth. Over in the lee scuppers a handful of men crouched at the rail, gasping and retching. Felix was not alone in his seasickness.

'Choppy for midsummer,' Castus said to Senecio as the navarch joined him before the stern canopy.

The old man smiled ruefully. 'Northern seas,' he said. 'Never can trust them! We'll be all right, even if the wind picks up some more. Another couple of hours, then we can give the oarsmen a rest and run north under sail. Only danger then's if the wind veers west and we get the shore under our lee – we need to keep enough sea room from the coast, and try not to stray too far northwards. Look there,' he said, pointing out into the wet darkness ahead. Castus peered forward, squinting, and made out the distant sparks of light dancing in the gloom. 'The other ships have got their lanterns up,' Senecio said.

The ship butted onwards, the rowing master crying out the stroke now, over the noise of the wind and the rush of the sea. Castus shed his linen vest and pulled a cloak around his shoulders. The total darkness that surrounded the ship was unnerving; he sensed the constant motion of the waves rather than saw then. When he looked up he could make out the bare mast and yard swaying against the sky, picked out by the scraps of moonlight. He had lost all sense of time, distance and direction.

Senecio at least seemed to have an idea of where they were. He paced up and down the gangway, sure-footed on the rolling deck, glancing up sometimes towards the faint moon, nodding, sniffing the breeze. Finally he cried out an order, and the deck crew rushed to the braces. The helmsman leaned hard on the tiller bars, and the *Bellona* swung steadily around, lurching a little, until the wind was under her stern and the racing waves foamed along her sides. The sail billowed out, the motion of the ship changing as she steadied on the new course, and men on the rowing benches relaxed with a vast groan and shipped their oars.

Castus seated himself on the stool just before the canopy, and took a mouthful of bread and a gulp of watered wine. Other men were creeping along the gangways, doling out food and water to the exhausted oarsmen. Above them the big canvas sail bellied, the rigging creaking. Scanning the sea ahead, Castus was glad to see the winking lights of the mast-lanterns on the other ships. He tried to count them, but the lights came and went. A short while later he could see nothing. Flurries of light rain spattered the deck around him.

Now they were moving more steadily, Castus felt the tiredness seeping through him. The events of the last few hours had drained his strength and harrowed his nerves. Even now, danger surrounded them. Once they got to the Rhine, he thought, they still had a long journey upriver, along a frontier under enemy attack. Would news of the threatened invasion have reached the towns and cities of the province yet? His tired mind conjured images of panic and disaster... All he must think about was getting himself and his men back to the river, back to Colonia. Back to where they might, perhaps, make a difference. But still the images came: Marcellina, who had survived the Pictish invasion in Britain that had destroyed her family, once more facing barbarian attack. His son, believing that his father had broken his promise to return, had forsaken him... *No*, he told himself. *Enough.*

'Dominus, lookout reckons he can hear breaking surf out to starboard.'

Castus snapped awake; he had dropped into a stunned doze on his stool. But the crewman was speaking to Senecio, not to him. He got up, stretching his limbs. The wind caught at his cloak and flapped it around his body. Senecio was giving quiet commands to the helmsman, telling him to steer a little more to port.

Spray burst suddenly over the deck, and a heartbeat later a juddering impact knocked Castus off his feet. Shouts all around him, screams from the men on the benches. Sprawled on the wet planking, Castus heard a ripping screech, then a noise like a thundercrack. He thought the ship had been hit by lightning – then the rigging was collapsing down onto the deck around him, the mast heeling over and toppling forward over the weather bow.

'She's struck!' the helmsman yelled. 'Rudders are dead! We're aground!'

Castus was back on his feet before he could think, bracing himself against the tilting deck. The whole forward end of the

Bellona was a mess of fallen timbers and flapping sail, the water bursting over the side. Senecio was standing amidships, legs braced, howling orders to the deck crew, but all seemed to be chaos, men stumbling and shouting, floundering between the rowing benches and across the gangway.

'Oars out!' Senecio cried. 'Rowers to the benches! Back her off! Deck crew and marines – clear the mast away!'

'What's happened?' Castus said. All around was blackness and racing water.

'Sandbank, I reckon,' Senecio said, his words tight and hard. 'Brought the mast down when we struck. Keel's bedded hard – you can feel it.'

The ship was buckling against the pressure of the water on her beam. Men scrambled along the rail now with axes and knives, cutting away the mess of rigging. Some of the upper oars were already working, threshing at the black water, but the lower-tier men had bolted up on deck when the ship struck.

A creak from below, then a bang, and the whole hull shivered. Castus could feel the old timbers groaning beneath him. A man came up the ladder from the hold.

'Bracing cable's parted!' he called out. 'Water flooding in from the bow!'

With a heave and a shout the deck crew wrestled the fallen mast over the side. The heavy baulk of timber swam for a moment, wreathed in strands of rigging, then a swell caught it and turned it, ramming it back against the hull of the ship. The men at the benches were heaving on the oars, cursing as they pulled, trying to drag the bows clear of the sandbank and off into open water.

Again the mast slammed against the hull. Castus saw figures tumbling from the opposite rail; he could not tell if they had fallen or jumped overboard. In his mind was nothing but stricken

318

terror and anguish. His chest heaved as he tried to draw breath, and his limbs felt dead.

'One more pull, boys, and she's free!' the rowing master cried. There were more men at the oars now, bending and then hurling themselves back across the benches. Castus saw Senecio, stamping along the gangway, waving his wooden hand at the deck crew and ordering them to fend off the floating mast before it rammed them again.

The whole deck heaved beneath him, and Castus staggered. For a slow sliding moment it seemed as if the *Bellona* was free once more in the water, the oars steadying her as the stern lifted with the swell. Then cracking sounds rippled through the hull, like dry sticks exploding in a fire. A surge of water punched at the side of the ship and she twisted, oars rising in disarray.

Castus staggered again as the deck sloped suddenly, flung out an arm to save himself and snatched only air. Wails and screams from the crew, another burst of spray, and Castus felt himself hurled sideways.

The rail struck hard against his hip. For a moment his fingers brushed slick wet wood, then he was tumbling in blackness. He opened his mouth to shout and water slammed against the back of his throat.

Panic gripped him. He was striking out with both arms, feeling the surge of the waves dragging him. The water pressed against him, and the next wave pushed his head under.

Pressure in his ears, rushing and murderous. He felt the water dragging him down, the heft of the cloak around his neck throttling him. With clawed fingers he ripped at the sodden wool until the gold brooch snapped and the cloak was gone. His throat was clenched tight, trapped breath punching in his chest. Then his head burst into air again and he sucked down breath.

No sign of the ship. Nothing but roaring air and surging water. Castus was kicking hard, thrashing with his arms, but his boots were weighing his legs and his injured bicep sent screaming pain through his shoulder. Once more his head went under.

Submerged, he felt a strange sensation of calm. All he had to do was stop fighting, let the water carry him. Everything was lost now. All his plans in ruins. Better to surrender to the fate that meant to destroy him. He felt buoyant, cushioned by the water. All he had to do was open his mouth and breathe it in...

Violent energy jolted him into motion, and he kicked hard. His head was above the surface, but only for a moment. He blinked, gasped, and then sank again. He knew his strength was ebbing now. Soon it would end.

Another gasping breath, and he sucked in water. His throat clenched against it, and he felt his lungs compressing, strangling him from inside. He blew out, and tried to hold his breath tight. No chance. His consciousness had shrunk to one single tiny point of light as the last strength died in his body.

The water surged again, carrying him.

As the spark of life flickered, he reached out and felt his fingertips brush through something beneath the water.

Sand.

PART FOUR

CHAPTER XXIV

They met the first of the refugees only a mile from Colonia Agrippina. Civilians with wagons and carts, some in carriages and many more on foot, moving fast away from the city, their faces blanched with fear. Luxorius nudged his pony to the side of the road and rode past them along the verge. Strangely, he had already seen a number of other people hurrying in the opposite direction.

'What do they think they're doing?' he asked. 'Some are going towards the city and others running away from it!'

'Civilians,' said one of the agentes in rebus riding behind him. 'Don't know what's good for them! Run about like chickens at the first breath of war!'

They had felt that first breath themselves only five miles back down the road, at the last posting station. The Chamavi and Chattuari, it was reported, and any number of other strangely named folk had crossed the Rhine and were already ravaging the countryside west of Tricensima. Or perhaps had already burnt Tungris. Or perhaps were rowing wildly up the river in canoes intent on massacring the population of Colonia. The Bructeri were rumoured to be massing in warbands to the east of the Rhine, ready to advance on the city.

Luxorius had taken the news calmly. He had not expected the invasion quite so soon, but barbarians, as he knew from his study of Roman histories, were passionate people and inclined to fly suddenly to arms. The threat of their imminent arrival gave a certain urgency to his mission, but he saw no reason yet to fear.

A little further down the road, and the trees fell away on either side. Across the flat plain, the red-brick walls of the city appeared. It looked formidable enough, the gates strong and the drum towers with their ornamental brickwork topped with battlements and artillery embrasures. But Colonia had been taken and sacked by the Franks just over forty years before, Luxorius remembered. He doubted that the defences had been much improved since then. Shows of strength could be deceptive. He rode up to the south gate, his two-man escort going ahead of him to clear a path through the people thronging the road. Both agentes in rebus were plainly dressed in military cloaks and tunics, but both were armed and carried imperial warrants. The guards at the gate allowed the party through without question.

In the streets of the city the same confusion reigned. Many of the shops already had heavy wooden shutters bolted in place, and the porticos were full of citizens and slaves milling around, some loading carts while others just stared in fearful indecision. There were soldiers, too, loitering at the street corners with no sign of command or control; some of them gazed at Luxorius as he passed, and some even saluted. With his dark complexion and fine clothing, he was clearly an imperial official of some sort. Perhaps, Luxorius thought, they believed he had come to take charge of the defence?

He remembered the city well from his last visit in the spring, and knew the governor had his residence in the north-east quarter, near the river. With the two agents at his heels he announced himself to the sentries at the door, and after only a short wait he was shown in.

'What can I do for you?' Tiberianus asked, with an impatient tone. He was in the main audience chamber of the house, pacing the rug as slaves and attendants came and went. 'As you can see, your arrival comes at a time of considerable urgency!'

'Myself and my escort have ridden three days from Treveris, clarissimus,' Luxorius told him. 'A bath and a meal would be most kind. Also, perhaps, a brief talk, in confidence if you please.'

'A talk?' Tiberianus said, pausing mid-pace. A brief quiver of concern crossed his face. Then he widened his nostrils at the eunuch, tipping his head back and sticking out his chest to try and appear taller and more imposing. 'Strange, I would say, for his eminence the prefect to send his own cubicularius and a couple of imperial agents on such a duty!'

'It is a matter of some delicacy,' Luxorius said, angling his head as he smiled.

The governor paused another moment, then ordered the slaves to leave the room and close the doors behind them. He composed himself.

'Well?'

'I'm somewhat curious,' the eunuch said, 'why you ordered the barbarian hostages to be executed in the arena recently. My master is also curious. Perhaps you could explain?'

'Explain?' the governor said, flushing slightly. Clearly he found the question impertinent. 'Why... what is there to explain? Our emperor, the Sacred Augustus himself, did much the same at Treveris a decade ago...'

'Ah yes, but the most blessed emperor had a large army in the field. Whereas you have only a scattered array of garrison troops and some cavalry. It might seem a rather bold gesture, one might say.'

'A what? A...' Tiberianus stammered. His anger was mounting, but Luxorius could tell he was nervous too. 'But your own master – his eminence Junius Bassus – agreed this course of action! I have the letter right here – I was only just consulting it once more...'

He pivoted from the waist, peering around the room, then snatched up a tablet from the side table. 'Here!' he said. 'Read it for yourself!'

Luxorius took the tablet between finger and thumb. He opened it, scanned the script briefly, then closed it again and traced the broken wax of the seal.

'Oh dear,' he said, shaking his head. 'Oh dear no. A crude forgery, I'm afraid. This resembles the seal of the prefect's office, but it's certainly not genuine.'

'Not genuine?' The governor's voice had risen to a cracked squawk.

'No. And in the circumstances,' Luxorius said, holding up the tablet, 'this might seem a rather treasonous item. And passing falsified documents is a serious offence, of course. I suggest you destroy it immediately.' He tossed the tablet down onto the couch beside him.

Tiberianus stared at the tablet, his mouth working as he tried to speak, or perhaps to breathe. 'But... But I acted in good faith. I... It wasn't even my idea – one of my friends, a very prominent citizen, suggested it to me! I was careful to seek the agreement of the relevant authorities before acting...'

'Normally,' Luxorius said, still smiling, 'I would be compelled to report this to the prefect himself. There is, however, another matter.'

'Another?' Tiberianus said, visibly trembling now. He made an effort to steady himself.

'Yes,' Luxorius told him. 'Several days ago, a letter reached Treveris, addressed to his eminence. I had the opportunity to see it. The letter was from one Julius Dulcitius, a local grain merchant, I believe, and contained some very troubling accusations, against yourself and several named others.'

The governor said nothing, his nostrils flaring as he struggled to remain calm.

'The letter alleges that you and these others conspired in the murder of Dux Valerius Leontius last year. That you arranged the, ah... *rerouting* of silver payments intended as subsidies to the barbarian tribes into your own private coffers.'

'This is outrageous!' Tiberianus broke in. 'Absolute lies. Dulcitius is a person of no account, a known fraudster. No doubt his wife put him up to this!'

'Nevertheless, such accusations require investigation, I'm afraid,' Luxorius said. The agents behind him shuffled their boots. The eunuch could understand their satisfaction; men of the agentes in rebus always enjoyed the humiliation of their betters.

'I... I can account for everything, I assure you...' Tiberianus stammered.

'I doubt that. However, I have a few other things to discuss with you, and perhaps we may reach some... accommodation. My escort of loyal imperial agents will quite happily wait outside, I'm sure.'

He signalled to the two agents, who nodded discreetly. Before they could move, the sound of rapid footsteps on tile came from the next room, and a shouted word of command. The double doors swung open and a man strode into the audience chamber. He was tall, with a robust air, in late middle age and wore an ornamented military cape and a swordbelt with a flashy scabbard. An army officer walked behind him, a drawn-looking man with a weak chin and bulbous eyes.

'Clarissimus,' the tall man declared to the governor, with an approximation of a salute, 'everything's prepared for my departure tomorrow. I have three thousand men waiting at Juliacum. Tribune Gaudiosus here will remain in charge of the city defences.'

The man stopped talking, noticing Luxorius and the two agents for the first time. He peered at them with a look of steely contempt.

'May I introduce Flavius Luxorius,' the governor said, 'cubicularius to his eminence the Praetorian Prefect of Gaul.'

'A chamberlain?' the tall man said, and chuckled to himself. 'So this is what the empire sends us in our time of need, eh? A gelding! And a pair of mules!'

The bigger of the two agents cleared his throat loudly, hoisting his swordbelt.

'And this,' Tiberianus went on hurriedly, gesturing to the tall man, 'is the distinguished Piavonius Magnius Rufus. On my own authority, in this situation of emergency, I have appointed him commander of all military forces in the province of Germania Secunda. It was his idea, in fact, to make an example of our barbarian hostages.'

'Indeed?' Luxorius said, smiling once more. Rufus drew himself up to his full height, hand on his sword hilt. 'Strange though,' the eunuch went on. 'I had believed that his excellency Aurelius Castus was commander in this region.'

'Aurelius Castus is a traitor!' Rufus snapped. 'He deserted his post on some spurious pretext and is currently either dead or collaborating with the enemy! I have taken over his command.'

'Did he not go to confront some pirates? I believed that was the case...'

'Ox shit!' Rufus said. 'There was only one witness to this supposed piracy, and he was an accomplice in the deception!'

'This witness, the sailor,' the governor said, his nerve apparently bolstered by Rufus's presence. 'I've had him arrested and questioned, on my own authority. Before he... *expired* he confessed that the whole thing was a ruse, invented by Castus and his confederates. I've also seized the former commander's household, and placed those of his staff remaining in the city in confinement. They too will be questioned!'

'I see,' Luxorius said, in as mild a tone as he could muster. 'How extraordinary. I suppose you must also have sent an urgent message to Treveris, to alert the Caesar to this threatened invasion and so on? I'm afraid no such message had been received when I left.'

'Why bother?' Rufus said. 'Here in Gaul we can look after ourselves! The empire's let us down too many times before. Now we look to our own defences.'

'And you have, no doubt, considerable experience in military matters?'

Luxorius saw the tall man bridle, the muscles in his neck bunch. Rufus had a powerful physique, but much of it was fat, and the taint of vanity lingered around him like rich scent. He took two steps towards Luxorius, glaring. 'More than you, I'll warrant,' he said, and then thumped his chest. 'I have true Roman blood in my veins – the blood of the Caesars! And when the hour of destiny arrives, men of true blood know their duty. But what would a creature such as you understand of that? What are you, an Egyptian? Aethiopian? You don't even have any *balls*!'

Luxorius merely raised an eyebrow. He remained smiling, moving his head slightly forward as he held the man's gaze. After a moment, Rufus gave a grunt of disgust and turned away.

'I leave for Juliacum at first light,' he told the governor. 'Gaudiosus will act in my name from now on. I suggest you keep this... *person*... confined within the city. For his own protection!'

He saluted once more, a curt aggressive gesture, then strode from the room.

A pause, the air seeming to settle back after the doors slammed. Tiberianus gulped, visibly, then drew in breath through his nostrils once more. 'You mentioned,' he said, in a rather tremulous voice, 'that you have something to discuss?'

Two hours later, Luxorius was descending the smooth stone steps into the cellars beneath the Praetorium. He held a scented cloth over his nose and mouth; the air down in the depths reeked of damp, stale urine and river mud. The sentry's lantern cast a wavering light over the ancient vaults above them.

Everything so far, the eunuch considered, was going well. The governor was clearly a weak-willed man, easily led, and the eunuch had little doubt that he could be bent to requirements. The letter from Bassus had been genuine enough; Luxorius had witnessed the prefect's secretary writing it, and had managed to slightly alter the seal before it was despatched. The execution of the hostages, of course, would provide due provocation for a barbarian attack, which in turn would give the Caesar opportunity to demonstrate his martial abilities. All the better if the governor could be blamed for the offence. Bassus would not care, and it gave Luxorius a useful bargaining tool.

Now all the eunuch had to do was ensure that Crispus was drawn into a position of danger, where he might meet an untimely demise without arousing suspicion; he had already despatched one of his agents with a message to Treveris. The appearance of Magnius Rufus was unexpected, but hopefully the man would soon be gone, off to command his scratch army. With any luck, the eunuch thought, Rufus would shortly receive a salutary drubbing on the battlefield.

The sentry turned a corner and led Luxorius into an arched corridor lined with heavy wooden doors. A pair of jailors stood before one of them, and a repeated thudding noise came from the far side of it. Luxorius halted before the cell and ordered the jailor to open the locks. The imperial mandate he carried gave him considerable powers, far more than the governor knew, but he was aware that he must use them discreetly.

A squeal of rusty hinges as the door swung back. From the noise, Luxorius had been expecting the prisoner to be some powerful brute of a man. Instead a balding and rather scrawny figure confronted him, blinking in the glare of the lamps.

'You are Musius Diogenes,' Luxorius asked, holding up a finger. 'Princeps officiorum to the dux, Aurelius Castus?'

The man nodded, baffled. He appeared slightly crazed. Luxorius was disappointed; he had wanted a more capable accomplice than this. But the man would have to do.

'Come,' he said. The jailers and the sentry had already retreated to the far end of the corridor. There was a table in an alcove between the arches, bread and a jug of wine set upon it. Luxorius waited while the prisoner ate and drank, then told him quickly and clearly what needed to be done. Diogenes listened, nodding. Now that the shock of his unexpected release had passed, he appeared a little more intelligent.

'Unfortunately,' the eunuch said, 'smuggling you out of both Praetorium and city undetected would be difficult. But there is another way. Follow me, please.'

He led the man along another, narrower, corridor and down some steps, the lantern lifted before him. The smell grew worse, and Luxorius pressed the cloth to his face with his free hand. At the bottom of a short flight of steps was a brick-lined pit, the heavy wooden cover that had sealed it shifted to one side. The stench rising from the pit was sickeningly intense.

'I'm reliably informed,' Luxorius said through the muffling cloth, 'that this leads to the main sewer of the city. It's quite large enough to wade through. Only a few hundred paces and it opens onto the riverbank below the city wall – I've arranged for the gate that bars the far end to be left open, and a boat is waiting at the bank.'

Diogenes swallowed, gagging slightly as he stooped over the pit.

'Could I?' he said, gesturing to the scented cloth.

Luxorius hesitated, but thrust the cloth at him. Diogenes tied it quickly over his nose and mouth, then with surprising agility dropped and swung himself down into the pit. A heavy splash came from below, then a gust of reeking air that sent Luxorius staggering backwards, almost tripping on the steps. He mastered himself, and heard the faint washing sounds of a body moving through fluid. Amazing, he considered, that all the great and glorious cities of the empire hide such torrents of filth beneath them...

With a shiver of repulsion, he put his foot against the wooden cover and nudged it back across to seal the pit. He had done all he could for Aurelius Castus, but now he had other matters to arrange. He climbed quickly back up the steps, eager for the clean air of the city above.

CHAPTER XXV

Sun on the back of his head. Then the hiss of surf, and the water surged over him. A cough racked his body; he gulped water, then choked. Flinging out his arms, pushing with his legs, he dragged himself up the slope of wet sand. It had been dark before, but now the day was here. When he tried to open his eyes the light was blinding, and the salt stung. His left arm was in agony.

Another incoming wave soaked him, and with a further effort of will he dragged himself on. The sand was dense and wet between his grasping fingers. He could taste it in his mouth, gritting between his teeth. He needed fresh water, wine, anything to ease the pain in his throat. Behind his closed eyes, images danced. He saw his son playing a ball game in the courtyard. He saw Ganna sitting by the open window, sewing a rip in the sleeve of his tunic. He saw Marcellina, as she had been many years before, in Britain. Then he saw once more the wreck of the ship, the tumbling mast and the twisting timbers. He groaned, reached out and grabbed again at the thick wet sand above the surf line, hauling himself further up the beach.

His cloak was gone, his shoulder belt and sword left in the ship. He was still wearing his boots, but they were filled with water and sand and felt like blocks of solid concrete. His waterlogged tunic and breeches dragged at his body as he tried to raise himself. The effort made him retch, and he choked up salt water, gasping and gagging until the spasms of nausea had passed through him. Then he lifted his head again, blinking, and looked around.

The beach was wide and grey-brown, the wet sand rippled with wave patterns. Inland, it rose to high dunes tufted with coarse grass. Squinting, Castus turned his head and gazed along the shoreline. Nothing but the hissing surf, the band of foam and black scraps of seaweed. Gulls whirled and cried. How had he lived? It seemed incredible – as if some sea god had lifted him in his palm and carried him to this lonely deserted strand. Sudden remorse rocked through him and he buckled into a hunched crouch on the sand. A groan rose from his chest, and turned into a sob. His eyes were filled with tears. *Please, immortal gods*, he prayed. *Please do not let them all be dead but me...*

Heaving breath, he shuddered and spat. When he raised his face he could feel the wetness on his cheeks. His left arm pulsed with pain, and when he glanced down he saw the sleeve of his tunic and the thick wad of linen binding his wound were red with fresh blood. His stitches must have torn open as he fought his way ashore. Gasping, swaying, he felt his own weakness. He had nothing now, not even a weapon with which to take his own life.

A moving shadow along the top of the dune caught his eyes, and for a heartbeat hope flared inside him. Then the two figures came into view, and despair welled up once more. They were not Romans. Both were bearded and long-haired, dressed in loose tunics of coarse wool, their legs bare. Both of them carried spears. As they caught sight of Castus they let out a yell and began running down the slope of the dune, weapons raised.

Castus staggered to his feet, bolts of pain coursing through him. He gazed around him, searching the tideline for anything he could use as a weapon – a bit of wood, a stone. Nothing. The two men slowed as they crossed the flat expanse of the beach, obviously finding him a less tempting target now they could see the size and bulk of him. But they were still advancing, cautious but steady. There were two of them, and they had spears. Castus stood, stooping, fists hanging. He was still wearing his broad leather waist belt; with fumbling fingers he undid the thick gilded brass buckle and doubled the belt, the cleats and studs on the outside. Holding it in his fist, he swung the weighted leather like a cosh.

The men were scavengers, he guessed. They must have heard about the wreck and come down to the beach to pillage the dead and kill any survivors. They looked desperate enough, their mouths open and their eyes wide as their lank hair blew in the breeze. Grimacing against the aches, he stooped and grabbed a fistful of sand.

Feinting with his spear, the first of the men edged closer, while his friend tried to circle around to Castus's right. Castus remained standing, shoulders down, with his wet tunic loose around his knees. He was breathing heavily in great bull-like gasps. The studded belt hung from his fist.

He moved suddenly, taking a long stride to his right as he turned and hurled the fistful of sand at the man trying to flank him. As the scavenger flinched back Castus lashed at him with the belt, striking him on the neck. The spear jabbed, but Castus dodged it and seized the shaft in his left hand, ignoring the screaming pain from his wound as he yanked the weapon from the man's grasp.

Spinning on his heel, he crouched low and whipped the belt out, the heavy spiked buckle catching the second scavenger behind the knee. With a yelp the man toppled backwards onto the sand. Castus was already up again, dropping the belt and taking the spear in his right hand, stepping in fast to strike. He jabbed the weapon down, stabbing the fallen man through the chest.

The other scavenger was already running, pelting away across the sand and up the dune, bare feet digging into the sand. Castus let him go. Breathing hard, he leaned on the spear and gazed down at the man he had just killed. The man lay on his back, arms flung out, his eyes and mouth open to the sky. Who was he? Castus had no idea. He had assumed this coast was uninhabited, but clearly there were still some people living here, scratching a life among the dunes and marshes. For a moment he felt a strange remorse. He had killed so many men in his life and thought nothing of it, but this stranger, this unknown inhabitant of a forgotten land, had died only moments after first setting eyes on him. It seemed unjust, somehow.

Gods, he thought. *Why get sentimental?* The man would have killed him, given the chance. He sucked his teeth, spat, then rebuckled his belt and began marching along the beach with the spear in his hand.

It did not take long before he found the first scraps of wreckage. What he had taken for dried mounds of seaweed was shattered wood, sea-sodden cloaks and coils of rope. A few more paces, and he found a shield face down in the wet sand. He took it, marched on. Then he saw the corpses.

The dead men were rolling in the surf. Some of them still wore their blue-grey oarsmen's tunics; others had stripped to their loincloths before they went overboard. Their tanned limbs flopped and waved as the surf turned them. Castus dragged the first few of them up onto the beach, checking for signs of life. But their flesh was cold and inert, clammy with death. A little further on, he found a small amphora washed up on the sand. He dragged out the stopper, heaved it up and gulped back vinegar wine. The taste of it made his head reel.

Something caught his eye, and he dropped the amphora and moved closer. A carved hand of dark wood lay in the wet tidewrack, seaweed trailing from the fingers. Castus reached down as if to take it, then straightened again. Senecio would not be needing it now.

Ahead of him the beach curved, an arc of sand rising to the inland dunes. Moving away from the surf, Castus began climbing the dune, forcing his waterlogged boots up through the dry sifting sand. As he climbed, he looked inland and saw a low drab plain, then a salt marsh beyond. Using the spear as a prop, he clambered up to the crest of the dune.

Something flickered past his head, singing in the air, and Castus hurled himself face down in the coarse grass. When he raised his head he saw men running up the reverse slope of the dune. Voices cried out. Startled, he recognised the words.

'Dominus!' Felix shouted as Castus dragged himself upright. 'You're alive!'

'Luckily. You almost killed me.'

'Sorry!' the optio said with a nervous grin. The sling was still dangling from his hand. 'Some god made me miss – I don't, as a rule.'

The wiry little man joined him on the crest of the dune, and Castus flung an arm around his shoulders, clasping him tight. 'Thank the gods,' he said. 'I thought I was the only one...'

'We all did at first, I reckon,' Felix said. 'There's not too many of us, even so.'

As the optio led him down the far side of the dune, Castus saw the small assembly of men sitting in the sandy hollow just above the beach. When he raised his eyes he saw the wreck of the *Bellona*, or what was left of it, about two hundred paces out. The waves were breaking over the mesh of shattered timbers, but the prow still stuck up, the gnarled old figurehead canted over to one side. Wreckage was spread all along the tideline, with the humped shapes of bodies pulled up onto the sand.

'We thought you were one of those scavenging bastards,' Felix was saying. 'Plenty of them out there. They've been sneaking all round us since dawn.'

'Who are they?'

'Fuck knows. Frisians, somebody reckoned, but I thought they'd all left this land years ago. Barbarian whoresons, whoever they are. They killed a few of our boys in the water just to steal their boots.'

The gathered survivors all rose to their feet as they saw Castus approaching, some of them calling out to him. Others stayed silent, watching him with sullen expressions. He made a rapid count: between twenty and thirty of the oarsmen had made it ashore, and about a dozen of the archers and the marines from the Second Legion. Few had weapons; none had armour or helmets. All looked ragged and terrified, or stunned into blank silence.

Castus leaned on his spear, looking from man to man. He saw Eumolpius among them, and hid his quick smile of relief.

'You've found a good position,' he told Felix. 'We can hold out here for a while, rest and work out where we are. I want lookouts on all the dune crests and men to scour along the beach in both directions looking for any more survivors, weapons and equipment, dry firewood, food and water. Anything we can find. Bury the dead too. Best remove their boots first.'

Felix nodded. Castus assumed he had begun the tasks already, but he needed to say something. Needed to show the men some command. All he wanted to do was sink down and cover his head.

An hour later the search parties had returned. They had found a few more of the amphorae of wine and water, and a cask of hardtack. A couple more survivors, too, who had been sheltering among the dunes further up the beach. Some of the men had gathered dry driftwood and sticks and managed to kindle a fire. It gave off more smoke than heat, but the survivors gathered around it, shivering in their wet clothes.

Castus sat on a roll of damp blanket-cloth, stripped to the waist, while Eumolpius knelt beside him, washing his wound and dousing the linen bandage with fresh water to remove the salt. At least he had managed to pull his boots off.

'So,' Felix said. 'What now?'

Castus sucked on his cheek. He gasped as Eumolpius tied the bandage tight.

'We're some way south of the Rhine mouth,' he said. 'Maybe ten miles, maybe more. We'll reach it if we follow the coast. From there we can head upriver, and hope we find some of our ships before the barbarians find us.'

The local scavengers had not troubled them yet. Felix had knocked a couple down with his sling, but many more of them remained concealed in the surrounding dunes and the marshes inland. The thought of them tracking his men as they marched, trying to pick off the stragglers, was not encouraging.

'Looks like we don't have many other choices,' Felix said. 'I'll pass the word among the others. When do we move?'

'Soon as we can. Let them rest another few hours. Then we get going.'

They moved off in a ragged column, keeping to the expanse of hard wet sand just above the surf. Castus went in the lead, spear over his shoulder and a shield slung on his back. His breeches and tunic had dried stiff and caked with salt, and rasped his skin as he moved. Eumolpius followed behind him, hefting one of the amphorae of water. The men with weapons and shields covered the inland flank; the scavengers were still following them, dodging along the dune crests, yelling and waving their spears. A couple of times a group of them descended to the beach, angling to try and intercept the column; Castus formed his men up tighter, and the few with slings pelted the scavengers with stones until they retreated.

The day was warm and as the men marched the breeze whipped sand at their backs. Every few hundred paces Castus raised his head and scanned the sea horizon, hoping to see the familiar masts and sail of a Roman warship, one of his own come back to search for them. But the sea was empty, the sun glinting off the waves.

They had covered nearly five miles, and the sun was sinking in the west, when Castus heard the cries from the rear of the column. He halted and turned, staring back along the beach. But the men were pointing out to sea, and when Castus looked southwards his heart clenched in his chest.

Four dark shapes on the glittering horizon. Slender raised prows, and the moving forms of men at the oars. The Frankish war boats had caught up with them.

'Pass the word,' Castus shouted. 'After me – we need to get off the beach.'

He scanned the line of the shore. Just to the north, two hundred paces away, the dunes rose to a grassy level area. A few wind-blown trees stood on the summit. He had no idea what lay on the far side, but it was the only defensible position along this stretch of coast. Slinging the spear over his shoulder, Castus set off at a labouring jog. He heard the stamp and gasp of the other men following close behind him.

'Slingers, anyone with weapons,' he called back over his shoulder, 'watch those fuckers on the dunes!'

Across the broad sweep of beach, he forged on up the slope of sand. Ahead of him he could see the scavengers as they darted from concealment. But they were running away, scattering back into the marshes behind the dunes. The sight of the Frankish boats had been enough for them. Scrambling up the last rise, Castus reached the level ground and jogged to a halt beside the first of the trees. When he looked to the east he saw the land dropping away into same expanse of dull green salt marsh. As his men stumbled up the slope after him, he knew that he could only hold out here for a short time.

The first of the boats had already turned to drive its prow up through the surf. With the sun low, Castus could see only dark shapes of men pouring across the bow and wading up onto the sand. The light caught their spears and the burnished ornaments on their shields. As the other boats came in he counted thirty warriors in each. He was outnumbered three to one, and the enemy were fully armed and equipped. Those of his own men who had no weapons had picked up lumps of driftwood or ship's timber as they marched, and hefted them now as improvised cudgels. But the battle, when it came, would not last long.

Felix was scratching around in the thin sandy soil, collecting round stones and pebbles he could use as sling missiles. 'Might get a few of the bastards as they come up the slope,' he said, baring his teeth.

Castus nodded. He licked his lips and tasted salt. The men gathered around the knot of trees had a look of grim resignation. All knew there was no retreat: the marshes behind them were the home of the scavengers, who would cut their throats if they got a chance. They stood in a rough half-circle, shoulder to shoulder, gripping their weapons as they stared down at the enemy assembling on the beach. Castus passed his shield to the man beside him. With his injured arm he could not have used it effectively. He had an anguished memory of the position he had tried to defend in Britain years before, when his unit was attacked by the Picts. That had ended badly, and this promised no better.

'May all the gods be with us now,' the soldier beside him muttered quietly. 'Mars and Jupiter watch over us. May Sol Invictus send his light against the darkness... May Fortuna bring us safely home...'

The Franks were not advancing straight up the dunes, but dividing into two parties and moving off to left and right. They would try and keep out of sight while they flanked the position, Castus realised. Nothing to be done about it. But the thought that his small tattered force still posed a threat gave him a nudge of pride. And there was still the chance that they would not attack.

'Nobody make a move until they show their intention,' he called.

He was watching the dunes to the left, where the larger of the two parties of Franks had disappeared. A moment later he saw them, moving slowly closer around the far side of the dune. Now he could make them out more clearly.

'They're closing in on the right,' Felix said. He had a stone in his sling, and was watching for a clear target.

'Wait,' Castus ordered. He held his breath.

A small group of figures was advancing from the left-hand group, picking their way forward through the grass and scrub.

'Everyone hold your position,' Castus said. Then he began walking.

Ten paces, and he halted, squinting. The leading warrior, a tall muscular figure dressed in red, with the sun on his yellow hair, was climbing the slope towards him. As he got closer, he lifted his head.

'Bonitus,' Castus called out.

The Frankish chieftain paused, braced against the slope of sand. 'You come to surrender to me, Roman?' he said.

'No. If you want a fight, you can have one. But I want to offer a truce.'

'Truce?' Bonitus snorted. 'You think you are in a position to offer anything?'

Castus stared at him. Despite the man's words, he felt that sense of connection he had known before. 'You followed us here?' he asked.

Bonitus shook his head. 'We go home. Quicker by sea. We leave this war behind us. It's not our fight. Gaiso is dead, but his people will choose a new leader. I do not want to argue with a man I don't respect.'

'We need to get off this coast,' Castus told him. 'Up to the Rhine, to find our other ships and men.'

Bonitus stared at him, the unspoken question hanging between them. Behind him, his warriors had gathered along the crest of the dune.

'Why should we help you, Roman?' he said.

Castus shrugged. 'If you do, Rome will be grateful. I promise you that.'

'Hah!' Bonitus laughed. 'We know your promises. Worthless!'

'The deaths of the hostages were not my doing, you know that. It was the governor, Tiberianus.'

'And you want to go and set this straight, hmm? Find this man who made you break your oath. Kill him. This is what I would do.'

343

'Then help me. You have four boats – how many extra men could each carry?'

Bonitus stroked his moustache with his thumb. 'Ten,' he said. 'Enough for all your little army, I'm thinking.'

Castus said nothing. The wind blew flurries of sand from the dunes. Behind him, Castus could sense his own men watching, anxious, prepared for anything. Bonitus looked back at his own warriors, then at Castus again.

'Very well,' he said. 'Our path is the same as yours. For now. But remember this, Roman. Your people forget promises easily. Mine do not.'

CHAPTER XXVI

They reached the mouth of the river by nightfall, the four Frankish boats turning and pulling in against the current. Each boat was packed with men. The rowing benches ran straight across the hull, with no open gangway, and the Roman survivors of the wreck sat perched between the shoulders of the Frankish oarsmen. Castus knew that many of his men had been unhappy about the arrangement. Putting themselves in the power of barbarians was not to their taste, whatever the alternative. But they had obeyed his order nonetheless. He rode in the lead boat, seated in the cramped space between the rear bench and the helmsman's post at the stern, where Bonitus himself handled the steering oar.

It was an unnerving experience to travel in such a small craft on the open sea. The waves rolled by at the same height as the topmast wales, but the shallow hull rode across them with only the occasional raking splash of spray. Castus watched the oarsmen, the warriors that he had expected to face in battle only a few hours before. Now and again he caught one of them watching him back, with an expression of guarded mistrust.

As the boats entered the river their motion changed, the keels levelling, but the current was strong and set against them. The oarsmen bent harder to their work, grunting and sighing in unison. Castus knew that they were putting on a show of

345

strength. It was impressive all the same; they appeared tireless, never missing a stroke. The dark land closed in on either side of the river channel, and the smell and sound of the sea faded from the air. Only the splash of the oars, the hiss of the water around the hull and the distant cries of gulls broke the night's stillness.

'You say your ships came this way?' Bonitus asked quietly.

'I hope so. How far upriver they are now I can't say.'

'Maybe others use this waterway. Maybe some who have no love for Romans.'

Bonitus called forward in his own language to the lookout who stood at the prow. The man raised his spear in acknowledgement, a brief flash of moonlight.

Silence again. Only the steady creak of the oars and timbers, the plash of water. Castus felt the ache in his body, the fatigue creeping through him. He had not slept for many hours, and there was an ocean of time ahead before he could think of rest.

A mile crept past, then another. Then the lookout hissed a warning, and the oars ceased their motion, the blades raised and dripping. Castus listened carefully; sound carried clearly across the surface of the river. Voices, the thud of wood.

Bonitus signalled with his hand and the oars dipped once more, slower now and almost soundless. The three other boats crept up on either side, until they moved abreast up the middle of the channel. Peering into the darkness ahead, the noise of his blood loud in his ears, Castus could just make out the shapes of other craft moored in the river. The lookouts at the prow of each boat had javelins ready.

Another voice, a shout, then a spark of light danced across the surface of the dark water. Castus caught his breath as he heard another sound: the distinct ratcheting click of a ballista slide being drawn back. He stood up, bracing himself against the bench ahead of him.

Cupping his hands around his mouth, he bellowed out into the darkness. *'Jupiter Dolichenus! Jupiter Dolichenuuuus!'*

An answering cry out of the darkness, the watchword acknowledged. Then a tumult of voices, the thunder of boots on planking. Moments later, the shapes of the moored vessels appeared out of the night.

Bonitus pushed at the steering oar, his men hauling hard, and the Frankish boat slipped the last distance through the water. The sharp prow bumped up against the hull of one of the big Roman troop barges, and Castus was already clambering forward, hands on the shoulders of his men as he stepped across the benches up to the bow and then over onto the deck of the barge.

'Aurelius Castus!' Modestus cried, his gnarled teeth gleaming in the moonlight. 'The gods are good!'

'At last,' Castus said. The sense of release was physical, almost overwhelming. Soldiers all around him, scrambling up from the deck to grasp his arms and shoulders and guide him down to sit.

'We've waited all day,' Modestus was saying. 'We were going to move on tomorrow morning, if we'd seen no sign of you... The *Bellona*?' he asked with a tentative note.

'Gone,' Castus told him. 'Foundered on a sandbank. I've got forty survivors with me, and Bonitus's men. Senecio was lost. How many of the other ships are safe?'

'All except *Pinnata*. We saw her light bearing away to the west around midnight last night. Reckon she ran for the coast of Britain. One of the troop barges is still missing too – sailed too far north up the coast, we think.'

Castus nodded, calculating. Three galleys and three barges left. Between two and three hundred men, not counting the Franks. He was still unsure whether Bonitus would agree to follow him any further. But he was alive, and most of his command was safe. It was a small victory, and a precious one. He shuddered, and for a moment he felt almost nauseous with relief. But the worst of the journey was still to come.

'How soon can you move? I intend to get as far upriver as we can under cover of dark.'

'Immediately, dominus. We're well rested, and we've foraged some provisions from the riverbanks.' Castus saw the crease of Modestus's brow in the darkness as he frowned. 'You need to see the surgeon though, I reckon.'

Castus raised his arm slightly, and saw the black stain of blood soaked through the fabric and the damp linen beneath.

The flotilla remained at its moorings another hour, while the Franks rested and the survivors of the *Bellona* climbed gladly aboard the other vessels. Castus stripped off his salt-caked clothes, and gasped as he stood on the wide flat bow of the barge while two soldiers poured buckets of cold river water over him, sluicing off the grime of the sea. Then he sat, patient and tight-jawed, while the surgeon cleaned his wound, stitched it again and applied fresh dressings. 'And this time, take care of it,' the surgeon said as he finished the job.

Dressed in a slightly musty old tunic and breeches, with a plain-looking standard-issue spatha slung over his shoulder, Castus climbed down into the Frankish boat again and made his way aft to speak with Bonitus. He found the chief sitting at the steering post; two of his warriors were with him, and moved away as soon as Castus approached.

'So,' Bonitus said. The water slapped around the stern of the boat, and the steering oar creaked in its bindings. 'You have your ships. You go to fight your war, I think.'

Castus nodded, flexing his bicep to ease the tightness of the new dressing. 'And you? You just... go home?'

Bonitus stifled a cough, and gazed off to his left at the flowing river for a moment. 'I have spoken with my people,' he said quietly. 'Some of them say that it is not good to sit at home like women while others fight.' He looked back at Castus. 'To fight our own brothers is not good either. But the Chamavi and Chattuari... we have warred with them before.'

'If all the Frankish people but you have turned against Rome, what then? Would you help us in our fight?'

'You remember your promise?' Bonitus's voice was barely more than a whisper now. 'This time, no more worthless words. I will follow you for my brother's sake, and my father's oath. But my people will expect reward.'

'They'll get it,' Castus told him. Bonitus extended his hand, and Castus clasped it. The bond of trust. He could only pray that he was not offering something he could not give.

All that night and through into the dawn they hauled on up the river. The strong current beat against them all the way, and the galleys could only make half the speed they could manage in still water. The heavy barges with their long sweeps slowed the flotilla down even more. The dark river twisted and curled, the helmsmen guiding the ships around the sinuous bends, trying to keep to the inner curves to take advantage of the slack current, steering clear of the treacherous mudbanks. Sometimes, when the river's meandering course allowed, the ships raised sail to give a little respite to the men at the oars. But each further bend turned them into the wind once more, and the sails flapped back against the masts.

Castus remained awake through the night, seated on the narrow triangular stern platform of the thirty-oared galley *Satyra*. The gangway was crowded with men, both marines and the surviving crew from the old *Bellona*, and every five or ten miles the soldiers and oarsmen changed places on the rowing benches, allowing a few at least to rest huddled on the gangway as the ship ploughed steadily onwards. It was hard labour, and the first light of the new morning showed the strain on every face.

As the sun rose the ships of the flotilla pulled into the bank where a grassy meadow came down to the river, the smaller craft beaching on the mud. The men stumbled ashore, most of them throwing themselves down at once to sleep wrapped in their cloaks. Castus posted sentries all around the camping ground, although there was no sign of life in any direction. The landscape that surrounded them looked identical to the dull flat marsh country, the pools and grassy plains he had seen from the coast the day before. It was as if all the night's efforts had availed them nothing.

They rested until noon; then they lit their fires and ate. As the smoke hung over the camping ground, Castus paced the perimeter. He had managed to sleep a little, two or three hours, but his body still felt heavy and clumsy with fatigue. He could only guess how the men who had worked the rowing benches all night were feeling. Watching the sky, he scanned the movements of the clouds. The wind had backed around to the south once more; it would be dead against them once they passed the confluence with the Vahalis.

Down at the riverbank, he found some of the galley crews already preparing their ships for departure. All of them, he knew, were eager to leave this barbarian wilderness and return to civilisation. A few recognised him as he passed and saluted, but he was dressed the same as them now, with no insignia of rank or status.

Castus found the rowing master of the old flagship aboard the *Satyra*. He was a veteran oarsman, with massive shoulders and arms corded with muscle.

'How long will it take us to reach Colonia, at the pace we've been making?' Castus asked.

The rowing master sucked his teeth and narrowed his eyes. 'At this pace, six days, maybe seven, dominus.'

'Too slow,' Castus muttered to himself. 'We need to be there in half the time.'

The rowing master shrugged. 'Then we must pull like Titans,' he said, grinning. 'And pray for a following breeze!'

By that afternoon they were back on the water, hauling east around the bends and reaches of the river once more. There were canopies rigged over the open decks of the galleys, but the sun reflected off the water into the eyes of the oarsmen; the men rowed with sweat pouring down their faces and soaking through their tunics. Water-carriers passed along the gangways, lifting skins so the rowers could drink without breaking stroke. Others hauled buckets up from the river and sluiced down decks and men alike, washing the swill of sweat, urine and faeces from below the rowing benches. Many of the less experienced oarsmen had tied rags around their blistered palms. The handles of their oars were sweat-dark and greasy with blood.

Castus made his way forward along the gangway of the *Satyra*, stooping under the canopy and stepping over bodies. Joining the bow-officer on the foredeck behind the curving dragon-headed prow, he watched the green riverbanks sliding steadily past. They had moved beyond the reach of the marshes now, and the land to either side was heavily wooded, the trees coming down to the water. There were signs of habitation too: a wooden jetty, a cluster of empty huts, a muddy scar on the bank where cattle had been driven down to drink. But no people. The land seemed deserted.

This was the country of the Salii, Bonitus's home soil. Leaning out from the bow, Castus saw the Frankish chief's boat coming up abreast of the galley.

'Where is everybody?' he called across the water, flinging out his arm towards the deserted riverbanks.

'Gone to the war,' Bonitus shouted back. 'Or fled north, away from it!'

Already they were in the hinterland of the invasion, Castus realised. And from here on they were in the enemy's country. He looked back along the length of the galley. The men were tiring, even after their rest. Many groaned as they heaved at the oars, or cried out in fatigue and pain. With every stroke, more of the oar-blades were clashing together as they rose from the water. It was not surprising; even trained oarsmen working in shifts could not keep up this sort of pace, rowing night and day, hour on hour with only short breaks. How long, Castus wondered, before their strength gave out? Already there had been casualties: men carried from the benches with sprained muscles, dislocated shoulders, sunstroke... And their morale could easily give way before their strength. Every officer aboard was alert for the mutterings of discontent, the first swells of mutiny.

'Come on, lads, throw yourself into it!' the sailing master was saying, clambering along the gangway beneath the awning. 'Those barbarian bastards are getting headway on us! Full pressure up the next bend, then we'll ease off... *Pull*, you sons of whores!'

Castus followed the man back to the stern deck. Behind him he could see the rest of the flotilla strung out along the reach of the river, oar-blades flashing in the sun as they beat against the current. He picked out the red and blue hulls of the scout galleys *Lucusta* and *Murena*, then the black shapes of the troop barges, with the Frankish boats cutting in between them. Every deck was packed with men. But they were moving so slowly. So maddeningly slowly.

Just behind him, a man on one of the starboard benches gave a sharp cry and slumped forward, his oar trailing slack in the water as he massaged his bicep. Already two of his comrades were dragging him over onto the gangway, one of them moving to take his place. Castus stepped forward and held the man back, then dropped onto the bench himself.

'Dominus,' the rowing master called from the opposite bench. 'You shouldn't – it's not your job—'

'Shut up and keep pulling!' Castus said.

He gripped the oar handle as he had seen the other men do, right palm under it and left palm over the top. Then he bent forward, breathed deeply and dipped the oar in time with the stroke.

At first the exercise was invigorating. After so many hours sitting in the cramped stern of the galley, it was a release to throw himself into hard physical labour. He wanted to beat at the river with all his strength, and had to hold himself back to remain in time with the other oars. Sweat began to tide down his back and drip from under his arms, and he felt his wound smart and ache.

An hour, then another. The pace was relentless. Castus had managed to settle into an easier rhythm, no longer digging his oar deep into the water but letting the blade flick just beneath the surface. But his arms were twisted ropes of pain, and his back screamed with every stroke. He blinked and shook his head to clear the sweat from his eyes, and felt the palms of his hands ribboned with blisters. His chest heaved as he drew in breath, and he kept his eyes locked on the naked back of the man ahead of him, a skinny youth in a loincloth. Every time the man swung forward the muscles in his back shifted beneath his tanned skin, his vertebrae showing clearly.

Castus was forced to admit that he was neither as strong nor as fit as he once had been. But his pride rebelled; he would not weaken. With every aching stroke of the oars he drew closer to his goal. The voice of the sailing master, the words of exhortation, became a low rumble in the back of his head. And as the sun slipped below the trees and dusk filled the channel of the river he ceased to think, ceased to notice the strain, and emptied his mind of everything but the heat of the oar-handle clasped in his hands, the grinding rhythm of the strokes, and the steady splashing of the blades in the water.

'Castra Herculis,' the rowing master said. 'That's what this place used to be called. One of our frontier forts, long ago. Not much to see of it now.'

Castus looked around him at the circuit of grass-grown rampart walls. The centre of the old fort was overgrown too, a thicket of tangled bushes and trees where there once would have been regular barrack blocks and gravelled roads. The sight brought him a strange melancholy feeling: loss, mingled with fascination. He remembered what the Caesar Crispus had said about restoring the old Rhine fortifications all the way to the sea. Roman troops had once lived in this place, holding the river frontier. Would they ever do so again?

He picked his way back down the grassy slope of tumbled wall and returned to the camp on the riverbank. It was noon, the second day since he had rejoined them on the river, and the flotilla had finally halted to rest ashore. It would only be a brief respite: this old fort now marked the boundary of the Chamavi domain, and Castus wanted to press on upriver under cover of night. His spells at the oars had left him exhausted, his back aching and the muscles of his shoulders and neck iron-taut. But he could not allow any delays now.

'Dominus,' Modestus said, striding up to meet him. 'A couple of the barbarian scouts have just come back. They say they found tracks leading up from the riverbank just upstream of here – thousands of men crossing the river and moving south, it looked like.'

Castus stared away to the south. There was a track across the wilderness in that direction, leading to the River Vahalis ten miles away and the fort and town of Noviomagus on the far side. He had considered disembarking the bulk of his men here and marching them onward by land, but with a strong enemy force now ahead of them that would be impossible. He peered at the horizon, looking for smoke trails, but could see nothing.

'This was where your last commander died, I think.'

Castus flinched, startled; he had not noticed Bonitus joining him.

'The interpreter told you that?'

Bonitus nodded. 'Maybe in this very spot, hmm?'

Suppressing a quick superstitious shudder, Castus looked around him at the dense green bushes, the stands of ragged trees. He was still grieved by the idea that Dexter, an officer he had liked and trusted, had been involved in the murder – but if Bappo had been present, that was surely the truth. Hard to imagine Leontius, a man he had known well, meeting his end in this forsaken place. *Struck down by his own troops.* He stared across the camp ground at the knots of tired men gathered around the cooking fires and the piquet of armed sentries beyond. So far, there had been no eruptions of insubordination, no whispers of mutiny. Or not as far as he knew. But they were still in no man's land, on the border of barbaricum. Once they reached more settled country, within reach of the Roman forts, would the men continue so gladly?

A cry from the far perimeter broke into his thoughts, and he glanced up to see a pair of horsemen approaching along the track from the southward. The sentry guards were already mustered to block them, shields ready and spears levelled. But even from where he was standing, Castus could see that the riders were Roman. Flinging his cloak back over his shoulder, he strode between the fires to meet them.

One of the men had already dismounted, while the other stayed in the saddle watching the surrounding land. Both wore green tunics, and Castus recognised the blazon on the shields slung on their saddle horns. They were men of the Numerus Batavorum, from Noviomagus. Had the garrison there managed to hold out?

The dismounted rider turned as he approached, but did not salute; Castus reminded himself that he was still dressed as a common soldier, and a very grimy and sweat-stained soldier at that. One of the sentries muttered to the man, and he stiffened slightly to attention, but still looked dubious.

'You're from Noviomagus?' Castus said.

'Yes... *excellency*,' the rider replied, cocking his head. 'We got reports of ships coming up the river, and the tribune sent us to take a look.'

'Have you seen the enemy?'

'Seen them? They've been pouring across the Vahalis for three days and three nights. Burned the town and slaughtered most of the people, never mind they're kin to them... They surrounded us in the fort, a good four thousand of them at least. We've only got two hundred of us left in the garrison, so we couldn't move out against them.'

Castus shrugged, nodding for him to continue.

356

'We saw their leader. Their king. Ragnachar. He rode all round the walls, just out of bowshot. If we'd had a ballista we could've picked him off. Then they moved away in bands, heading south.'

'When was this?'

'Yesterday, the last of them cleared out. We've been scouting and bringing in survivors ever since.'

Ragnachar. Castus remembered the name well, and the proud figure that had stood on the riverbank the previous summer as he made his demand for hostages. He remembered the man's distress and humiliation too. Had his son, Conda, joined him on this invasion? Both would be eager to avenge themselves on Rome, and on Castus himself in particular. Calculations flickered through his mind. Time and distances. If this was the main attack from the north, and it had passed through only the day before, was there still time to reach Colonia ahead of them and regain command of the defences?

'Get back to your tribune,' he said. 'Give him my congratulations on his defence, and tell him to hold his position until relieved.'

'Yes, dominus,' the scout said, saluting. 'We will do what we are ordered, and at every command we will be ready!' He still had a quizzical look. 'Funny thing is, though,' he said, 'everyone's been saying you're dead.'

CHAPTER XXVII

Twenty-four hours later, the flotilla hauled around the last bend of the Rhine and came into sight of the fortress of Tricensima. A parched cheer went up from the men on the rowing benches as they craned back for a glimpse of the reassuring battlements and buttress towers. No plumes of dark smoke rose from within, and the banner still flew above the northern gate. All appeared calm; the fortress still remained in Roman hands.

In fact, Castus thought as the galleys swung across the broad reach of the river and backed towards the muddy shore, there was little sign that the people in the fortress were even aware of the barbarian attack. No patrols guarded the riverbank, no horsemen rode from the gates to meet them. As the weary oarsmen from the galleys clambered ashore, Castus left Modestus in charge and marched up the track towards the fortress gates. He took Felix with him, and Eumolpius, with a trumpeter and six men of the Second Britannica as an escort. His personal draco standard had been lost in the wreck of the *Bellona*, and none of the other units under his command had one.

The track led them up through the overgrown ruins of the city that had once stood here, before the fortress was rebuilt on a smaller plan. Away to the left, Castus could make out the hulk of the old amphitheatre, now almost lost in a thicket of trees; the old grid of streets now formed the divisions between vegetable plots. Though only a vestige of the old legion fortress it replaced, Tricensima was still the most powerful stronghold on the Rhine frontier. Impossible that the commander here should not have learned of the barbarian assault.

'Halt and identify yourselves!' a voice cried from the gatehouse tower. The gates remained closed. Castus peered upwards and saw helmeted heads along the rampart walkways, and the iron arches of ballistae.

'Shall I do this?' Felix asked.

Castus nodded. Behind him, the trumpeter blew three sustained notes.

'Open the gates, in the name of the emperor!' Felix shouted, in a surprisingly powerful voice. 'Open the gates for his excellency Aurelius Castus, vir perfectissimus, Commander of the Germanic Frontier!'

Shouts from inside the gatehouse, the sounds of argument. Castus waited. Then the noise of the heavy timber barring the gate grating against wood. The gate creaked open, and a figure walked out into the sunlight.

'Dominus!' Diogenes said with a pale smile. 'My apologies – the prefect here ordered them to keep the gates closed. They thought the barbarians had killed you all and stolen your ships!'

'Diogenes...' Castus said as he paced closer, surprised recognition turning quickly to acid dread. 'What are you doing here? Why are you not at Colonia...? *Where's my son?*' He seized the man by the shoulders, then flinched, choking. 'And what's that fucking awful stink?'

'Sorry, I can't seem to wash it off... Many things have happened. Come inside. We need to talk. Things are not good, brother.'

The tone of Diogenes' voice was quite enough to confirm Castus's apprehensions. He set his jaw, nodded, and then followed the secretary into the fortress with his escort marching behind him.

Inside the walls, they moved swiftly along the broad central avenue towards the headquarters building, which occupied a converted wing of the enormous old bathhouse. All along the street, soldiers of the garrison lined the wooden porticos. Some saluted, while others just stared, either with hopeful smiles or expressions of confusion. As they walked, Diogenes spoke quickly and quietly, telling Castus about what had happened at Colonia: the governor seizing power, Rufus's appointment as commander, the arrest of Diogenes himself and Castus's remaining staff. 'They sent men into the Praetorium to take us,' he said. 'We thought of resisting, but... they already had your son.'

Castus's step faltered, and he pressed a fist to his mouth to stop himself crying out. 'Where have they taken him?' he managed to say.

'Tiberianus took him to his own residence. So I heard afterwards. They've declared you an enemy of the state too – all troops at Colonia have been ordered to seize or kill you.'

'Ha!' Castus shouted. He smacked his fist into his palm.

As they covered the last distance, Diogenes quickly told of his escape, the stumble through the sewer and his voyage downriver in a canoe with only a single oar. 'I arrived this morning. Haven't had time to wash properly or change my clothes...'

'The eunuch freed you, you said? Luxorius, the prefect's chamberlain?'

'I'm sure it was him, yes. The gods alone know what he was doing there. He told me specifically to find you and

360

report everything that had happened, so you don't walk into a trap.'

What was the eunuch's game now? Castus remembered meeting him that night at Noviomagus, before the Caesar's meeting with the barbarians. He had suspected him then. He shook his head – there were enough other things to worry about without considering the schemes of eunuchs.

Inside the headquarters building, they found the commander of the fortress waiting for them in his private chamber. He already had a pale and queasy look of apprehension. As Castus entered he stood up from behind his table, saluting awkwardly.

'You've kept your garrison within the walls,' Castus declared, without a word of greeting. 'You've made no effort to patrol the surrounding area or secure the river. Why?'

'Excellency,' the commander said, his jaw trembling. He rubbed his balding scalp. 'Until we received better intelligence, I thought it prudent...'

'Where was this *better intelligence* supposed to come from?' Castus growled. He took four paces across the room and planted his fists upon the table. The commander sank back down into his seat. Castus glared at him, until the man quailed and looked away.

'You are hereby stripped of your command,' Castus ordered, striding away from the table again. 'Your drillmaster, who I believe is a capable man, will take charge of the fortress in your place.'

'Excellency!' the commander said, his stool toppling to the floor as he stood up. 'I must protest! I've done nothing...'

'Exactly, you've done *nothing*!' Castus bellowed, turning on his heel and stabbing a finger at the man. His words echoed around the chamber. 'Now – one more word from you and I'll have you arrested for mutiny. And I'll execute you my-fucking-self!'

Striding outside, Castus stood in the bright sunlight at the head of the steps, flexing his knuckles. He had a strong desire to hurt somebody. But he knew that his real target was still many miles south, at Colonia. A wave of fatigue passed through him, darkness filling his mind. He blinked, and saw a party of soldiers from the Thirtieth Legion in mud-stained tunics filing across the gravel yard, heavy baulks of timber across their shoulders. The fort commander had apparently decided to take this opportunity to strengthen the defences. The officer leading the work party was a lean, rangy man with a bristling black beard. Even without the fur hat he had been wearing before, Castus recognised him.

'You, centurion,' he called from the top of the steps. 'Formerly of the Fifth Praetorian Cohort and Thirteenth Legion Gemina. Am I right?'

The bearded man halted, the file of men behind him dropping their loads to the gravel. 'You're not wrong,' he said, with a smile. 'I remember a face too, excellency. Though you're not looking your best, if I may say so.'

'Could say the same for you,' Castus replied.

The ex-Praetorian spread his arms, peering down at his shabby tunic with an exaggerated grimace. The men behind him snorted with laughter; most of them were clearly older veterans of the Guard as well.

'How many of you are there here?' Castus asked.

'From the old cohorts? Three hundred of us left here, more or less. Fewer with every winter.'

'I saw barges down by the river. Can your men row?' He saw the centurion's quick look of disgust at the prospect. 'We're a long way from the Palatine now,' he added.

'If you're taking us to war, dominus,' the centurion said, with a wry smile, 'sure, we'll row all the way to the Alps if you want.'

Back inside, Castus gave the orders to Diogenes and the new commander of the fortress. His men needed to be resupplied with food, arms and equipment, the wounded men taken to the hospital and replacements drawn from the garrison, and barges prepared to embark three hundred men of the Thirtieth for immediate departure. While his secretary and the commander's staff set to work, Castus paced across to the window. He pushed open the shutter and gazed across the roofs of the barrack buildings towards the gatehouse, and the banner hanging slack in the midday stillness. His back and shoulders ached from rowing, and soon the torment would begin again.

More than eighty miles of river separated Tricensima from the city of Colonia. How long would it take them, at their present speed? More importantly, Castus thought, did his men still have the strength to do it? Most were already ground down to their last reserves of stamina. Push them any harder, and the number of injuries would increase; the number dropping from heat and exhaustion would increase, too. If he ever reached Colonia, his troops would be too fatigued, too depleted, to fight.

He felt the darkness sinking through him. All of his plans, all of his desperate energy, had led to nothing. Failure on every side. The barbarians and the men who had seized control of the province would fight it out between them, and there was nothing that he could do about it.

Then, just as he turned away from the window, a flicker of movement caught his eye. He glanced back. The banner over the gate was lifting, eddying on the breeze. Castus stared, frowned, uncertain of the direction. Modestus and two oarsmen were running across the gravelled yard, waving up at him.

South, he realised; the banner was blowing towards the south. He slammed his fist down on the sill of the window, with a shout that brought Diogenes and the clerks to their feet. They had their following breeze.

Under cover of darkness, the ships ghosted up the wide channel of the Rhine with slow strokes of their oars. The wind that had carried them southward for two days had almost died away now, but it had served them well; Castus had vowed to sacrifice to the gods for it, if ever he got the chance.

The long bridge that connected Colonia Agrippina with the fort of Divitia on the eastern bank was a tracery of blackness across the moon-grey river. Beyond the fort, fires were burning. Inland too – trails of sparks were lifting from the darkened land, and the fort's walls showed clearly in the glow of the flames. There were a few scattered fires on the opposite bank, also; some of the barbarians must have paddled over in boats to pillage the area around the city. Bructeri, Castus guessed. Ganna's people, from the densely forested hill country to the east. In the still air, the men on the ships could hear the distant roaring of the barbarians around their camp fires, the bursts of laughter and anger, the shouts of defiance. Both fort and city remained silent.

The galleys slowed, then took up position with the oars working to hold them in the current. Castus climbed from the deck of the *Satyra* into one of the smaller scout vessels, the eighteen-oared *Lucusta*. Beyond the galleys, his three original troop barges had been joined by five larger vessels carrying the ex-Praetorian veterans of the Thirtieth Legion. Bonitus's Frankish war boats slipped between them, lookouts at every prow.

'Take us upstream, as close to the bridge as you can get without being spotted,' Castus told the helmsman, as Diogenes and Felix dropped down into the scout galley behind him. The rear oarsmen fended off at once, and the narrow hull of the *Lucusta* moved smoothly against the current with only a ripple of water. Castus clambered forward, stepping over the rowing benches, until he could stand braced behind the prow of the galley and watch the riverbanks, the walls of the city and the fort, and the bridge between them.

He remembered the last time he had tried to get into a besieged city in darkness. That had been many years ago, back in Britain, when he and Marcellina were escaping from the Picts. He had narrowly escaped death, then, only to be imprisoned as a deserter. He wasn't about to make that mistake again, especially now the defenders had orders to kill him: marching up to the gates and demanding entry was a good way to get himself shot with an arrow or ballista bolt. During the long hours of the voyage south from Tricensima he had thought over his options. The fetid sewer that Diogenes had used as an escape tunnel was too narrow for a large force of men; and there were too many chances of being discovered and trapped down there: a terrifying thought. But perhaps the bridge was the key. Castus knew that the garrison in the fort on the east bank must have an open supply route across the river from the city. The trick would be to get between them somehow.

'Ready to go,' a voice said, and Castus turned to see Felix crouched in the scuppers. The optio wore only a dark tunic, and his long sinewy arms and bony face were smeared with black river mud. He looked like a creature from nightmare as he grinned. His sling was wrapped tight around his fist. Castus had guessed that his unusual collection of skills might come in useful; now he would be proved right.

A small skiff pulled up beside the bow, and Felix climbed across into it.

'Sure you know what to do?' Castus hissed.

'Don't worry about me, dominus,' Felix said. 'Be back before you know.'

'And no blood, if you can...'

'I've never killed a man yet who wasn't asking for it!' Felix said, before telling the single oarsman to shove off from the galley.

Castus watched the boat moving away upstream, then the men of the *Lucusta* lifted their oars and let the river's current carry them gliding back down to where the other ships of the flotilla lay waiting. Small boats moved between them, carrying Castus's orders for the night ahead. It would be another gamble, he knew; his men could find themselves caught out in the open, trapped between the fort and the city, with barbarian raiders closing in around them. Back on the stern deck of the *Satyra* he breathed deeply, then exhaled, trying to subdue the churning anxiety in his gut.

One of the troop barges bumped alongside; Modestus and eighteen men of the Second Legion leaped over onto the galley's deck. All wore light kit, leather covers concealing their shield blazons. Some carried grapnels and ropes. The other barges and the Frankish boats had already pulled over closer to the western riverbank, ready to close in and disembark when they heard the signal. With a nervous jolt, Castus checked that one of Modestus's men was carrying a trumpet.

'Boat coming in,' a hushed voice called from the bow. A moment later, and Felix was hauling himself aboard.

'*Sunrise of Liberty!*' he said with a wry smile. 'Nice watch-word, eh? Lucky me – they changed the sentries just after I got up to the road. One of them might wake up with a sore head tomorrow, but no real harm done.'

'Good,' Castus said. He clenched his jaw – now for the throw of the dice. Already the men on the benches were bending to their oars, the *Satyra* beginning to haul upriver towards the bridge. On deck, the legionaries removed their helmets and squatted down, covering their spear blades. With any luck, the sentries would be half-blinded by the glow of the riverbank fires, but any glint of metal in the moonlight could be fatal.

Slow, then slower, the galley crept up towards the bridge. Now the men on deck could hear the rushing flow of the river's current around the massive stone bridge piers. Above the piers rose the lattice of heavy wooden beams that supported the roadway twelve feet overhead. Castus kept his eyes on the railing of the bridge, alert for a sentry's movement against the dark sky. With silent oars the *Satyra* pushed against the current, until the bridge was almost directly over her bows. Hauling himself up, one of the crewmen scaled to the masthead with a grapnel in his hand. As the mast approached the bridge timbers he swung the hook; at once the men on the benches below lifted their oars, the current carrying the galley back until the grappling rope ran taut. Other men heaved on the line, pulling the hull of the ship up against the massive sloping stone blocks of the bridge pier.

Felix was first to leap. He was up onto the lowest masonry ledge before Castus had seen him move, another grapnel and rope trailing after him. Others climbed up behind him, the ship held now in a web of taut cables as the soldiers clambered from the deck and up the bridge pier, shields slung on their backs. Castus followed, his boots kicking at the mossy, weed-slippery stones. From a distance the piers had looked as smooth as marble; now he saw that there were handholds and ledges all the way up, left by the engineers who had built the bridge less than ten years before. Swinging his arms, he hauled himself upward, trying not to think of the fast-flowing black water beneath him.

Muscles burning, his wounded bicep flaming, Castus dragged his bulk up the lattice of timber girders. All around him echoed the grunt and thud of climbing men, boots grating on stone and wood. Felix had reached the bridge railing and was checking the roadway in both directions. Another heave, a sliding scramble up a slanted timber, and Castus followed him. Breathing hard, he crouched at the side of the road as the last of the men piled across after him. No figure appeared from the darkness. No call of challenge. The river was quiet beneath them.

'Form up,' Castus said.

As the men assembled on the roadway he took his place at their head, then swung his arm and marched forward towards the western bank and the city beyond. The sound of boots on gravel and timber was loud in the night's stillness. They were approaching the far end of the bridge when they heard the sentry's challenge.

'*Sunrise of Liberty!*' Castus called back, not breaking step. He could make out the forms of the sentries, now, and the spectral white figures of Minerva painted on each shield.

'We didn't see your signal, mate,' the first sentry said. 'You're supposed to let us know before you come across!'

'Urgent message for the governor,' Castus said from the side of his mouth.

'Seems like a lot of you to be carrying a messa—' The sentry's voice choked as three men grappled him; three more subdued the second sentry, felling him with a muffled volley of thuds and kicks. Castus kept moving.

Off the bridge, he marched up the muddy road that crossed the dock area to the Mars Gate of the city. To either side in the darkness he could make out the tangled wreckage of demolished warehouses. Destroyed by the defenders, he guessed, to avoid giving cover to anyone assaulting the walls. His breath was tight as he came up the last inclined causeway towards the gate.

'Halt and declare yourselves!' The cry came from one of the high arched windows of the gate tower. Castus gave the watchword, then waited. Above him the arches glowed with faint firelight. He thought of the artillery on the towers, the archers standing ready. Bolts and arrows were no doubt aimed directly at him.

The men behind him shuffled and stamped. Some had shifted their shields to the front, ready to block any missiles. Still the gates remained closed.

'Come on, lads!' Felix yelled. 'I need to piss! Open up or I'll do it on your doorstep!'

A stir of laughter. Castus broke into a grin. He felt the nervous energy inside him jump and flutter. Then he heard the echoing clatter of the great wooden portcullis lifting inside the gate passage, and a moment later the shunt and bang as the locking bar of the gate was lifted.

They moved in a rush as soon as the first opening appeared between the gates. The men in the passage could do little to oppose them; they fell back, raising their hands as the soldiers stormed between them. Felix slammed the optio in charge against the wall with his shield.

'Modestus, secure each tower,' Castus said. His heart was thumping. 'Hold the gates until you're relieved, then take a force into the city and take the other gates. Felix – bring four men and follow me. Trumpeter – whenever you're ready.'

The young man with the trumpet coughed, spat, then raised his horn and blew a long sustained note. Already Modestus and his men were into the towers on either side of the gates, rushing up the steps and raising screams and cries of alarm from within.

Striding up the dark street from the gate, his nailed boots crunching on the cobbles, Castus saw figures appearing from the doorways and porticos on either side, drawn by the noise and the trumpet's call. Some of them cried out questions as he passed. He had known cities under siege, before, and all of them had this same feeling of tense anticipation, everyone on the edge of panic. He felt it himself. But at least now he was inside the walls. He had a chance. And he could finally confront Tiberianus.

He turned the corner opposite the high wall of the Sacred Precinct and marched north, passing the front portico of the Praetorium. There were groups of soldiers in the streets, some of them on sentry duty and others just loitering around the watchfires. None of them challenged him. He was moving fast, with an escort and a sense of purpose. The lack of morale in the city as a whole was almost palpable.

At least the soldiers on duty at the doors of the governor's residence appeared alert. They stepped forward as Castus approached, barring the way with their spears.

'Move aside,' Castus ordered. 'I'm going in to speak to the governor.'

'What's this, boys, a mutiny?' said one of the guards. He looked as if he might be tempted himself.

'I am Aurelius Castus, Commander of the Frontier, and my troops are taking control of this city. Right now there's two of you and six of us. Make a decision.'

The guards exchanged a glance. One of them shrugged, and they moved aside. Felix was already shoving between them to bang on the inlaid panels of the door with his sword hilt. A moment later the locks clashed and the door edged open. Felix threw himself at the gap, and Castus followed him into the house.

Lamplight shone off the marble in the vestibule, slaves in patterned tunics falling back from the doorway in shock as Castus and his men marched through them. Two pillars at the far end framed an opening to the moonlit central garden; between them stood a grey-bearded man in a red silk robe. Castus recognised him from his previous visits: Tiberianus's major-domo.

'Where's the governor?' he demanded.

The old man stretched out his arm, pointing to the bath suite at the far side of the garden. 'But I'm afraid you will be unable to speak to him,' he said. Castus noticed that the man's face was wet with tears.

'What do you mean?'

'I regret to report, excellency,' the major-domo said, 'that the clarissimus Claudius Basilius Tiberianus... has taken his own life.'

CHAPTER XXVIII

The body floated in the centre of the circular pool, arms spread wide, and the water was dyed rose pink around it. A little steam still coiled from the surface in the light of the lamps set in niches around the room; Tiberianus had clearly ordered his bath heated before he cut his own wrists. His flared nostrils floated just above the bloodied water, his face submerged. Castus stared at the dead man, the fierce energy that had propelled him from the river dying away into a distant sense of loathing. The governor had removed himself from the reach of vengeance.

'Disappointing,' a voice said. Castus turned sharply. The man beside him had a familiar dark complexion and a shaved head that gleamed in the light of the lamps. 'A tool of flawed metal,' the eunuch went on, nodding towards the body in the pool. 'The slightest pressure, and he bends. He bends and breaks.'

'What are you doing here?' Castus said, frowning, his voice jagged with frustration and fatigue. The major-domo had followed him into the bathing chamber, still sniffing back tears.

'I'm what you might call a guest,' Luxorius said. 'Though not a willing one. Confined to the city by the orders of the governor. Although those orders do seem to have lapsed with his demise...'

Before the eunuch could say more, Felix came stamping back in from the garden, one of the soldiers trailing him. 'We've searched the whole house, dominus. Nobody here but the governor's staff and slaves.' He raised an eyebrow as he noticed the corpse floating in the bath, and let out a low whistle of interest.

Castus seized the major-domo by the arm. 'Where's my son?' he demanded. 'Where's Sabinus?'

'I believe I can answer that,' Luxorius said. 'Your son was here, but he was removed three days ago by the slaves of Magnius Rufus. They said they were taking him and some others – refugees, they called them – to Juliacum.'

Castus felt a ringing in his head, as if he had been struck. He clenched his fist and pressed it to his brow. Then he snatched up one of the lamps and flung it with a snarling cry of rage at the body floating in the pool. 'Bastard!' he shouted, and the word echoed back at him from the vaulted ceiling.

In the governor's reception room, Castus sat on the edge of a couch with his shoulders slumped, his head gripped in both hands. His skull felt tight with nausea and anger; his whole body was coursing with it. How had he allowed this to happen? What mistake had he made? And what – the thought spun in his head, maddening – what should he do now? A voice spoke at the edge of his mind. Sabina's voice, asking where their son had gone, what had been done with him...

'I'm sorry,' he whispered hoarsely into his cupped hands. 'I'm so sorry. There was nothing I could do...'

'I hope I'm not disturbing you, excellency,' the eunuch said, appearing in the doorway. He smiled as he entered the room and seated himself on the facing couch. Two slaves followed him, carrying platters of food and glasses of wine. 'I thought you might like refreshment. You certainly appear to have had quite a journey. I'd suggest a bath, too, but in the circumstances…'

Castus stared at him, his jaw slack. But his stomach was growling at the thought of food; he had not eaten or drunk for many hours. Ignoring the eunuch, he snatched up one of the platters and began to eat. Slices of cold meat – smoked pork, perhaps, or venison. He could barely taste it. He grabbed one of the glasses and gulped back wine.

From the garden portico outside he could hear the clashing sounds of hobnailed boots on mosaic tiles. The rug on the floor was already soiled with muddy prints. Strange to see fully armed soldiers, sweat-stained unshaven men with shields and spears, thronging the governor's tastefully appointed residence. Only a shame, Castus thought, that Tiberianus did not live to appreciate it. Felix and his men were still searching the governor's rooms; Castus had sent a message to Diogenes, telling him to find the house of Julius Dulcitius and bring the grain merchant and his family to the governor's residence. Even from the depths of his angry despair, he knew he had to remain in control, keep people moving. Soon he would have to summon the city councillors, the duumvirs and the curator. And then there was the city itself to contend with, and the barbarian horde camped on the far side of the river… He felt age weighing upon him, the aggressive stamina that had carried him so far now almost drained.

'I expect you'll be marching towards Juliacum very soon,' the eunuch said. 'We received a message earlier today – or yesterday, I suppose – that the main force of the Chamavi and Chattuari were plundering the whole area. If you decide to move in that direction, I would be happy to join you.'

'Why would you want to do that?' Castus asked, his mouth still half full of meat. It was salted ham, he had decided.

The eunuch gave him a rather cat-like stare. 'The governor killed himself because he learned that four days ago I managed to smuggle a message out of the city to the Praetorian Prefect at Treveris. By now the most blessed Caesar will have mustered his field troops, and already the advance units will be on the road. If your force can hold the barbarians at Juliacum, the field army can destroy them utterly. I would like to be present to share in the triumph!'

'You seem very confident we'll win.'

'I'm not a very military person,' the eunuch said, 'but I have faith in the power of our armies. We do have the true God on our side, I think!'

'You're a Christian then?'

Luxorius lifted the small gold pendant he wore around his neck. But he was still smiling and Castus could not tell whether there was a certain mocking irony in his gesture. He recalled the last time he had seen the eunuch, at Noviomagus on the night before the Caesar met the Salian chiefs.

'You always seem to turn up in unusual places, don't you?' he said. 'I knew a man like that once. He came to a bad end, so I heard.'

The eunuch just shrugged.

Castus stood up and crossed the rug to stand beside him. 'I'd like to know quite what sort of game you're playing here. You're the prefect's servant, right? Or is somebody else giving you orders?'

For a moment Luxorius smiled again, half closing his eyes, still with that look of subtle irony. Castus drew the knife from the sheath on his belt and slapped it down on the table beside the couch. At the sight of the blade the eunuch flinched, his smile vanishing. A quick tremor of fear passed through him, but then he composed himself.

'There's no need to threaten me,' Luxorius said quietly. 'I assure you, I have lost more in my life already than any man would care to lose. You won't break me so easily.'

'Tell me why you're here then,' Castus said. 'Who sent you and what are you doing?'

'Could we just say that I serve a higher power?' Luxorius smiled again. 'A power that bears you no malice, Aurelius Castus. I freed your assistant, the soldier called Diogenes. I can help you again, if you'll let me.'

The lamps had burnt low and a trembling shadow was filling the room. Castus laid his hand on the knife blade, then picked it up and returned it to his belt sheath. 'I need no more of your help,' he said. 'Come with me if you want – you're still the servant of my superior officer, supposedly. But I don't want you getting in my way, understood?'

'Absolutely.'

Voices from the dark portico outside, and a moment later Diogenes and two soldiers marched into the room and saluted.

'We found Dulcitius's house, dominus,' Diogenes said. 'But somebody else had got there first. The doors were broken and everything inside was in chaos. There was a body laid out in the dining room, under a sheet. Stab wounds to the chest and neck. Priscus here found one of the household slaves, who told us that the dead man was Dulcitius himself. Soldiers killed him, the slave said, and seized his wife and daughters. Apparently they said they were taking them west to join Magnius Rufus at Juliacum.'

First light of dawn, and Castus stamped heavily up the wooden stairs to the rampart above the gatehouse of the bridgehead fort. The sun was still below the wooded hills to the east, but a seeping grey luminescence showed him the blackened waste of land stretching away from the fort walls towards the belt of trees, the charred stumps of the outer palisade and the burnt ruins of the buildings that had stood along the roadside. Low mist clung in hollows of the land, threaded with smoke.

'They're camped in a wide arc, just beyond the trees,' the tribune said, sweeping his arm across the expanse of open ground. 'Probably four or five thousand of them. Bructeri mostly, as far as we can tell, with some of the Lanciones and others. They made a couple of attempts at the walls, but mostly they've just plundered whatever they could get their hands on and burnt the rest.'

Castus grunted. His impression of Tribune Gaudiosus had improved since he reached the fort. The officer had presented himself at once, surrendering his sword and submitting to any punishment that Castus decreed. He had already heard of the governor's death, and the change of command in the city. The languorous, haughty pride he had once exhibited was gone now; he was a loyal soldier, he said, and had been following orders. Castus had been inclined to have the man punished, even executed. He had crossed the bridge with murder in his heart. But he was short of officers, and Gaudiosus had clearly led the defence of his position well. He had pardoned the man, for now. Hopefully Gaudiosus would come to earn his mercy.

'What's your total strength, here and in the city garrison?'

'Nearly three thousand, dominus,' Gaudiosus said. 'The detachment of the First Minervia, a few of the Thirtieth, the Fifth Valeria Thracum, and a small unit of Dalmatian cavalry who rode in from Bonna just before the barbarians came.'

Staring out over the wasteland of burnt ground, Castus could make out the figures of the barbarians beginning to emerge from the woodland. Were they massing for a fresh assault? It seemed unlikely – their dead still lay heaped around the walls, and they must have realised by now that they lacked the numbers or the skill to storm the Roman fortifications. A deadlock, then. The resolution he had considered as he crossed the river became firmer in his mind.

'Find me a green branch, if you can,' Castus said, and turned towards the stairs.

'You're going to *talk* to them, excellency?' Gaudiosus widened his eyes.

'Would you rather *fight* them, tribune?'

At least, Castus thought as he descended the wooden flights of stairs, he was able to make a better impression now. His private quarters in the Praetorium had been ransacked by the governor's men, of course, but Eumolpius had managed to locate a chest of clothing and the armour and equipment that Castus had left behind when he departed on his mission down the river. Now he was dressed in a fresh white tunic and breeches, clean dry boots and a white wool cloak. He wore his gilded muscled cuirass, and his burnished helmet with its tall black feather plumes. His imperial brooch and eagle-headed spatha had been lost in the wreck of the *Bellona*, but he had found temporary replacements. He was still achingly tired, beyond sleep, but he was dressed for command.

Castus's mounted escort was waiting just inside the gateway. His familiar old grey mare was there, too; Eumolpius had found Dapple in the Praetorium stables, under the care of the drillmaster Tagmatius. Castus rubbed the horse's nose and patted her neck, then swung himself up into the saddle. The stocky youth mounted behind him was the *draconarius* of the First Minervia, newly appointed as Castus's personal standard-bearer, the banner that trailed behind the gilded dragon's head now replaced with imperial purple silk.

Turning in the saddle, Castus made out the figure of Bonitus in the shadows beneath the gatehouse. The Frankish chief was gazing upwards at the portcullis mechanism and the iron-bound gates. He had a look of intense appreciation; probably, Castus realised, he had never studied the interior of a Roman fort before. The circuit of powerful walls had clearly made an impression on him. He noticed Castus and his party mounted in the roadway, and with a last upward glance strolled over to join them.

'Will you ride out with me?' Castus asked. 'I'll need a translator.'

Bonitus gave him a cold smile. 'And it looks good, heh, to have me there too?'

'It might help, yes.'

'Well...' Bonitus said, nodding briskly. He adjusted his gold-buckled belt and the array of weapons he was carrying: knife, axe and sword. Then he vaulted up onto a spare Roman cavalry horse, settling himself in the saddle with the ease of a skilled rider. 'Maybe we see!'

Trumpets sounded from the battlement walkway above them, then the portcullis shuddered upwards and the gates began to creak open. Nudging the horse's flanks, Castus led his men out through the dark tunnel and into the morning sun.

They rode only a short way from the walls, along the paved road that ran due eastwards towards the hill country, the very limit of Roman control. Then Castus raised his hand and signalled a halt. One of the men behind him was carrying the green branch, the symbol of parley. Now they had to see whether the barbarians would respect it.

Mist and smoke curled through the wreck of charred timber and burnt tree stumps beside the road. From the forest at the far side of the cleared land, Castus could hear the calls of the

Bructeri warriors, the braying of their horns summoning their chiefs. He sat firmly in the saddle, kept his back straight, and waited.

The shapes of men seemed to form out of the mist, thronging along the margin of the forest. As Castus watched, a band of them moved forward along the road towards him. They were mounted on horses and ponies, five or six well-armed, powerful-looking warriors, either chiefs or war leaders. The others following on foot appeared to be members of their household retinues, with their slaves or spear-carriers. The mounted band came to a halt only fifty paces away. In silence the warriors stared at him. Castus thought of the campaign he had fought against these same savage people ten years before. The dying men writhing as the poisoned arrows bit their flesh. He was surely mad to extend trust to them now.

'Tell them that the governor, Tiberianus, the man who executed the Chamavi hostages and started this war, is dead,' Castus told Bonitus. He waited while the Salian chief translated his words in a rather casual-sounding tone.

'Tell them that I am Aurelius Castus, Commander of the Germanic Frontier, and I have taken charge of this city in the name of the emperor. The emperor's son, Caesar Flavius Julius Crispus, will arrive in one or two days with a powerful army to destroy those of our enemies who remain in the field.'

Bonitus gave him a glance, a raised eyebrow and a quick smile. Then he called out the translation. It seemed to go on for longer than Castus had expected.

'What are you telling them?'

'I also add that I myself lead a powerful force of Salii, thousands strong, in the service of the Roman emperor!'

'Don't overdo it.'

'Heh, sorry!'

'Tell them that we know they cannot take our fort or city. They waste the lives of their men in this assault. Instead I offer them a truce: if they withdraw their raiding parties, collect their dead and go back to their homeland there will be no reprisals against them. They have satisfied the demands of honour. Now let them return to the treaties they agreed with Rome.'

Bonitus took his time over the translation; Castus hoped he was adding no more boastful flourishes of his own. A silence followed his words; then the Bructeri leaders began to talk among themselves in low urgent voices.

'Can you make out what they're saying?' Castus asked from the corner of his mouth. Bonitus shook his head.

The Bructeri group parted a little, and a boy on a pony rode up between them. Aged about twelve, he carried a light javelin across his shoulder. At the first sight of the boy, Castus felt a jolt of recognition pass through him. It could not be possible, he thought, but still he leaned forward over the saddle horns, studying the boy. Just a close resemblance, perhaps – understandable within a single tribe. Then the boy raised his hand to brush the blond hair from his face, and Castus caught the wink of a blue bead on his wrist. The same amulet that Ganna had given him, and that he had returned to her only last winter. The boy was her son: he was sure of it.

And now one of the leading warriors was leaning from his horse to speak to the boy. Together they glanced towards Castus, and the boy nodded. Frowning, still half disbelieving, Castus remembered Ganna's words: *My brother has taken him into his household. He is a great man, now, my brother. The high chief's bodyguard.*

Dapple stamped at the ground and shook her mane, the stink of smoke and charred timber beginning to unnerve her. Castus tightened his grip on the reins, still gazing at the group of Bructeri, and at the boy he knew must be Ganna's child. The child was staring back at him, and Castus tried to read his expression. How would he feel, he wondered, in this boy's place? He had no idea – his own mother had died when he was born, and he had hated and feared his father. But this boy must know that the Romans had slain his father, taken his mother as a slave and held her for nearly ten long years. How did he feel, knowing that the enemy commander who had kept his mother in servitude for so long now confronted him?

The warrior who had spoken to the boy – Ganna's brother, Castus assumed – now urged his own horse forward. Three other men followed him. As he drew closer, Castus saw the resemblance despite the blond beard combed out over his chest, the fierce warrior garb and posture: the man had the same clear blue eyes, the same proud bearing that he remembered in Ganna herself. He halted, and for several long moments he fixed Castus with his gaze.

'You,' the warrior called in thickly accented Latin. 'You – Aurelius Castus.'

'I am,' Castus told him.

Another long pause, then the warrior glanced back towards the group behind him, nodded, and looked at Castus again.

'My king say. We accept.'

The warrior raised his spear, then turned his horse and rode back with the others towards the distant trees. Castus let out a long-held breath. He heard Bonitus doing the same.

A low cry went up from the barbarian host, building to a roar that resonated between the trees. A single horn sounded a long braying note. Then, as Castus watched, every man turned and raised his shield, moving back into the forest's darkness, until the drifting smoke and the last haze of mist obscured them entirely.

Was Ganna herself out there somewhere? Castus had no way of telling. But as he sat in the stillness, the early sun warming his face, he could almost sense her looking back at him from the trees. He raised his hand, palm outwards. Then he gave the signal to return to the fort.

CHAPTER XXIX

So much delay, and so much still to lose.

The sun was setting once more by the time the assembled troops marched out through the west gate of the city on the long straight highway towards Juliacum. To have lost a day now was almost more than Castus could endure, but it had been necessary. He had given orders to the city councillors and his own commanders, and toured the defences; only then had his last reserves of energy given out, plunging him into deathlike dreamless sleep on the couch in his quarters. Six hours later Diogenes had woken him with the report the scouts had brought in: the Bructeri had withdrawn completely. The city was safe, but Castus's son was still in danger, still a virtual hostage in the hands of Magnius Rufus. Marcellina and her daughters too. He knew he could not lose any more time.

Along the highway the troops marched through the warm summer night, spreading out into a long column. Each man was fully armed and equipped, with eight days' rations in his pack. Castus had withdrawn men from the garrison of Colonia and added them to his own force; now he had just short of two thousand under his command, but only a handful of them were mounted. Strong enough to smash any raiding bands they met on the road, but a meagre force if they had to confront King Ragnachar and his main Chamavi host.

Castus had ordered his men to bring every trumpet and horn in Colonia, even those sacred instruments kept in the temples. He hoped the gods would not be angered by the sacrilege. But the men were rested and eager, and marched with a purpose now. The flat arable lands around them appeared empty in the darkness, only the flicker of distant fires along the horizon showing the presence of war.

An hour after midnight they reached a crossroads with an inn, a posting station and a clutch of houses, and Castus ordered a halt. Tiberiacum, the place was called. The similarity with the name of the dead governor seemed ominous. He was moving back down the column, checking the situation of the troops and their officers, when a scout brought news of cavalry on the road ahead. The Sixth Equites Stablesiani, riding in from the west.

'Tell their tribune to station his men with my vanguard,' Castus told the scout, 'and then report to me.' As the man rode away he clenched his back teeth and stared into the darkness. He had not expected to meet Ulpius Dexter again so soon.

In the rear chamber of the posting station he sat at a rough plank table and waited, tapping his fingers. The lamp on the table gave a feeble sputtering light, casting slanted shadows around the graffiti-scarred whitewashed walls. Diogenes stood beside the door, with Felix and two dependable soldiers of the Second Legion. Voices came from the lobby outside, then the door opened and Dexter entered, stooping under the low lintel. He was still dressed in his cloak and scale cuirass, his helmet clasped under his arm, the road's dust clinging to him. He grinned as he saluted, the muscles of his tanned face tightening.

'Good to see you alive, excellency! We heard rumours otherwise...'

Castus nodded. The man had no idea, clearly. He gestured for the tribune to continue.

'I've got two hundred of my riders with me,' Dexter said. 'We came in from the Tungris direction, fighting running battles all the way to Juliacum, but the town was surrounded by the enemy – too many of them to break through. Most of the ones we met were slaves, freed from the fields and armed against their masters. I was aiming to reach Colonia by dawn and join the garrison there. We've taken losses, but I can turn the men around at once if you'll lead them.'

Castus splayed his hands on the table. He felt a low pain in his chest at the thought of what he had to do. He had trusted this man once, considered him the best of his officers. But the guilty are often not the worst of men. Standing up, he circled the table until he stood before Dexter.

'Surrender your sword, tribune.'

Dexter blinked, and then grinned, as if at some joke. But when he saw Castus's grave expression, a look of hunted fear flickered in his eyes.

'I don't understand,' he said. 'I don't... What...?'

The slightest nod from Castus, and the two soldiers stepped forward and seized the tribune's arms. Felix reached in nimbly from behind and took Dexter's sword, slipping it from the scabbard. Dexter's smile died.

'Last year,' Castus said, 'my friend Valerius Leontius, Commander of the Frontier, was murdered at Castra Herculis. You were there. What happened?'

The tribune's expression shifted between feigned outrage and guilty fear. 'Leontius was killed by the barbarians!' he said.

With one sweeping movement Castus drew his sword and swung it up against the tribune's neck. Dexter flinched as the honed steel touched him, the muscles of his throat pulled tight.

'Your interpreter already told us everything,' Castus said, conscious of the lie. It had been a hunch, an intuition, and he had prayed that he was not mistaken. But Dexter's look of panic told him all he needed to know.

'Bappo? He's a liar...! Where is he now?'

'Bappo's dead. As is Governor Tiberianus. And you won't leave this room alive unless you talk.'

'I...' Dexter began, and then swallowed heavily. He looked sick, trying for a defiant tone but failing. Resignation was stealing his resolve. This was his fate, and he knew it. 'They gave me money,' he gasped. 'Leontius was never popular – he was harsh, unforgiving... Tiberianus and Magnius Rufus promised me money, and I needed it. I had debts.'

'Any decent officer can live on his pay. What was it? Gambling?'

'Yes, and... other things. They threatened me – said they could have me dismissed from the army, even seized and tortured. Of course I went along with it...'

'Of course. And you murdered Leontius yourself?'

Dexter closed his eyes as he nodded. Castus felt a hot rush of satisfaction rise through him. For the first time, he held justice in his hands. But he knew that it was not that easy: Dexter was the sole witness to the treachery, and Castus needed both him and his troops.

'And then you stood by and did nothing when Rufus tried to have me killed. That night at the villa, when I was attacked in my room – you knew what was going to happen...'

'No!' Dexter cried. 'I was as shocked as you. I never expected him to go that far...'

'But you did nothing. You said *nothing*.'

He lowered his sword. Dexter's eyes were wet, and he blinked away the tears with an expression of disgust. 'I'm sorry,' the tribune said. 'I've lived with this crime for over a year. I deserve your punishment, but my men were only following orders.'

Following orders, Castus thought. How many times had he heard those words? How many times had he used them himself?

'We have a battle ahead of us,' he said quietly, leaning back against the table. 'If any shred of honour remains to you, you'll do your duty. Perhaps you'll find a soldier's death, and all this can be forgotten. For now, I return your sword on trust. See to your men. We rest here for two hours, then we move.'

Dexter's face reddened, and he stammered as he tried to speak, and then fell silent. Drawing himself up straight, he gave a military salute. 'We will do what we are ordered, and at every command we will be ready!'

When the tribune was gone Castus seated himself once more at the table. There was a flask of watered wine beside him, and he poured himself a cup. A tap at the door, the sentry's voice, and then Luxorius entered the room.

'Forgive me. I overheard your conversation,' the eunuch said in a conciliatory tone. 'A startling disclosure! My master the Praetorian Prefect will, of course, wish to learn more about it. If you don't mind, I will accompany the tribune myself, and ensure that he does not, ah, attempt to escape.'

'He won't,' Castus said. He felt dirty inside, all the satisfaction of Dexter's confession washed out of him. Death in battle was the best the tribune could hope for now. 'But go with him if you want, I can't stop you. Just try not to get killed, eh?'

'Juliacum up ahead, dominus!' the scout reported. The night was already fading towards dawn, and in the greyness Castus could make out the column of footsore troops stretching away behind him, stationary as they waited for the order to advance once more. Twenty-five miles they had marched under cover of darkness; all were tired, blistered, eager for food and rest. But all knew that the enemy were close now. He could sense the men watching him, waiting for his decision.

'What's the situation over there?'

'The fort garrison's still holding out, it looks like,' the scout said. 'But they're surrounded on all sides. The cavalry have already hit some of the enemy piquets and outlying encampments. A lot of the ones we killed are escaped slaves – they've still got the shackle scars on their ankles.'

Castus remembered the Frankish prisoners he had seen working on the estates of Magnius Rufus. He could hardly blame them for their revolt. Was Rufus himself now trapped inside the fort, with the troops he had gathered under his command and the refugees he had taken from Colonia? He would find out soon enough.

The ground ahead rose slightly, the barest swelling of the flat plain but enough to hide the column of troops from the horde encircling Juliacum. Castus nudged his horse forward, riding up the slope of the road; then he dismounted and sent an order for his commanders to join him at a stand of trees overlooking the plain to the west. As he waited, Castus walked forward, screened by the trees. In the faint pre-dawn light he could make out the brown brick circle of the fort walls and the civilian settlement along the road with ribbons of smoke still rising from the plundered buildings. In the fields and open country surrounding the settlement he could see the scattered encampments of the barbarians.

'Form up in close order,' he told the commanders. 'All standards to the fore. Horns and trumpets ready on my command, cavalry to fan out on either flank. Once they see us, we keep moving until I order a halt. Slow and steady.'

Nods and mutters of acknowledgement from all around him, and the men returned to their units. Dexter alone lingered for a moment more, his face grave as he saluted. Striding back down the slope, Castus mounted and led his small party of mounted troopers, with his staff officers and standard-bearer, off to the right. The sky to the east was already flushed with the rising sun. He raised his hand, then let it fall.

A single horn sounded from the vanguard of the column, answered at once by another, then more. With a crash of boots on gravel the column began to move.

Sunlight flashed through the leaves of the trees overhead, then the full burst of dawn lit the plain. The brassy clamour of the trumpets was almost deafening, one horn answering another, a wild cacophony of command calls as the troops marched over the rise. Their standards caught the sunlight: the glinting eagle and the ram ensign of I Minervia, the *vexilla* of the II Britannica, XXII Primigenia and XXX Ulpia Victrix detachments, the flags of the cavalry units and Castus's own purple draco streaming in the breeze.

Already the plain was stirring into life and motion, as the mass of barbarian raiders and freed slaves camped around Juliacum looked into the rising sun and saw a phalanx of troops bearing down on them, with all the standards and the wild screaming trumpets of a field army on the march. They could see the cavalry fanning out along the crest of the rise, dark against the brightening sky, and the dust raised by the marching men. Already they were scattering in disarray, abandoning their encampments and fleeing westward, away from the advancing doom.

As the last men of the column crested the rise, Castus signalled a halt. A single trumpet call, and all two thousand men raised their spears and let out a ringing battle cry. The noise died across the plain, but it was enough: their enemies were fleeing, masses of them streaming away on foot or on stolen horses. The cavalry were riding down the stragglers as the troops advanced along the road towards the gates of Juliacum.

It was four hours later that he saw her, at the end of a stable portico crowded with wounded men. She stood in a patch of sunlight falling between the wooden pillars, wadded linen and a water jug in her hands as a surgeon knelt beside her attending to one of the injured. Dressed in a plain long tunic, her hair bound in a cloth, she could have been one of the slaves, but Castus knew her at once. He strode forward, stepping over the straw pallets where the wounded men lay, the heaps of equipment and weapons piled beside them.

Just for a moment, he felt that he could walk right up to her, close the distance between them and take her in his arms. The noise around him, the groans and cries of the injured and the clatter from the stable courtyard, fell into silence. She saw him, her eyes widened and she set down the jug and stepped back. He halted just in time. The noise rose up between them once more.

'Excellency,' Marcellina said with awkward formality. In the sunlight he could see the lines of weariness scored into her face, the dark smudges beneath her eyes. 'I heard you were here. I... was going to find you, but I needed to help...'

She gestured at the scene around her. Castus understood. To wait passively at a time like this would have been unbearable; without the constant pressure of decision and action, he would have fallen into despair days ago. But he could hear the strain in her voice, the desperate need to remain focused and not give way to grief.

'Your son,' she said. 'Magnius Rufus took him. My daughters too.'

Castus felt his throat tighten, his shoulders lock with anger. He had already learned what had happened here: how Rufus had ridden out against the invaders with his three thousand men and fallen into successive ambushes all along the road west towards Tungris. How the troops had become split up, their morale shattered, and panic taken hold. Rufus himself had fled back to Juliacum with the horsemen, and the survivors of his force had come in over the following hours, many of them wounded and lacking commanders, until the enemy had sealed the roads.

'Where is he?' he asked, unable to keep the jagged edge of rage from his voice.

Marcellina drew herself upright, speaking with a crisp hauteur. 'He left for his villa yesterday night. He intends to defend his own lands, and let the rest of us suffer for his mistakes.'

Castus looked away, stifling a curse. *Yesterday night...* if only he had been quicker, had pushed himself and his men harder... But there was nothing he could do now. The entire space within the walls of Juliacum was packed with people, the parade ground turned into horse lines, the barrack porticos and stables, the posting station and the storage sheds all turned into billets for thousands of soldiers and the civilians who had fled from the surrounding lands.

'I've set up my quarters in the western gatehouse,' he said quietly, stiff with the sense of propriety. 'Can you visit me there later? Once your duties here are done?'

She gave him a quick nod, then knelt beside the surgeon to help him bandage the bloodied cavalry trooper at her feet.

It was midday before she came to him. Castus had slept briefly, and even managed to take a hurried lukewarm bath.

He was sitting on a stool with his back to the door, stripped to the waist as Eumolpius changed the dressings on his wound. The sentry showed Marcellina in, and she gasped as she saw him.

'Oh, I'm sorry! I'll wait...'

'No,' he said, standing quickly and snatching up his sweat-stained tunic. Marcellina had turned away, staring into the corner of the room as Castus dressed himself and buckled his belt. With a quick wave of his hand Castus dismissed his orderly and the sentry.

'I didn't know you were hurt,' Marcellina said, turning to face him once more.

'Just a thorn scratch,' Castus told her, and smiled as he saw her frown. She seated herself on the stool, and he crossed to the curve of arched windows at the far side of the chamber and leaned on the sill. Outside he could see parties of Dexter's tireless cavalry troopers, returning from hunting the barbarian stragglers across the plain.

'Rufus murdered my husband,' Marcellina said. Her voice caught, and when Castus glanced back he saw her cover her face with her hand, wiping away tears.

'I know,' he told her.

'It was my fault. I persuaded Dulcitius to write to the Praetorian Prefect and tell him everything. About Rufus and the governor, and what they'd done to the last commander, what they were trying to do to you. But they found out. I don't know how.'

'It wasn't your fault,' Castus said, in a gruff whisper.

'My husband wasn't a bad man,' she said, and sniffed back a sob. 'He tried to do what was right. But he was in debt to them – everything we owned.' She pulled off her headcloth, her hair tumbling loose as she scrubbed her face. 'And now he's dead, and Rufus – Rufus! – you know what he did?' She was sitting upright, her face burning with anger.

'What?'

'He offered to marry me! *Him* – the man who had killed my husband… He knew my father once held high military rank in Britain and my mother was of good family there. He told me that a woman with my heritage – with my *blood* – deserved more than to be the wife of a merchant…' She choked a cry of disdain. 'I deserved a husband who was descended from an emperor!'

Castus flinched as he pushed himself away from the window. 'What did you tell him?'

Marcellina glared at him for a moment. 'What do you think I said? I'm a widow, thirty years old, with two young daughters to support and nothing to my name. What could I say?' She tightened her lips, alight with fury. 'I told him to crawl back into whatever filthy pit of Hades he'd come from!'

Castus snorted a laugh, unable to stop himself. Marcellina drew in a shuddering breath, then smiled as the boiling anger subsided in her once more. 'But then,' she said in a quieter voice. 'Then it was chaos. Nobody here knew what they were doing, nobody… They haven't seen anything like this before. But *I have.* I lived through all of it, back in Britain. My children are all I have left to me now – he knew that, so he took them when he fled south. He knows I'll go after them.'

'And my son?' Castus said, pulling up a stool and sitting down to face her. 'Why did he take Sabinus?'

Marcellina looked away, her hair falling across her face as she pressed her fingers to her brow. 'I believe he intends to use your son,' she said. 'Use him as a hostage. Trade him for his own life, if necessary. Either to you, or to the barbarians.'

Castus gave an anguished groan, folding his arms tight to his chest. He had guessed as much, but hoped it was not true.

Hoped there might be some other reason, some less hideous truth. He thought of the Chamavi leader, Ragnachar, standing at the riverside as Castus threatened his captive son with death. Now he shared that sense of helpless pain.

'What happens now?' Marcellina asked, her voice grown tender.

Castus took a long breath, exhaled, tried to think clearly. 'We've had messengers from the south,' he said. 'The young Caesar and the advance units of his field army are nearly at Icorigium. I've sent messengers requesting they divert onto the direct road to Aquae Granni. They could meet up with me a march west of here in a day – maybe two days.'

Marcellina nodded, uncertain. Both of them knew that it was a hard and dirty road to Aquae Granni, through the dense forests of the Arduenna. A large force travelling that way could easily be held up.

'And you? What will you do?'

For a long while he could not answer. He knew what he wanted to do. Rufus's villa lay only five miles south of Juliacum; if he took a small mounted escort and rode fast he could be there within an hour. He could rescue his son, and Marcellina's children, and return in time to lead his men... But that could not happen. Dealing with Rufus could take time, and every moment his troops delayed at Juliacum, the main barbarian horde would be free to plunder the lands to the west. As soon as the Chamavi and Chattuari heard of the field army's approach they would surely swing north along the valley of the Mosa, heading for the frontier and their own territories beyond. He was the supreme commander, for now at least, and he could not desert his men while the enemy were in the field.

'I march west before sundown,' he said, with a pained downward glance.

Marcellina nodded slowly. She appeared breathless, a blush rising to her cheeks.

'Then I will go to find Rufus myself,' she said. 'I still have a carriage in the yard outside, and I can find horses...'

'No. You stay here. It's not safe to travel the roads without an escort.'

'You don't give me orders!' she said, with a flare of anger. 'I'm not one of your soldiers!'

She had said something very similar to him many years before, Castus remembered. He shrugged an apology. 'I'm sorry. Command gets to be a habit after a while. But please, stay here. Just a day, two days more...'

'I'm going to find my children,' she said, with slow emphasis. 'And you'll have to lock me up if you want to stop me.'

For a moment they stared at each other. Castus heard the heavy tread of a sentry climbing the stairs to the battlements in the next room. Then he let out a long sigh, leaned forward and took her hand. She ran her fingers over his palm, lightly tracing the pink calluses of blister-scars left from the hours of rowing.

'At least let me send some of my men with you,' he said.

'No. Rufus has his guards all around him: they'd attack anyone trying to get to him – but he wouldn't harm me, I'm sure of it. I think maybe I can talk to him, make him see reason.'

Good luck with that, Castus thought.

Marcellina lowered her head, then looked up at him again. 'He's mad, I know. He really believed that he could lead an army and liberate the whole province. He believed the troops would salute him as their triumphant leader and he could stand equal with the emperor himself, like his mighty ancestor... *Great gods!*' she cried, casting a wild glance at the ceiling. 'These men with their dreams of power! Why do they have this lust for it...? Do you have it too?'

'No,' Castus said. 'I've never wanted power. But it's been given to me anyway.'

'Because you use it wisely, maybe.'

'You think I'm wise? After all this?' He grinned, and felt the warm pressure of her hands, the tightened clasp of affirmation. Standing, he drew her to her feet.

'I know what you're planning to do,' she said with a quick stammer. 'I know that the barbarian king wants to kill you for breaking your vow about the hostages... You're going to use yourself as bait, aren't you? March out into open country and wait for him to come and find you.'

'That's the only plan I've got,' Castus said. 'Seems like a good one.'

'It's too much to risk,' she whispered. She stepped forward, pressing herself against him and stretching up to kiss his lips. 'Please be careful. Come back alive.'

'I'll try,' he said. But he would promise nothing. He had broken too many promises already.

CHAPTER XXX

S omehow he had always known that this would be the place.
As he climbed the wooden ladder to the upper chamber
of the isolated watchtower, Castus remembered the last time
he had been here; his observation then had been inspired, a
god's whisper. This was a place of war. And this was where he
would fight his battle.

It had been winter then, the land bare and cold. Now it was
high summer, and from the window of the tower he looked out
over rolling pastures filled with wild flowers, scattered stands
of trees along the horizon. Still early, the sky a pale eggshell
blue, but the sun was already bright. It was going to be a warm
day, a beautiful day. Cool air breathed in his face as Castus
stepped out onto the walkway and gazed to the west. From
the low ridge where the tower stood, the land sloped gently
to the marshy valley of a river that fed into the Mosa. And a
few miles along the valley, moving towards him, he could see
the war host of the enemy. Men in their thousands, driving
animals with them: horses, herds of cattle and flocks of sheep
plundered from the surrounding lands. Captives, too, no doubt.
They moved in dark streams that flowed together into a single
moving mass. The sun glittered on their spears.

Castus gripped the wooden rail of the walkway, letting
the shudder ripple through his body. Fear had its place, and

he knew it well. Crossing to the eastern side of the tower, he stared up into the dazzle of early light and raised his palms to the warmth, muttering a prayer. It was a familiar prayer, one he had spoken many times before. *Sol Invictus, Lord of Light, greatest of the heavens...* But he did not pray for himself. He prayed for the men under his command, for Marcellina and her daughters. For his son. For all the people of this province that had been placed under his protection. *Your light between them and darkness...*

Down on the road and around the watchtower itself he had 2,500 men. They had marched hard, another night advance, mile after mile across the flatlands from Juliacum, past the burnt villages and the smashed ruins of the roadside settlements. This tower alone had withstood the tide, the small garrison of cavalry driving off the raiding bands that moved west, then back east again. Moving around the circuit of the walkway, Castus scanned the country in all directions. He sucked at his cheek, raising his hand to shade his eyes, judging the lie of the land.

From the palisaded compound below him he could smell the smoke of the cooking fires, the scents of frying bacon and steaming porridge. He heard the voices of the men at the fires rising up to him, their tired laughter and their nervous boasts. The familiar voices of men facing battle. He had summoned them here, he thought, just as the Frankish chieftains had summoned their warriors to this confrontation. He could have remained with them in Colonia or in Juliacum, safe behind the walls, waiting until the barbarian storm had passed. But they were fighting men, just as he was. This was what they had been trained to do. This was how they earned their gold.

A rattle of feet on the ladder, and Castus stepped back into the chamber as Bonitus appeared through the trapdoor. He was yawning, his chin hazy with blond stubble. Like many of his warriors, he had found the night marches a trial.

'You see something good from up here?' he asked with his familiar crooked smile. 'You see your young emperor, maybe, coming to rescue us, hmm?'

Castus cleared his throat, leaning into the frame of the open door. 'You don't have to stay,' he said. 'I've brought you far enough. You've proved your loyalty. If you want to take your men and go, do so.'

Bonitus shrugged. 'Enough walking,' he said. 'You Romans love to walk, heh! All night, looking at the stars... No, we walk enough. Now is the time to fight. We stay.'

Castus felt oddly moved, but did not want to show it. He went outside again, onto the walkway, and Bonitus followed him. They stood at the rail, watching the distant swarm of the enemy assembling in the valley.

'Ragnachar,' Bonitus said. 'The wrath of the Franks!'

It was Gaiso who had said that, Castus remembered. On the muddy shore of the Vahalis estuary, in the moments before the arrows and javelins cut him down. *Kill their leaders*, he thought. *Kill their leaders and they are nothing but a rabble.*

'You see where the land dips, just to the north of us?' he said, pointing. 'Looks like a dry streambed, or a sunken track with bushes around it. Ragnachar'll want to send a force up there to try and outflank us. I want your men to stop him.'

'Holding the position?' Bonitus said, with a vague sneer.

'You'll have a hard fight if they come that way. If they don't, you can attack them from behind. I'll send some archers and light infantry to support you. Oh – and tell every one of your men to tie a red cloth around his head. Wouldn't want any of mine killing them by mistake. The watchword's *Concordia*.'

'You know,' Bonitus said, cocking his head. 'I begin to understand why my brother called you a friend.'

'You do?'

'Yes!' Bonitus laughed, then clasped Castus's right shoulder. 'I go now,' he said. 'We must get into position unseen. If we don't meet again in this world...'

Castus nodded. There was nothing else to say.

Once the Salian chief had left him, he called down to the sentry in the lower chamber to summon his unit commanders. The troops were already moving away from their fires and assembling in the open ground surrounding the tower. As he waited, Castus peered down at the small compound below him. The palisade had a single gate, stables and barracks lining the inner wall, a ditch filled with spiked stakes outside. Not enough space within the enclosure for even a quarter of his force, but the little strongpoint could be a last redoubt if he needed one. The idea brought a spasm of cold horror: he pictured a mass of desperate men trying to funnel back through the narrow gateway, the panicked chaos in the churned mud of the compound, the enemy storming the palisade... Better not to consider such things at all.

One by one the officers came up the ladder into the chamber: Modestus, Dexter, the prefects of the Dalmatian cavalry and the Fifth Thracians, the staff tribune who commanded the First Minervia, and the senior centurions of the Twenty-Second and Thirtieth Legion detachments. Castus led them out onto the walkway. Simply, and briefly, he told them what he intended, pointing out the positions and the probable angles of attack.

'Questions?' he asked. There were none. If any of the officers doubted the wisdom of his plan, they would not express it. They had less than an hour before the advance groups of the enemy reached them. In silence they filed back down the ladder and rejoined their men.

Outside the circuit of palisade the grass was steaming as the rising sun burned off the dew. Castus mounted his horse and rode out through a gap in the front line of the formation. The ground sloped ahead of him, and two hundred paces to the west it fell more steeply. Mist in the valley below, and as it faded he could see the enemy horde already gathered on the banks of the river. Even without the captives they had herded with them, Ragnachar's host must number nearly ten thousand. As Castus watched, the warriors grouped into attack columns, each headed by the household guard of one of the chiefs. So much, he thought, for his idea of a disorganised rabble. The noise of their battle cries, their jeering shouts, rose on the morning air.

Returning to the Roman position, Castus turned his horse and rode slowly along the front line. His men formed a hollow square, eight deep, with locked shields, surrounding the ditches and palisade of the watchtower. To the west, facing the direction of the barbarian assault, were the veteran soldiers of the Thirtieth, the former Praetorians. With them stood the remaining men of the Second Britannica, under Modestus's command. The detachment of the First Minervia, most of them untried recruits or older men, formed the two sides of the square; at the rear were the lighter-armed troops of the Twenty-Second and Thracians. The Stablesiani and Dalmatian cavalry were stationed there, too, ready to ride out on the wings against any attempts to encircle the position. All they had to do, Castus thought, was to hold formation and not give ground. A bulwark of men, against the rushing Frankish tide.

He tried to recall the speeches he had heard, from emperors and commanders, in the moments before battle. Their words poured through his mind, but would not hold. How to find the right phrases, to give heart and courage, to avoid anything of ill omen? He cleared his throat, drawing in his reins.

'You've marched a long road with me,' he cried, feeling every man's gaze upon him now. 'You've proved yourself soldiers of Rome, every one of you. Now we're facing the last test. Those men down there,' he shouted, pointing, 'those *barbarians*... all of them swore oaths to keep our peace and respect our frontiers. Now they've broken their oaths, and come into our province to pillage and burn. To rape and plunder. They thought they could escape our justice. They're noisy enough now, but most of them've never faced Roman steel!'

A massed growl rose from the ranks. Castus nudged his horse forward.

'Already,' he shouted, 'the Caesar Crispus, son of our emperor, is approaching with his field army. But we need to hold the enemy until he arrives. We hold them *here*. Only a few hours, brothers! Do not yield; do not flinch. They'll be advancing uphill with the sun in their eyes. Hold your positions, and may the gods reward us with a righteous victory!'

Now the growl turned to a roar of acclaim, the troops raising their spears in salute as Castus kicked his horse into a canter and circled the formation. The noise faded as he passed back between them. Dismounting, he passed the reins to Eumolpius.

'Find me a shield,' he told the orderly, 'and strap it to my forearm.' His left arm still ached with every movement, and he knew he could not grip and heft a shield with his hand alone. When Eumolpius returned with the shield, Castus was glad to see that it bore the red sun-wheel on gold, the emblem of Legion II Britannica. He had fought behind that blazon many times. A good sign.

'Take my horse inside the palisade,' he told Eumolpius as the young man fastened the straps. 'Then I need you up in that watchtower with Diogenes and a pair of hornblowers. You'll be my eyes up there, understand? Any movement on the flanks, let me know. And look out for my signals – you'll need to relay them.'

'Yes, dominus,' the orderly said. He took the reins again.

'How old are you?' Castus asked.

'Twenty-eight, dominus.'

Two years short of the legal age for manumission. It did not matter now. 'Live through this,' Castus told him quietly, 'and I'll see you're freed. You've served me well for long enough.'

'Thank you, dominus,' Eumolpius said, his doleful face looking more than usually bleak. Then Castus flicked his hand, and the orderly led the horse away towards the gate in the palisade. As he watched them go, Castus noticed the eunuch leading his pony towards the fortification. Luxorius had been riding with Dexter and his Stablesiani since Juliacum; Castus wondered what the smoothly urbane eunuch and the weathered cavalry commander had found to talk about. 'Get up into the tower and stay there,' he called, and Luxorius raised a hand in acknowledgement, smiling. At least he would be out of the way.

There were spare weapons piled beside the ditch: spears, javelins and darts. Castus selected a spear, weighed it in his hand and with a nod of approval slung it over his shoulder and marched across the trampled grass to the centre of the front line.

'Joining us again, dominus?' Modestus said with an apprehensive frown.

'They'll need to see me,' Castus told him, nodding towards the barbarians in the valley. 'That way they'll bunch towards our centre.' His draco-bearer ran up behind him, taking a position at his side with the long purple snake-tail of the banner curling in the air above him.

'Nice to know we'll be close to the action,' Modestus muttered.

All along the line, men waited in formation. The low sun stretched their shadows before them. Castus knew this time well. How often had he stood in the battle array, waiting for the killing to begin? The sound of the barbarian approach rose from the valley. Men tipped canteens and swigged water; others spattered their last urine onto the grass.

Now the sound from below the slope grew, a clamour and boom of voices, spears rattling against shields. As they emerged from the valley's mist into the level glare, the Frankish horde appeared to glitter and glow. The sun caught their brightly ornamented shields and dyed tunics, their red and blond hair tied in braids and topknots, their faces shining with sweat. They made no running advance, no wild charge up the slope towards the Roman line. Instead they came on at walking pace, bellowing out their battle cries, keeping to the dense formations of their attack columns. At their centre was a mounted group, riding beneath a standard of what looked like red-dyed horsehair tied to a pole, with a ram's skull mounted on the top. It was not horsehair, Castus realised. The standard was decked with the scalps of enemy warriors, and below it rode Ragnachar, war chief and King of the Chamavi.

The horde advanced until only two hundred paces lay between them and the Roman square. Other groups pushed further, to the left and right, moving up the flanks until the sight of the cavalry on the wings brought them to a halt. The men in the Roman formation stood immobile, silent. Scanning the front of the Frankish columns, he picked out Conda, son of Ragnachar, the youth he had captured the previous summer and permitted to return home. Other leaders headed each column: the chiefs and Kings of the Chattuari and the Lanciones, the

Tubantes and the Amsivarii. Over to the right Castus was surprised to recognise Flaochadus of the Salii. He must have led his men up the Scaldis and then swung west to join the others.

Ragnachar dismounted and strode forward to stand before his warriors. His silvered scale cuirass and high-crested helmet gleamed in the sun, and he carried a heavy-bladed spear. Raising his fist, he began to shout, pummelling the air and thrashing his spear. Castus heard a mangled version of his own name.

'I believe he's challenging you to single combat,' Modestus grinned over his shoulder.

'So I see,' Castus said. He could hear the hatred in the Frankish leader's voice. The summer before, Castus had humiliated this man in front of his people and now Ragnachar wanted revenge. He wanted to drive that massive spear straight through Castus's body and then gloat over his corpse.

'Hope you're not thinking of accepting?'

'Wouldn't dream of it,' Castus said. 'Let him shout himself hoarse.'

A burst of laughter came from the right of the Roman formation. Castus peered over the shoulders of the men beside him and saw one of the soldiers of the Thirtieth step out from the line and turn his back to the enemy. He raised his tunic, bent over, and loudly slapped his buttocks. The man darted back into the ranks, hilarity all around him, as an outraged yell burst from the enemy. Castus was smiling through gritted teeth.

Horns thundered from the rear of the Frankish horde and at once the attack columns lurched forward. Shields raised, spears and axes and knives flashing, the barbarians broke into a rolling charge.

Archers and slingers sprang up from concealment in the long grass ahead of the Roman line, loosing their missiles at the charging enemy and then running back, turning to loose again before dodging in through the shield wall. Already a few of the barbarians had fallen, but the volleys of arrows and shot had not slowed them. They quickened from a jog into a run. All around him Castus felt the shield wall tense and lock tighter.

And then the first screams of pain came from the charging horde. Warriors toppled suddenly, sprawling, while others threw up their arms and buckled, as if struck by some unseen dart. The Roman troops began to yell in satisfaction as the pits that Castus had ordered them to dig in the hour before dawn took effect. The pits were small, but concealed a sharpened stick jutting from within. The luckier barbarians just tripped and fell; others were spiked though the foot as they ran. As the Franks realised their danger, the impetus of their charge faltered and died, men halting to gaze around them in sudden fear, as if some hidden enemy lurked in the grass.

Castus heard the centurions cry out the order, and instinctively lowered his head. Every man in the rear four ranks drew back his arm, then in one swinging motion they hurled their javelins and lead-weighted iron darts. Behind them the bowmen and slingers added their own arrows and shot to the volley, and for a moment a flickering shadow fell across the Roman lines as the rain of iron arced over them and slammed down into the mass of men trapped between the pits. Already the rear-rank men were hurling their second javelins, then their third: a ceaseless torrent of barbed metal plunging into the chaos of the Frankish horde.

The barbarians howled in confusion and horror as the volleys fell at them out of the sun. A few of them had managed to charge past the pits, but the javelins cropped them down like wheat under a harvest sickle. Staring between the ranks, Castus saw one warrior struck straight through the head. Another dropped, screaming, the long shank of a javelin pinning him through both thighs. Others staggered back as the stinging darts hissed around them, the barbarian columns breaking and spilling away down the slopes.

'Hold!' Castus yelled, raising his hand. He heard the order repeated down the lines, and the rain of missiles died away. Agonised groans were coming from the bloodied grass all around the Roman square. From over to the right, where Bonitus and his men had been concealed in the gulley, Castus could still hear the clash of fighting. But a few moments later there was silence there too. *Is this it?* Castus allowed himself to think. *Have we broken them at the first attack?* Joy surged inside him; pre-emptive, he knew, but it gave him new energy. His men clearly felt the same.

'*Roma Victrix!*' the men in the ranks shouted. And now it was their turn to batter spears against shields, to stamp and yell. '*ROMA VICTRIX!*'

They had taken almost no casualties in the first assault. Too good to last, Castus thought grimly. He sat on the grass, shield still strapped to his arm, running a whetstone along the cutting edges of his sword. He was still using the weapon he had been given when he rejoined his ships at the mouth of the Rhine, a simple blade with a wooden hilt and a worn ivory grip, the product of some legion armoury. But it was a good tool, he thought, a soldier's weapon. Three feet of Roman iron, twin fullers and a good edge. It was a little notched, and the tip was blunted, but it would serve.

Shouts from the right flank, '*Concordia! Concordia!*' and Castus stood up to see Bonitus's warriors streaming up from the gulley and along the avenues left clear of pit-traps. For a few moments the Roman line remained closed to them, but at a command from one of the tribunes the troops raised their spears and parted shields to allow the Frankish allies into the square.

'Hot work down there!' Bonitus cried as he saw Castus. The Salian chief had blood crusted over his left temple, and more blood running between the knuckles of his sword hand. 'I killed that pissing bastard Conda of the Chamavi,' he said with a grin. 'This is a good day!'

There were fewer than a hundred of the allied warriors remaining, most of them wounded, but all of them exultant after their victory over their fellow Franks. Castus ordered them to join the troops at the rear of the square to reinforce the line.

'You saw Ragnachar?' Bonitus asked as he turned to go. 'He's thirsty for your blood, my friend!'

Castus nodded. Particularly thirsty, he thought, now that the last of his sons had been killed. Ragnachar had given away fifty hostages to secure Conda's safe return the previous summer. Now the hostages were dead, and Conda too.

'Keep your shield up if you meet him, hmm?' Bonitus said. 'He has a long reach!'

As the Franks filed away, still laughing and boasting of their exploits, Castus looked up at the position of the sun. Nearing noon, he realised. How long until they began running short of water? Every hour they could hold out here, keeping the Frankish horde in one place, brought Crispus and his field army closer. But Castus was tormented by the thought of his son, left in the power of Magnius Rufus. Every passing hour increased the chances of Rufus turning his frustrated rage on Sabinus, or even on Marcellina.

A trumpet cried from the watchtower, and Castus glanced up to see Eumolpius waving towards the west. The Franks were forming up for another attack. He pushed his way forward through the ranks once more, until he was just behind the front line of the Second Legion men. Within moments, the barbarians appeared up the slope, moving in their dense attack columns, howling and clashing their weapons as they came. Their skirmishers had already moved forward, crawling through the long grass to hurl light javelins and slingstones at the Roman line. Castus flinched as a missile passed over him; then again as a man in the rear rank was struck down.

Then a great roar went up from the Frankish horde, and the columns broke into motion. And at the head of the main column, charging directly towards Castus's position, was the Chamavi king, Ragnachar.

CHAPTER XXXI

'Hold! Hold your formation!'
The Roman ranks shuddered as the men closed up,
the troops at the rear pushing forward with their shields to
strengthen the line. There was no measured advance this time;
the Franks were closing the distance at a run, trying to evade
the shower of darts and javelins they knew awaited them.

'Loose!' The command bellowed out, and once again the sky
filled with flung missiles – but too few to break the impetus of
the barbarian assault: the Franks were leaping over the bodies
of their slain comrades, sure-footed between the pit-traps.
Javelins cut down a dozen of them, a score of them, but still
they closed, thousands strong. With only ten paces before the
Roman line they screamed out a battle cry, the noise bursting
back from the wall of shields. And then they struck, with the
violence of a hammer blow.

Bodies collided, shields battering together as the Frankish
charge rammed against the Roman defences. Castus felt the
formation around him buckle as the men took the impact, then
surge forward again as the rear ranks pushed to straighten
the line. Boots stamped and skidded on the muddy grass,
bodies tumbling between them as the two opposing masses of
men ground against each other. Spears stabbed out from the
Roman wall, clashing against the Frankish shields, or sinking

into flesh. Any man who could raise his right arm from the crush hacked and thrust wildly, screaming into the face of his opponent. It was a brutal fight of attrition, but the Franks were piling more men in from the rear, clambering over the bodies of their injured and their slain. Castus saw a warrior leap up onto the shields of his comrades and hurl himself over the heads of the front line onto the packed ranks behind; he died instantly, pierced by a mesh of blades. But the pressure was too great to allow the Romans to push the enemy back. The slightest breach in their line, and all would be lost.

Craning his head up, Castus peered back at the inner face of the square. Fighting on both flanks: the Franks had sent attack columns curling around like horns to strike at either side. Only the rear was secure; Castus could see the lances and pennants of Dexter's cavalry troopers as they charged and rallied, driving back the enemy wings. But even there the press of barbarians was too great to allow the horsemen to break through.

A surge of violent motion from the right, and Castus saw the ranks of the Thirtieth driven inwards. The Frankish attackers had found a weak point in their front line and smashed their way through it; now the broken formation was a churning mass of struggling figures, reinforcements rushing from either side to try and close the gap. Castus opened his mouth to shout an order, but the noise was too great. No voice could rise above the clash and grate of iron, the banging of shields and the screams of pain. As he watched, the veterans of the Thirtieth, the former Praetorians, fought back against their attackers, dying where they stood until their comrades could heave the breach closed over their stricken bodies.

A messenger came struggling through the ranks. 'Dominus! The left flank can't hold – there's too many of them...' Castus shoved the man aside and stared back across the interior of the square; the line of the First Minervia was already bowing inwards. At any moment the pressure of the attack would breach the formation, and the barbarians would rush inside the defences like floodwater through a broken dam.

Through the crush of defenders ahead of him, Castus saw the ram's skull totem raised above the centre of the Frankish horde. Beneath it, he knew, was Ragnachar. He began pushing his way forward, as a stream of injured men were carried to the rear. Two ranks back from the front line and he could press forward no further, his body tight in the crush of mailed shoulders and wedged shields. A spearhead clashed against his helmet crest, making his head ring, but he got his arm up and levelled the shaft of his own weapon, thrusting between the men ahead of him. His draco standard whipped above him, and he saw the scalp-decked skull totem dip forwards as the Frankish leader caught sight of him.

Ragnachar was forging his way towards the Roman line, bellowing, his spear raised in both hands and his eyes flecked with blood. If he stretched forward, Castus could almost have touched him. But the press of men between them was too great, the bodies underfoot forming a heaving mound with the shields and spears clashing above them. *Kill their leaders and they are nothing but a rabble...* Castus lifted his arm, drew his spear back, and waited until he next glimpsed the Chamavi king through the tide of struggling bodies. Then he threw. At the last moment Ragnachar parried, and the shaft of his own spear deflected the missile.

'Modestus!' Castus yelled. 'On my command, attack from the centre!'

For a heartbeat the centurion stared at him, uncomprehending. Then he followed Castus's eye, and saw the figure of the Frankish king in the ruck of enemy warriors. With a savage grin he shouted the order to the men around him.

Castus had his sword in his hand. Ragnachar was pushing towards him again, heaving aside his own bodyguards. A shout of command, and Castus felt the shields locking around him, the surge from behind bearing him forward as the Roman line punched outwards into the mass of the enemy. Screams on all sides, the battle cries of the legionaries amplified by the hollows of their shields. Castus kicked forward, stamping over fallen men, the relentless momentum of the assault splitting the Franks and laying open a path to their leader.

Ragnachar reared back, his spear raised, then struck out. His spearhead slammed against a Roman shield; one of his bodyguards aimed a blow beneath the rim and cut down the man to Castus's left. The Frankish leader stabbed again, aiming directly for Castus this time. Heaving his left shoulder up, Castus took the blow on his shield and rolled beneath it. He stabbed, and the blunted tip of his sword grated across the king's scale-armoured chest. Now they were face to face, the combat at the front line seething around them. Ragnachar lifted his spear directly upwards, his mouth stretched in a howl of rage as he aimed his thrust. Castus took a long step forward, his shield lifted above him, then slashed at the king's unprotected leg. The blade sheared through muscle and tendon. He felt the spear jab down against his shield, but Ragnachar was already reeling backwards as his injured leg gave beneath him.

For a heartbeat the fighting around them seemed to grow still, the warriors of the Frankish bodyguard staring in horror at their crippled leader. Castus took another step, stumbling, lifted his sword and then hacked down. He felt the impact up his arm, the notched blade biting into Ragnachar's neck between mail shirt and helmet. Wrenching the blade free he chopped again, and this time the king grunted in shock, his reddened eyes widening as he stared up at Castus. Blood spilling down his chest, the Chamavi leader collapsed back against the heaped bodies of his fallen warriors.

'Back!' Modestus was shouting, 'Back to the line!' Castus felt himself gripped and dragged. He had not realised that he had fallen. Hands lifted him, shields closing around him as the wedge of legionaries retreated. He got his legs beneath him, struggling to raise his shield. Spears jabbed and slashed around his head, and the roars of triumph and rage were deafening. Then the line closed, the front ranks locking together once more. Only then did Castus feel the burst of fear, the sudden exhilaration of victory. His standard-bearer caught his arm, pulling him back between the ranks. As he looked behind him, Castus felt his joy veer into sickening horror. The interior of the square was a chaos of fighting men, Franks who had burst their way through the flank locked in fierce combat around the ditches and palisade of the watchtower. On the far side of the position Castus could see Bonitus and his men pushing back against the invaders, while other bands of soldiers tried in vain to seal the gap in the line.

It was over, he thought. Another rush from the enemy and the formation would be torn apart. The enemy were already butchering the wounded men left inside the square.

He heard Felix screaming: 'Rear ranks, *face about*!' The men to either side of him turned, raising shields and spears against the enemy that now threatened to engulf them. The high bleat of the trumpet came from the top of the watchtower. *Too late*, he thought. It was all too late...

But then, as the last reserves of strength burned in his body, he heard cheering from the far side of the broken square. For a few moments he stared, uncomprehending. Then he saw the streaming banners, the sun glittering on the scale trappings of armoured horses. Cavalrymen were pouring along the slopes to the south, driving into the Frankish horde with levelled lances. Castus looked up at the tower and saw Eumolpius waving back at him and pointing. In the bright glare of the noon sun, he saw the purple banners of the imperial Horse Guards, the Schola Scutariorum, streaming along the disarrayed margins of his formation. And behind them, away to the east, the rising brown dust cloud of the advancing field army.

The cavalry trumpets were sounding *general pursuit* by the time Castus reached the gateway in the watchtower's palisade. The ditches to either side were scattered with dead men, bodies of Romans and Franks tumbled on the earth banks or impaled on the stakes. In the gateway he stood braced on his sword, the sense of relief still seeping through him, mingling with the slow afterwash of nausea and loss. Eumolpius joined him, and Bonitus; the allied Frankish warriors had already taken shelter inside the palisade, to avoid being cut down by the lances of the cavalry.

All across the interior of the Roman square there were bodies, the grass churned with blood and bootprints. But the enemy attack was broken; the death of their leader and the sudden arrival of the field army had robbed them of their courage and cohesion. With their comrades fleeing away down the slopes, any warriors remaining within the square had been surrounded and cut down, and the flanks of the formation now stood firm once more. A gap opened at the rear of the square, and the men in the battle lines raised their spears in the sunlight and yelled out the salute as the young Caesar Crispus rode between them at the head of his mounted staff and bodyguard.

Castus waited, still short of breath, his blood hammering. Crispus was riding a powerful horse, and his gilded cuirass and helmet shone almost painfully bright. An enormous draco of purple and gold roiled in the air above him. As he approached, his horse stepping carefully over the bodies, Castus saw a look of something like horrified awe on the young man's face.

'Aurelius Castus!' the Caesar cried, raising his hand with two fingers extended in greeting. 'You've been hard pressed here, I see... I salute you!'

Castus walked forward, sheathing his sword, then dropped to kneel beside the young man's horse. 'Majesty,' he said. 'I thank the gods you arrived in time.' He was kneeling in blood, and felt it soaking through the cloth of his breeches. 'There are spiked pits all around our position,' he went on. He was yelling, he realised. 'You must keep the cavalry back from our flanks – the road ahead's clear of them...'

'Good!' Crispus said. His horse was growing nervous of the blood and slaughter, and he fought to control it with the reins. 'Then that's the way we'll go!' As Castus rose to his feet he saw that he had been mistaken: the look on the young man's face was not horror, but a wild adolescent enthusiasm. He remembered the boy he had seen, only a year before, puking on the wheel of a carriage after the attack in Raetia. Crispus was a changed man now, an emperor on his first field of battle.

'Find a horse and follow me,' the Caesar called, his voice cracking. 'You will tell me of your battle once victory is ours!'

Before Castus could say another word, the young man spurred his horse forward and the far side of the square opened to let the imperial cavalcade through. Castus breathed a curse as the horsemen streamed past him.

Striding back to the palisade, he snatched a waterskin from Eumolpius and drank deeply. He needed to be away from here; his part in the fight was over, and he could think only of his son, of Marcellina, and of Magnius Rufus. But he could not desert his command just yet. Diogenes joined him in the gateway, leading Dapple by the reins, and Castus swung himself up into the saddle with a grunt of effort.

'Find me half a troop of the Dalmatae,' he told Diogenes, 'and make sure they're mounted and ready to move as soon as I return.'

Then he pulled at the reins, kicked with his heels, and rode after Crispus and his retinue. From the corner of his eye he noticed the eunuch, Luxorius, galloping from the palisade gate behind him on a pony.

Only when he cleared the front line of his troops did Castus realise the extent of the slaughter. The ground around his square was heaped with Frankish dead, thickets of javelins, darts and arrows jutting up from the bodies. Dapple picked her way carefully along the road, following in the wake of the imperial advance. When Castus glanced down he saw the body of Flaochadus, the Salian chief, lying wide-eyed among the slain. Beyond the range of the javelin storm the ground was clearer, and Castus urged his horse into a gallop. Even here there were bodies, fugitives cut down by the armoured lancers of the Equites Cataphractarii as they swept around the square. Reaching the brow of the slope, Castus looked down across the marshy river valley and saw the remains of the barbarian horde streaming away in confusion. In places knots of warriors had turned to make a stand; horse archers surrounded them, showering them with arrows until they broke, and then the lancers rode down the survivors.

Crispus and his mounted retinue had already caught up with one of the Frankish groups. As Castus watched, the Caesar plunged in among the fugitives at the gallop, his sword raised high. With the troopers of his bodyguard following close behind him, the barbarians did not stand a chance. The retinue rode straight through them, leaving a trail of hacked bodies.

Reining in his horse, Castus turned in the saddle and gazed up the hill behind him. The infantry of the field army were already deploying from their line of march, ready to move down the slope and crush any last pockets of resistance. This was no battle now, only slaughter; just for a moment Castus felt a tight sensation of shame in his gut. The proud warriors being massacred in their hundreds all across the valley were kin to Bonitus, to his old friend Brinno. The cousins of Ganna's people. If things had been different, they could have served in the Roman army themselves. Now they were just carrion, mauled and bloodied flesh for the scavenging birds and the wolves. But he could not allow himself to feel any sympathy for the slain.

He turned again towards the valley, and saw the gilded figure of Crispus sitting motionless on his horse. The young man had ridden clear of the cavalry fight swirling away down the slope, and for a moment it appeared that he was surveying the scene of his triumph; then Crispus leaned forward in the saddle, reaching up to tug at the fastenings of his helmet with clumsy fingers. There was blood flecked on the forequarters of his horse, and he had dropped his sword. As he pulled his helmet off and swayed back in the saddle, he looked dazed and sick.

'Caesar!' Castus called out, spurring his horse forward. As he did so, he noticed another rider galloping along the slope towards Crispus – a messenger, he assumed, or one of the staff officers. Crispus raised a hand and wiped at his brow, but did not turn around.

The other rider was coming up fast, his cloak whipping out behind him. Beneath his helmet he wore a cloth tied over his nose and mouth; with only twenty paces between them, Castus recognised the man by his armour. What was Dexter doing so far from the rest of his unit? Even as the question passed through his mind, Castus saw the tribune turn his horse and lean in the saddle, a Frankish javelin raised to throw.

Shock chilled his blood: he saw the weapon's aim, its clear target. With a choked cry he hauled on the reins, swinging his horse to the right. Dapple kicked air with her hooves as she swerved, champing at the bit; Castus saw the tribune's widened eyes as he turned, and a moment later the two riders slammed together. The impact drove him forward in the saddle, and he grabbed at Dexter's arm. Hurling aside his javelin, the tribune reached for his sword hilt, but the two horses were pushing against each other and he was thrown off balance. Castus managed to get a grip on the other man's belt, trying to haul him from the saddle. Another rider came up behind them, leaning to grapple the tribune. One hand seized Dexter's helmet and dragged his head back; the other plunged a short knife into the side of his neck. Castus felt the spasm run through the tribune's body, then Dexter slumped sideways and toppled from the saddle, down between the kicking hooves of the horses.

Luxorius was already backing his pony away from the confrontation. He had thrown down the knife, and hid his right hand in a fold of his cloak.

'A madman!' the eunuch exclaimed, and tried to smile. 'Who would have known?'

'Who indeed?' Castus snarled. He could see the fear and disappointment on Luxorius's face. The whole incident had taken only a few heartbeats; had anyone else even seen what had happened? Castus shook at the reins, spurring Dapple to ride the last distance towards Crispus.

Only now did the Caesar turn to look back at him, still confused and blinking. As Castus approached he saw the smear of blood on the young man's face where he had wiped the sweat from his eyes.

'Majesty – are you injured?'

'No, I...' Crispus raised his right hand. The palm was covered with blood.

Castus gripped him by the shoulder, steadying him in the saddle. There were other riders around them now, staff officers and bodyguards galloping up to surround them.

'Is the battle over?' Crispus asked, stammering slightly. 'Is this victory?'

'Victory, majesty!' one of the staff officers cried, saluting. 'The enemy are driven from the field!'

Crispus was nodding, still gazing vaguely at the blood on his palm. Castus tried to remember the first time he had ever fought in battle, ever killed a man. So many years ago: the vague memory slipped through his mind and was gone.

'I need to leave you,' Castus said quietly, bending closer. 'I'm taking an escort and riding south. I'll meet you again tomorrow at Juliacum, do you understand?'

'Yes, yes,' Crispus said, as if to himself. He reached out suddenly and grabbed Castus's hand. A grin lit his face. 'We won, didn't we!' he said.

Hypatius, commander of the field army troops, rode up and took the reins of the Caesar's horse. He glanced at Castus. 'What's this? You know of another enemy force in the field?' he demanded.

'No, dominus. Something I have to do. A private matter.'

Hypatius peered at him for a moment, stern-faced. Then he gave a curt nod. 'Juliacum, tomorrow,' he said.

CHAPTER XXXII

They were still three miles north of the villa when they passed the first of the dead bodies. It was lying in a field beside the track, and Castus would have taken it for a bundle of rags thrown down by some fugitive, except for the pair of crows that flew up from it as the riders approached. A few hundred yards further and there were more, sprawled in a ditch. Slaves, they looked like; Castus turned to look at them as he rode by, and saw the red welts left by shackles on one exposed ankle. The next dead man wore the grey tunic and cap of Rufus's private bodyguard of freedmen and mercenaries. Beside it lay the sprawled and bloodied corpse of the landowner's thin-faced neighbour, Fabianus. Castus kicked his horse into a gallop.

Behind him, the biarchus and sixteen troopers of the Eleventh Dalmatae followed without a word. He had told them little of their mission, and they had ridden without question or complaint. Light cavalrymen mounted on small tough horses, they had been with him since he left Colonia, two nights and two days on the road with not much rest. Castus himself could barely remember the last time he had slept. His body ached, his left shoulder was numb and the motion of riding drove shocks of pain up his spine. But he was burning with a hard aggressive energy that conquered all his weariness.

They had covered the distance from the battlefield in only four hours, riding as fast as they could without exhausting their horses. Branching off the highway several miles west of Juliacum, they had crossed a rolling countryside of fields and orchards, tranquil in the early-evening light. But the raiding bands had passed this way too; the few settlements along the way were deserted, their huts plundered. Castus had hoped that the barbarians, and the hordes of liberated slaves that followed in the wake of their destruction, might have avoided this part of the country. He saw now that he had hoped in vain.

As they rode through the last screen of trees that masked the valley, Castus saw thin trails of black smoke rising from the villa. There were figures on the track in front of them, but they melted away into the trees as the riders galloped into the sunlight. Below him, Castus saw the slope towards the causeway and the low bridge that crossed the fish pools. Across the valley, he could see that one wing of the villa was still smouldering, but the rest seemed intact. In the evening light the scene appeared almost gentle, hazed by drifting smoke. Then he narrowed his eyes against the low sun, and made out the smashed railings along the front portico, the gaping openings of the staved-in doorways. At the far end of the building stood the stone tower that Rufus had constructed as a redoubt, and a mass of sticks and straw had been heaped around its base.

Sparks raced through the shadows beneath the front portico as men ran with torches to fling onto the mound of dry tinder. Even as he watched, Castus saw the smoke billowing around the base of the tower. And all around, spreading across the garden terraces below the villa almost as far as the gazebo where Castus had talked with Rufus, was a vast armed mob. As the first flames licked against the stones they raised a baying cheer that carried across the valley to the band of horsemen on the far side.

'Fuck,' the biarchus said. 'There's hundreds of them!'

'Most of them slaves, brigands, runaways,' Castus replied, raising his voice so all the troopers could hear him. 'They won't stand against us. Trumpeter – let them know we're here.'

The *tubicen* raised his polished brass horn to the sunlight and sounded a long keening note. At once Castus saw the mass of people gathering around the tower thrown into confusion, many of them pausing only a moment before flight. But many more remained.

'Check your tack and kit,' he said, 'then form into double column. Once we're across the bridge we deploy into line abreast and push up the slope and along the terraces. Go in hard and we'll scatter them.'

Or so he hoped. He had left his heavy cuirass and helmet, his shield and greaves with Eumolpius. As the Dalmatian riders swung their own shields and lances into position, Castus tightened his belt around the linen vest he wore over his tunic, then drew his sword. The trumpeter sounded the signal to advance, and the riders formed up and began cantering down the track towards the bridge.

By the time they reached the slope on the far side, the mob around the tower had already thinned. Fugitives were scattering along the valley, into the shelter of the woods to the south, or wading across the lower fish pools. The fire had only taken hold around the far side of the tower; it produced more smoke than flame, and the black fumes rolled along the terraces beneath the villa. Those rebels that remained were all armed, many with shields and spears, or thick wooden cudgels; they screamed their defiance as the cavalry deployed and climbed the slope towards them at the trot. When he glanced up, Castus saw two men in grey tunics on the wooden walkway at the top of the tower aiming hunting crossbows down into the milling horde below.

'*Dalmatia!*' the biarchus cried, raising his spear as he kicked his horse into a gallop. The troopers howled back their battle cry, urging their mounts up the slope almost knee to knee, each man drawing the first of the javelins from the sheath he carried behind his saddle. Castus rode at the centre of the line, trusting to Dapple's weight and training to forge a path through the enemy. He dipped his head towards the mane as a flung spear darted past him, then tugged the reins to send the big grey mare barrelling into one of the rebel fighters and trampling him beneath her hooves.

There was only time for a single volley of javelins from the horsemen, then the men of the Eleventh Dalmatae slung the spears from across their shoulders and rode into the rebel horde, striking down anyone who opposed them. Castus saw one of them knocked from the saddle by a swinging cudgel; the trooper beside him stabbed down with his spear, slaying the attacker. A small band of the rebels had fled to the portico of the villa and were pelting slingshot down at the horsemen from between the pillars; two riders peeled away from the line and rode their horses straight up the front steps and onto the portico pavement, hunting down the slingers and spearing them.

Castus swung his horse to the left, forcing another of the rebels to dance back from the kicking hooves. A second man stepped in, roaring, from the right. Castus slashed down with his sword, chopping through a spearshaft. Slashed again, and the man fell back with a scream. He could hear the biarchus calling his men to re-form.

The rebels that faced them were indeed mostly slaves, clad in rough tunics and armed with improvised or stolen weapons. There were a few Frankish raiders among them, but not enough to stiffen their resolve. Castus remembered the fight that Rufus had staged for the entertainment of his dinner guests; these men were similar to those luckless amateur gladiators. He looked around for the pale-haired man, the killer who had attacked him in his room, but he was nowhere to be seen.

Now the cavalry's advance had taken them around the lower flank of the tower, trapping a band of rebels between the horses and the fire. Troopers split away in pairs to hunt down the scattered few still carrying arms, while the rest formed a cordon with levelled spears. Smoke billowed and fogged the air around them.

'Take some of them alive!' Castus shouted to the biarchus. 'Get them to put out that fire!'

He glanced up, and his heart leaped in his chest. Thirty feet above him, Magnius Rufus stood at the wooden parapet of the tower's walkway. Beside him, clasped to his side, was Castus's son. The landowner's bodyguards flanked them on either side.

A shout from one of the troopers, and Castus turned to see the heavy door in the tower's first storey swinging open. A ladder jutted from within, and as soon as it had dropped into position three grey-clad figures came scrambling down from the tower, coughing through the smoke. As soon as they reached the ground they scattered, running for the trees.

'Let them go,' Castus called. 'Biarchus – hold the perimeter of the tower. Two of your men dismount and follow me.'

Swinging down from the saddle, he tossed the reins to one of the mounted men and ran, sword in hand, up the slope to the foot of the ladder. As the two soldiers followed, he hauled himself up the wooden rungs. The lingering smoke made his eyes smart, but he could see the men gathered just inside the tower's doorway, more of Rufus's bodyguard. They looked terrified, irresolute, gripping their swords with slack fingers.

'Weapons down!' Castus shouted to them as he reached the top of the ladder and pulled himself in through the doorway. The lower chamber was dark, thick with smoke. The bodyguards had retreated to line the far wall, raising their hands as they dropped their swords. In the centre of the chamber, a wooden stairway climbed to the next floor.

'After me,' Castus told the two troopers at his back. He stamped his way up the stairs, peering through the smoke into the dim light of the upper storeys. At the top of the stairs was another chamber, with weapons stacked around the walls. Big wooden chests as well, some of them flung open. Castus kicked something on the floor: a twist of metal caught the light. A hacked chunk of silver. The chests were full of it.

'Excellency!' a voice called from above. Castus knew it at once. 'I must ask you to come no further!'

At the far side of the chamber, a narrower stairway climbed the wall, rising to the topmost storey of the tower and the doors out onto the walkway. Castus paused while the two Dalmatian troopers climbed the stairs behind him.

'Rufus!' he shouted, his voice booming in the confined space of the chamber. 'You've got my son up there. Send him down, and then we can talk.'

'I'm afraid not,' Rufus replied. His voice sounded very close now – Castus guessed he was leaning across the railing of the stairway. 'I thank you for disposing of my rebellious slaves, but now your job here's done and I must request that you leave my property. I'll have your child delivered to you unharmed once you reach Colonia again. My only discussions will be with the Caesar and his prefect.'

Pressing himself against the wall, Castus edged towards the base of the last stairway. Where was Marcellina? He had no idea who might be in the upper chamber with Rufus, or how many of his guards still remained up there. Silently he signalled to the two Dalmatian troopers to move up behind him. One of them, a squat bowlegged soldier with a broad scarred face, grinned and motioned upwards with his spear. Castus shook his head. Storming the stairway might work, but with his son in Rufus's power he could not take the risk.

Slowly, quietly, he began to climb the stairs, keeping his back against the wall of the tower and leading with his right shoulder, sword ready. The wood creaked beneath him, and he could hear shuffling footsteps on the planked floor above. He was halfway up the stairs when a scream came from the upper room.

'Castus!' Marcellina's voice cried out. 'Be careful – he's coming for you!'

The warning saved him. Castus dropped back two steps and got his sword up as a figure plummeted from above, dropping from the upper floor onto the stairs. The knife that would have struck him in the head gashed against the wall, striking sparks from the stones. Castus recognised the pale eyes, the paler hair – Rufus's killer, the freed slave. A Saxon, he now realised. The heavy knife slashed again, raking along the blade of Castus's sword as he parried the blow. Forced back against the wall, the killer perched on the steps above him, there was nothing Castus could do except defend himself.

The killer moved fast, dodging in beneath Castus's longer blade to slash at his side. Castus felt the knife slice the linen vest, but it did not penetrate. He was trying to angle his sword to stab at the Saxon, but the confined space of the stairs favoured the shorter blade. Behind him the two troopers had closed up with spears ready, but his body was blocking them.

With a springing leap, the killer dodged up three steps, then twisted and slashed down at Castus again. Castus flung up his left hand to parry, an instinctive movement, remembering too late that he was not holding a shield. The knife flashed, and for a moment Castus felt nothing. Blood spattered the wall. Then he felt the searing pain up his arm, and bellowed. The knife had severed the smallest finger on his left hand.

With a snarl of triumph the Saxon leaped from the upper stair. With agony bursting through him, Castus buckled forward, banging the pommel of his sword down on the step as he hurled himself against the man's legs. The killer snatched for the handrail as he was knocked off balance; then Castus felt the weight of the body falling over him, his upright blade driving beneath the man's ribs. The killer coughed once, groaned and fell slack. Castus shoved himself free, kicking the dead man away from him and dragging the sword from his body.

Raising his left hand, Castus saw what the knife had done. He slumped on the stair, back to the wall, as the sickening agony tore through him. Blood was welling from the wound, and he clenched what was left of his hand into a fist and pressed it hard against his belly. The two troopers were hanging back, stunned.

'Fuck!' Castus yelled, pained breath bursting from his heaving chest. He snarled against clenched teeth. '*Fuck!*'

Then he heard the scream from above. Marcellina's voice. 'Get away from him! Get back – *leave him alone!*'

His head reeled, but Castus managed to shove himself upright against the wall and climb the last few stairs into the top chamber of the tower, his hand still pressed against the bloodsoaked linen of his vest. A single glance took in the scene: a square room, doors to either side opening onto the walkway. Rufus stood at the centre, holding Castus's son before him in a tight grip. One hand covered the boy's face, the other held a short knife to his throat. Two more guards stood with Rufus, both of them with loaded crossbows. At the far side, against the wall, Marcellina crouched with her two daughters huddled in her arms, wide-eyed with shock and horror.

'Stay back,' Castus hissed to the soldiers below him. He advanced two steps into the chamber. His eyes were locked on the knife pressing into his son's flesh. Sabinus appeared paralysed, terror-stricken.

'And you stay back also,' Rufus said. 'I'm not a cruel man, but you're pushing me.'

The landowner looked haggard, his face grey and lined but taut with stress. Castus noticed that he had a bandage around his upper arm, and when he moved backwards he appeared to limp slightly. Castus flicked a glance across to Marcellina, who stared back at him. She had a bruise on her face, he noticed; Rufus must have struck her. The two girls were shivering in her arms, gasping back tears.

'You two,' Castus said to the guards with the bows, teeth gritted against the pain of his injured hand. 'Get out of here.'

He stepped aside, and the two guards exchanged a look. Then they dropped their weapons clattering to the floor and bolted down the stairs.

'I know...' Castus said, fighting to speak as the breath heaved in his throat and agony racked his body. 'I know all about what happened... to Leontius. The prefect knows too. It's over for you.' He could feel himself weakening, the blood dripping down his legs and onto the plank floor.

Rufus was backing away towards the door to the walkway, pulling the boy with him. Castus took a step after him, then another.

'Put... down... your... sword,' Rufus said, forming the words with aching care. Then: 'Put it down!' he cried suddenly. 'I'll kill your boy!'

Now he was at the door, and moving out onto the walkway that ran around the top storey of the tower. Castus followed him. The evening sunlight had a reddish tint, and when he glanced over the railing he could see the cordon of mounted troopers below him, and the disarmed slaves in a huddle around the tower base where they had been working to put out the fire.

Trying to keep his breathing steady, his mind clear, Castus shuffled forward again. Rufus seized the boy around the waist, keeping the knife to his throat, and heaved him up onto the wooden railing of the walkway.

'No closer!' he said. 'If I release him now, he falls!'

Sabinus let out a thin cry, but his body was stiff with fright. Rufus must have drugged the boy, Castus realised, to keep him quiet. Fresh anger swelled inside him.

'Put down the sword,' the landowner said. 'Put it down and kneel...'

Castus leaned against the wall of the tower. Sweat was running into his eyes and he felt dazed and faint. He could not use the sword against Rufus for risk of striking his son. Leaning forward with a grunt of agony, he let the blade fall from his hand. Keeping his eyes on Rufus, he eased himself down onto one knee.

'Good!' Rufus said. 'Good – we're in our proper places at last, *excellency*!'

'You really thought you could rule?' Castus gasped. He was watching Rufus, his son, the knife. *Never take your eyes from the knife.* Shouts came up from below – the biarchus and his men calling to him.

'It's in my blood, didn't you know?' Rufus said. 'True blood will always rise when the hour comes...'

A cry from the right, around the angle of the tower. Rufus turned his head, just as Marcellina stepped onto the walkway

431

with one of the loaded crossbows in her hands. She must have left the chamber by the opposite door, Castus realised... It was enough. With one surge of energy he propelled himself upwards, snatching at Rufus's wrist and pulling the knife away from the boy's throat.

Rufus hissed in fury, trying to keep his grip on the child.

'Bastard!' Marcellina yelled. The crossbow *thwacked*, and the short bolt spiked Rufus deep in the muscle of his shoulder. He screamed through his teeth, arching his spine as he reached for the wound. Castus flung his bloodsoaked left arm around Sabinus, pulling the boy from the landowner's grasp, and together they fell sprawling onto the timbers of the walkway.

Hugging his son to his chest, Castus dragged himself backwards. 'Lie down,' he told the boy. 'Lie still and keep your eyes closed.' Sabinus just let out a dazed groan. Castus's reaching hand found the fallen sword, and his fingers closed around the grip.

Rufus was still on his feet, still holding the knife. He slumped sideways against the railing, a strangled cry of pain wrenching from his throat. Castus struggled upright again, his wounded hand clasped tight beneath his arm as he held the sword levelled.

'Yield,' he demanded.

Turning to stare at him, Rufus let the knife drop. Marcellina was edging towards him too, the heavy stock of the crossbow held like a club. With a long shuddering sigh the landowner straightened, drawing himself stiffly upright against the railing.

Then he leaned, and pushed himself backwards over the side.

Castus leaped forward, but he was too slow to grab Rufus with his injured hand. When he peered over the side, he saw the body strike the ground thirty feet below him. For a moment the broken limbs writhed. Then, as Castus watched, the crowd of disarmed slaves gathered around the tower gave a cry and dashed towards Rufus, snatching up sticks and sickles, pitchforks and cudgels. The cordon of troops, baffled, made no move against them as the ragged horde closed around their former master with wails of vengeance. Even from the top of the tower, Castus could hear the sounds of hacking, of flesh pummelled, stamped and gouged.

His son had joined him at the railing and Castus hid the boy's eyes with his palm. The troopers were closing in now to drive the slaves away. Two staggering steps back against the wall of the tower and he slid down into a crouch, his wounded left hand clasped tight to his belly, his right arm gripping his son as the boy emerged from his stupor and began to tremble.

Marcellina knelt beside him, calling to her daughters. She laid a palm on his cheek, leaned closer and kissed him. Then she began tearing her headcloth to use as a bandage.

Lying back against the wall, his legs stretched before him, Castus felt his son pressed against him, Marcellina easing his maimed hand from the mess of blood and binding it with cloth. Exhaustion ached through him, shards of pain drove through his skull, but when he closed his eyes to the red glaze of evening sunlight he felt only a vast and liberating sense of peace.

CHAPTER XXXIII

To the victors, the spoils.

Three days after the total destruction of the Frankish invaders, Flavius Julius Crispus, Caesar of the West, rode back into the city of Colonia Agrippina at the head of his army, to the riotous acclaim of the people. He sat upright in his carriage, dressed in his gilded armour and jewelled helmet, his embroidered purple cloak, and he gripped a gold-tipped lance in his right hand. He kept his eyes straight ahead, never acknowledging the cheers and salutations of the crowds, and as he passed beneath the western gate he dipped his head slightly in the traditional gesture of magnificence. But all could see the grin on the young man's face, the look of joy in his eyes.

Beside the carriage, ahead even of the imperial banner-bearer, rode Aurelius Castus, Commander of the Germanic Frontier. His left hand was wrapped in a thick linen bandage, his arm held against his chest with a sling. But he rode steadily, head up and jaw set hard. The timber porticos lining the street were packed with people, all of them cheering; Castus heard his name called, and saw the old drillmaster, Tagmatius, waving from a street corner. He raised his right hand and smiled.

They passed through the city to the forum, the troops of the victorious army marching beneath their eagles and vexilla, their streaming draco banners. All the field legions and the frontier units that had participated in the campaign had sent their detachments, and between them rode the armoured cavalry of the Cataphractarii and the Horse Guards of the Schola Scutariorum. And at the heart of the Roman array came Bonitus of the Salii, with a guard of his own warriors marching around him.

In the great hall of the basilica, Crispus sat enthroned upon the dais while the orators declaimed their panegyrics on his glorious victory. Castus stood in the front row, his mutilated hand itching inside its dressings, his left arm numb. He was still weakened from loss of blood, but since the events at the villa of Magnius Rufus there had been little time to consider what had happened. The surgeons at Juliacum had cleaned and dressed his wound, but he would never be able to use a shield effectively again. He wondered whether he had stood in the front line of battle for the last time. But the near-ceaseless violent struggles of the last two weeks had rid him of the lingering darkness of Sabina's death. He felt fully alive once more, awake in his body. He had his son back, and that meant more to him than any reward.

A hush had fallen over the great hall, the assembled masses silent before their enthroned young ruler. Castus glanced up at Crispus, and saw how the boy had changed. He was more at ease with himself now, the relief of having proven himself in battle giving him a look of genuine confidence and command. One by one the officers of the field army approached the throne, kneeling to kiss the imperial robe and receive their tokens of favour. Castus heard his own name called, and shrugged himself out of his trance.

Slowly he paced across the marble floor, saluted, and then took the few more steps to the dais. He stifled a groan as he knelt, gathered the hem of the robe and raised it to his lips, then offered his right hand. An attendant placed white silk across his palm, and then Crispus leaned forward and placed the ivory tablet upon it.

'Aurelius Castus,' the herald declared, 'for your courageous service in battle against the enemies of our state, we elevate you to the dignity of *comes rei militaris.*'

Companion in military affairs. One of the senior officers of the army of Gaul. Castus kept his head bowed as he raised himself to stand and retreat backwards down the steps. He had known of his promotion, but to hear the words, to hold the official symbol of rank in his hand, was a rare and potent blessing. He was trying not to smile too openly as he took his place at the front of the assembly once more.

Now Bonitus's name was called. The Salian chief advanced across the floor to the dais, dressed in his finest embroidered tunic and breeches. He knelt, and performed the adoration with impressive ease.

'Bonitus, son of Baudulfus, for your loyal service to the Roman state we grant you citizenship, and the dignity of *praefectus gentilorum*, to rank with the Ducenarii of Protectors. Furthermore, we decree that your people shall be settled on vacant land within the province of Gaul, as subjects of Rome.'

Castus felt a beat of satisfaction in his chest. Bonitus's reward had been his doing; he had insisted on it, argued for it to the Praetorian Prefect. As the Frankish chief paced back to join the assembled officers he glanced across at Castus. The slightest nod, the briefest smile, then he raised his head proudly and walked on.

Once the Caesar had made his departure, the assembly broke up. Castus was relieved; there would be feasting later that day, probably more speeches, more stiff formality, but for now he was free. As he moved through the crowd towards the doors of the basilica, he sensed a presence beside him.

'Allow me to be the first to congratulate you,' the eunuch said in a smooth quiet voice. 'A well-deserved promotion!'

Castus glared at him, his mood of liberation souring. He had seen little of Luxorius since he left him on the battlefield, moments after Dexter's death. The eunuch had chosen his moment well: they were surrounded by people, the noise of voices echoing in the vast marble hall. There could be no confrontation here.

'I know what you did,' Castus said through narrowed lips. 'But I don't know why. What did you offer him? Dexter, I mean? A purse of gold, if he committed one last crime?'

'I'm sure I don't know what you're talking about!' Luxorius said with a smile. 'And if I did, I'd have to wonder what evidence you possess...'

'None. As you know. And no evidence for the attack last year in Raetia, or the Frankish killers you hired at Noviomagus. You won't get another chance, I promise you that.'

Luxorius raised his eyebrows, still smiling. 'As for that, you need not worry,' he said briskly. 'His eminence the prefect has very kindly accepted my request to leave the province and rejoin the court of the Augustus. The climate here, I find, doesn't suit me.'

They were still walking, but as they passed through the doors into the vestibule Castus halted and turned to face the eunuch, leaning closer as he spoke. The crowd around them had thinned. 'So tell me why. Who's giving you orders? Licinius?'

'Oh no,' Luxorius said, glancing away. 'But duty compels us to some strange things, as I'm sure you know. Perhaps one day you'll discover the truth, and then you might understand.'

He bowed slightly, then paced quickly away.

Castus exhaled, frowning as he watched the eunuch melt into the crowd around the doors. It was true: he had nothing to prove his suspicions – his certainties – that Luxorius had made several attempts on the life of the Caesar. Reporting those suspicions could do more harm than good. All he knew was the attempts had failed. And now the eunuch would vanish once more.

'To Hades with him,' Castus said under his breath.

The vestibule was emptying and, as the slow tide of finely dressed figures flowed out through the tall main portal, Castus noticed the group standing near the smaller doors at the far end. He turned at once, pacing quickly towards them. As he approached, Sabinus broke away from his tutor and his nurse and ran across the polished marble floor to greet him. Castus knelt, hugging the boy with his right arm.

'Father! I saw you up on the stage. I wanted to shout out, but Bissula said it wasn't allowed...'

'Not a stage, lad,' Castus said, grinning. 'It's called a *dais*. Stages are for pantomimes!' But the boy was right, he thought. It was all theatre, all performance.

Standing, holding his son clasped to his side, Castus walked over to the group remaining near the doors. Marcellina stood with her daughters on either side of her, a pair of slave maids keeping a discreet distance. She was dressed once more in her elegant tunic and mantle, her braided hair covered by a light shawl, the very image of respectable Roman femininity. A smudge of cosmetic hid the reddened bruise on her temple. But when she smiled, Castus saw the warm light in her eyes.

'Comes rei militaris,' she said, pronouncing the title with slight, amused mockery. 'You deserve it.'

Castus could only shrug. The two girls were gazing at him, the older one with an air of mature formality. The younger girl stared at his bandaged hand with open curiosity, sticking her tongue from the corner of her mouth. They were still recovering from their ordeal, Castus knew, as his son was too. But children are resilient, he was learning. It would take these girls a long time yet to digest the reality of their father's death. Longer still before they saw Castus himself as anything but a stranger. But he was willing to give them all the time they needed.

'I suppose soon you'll be leaving us,' Marcellina said, a catch in her voice. 'Going to Treveris, to the Caesar's court.'

Castus nodded. 'It's not such a bad place.' He drew a breath, then lightly brushed her cheek with his fingers. She closed her eyes.

'Come with me,' he said.

'A merchant's widow with two children?' she replied, trying to laugh. 'You're a great man now, a wealthy man. I—' She broke off, then silently took his hand, raising it to her lips and kissing his scarred knuckles.

He spoke again.

'Come with me.'

EPILOGUE

Aquileia, August AD *318*

The laurelled letter arrived at the beginning of the month, carried by a dust-covered messenger who had ridden by horse relays all the way from Colonia Agrippina. Word of the Caesar's triumph over the Frankish invaders spread fast. Constantine himself, it was reported, had greeted the news with a cry of joy, falling on his knees and raising his hands in thanks to heaven. His son had won his first victory; he had been blooded in combat and saluted by the troops on the field of battle. He was a man, and an emperor. At once the palace decreed a five-day festival to celebrate the achievement and a new coin issue to commemorate the vanquishing of the barbarians.

Fausta kept a smile on her face the whole time, and even managed a show of enthusiasm when she congratulated her husband. Not that Constantine was paying her much attention; between the glad tidings from Gaul and the rumours of Sarmatian and Suebic threats on the Danube, the emperor had little time for domestic affairs. He spent all his time closeted with his military commanders, or storming about the polished corridors of the palace snapping out orders. Soon the mobile court would travel on to Mediolanum, and perhaps after that they would return east to Sirmium. Even so, Fausta had to endure several days of banqueting and an endless series of

441

races and games before she could retreat to the sanctuary of her own wing of the palace.

August in Aquileia was hot, and in the evenings the breeze filled her chambers with the smell of the salt lagoons around the head of the Adriatic. She felt, she thought, rather empty now. For so many months she had been hoping for a different sort of news from the west. Yet now Crispus was not only alive, but triumphantly assured in his father's eyes. Constantine could speak only of him; he seemed to have forgotten the two infant sons that Fausta had given him.

'So, you failed,' she said.

The eunuch merely smiled and inclined his head. He had arrived several days after the messenger from Gaul. Clearly he had travelled at considerable speed himself, Fausta thought, although his appearance at the palace was so quiet that it had caused barely a ripple of notice.

'It was... somewhat more difficult than I'd anticipated,' Luxorius said. 'Although there were a number of occasions when I came close to bringing the matter to a conclusion.'

'Close isn't good enough.'

They were sitting in her private chamber, on facing chairs, the windows open to the dank salty breeze. Fausta fanned herself gently, and sipped wine from a glass goblet. She had been drinking heavily these recent days; alcohol helped her maintain an appearance of tranquillity.

'And now my husband's golden bastard is the pride of Gaul,' she said, unable to keep the sour resentment from her voice. She inhaled sharply, regaining her composure. She would not appear weakened by this, especially not in front of a eunuch. She was still an emperor's wife.

'He made quite an impressive show, the young Crispus,' Luxorius said with a slanting smile. Was he goading her? Fausta fought down her irritation. 'He marched back into Colonia Agrippina at the head of his troops, you know... Though I dislike military spectacles, it really was quite thrilling. Having been on the battlefield myself...'

'You? On a battlefield?' Fausta snorted a laugh, then covered her nose with the back of her hand.

'The things I do for you,' Luxorius said, shrugging.

She had expected him to make some claim on her sympathy. Fausta had been all too aware of the risks she ran employing the eunuch like this. Now that he had failed, the risks remained. If it were ever discovered... Ever since his arrival was announced, she had been contemplating having him disposed of, fingering the murderous thought in her mind. It was an almost irresistible temptation. But even with her fears, her night terrors and the plots they bred, Fausta still believed that she was a good person. A virtuous person, despite everything. Certainly she had planned to have Minervina killed, as she had planned the death of Minervina's son Crispus. She had prayed for it – the memory gave a cold thrill of guilt. *Destroy them both, kill them, exterminate them, O wrathful gods. Cleanse the earth of them entirely...*

But to kill a loyal servitor, just because he had failed her, was the sure mark of tyranny. Her father and her brother would not have hesitated. Constantine would not have hesitated. But she was not them, she told herself that. And the eunuch may still have his uses. He owed her his life, although he did not know it yet.

'So why did you leave Gaul? And so promptly too...'

'I came to believe my position had been, shall we say, *compromised*,' Luxorius said.

Fausta tried to hide her dismay. 'You were discovered? How?' *Gods*, if the fool had allowed her name to be mentioned in connection with this... Panic fluttered against her breastbone.

But the eunuch appeared unconcerned. He shrugged, and made a vague circling gesture. 'Nothing so alarming,' he said. 'But my activities had come to the notice of certain figures. Including your... ah... *friend*, Aurelius Castus.'

'He's not been harmed, by... anybody?'

'No! And certainly not by me, if that's what you mean. He was slightly wounded, but such is the way with soldiers. No, in fact he's been honoured by the Caesar. Promoted to his military council, no less. I ought to add that it was this same man who personally defeated two of my attempts to accomplish our design. I believe he suspected me, or had some intuition at least.'

'He had evidence?'

'None,' Luxorius said, with a slight wince, as if appalled that she had underestimated him. 'But if he guessed my purpose, I sincerely doubt he knew *why*. In any case, if he'd made any report of his suspicions, I would never have reached this place alive.'

No doubt, Fausta thought. The agentes in rebus would have left the eunuch's body lying in some mountain valley, to be gnawed by wolves. But the knowledge that a man she had trusted, a man she had felt warmly towards, had been the cause of the eunuch's failure was bitter news. Now, she realised, Castus would surely be the Caesar's loyal supporter. And Crispus would have many others like him, officers of the army of Gaul, devoted to his service and more than ready to back his claim to rule when the time came. Ready, even if the boy himself was not, to eradicate anyone who stood in his way.

But perhaps, she thought, it did not have to be like that. She swallowed down the gall of her disappointment. Wallowing in failure would do her no good – that path led to surrender, to passivity and defeat.

An idea was taking form in her mind. Something new, something she had not considered before. Aurelius Castus had frustrated her plans in Gaul, but sooner or later Crispus would need to return eastwards to join his father. A dependable officer, securely placed within the Caesar's own staff, the Caesar's own trust, could be useful to her... Fausta had always considered Castus an ally. Could she turn him more deliberately to her cause? If the eunuch's plans had failed because of this man, could she somehow compel him, even trick him, into doing what Luxorius had found impossible? A slight sweat prickled on her brow. But the eunuch had guessed what she was thinking.

'It occurs to me, domina,' he said, pressing his fingers together beneath his chin, 'that the imperial court is a precarious place. The higher one rises, the more mutable one's allegiances become. There's no telling to what ends a man might be driven, if enough pressure is exerted. You might do well to study the affairs of this Aurelius Castus very closely in future.'

The breeze through the windows freshened, making the shutters creak. Fausta smelled the lagoons and the open sea beyond.

'Yes,' she said quietly. 'Yes, perhaps I shall.'

AUTHOR'S NOTE

The surviving history of the early fourth century AD is essentially the story of the emperor Constantine. Our written sources follow him almost exclusively, as a spotlight follows the leading actor on a stage. Beyond the radius of their illumination, there are only suggestive shadows and the vague echoes of distant events.

While we know that Constantine's teenaged son Crispus was promoted to Caesar in AD 317 and sent to govern Gaul soon afterwards, what happened there is harder to establish. He (or, more likely, his military commander) seems to have won a war against the Franks some time before AD 320; the orator of Panegyric IV refers to an 'enormous victory' over the barbarians from beyond the Rhine. This may be exaggeration, but it is noticeable that after this date the Franks, who appear repeatedly as enemies of Rome in preceding years, fall silent for nearly three decades. In fact, when we hear of them again they are acting as allies of the empire.

In composing my own depiction of events, I have freely adapted some episodes from later history, and in particular from the campaigns of the Caesar Julianus (later the Emperor Julian 'the Apostate') in the AD 350s. Ammianus Marcellinus gives a detailed account of the Caesar's wars, while Eunapius of Sardis describes his negotiations with the Chamavi conducted

447

from a vessel moored in the river. The later Greek historian Zosimus mentions a settlement of Saxon pirates on an island near the mouth of the Rhine. I have chosen to believe that similar events could have happened more than once in Roman history.

Considering their later importance, it is perhaps surprising that we know so little about the Franks at this time. Scant archaeological traces remain from the fourth century. Beyond a few lists of different tribal groups in Roman sources, most of what we know of them comes from the later 'migration era', when the Franks moved across the Rhine to establish the kingdoms that would one day become the heartland of medieval France. The Saxons, who lived around the mouth of the Elbe and southern Jutland during this period, are similarly elusive. Edward James, in his books *The Franks* (1991) and *Europe's Barbarians, AD 200–600* (2009), sets out what little we know or can determine. The 'war boats' of the Franks and 'longboats' of the Saxons I have based on the fourth-century oared Germanic vessel excavated at Nydam in Denmark, and to a lesser extent on the much later Anglo-Saxon ship from Sutton Hoo in England. John Haywood's *Dark Age Naval Power: A Reassessment of Frankish and Anglo-Saxon Seafaring Activity* (1991) is a wide-ranging survey of the ships and seamanship of the various Germanic peoples of the era.

The situation in the Roman provinces of the north-west during this period is only slightly clearer. Older theories about barbarians entirely driving out the inhabitants, and a rise in the level of the North Sea inundating the land, have been challenged by more recent studies. But it does seem that large tracts of the Roman frontier territories were abandoned after the later third century, for one reason or another, and the coastal regions were partially claimed by the sea. Even so, the lands of northern Gaul did not become a desert, and the cities continued to thrive, protected by a strong military presence. Nico Royman's *Villa Landscapes in the Roman North* (2012) argues for a continuation of at least some of the big villa estates of Belgica and Germania into the fourth century.

As this story is so much concerned with frontiers – geographical, social, even psychological – the wealth of literature on the Roman *limites* has proved invaluable. There isn't space here to list too many titles; suffice to say that Harald von Petrikovits' 1971 paper *Fortifications in the North-Western Roman Empire from the Third to the Fifth Centuries* A.D., while slightly dated in places, remains a solid guide to the military situation. Philip Parker's *The Empire Stops Here* (2010), meanwhile, provides an engaging tour of the state of the frontiers today.

The Roman presence on the lower Rhine has left many visible traces. The excavated ruins of the riverside Praetorium of Colonia Agrippina (Cologne) are exhibited in a basement gallery below the modern *Rathaus*, while the city above still shows evidence of the ancient grid of streets and the circuit of the Roman walls. The Römisch-Germanisches Museum, near the cathedral, is built over the remains of a palatial third-century townhouse with fine mosaic floors. In Mainz (Roman Mogontiacum), the excellent Museum für Antike Schiffahrt displays full-size reconstructions of two late-Roman river galleys; the remains of these and several others were discovered in a riverbank harbour excavation. The smaller of the warships described in this novel would have resembled these vessels.

Most of the characters mentioned in this story are fictitious, although a few have their roots in history, and I have tried to do them justice. Lactantius, the Christian writer who acted as tutor to the young Crispus, did indeed argue that the world is flat; I have paraphrased the relevant sections from his own text *Divine Institutes*. However, it was an eccentric opinion even at the time, and was not adopted by the wider Church.

Once again, I must thank all those who helped me in the writing of this novel. My agent, Will Francis, and my editor, Rosie de Courcy, provided some very helpful discussions on structure, while Ross Cowan's comments on aspects of the military organisation of the era were again invaluable. I am also very grateful to Mark Hebblewhite for allowing me to read some of his unpublished, and highly inspiring, work on the later Roman army.